# THE ST. LUCIA ISLAND CLUB

TURNER
PUBLISHING COMPANY

# THE ST. LUCIA ISLAND CLUB

A JOHN LE BRUN NOVEL

by

Brent Monahan

Turner Publishing Company
Nashville, Tennessee
New York, New York

www.turnerpublishing.com

The St. Lucia Island Club, A Novel



Cover design: Maddie Cothren
Book design: Glen Edelstein

Library of Congress Cataloging-in-Publication Data

Names: Monahan, Brent, 1948- author.
Title: The St. Lucia Island club / by Brent Monahan.
Description: Nashville, Tennessee : Turner Publishing Company, [2016] |
Series: A John Le Brun novel ; book 5
Identifiers: LCCN 2015047650 | ISBN 9781681620411 (softcover)
Subjects: LCSH: Le Brun, John (Fictitious character)--Fiction. |
Murder--Investigation--Fiction. | GSAFD: Mystery fiction.
Classification: LCC PS3563.O5158 S69 2016 | DDC 813/.54--dc23
LC record available at http://lccn.loc.gov/2015047650

Printed in the United States of America
15 14 13 12 11 10 9 8 7 6 5 4 3 2 1

*For Caitlin*

# CHAPTER ONE

## May 23, 1910

JOHN LE BRUN STROLLED INTO Gramercy Park, smiling at the sudden softening of city noise. In the past five years, as automobile and truck traffic replaced the rhythmic clip-clop of hooves and the soft squeal of wooden wheels, the mechanical din on thoroughfares such as Park and Lexington Avenues had become truly annoying to the man who spent most of his life in the "sleepy South." After more than a few days on Manhattan Island, he invariably sought out isolated, bosky squares, to remind him of Brunswick, Georgia, his relaxed, refined hometown. He tipped his hat to an elderly couple descending the steps of one of the dignified brownstone residences.

Le Brun had retired from the position of sheriff of the southern seaport in 1906, but a series of opportunities had allowed him to open a lucrative detective agency in New York

City. This, and the fact that his wife, Lordis, had been anchored to Manhattan by a solemn promise until only a month earlier, fostered train trips to and from Georgia approximately four times a year.

The periodic shuttling was not in the slightest perturbing to the Southern gentleman; for most of his life he had longed to live where libraries, museums, bookstores, and theaters abounded. He was less enamored of the proliferation of American men's clubs, slavishly based on the London mania, but he was quite proud of the fact that the Player's Club had made him an honorary member. Housed in the converted Gramercy Park residence of departed god of the American stage Edwin Booth, the all-male club was the gathering place of the creative arts elite. The club also accepted accomplished men of other professions who enjoyed rubbing shoulders and hoisting drinks with actors, singers, writers, painters, poets, and the like.

After being vetted by the club's doorman, John descended to the bar, where he encountered one of his favorite members. Henry Fisk Carlton was the author of popular American historical books. Upon spying Le Brun, Carlton flung his arms wide.

"John! What a wonderful happenstance!" He crooked his fingers to encourage Le Brun's advance. Tugging on the sleeve of his drinking companion, whom John did not recognize, Henry drew him from the bar. "Cleveland, this is Mr. John Le Brun, the preferred detective of the New York rich and the solver of several impossibly thorny murders."

Before John could soften the introduction with a bit of self-effacement, the historian said, "And this is Cleveland Moffett, editor of the Sunday *Herald*."

"Until recently," the man disclosed, nodding stiffly from the waist. "At liberty right now." John noted that he parted his hair high on his head and slightly to the left and that he did not trim his bushy eyebrows. Beneath the twin caterpillars, his fixed stare and protruding lower lip gave him a hawkish demeanor.

His starched collar was so wide that he seemed to be wearing a neck brace.

"But more appropriate to the wonderful happenstance," Carlton continued, "Mr. Moffett is the author of several celebrated mystery shorts. Have you read 'The Mysterious Card'?"

John shifted uncomfortably at the situation his friend Henry had put him in. "I'm sorry. I can't say that—"

"I'm surprised, given your omnivorous reading habits," Carlton declared. To Moffett he said, "But then again, John lives in Georgia, and *The Black Cat* is published in Boston, is it not?"

"Correct," said the mystery writer.

"A corker of a periodical," Henry Carlton assured. "At any rate, Cleveland's unique angle is not revealing the answer to whatever puzzle he poses. The printed speculations and public clamor for solutions have made him quite a literary celebrity." As an afterthought, Carlton said, "Like Frank Stockton's 'The Lady or the Tiger,' which you surely have read."

"More than once," John responded. "The first time was at least a couple decades ago, in *The Century*. But Stockton did not withhold his solution."

"He most certainly did!" Carlton insisted. "He went to his grave without revealing whether the princess signaled for the young man to open the arena door that exposed her rival or the man-eating tiger."

Cleveland Moffett's eyes narrowed, and the corner of his mouth curled into a slight smile. "I was under the same impression as Henry. What makes you believe Stockton revealed the answer to his puzzle?"

"It's right in the story, as are the solutions to all well-written mysteries," Le Brun replied. "If memory serves, Stockton's openin' line is somethin' like 'In an ancient time, there lived a semi-barbaric king.' Everythin' in that first sentence comes right out of fairy tales, epics, and legends. Everythin' but the unusual word 'semi-barbaric,' which makes the adjective vitally important. The story is very short, yet 'semi-barbaric' and 'barbaric' are used at least ten times. The king's daughter, who has paid to know behind which doors stand the tiger and the lady, is point-blank told to be 'barbaric.' Such a woman would not allow her assumed rival for the young man's affection to win the day. She nods to the door on the right, behind which waits the tiger."

"You're absolutely convinced that he will die," Moffett said.

John caught the eye of the bartender. "Bourbon and water, if you please." Then he returned his focus to the writer of mysteries. "No, that I cannot determine." Before his response could settle in, he added, "Because the author does not tell me if the young man was clever enough to understand that the practices of a land come from the attitudes of the person in charge. Therefore, the child of a man who is barbaric will learn the way of her immediate world from her father's lap."

"Hmmph!" exclaimed Henry Carlton.

John concluded, "That's the reason behind the sayin' 'If you want to kill a snake, chop off its head.' I live in a port town, with many warehouses. Over the years, I've observed that if the owner is nasty, the workforce becomes nasty all the way down the peckin' order; if he's kindly, the workers tend to reflect his behavior. Stockton's imaginary land is barbaric all the way down."

"Well, it's a pleasure to meet such a thoughtful man, whether you're right or not," said Cleveland Moffett, offering his hand. "I shall have to re-read Stockton's story very carefully."

---

THE HEADQUARTERS OF the John Le Brun Detective Agency was well concealed. It was located on a West Side Midtown block containing several street-level businesses that promoted themselves with large, sometimes-garish signage. The agency, run with no outside advertising, also served as the parlor of Mr. and Mrs. Martin McMahon. Mary McMahon was the manager of the operation, with all other employees working part-time as demand warranted. The investigators were almost all retired New York policemen who enjoyed a periodic infusion of extra cash from investigating the backgrounds of would-be fiancés of the daughters of wealthy families, exposing cheating husbands and wives, guarding the guests and presents at weddings, or protecting masquerade ball attendees from the starving masses who waited for them with rotten produce on hotel sidewalks.

Le Brun climbed the front stoop of the McMahons' three-story tenement. The backfire of a passing motorized van caused him to pivot toward the street, drop into a crouch, and reach under his suit jacket tails, where his revolver was holstered. He realized a moment later what had caused the sharp report, straightened up, and continued to the double doors.

When he entered the parlor, John saw from her amused expression that Mary must have witnessed his skittishness from one of the two front windows. He had hired Mary for her sharp mind and eyes and her inquisitive nature, which caused her to check on the busy street beyond the panes of glass far more than surrounding inhabitants were wont to do. Irish lace hung inside the windows, offering ample spaces to allow Mary to use her keen vision even as the lace protected those outside from seeing her.

"Listen, John, I don't know that it will bring any money into our till," Mary said as Le Brun hung his hat on the coat tree next to the parlor door, "but I was over at Maeve McGillicuddy's this morning and I saw something peculiar."

"Do tell," John said, inviting the rest of her tale. He knew that Mary was not the long-winded type, given to holding attention with protracted, one-sided conversations. However, her observational powers and penchant for detail sometimes turned a short report into a novella.

"She lives a block south, on Thirty-seventh. The shade side, same as us. So it's easy to observe not only what goes on across the street but often a distance into certain shops and businesses. We were having a nice cup of tea by her front window, and I look out and see a delivery wagon pull up in front of the print shop directly across. The wagon is from Aycliffe & Easterman. Do you know the company?"

John sat at the dining table. "Can't say as I do."

"They sell the finest papers, for personal stationery, top business correspondence, and the like. Beautiful stuff to the eye and the touch. We often get requests for our services written on Aycliffe & Easterman paper."

"I see," John said, expecting that by now Mary would have offered him a "nice cup of tea."

"I understand what makes their paper so rich is the finely shredded rag content. But the print shop is a dank hole in the wall. Down five steps below the pavement. So I ask Maeve how often she sees this wagon delivering to the place."

"And she says 'often,'" John said.

"'Regular,' is the word. Her exact words were, 'I think that wagon is there every Monday morning.' Maeve's not as concerned as I am with people who aren't neighbors." Mary straightened the crucifix hanging between the two front windows. "But I myself seen . . . saw . . . at least two reams carried in. Not in small boxes but long, wide ones. Made the deliveryman walk bow-legged, they did."

John had apprehended Mary's suspicion since her mention of the quality of Aycliffe & Easterman paper. "So, you suspect the print shop owner is—"

"A coneyman," Mary finished his sentence, using the New York slang for counterfeiter. "Printing the queer," she added, using more of the criminal parlance she had picked up from their policeman associates. "He ain't printing handbills with paper that size and quality, I'll tell you. I figure it's sheets of paper money."

"Why don't I take a look-see?" John said, rising from the chair.

"It's 413 West Thirty-seventh," Mary told him, grinning at the ready willingness of her respected employer to follow up on her observation. "Although we don't stand to make a dime if I'm right."

"But we would prevent losin' far more than a dime if we were to accept this shop's fake currency in the future," John noted as he grabbed his derby.

"Right you are, right you are!" Mary chirped.

---

THE PRINT SHOP was indeed "a dank hole in the wall." A display window bore the legend "Erik Apfelbaum/Printing and Engraving." The glass expanse was backed by black curtains, which had been drawn apart. John entered the business expecting to hear the steady thump of an electric printing press. Instead, the sounds of several male voices speaking in low tones issued through another black curtain, which hung lintel to floor across an open doorway and completely blocked the view of the space beyond. Several samples of print work had been tacked to the wooden wall behind the service counter.

Le Brun tapped the counter bell. The voices grew silent. A heavyset man who John judged to be in his early forties appeared. He wore an apron impregnated with the ink of many printing sessions. His face bore the ancestry of eastern Germany. His fingertips were lightly stained a peacock green.

"May I help you?" he asked.

John rested his elbow on the counter, reminding himself to swap his Southern drawl for a Yankee accent. "Perhaps. I recently purchased a warehouse over in Jersey City, and I'd like to make my services and rates known around Manhattan." He stretched out his hands. "I'm thinking about posters so big. At least five hundred. Maybe a thousand, if the price is right."

"Dry glue on the back?"

"Yes."

"Printed in how many colors?"

"Black print and red borders."

"Do you need any illustration or design work?" asked the man behind the counter, jotting notes on a piece of scrap paper.

"Just words," John replied. "Your top- and bottom-end charges for five hundred will do for comparison right now."

As he spoke, Le Brun heard two male voices speaking in short, low exchanges just behind the black doorway curtain. A moment later, the men passed through the opening. Both were somber-faced, in their thirties, and dressed in ready-made suits of reasonable quality. John noted that they held identical black leather document clutches, about twice the size of normal wallets, identically stuffed. One, who was on the thin side and about John's height, had reddish hair and sported a military-style moustache. The other was a bit shorter than John's five-foot-eight stature and wore wire-frame eyeglasses, well supported by the full cheeks of a round face. Both men moved through the front of the shop with speed, pointedly avoiding eye contact with Le Brun and the shop proprietor.

The man behind the counter offered a base quote, then began detailing particulars and add-on charges.

"That's good enough for now, thank you," John said. "You'll probably see me again." Before the printer could renew his pitch, Le Brun turned and exited the shop, climbing the steps to street level.

The pair of men strode away at a good pace. John matched them, keeping two hundred feet back. His quarry, walking abreast, turned south on Eighth Avenue. When they reached the corner of the nearly completed Pennsylvania Station at Thirty-third Street, the two turned west, strolling along the two-block length of the ancient Greek revival wall, chatting amiably. The man with the flaring moustache tipped his hat to his companion and continued south toward the central Manhattan post office, which John knew would soon be demolished and replaced by a monumental structure that would complement Pennsylvania Station.

The full-cheeked fellow continued to the temporary ticketing and waiting areas of the Pennsylvania Railroad, not far beyond where the trains emerged from a double tunnel under the Hudson River. John shadowed him until the man queued up at one of the ticket windows. The detective took his place in the same line, allowing a young man who carried a bouquet of flowers to separate them. John stepped slightly to the side to be able to watch the bespectacled man's actions. As the object of his focus finished the transaction and moved toward a set of iron stairs, Le Brun pivoted and presented his back. The young man completed his purchase, and John advanced to the window. He flashed his detective's credentials at the ticket vendor and said, "The man with the spectacles who just left your counter paid you with paper currency."

"Yes, sir. A five-dollar bill. He paid for one way to Newark."

John calculated that the man would have gotten more than four dollars in coinage. "I'd like to purchase that bill."

"Here it is." The ticketing agent pulled the bill from his till.

John extracted two two-and-half-dollar gold pieces and set them on the counter. "An even exchange, and I thank you."

Le Brun headed out onto the street, not wanting to be seen by the man whom he strongly suspected of being a "passer." He imagined the character with the fancy moustache was at that moment purchasing sheets of postage stamps, which could easily be resold to larcenous businessmen for up to 80 percent of their value. He judged that the two men's oversized wallets could comfortably hold one hundred identical bills, totaling enough together to purchase a new automobile. If the print shop owner used one passer each to cover Manhattan, the Bronx, Queens, Brooklyn, Staten Island, and New Jersey, $3,000 in bad currency could be put into circulation in a week or less—what it took a competent New York lawyer an entire year to earn. The amount was the proverbial drop in the bucket in one of the major metropolises of the world, yet John knew that as much as 3 percent of paper money in national circulation was counterfeit. Many drops from many dirty buckets could gradually pollute an entire system, causing inflation and enough suspicion among citizens that gold and silver might need to return as the standard species of commerce.

The fault lay in the national monetary system, a failing that Le Brun had railed against many times, especially to the rich and influential that his agency served and with whom he occasionally shared a drink and a conversation. The United States needed centralized mints and standardized paper money. Back when John was a boy and thousands of small banks existed, each one issued its own currency. During the Civil War, somewhere between one-third and half of all the paper money was false. In response, the federal government established national banks, which were chartered to print money backed by U.S. bonds. But with hundreds of banks participating in the program across the country and in U.S. territories, it was impossible for the average individual to know all the designs and to be able to declare any single example counterfeit.

The $5 bill John stared at was ostensibly issued by the Vineland National Bank of Vineland, New Jersey. It depicted several scenes showing Christopher Columbus in the New World. The obverse side was sharply printed in black and shades of gray, with national charter and series numbers in red. On the reverse side, the border work was in peacock green. It was the same color as the stains on the print shop owner's fingertips. The bill had been folded several times and crumpled but showed no true signs of wear. Clucking at his observations, John tucked it into his inside suit jacket pocket.

"Good on you, Mary McMahon. Now, where precisely is the New York office of the Secret Service?"

# CHAPTER TWO

## May 30, 1910

"WE'VE ARRIVED," John told Lordis Goode Le Brun. "Do not look across the street."

Lordis nodded. She climbed the tenement steps with haste and passed through the door that her husband held. Her eyes sparkled with excitement. In her four-year relationship with John, he had never before invited her to witness the arrest of criminals. True enough, he had discussed elements of cases with her during investigations and solicited her opinions, but he did not involve her physically. The one case in which she had been taken hostage by an adversary had been excuse enough for Le Brun to adamantly demand separation of his married life and profession. She had pressed him so relentlessly, however, that he had finally brought her to witness a capture that he expected would present no danger.

Lordis entered the tenement hallway. A door opened on the right. Lordis recognized the small, button-eyed Mary McMahon immediately. In her left hand the agency manager held a pair of binoculars.

"Mrs. Le Brun, come in, come in! You've missed some of the prelude, but the main act is yet to come." She tugged Lordis gently into the tiny parlor. "This is Maeve McGillicuddy, the concierge of the building."

In response, the redheaded resident rose, as if to royalty, and executed a small curtsey. "Pleased to meet you, ma'am. Take my seat, please!"

John had told Lordis to wear nothing finer than a plain day dress so that she would not stand out on the Tenderloin streets, but even so, her apparel was clearly of finer quality than that worn by either Mrs. McMahon or Mrs. McGillicuddy. She also stood taller than both and walked with the carriage of one educated in a Southern finishing school. John had advised her not to wear a hat, the absence of which only served to show off her wealth of light-brown hair, cut and coiffed the day before by a Fifth Avenue beautician. John was proud of having married a true lady, still turning heads in her late forties, but he had realized as they approached Thirty-seventh Street that her arresting beauty could in some instances prove a liability.

"What happened so far?" Le Brun asked.

"You were right when you guessed the passers receive the goods on Mondays," Mary replied. "One young dandy entered about a quarter-hour ago and has yet to reappear. Apfelbaum must do his special printing on Sundays so no walk-ins can interrupt him. The godless miscreant."

"Printing and passers?" Lordis said. "Is this about a counterfeiting operation?"

"You're quick," Maeve praised.

"Four men entered the place right after the owner opened," Mary said. "I expect they were all Secret Service agents. A woman went in briefly and then came right back up. She looked confused."

"They no doubt shooed her away," John said.

"I want to hear about this from the very beginning," Lordis solicited.

The detective agency manager obliged her, in her thorough yet no-nonsense manner. When Lordis posed a question to John, he declined to speak and rather smiled and turned his hand, palm up, toward Mary.

"Nice work that printer did," Mary concluded. "Leastways, that's what your husband tells me."

Le Brun, who remained standing, nodded. "I paid my second visit to the New York branch of the Secret Service Thursday," he told Lordis. "Took them a day to find a genuine Vineland National bank note. To tell the truth, the engravin' work was so good that I could scarcely see the errors. The printer is something of an artist. May I borrow those binoculars?"

"Why talented people turn to crime instead of honest labor is beyond me," Mrs. McGillicuddy said.

"It's usually a matter of laziness and the temptation of big payoffs." Le Brun focused the lenses. "If this man were to print phony money for a single year, he might net a profit of sixty thousand dollars. Enough to buy a buildin' such as this outright, with enough left over to furnish it."

"Somebody's coming down the sidewalk," Lordis said, "wearing spectacles on a round face."

The figure came into the viewing field of the binoculars. John recognized the man he had tailed to the train station. The passer looked down at the display window of the print shop. He took a slight hitch in his step, glanced briefly up the street and then behind him, and continued on his way.

"Apfelbaum has used the window curtains as a signal," John said, lowering the binoculars and handing them to Mary. "Durin' business hours he draws the curtains back. They're still closed." He plucked his hat from the wall rack where he had hung it. "I'll tail this Jasper. Someone needs to inform the agents across the street."

"I can do it!" Lordis volunteered in an insistent tone.

"No, Mary should," John replied. He saw the knotting of the muscle at the back corner of Lordis's jaw and knew she was swallowing words behind the curve of her tongue. "Lordis, you telephone the local precinct, tell them what I look like, and have them meet me at the Pennsylvania Station southbound tracks." He did not wait for reply from either woman but accelerated his movements as he turned into the hallway and dashed out the tenement front door.

The counterfeit passer had headed east, toward the center of Manhattan Island. From the top of the tenement stoop, John saw that the man had begun to lengthen his stride. Le Brun broke into a trot in order to shorten the distance between them. When his quarry reached Seventh Avenue, he turned the corner, heading south. John settled into a pattern he had read about regarding Indians of the eastern tribes, whereby they alternated fifty long steps with fifty trotting paces and were able to cover as many as fifty miles in a single day. By the time the counterfeit money passer reached Thirty-third Street and turned west, however, John was sure such Indians were braves in their twenties and thirties and not chiefs in their early sixties. John slowed with relief as soon as he satisfied himself that the man was intent on crossing the Hudson River to his home ground.

As he had done the previous week, the plump-cheeked man purchased a ticket to Newark. When he turned from the counter and saw Le Brun, his eyes fixed on the detective. An expression of concern pinched the skin above his nose. John casually redirected his attention to the nearest call board, which indicated that the next train stopping at Newark would not depart for another twelve minutes. John noted that the clutch in the man's hand was identical to the one he had carried the previous

Monday. It bulged less than on that day, however. John figured that it contained the printer's share of genuine money from the passer's labors.

Four minutes dragged by, with the passer and the detective leaning against adjacent guardrails, both staring down at the tracks and the lines of cars, both pointedly avoiding the other's eyes. The next minute, two beat policemen entered the makeshift terminal, chests heaving and faces red from exertion. John raised his hand.

"Officers!" he called out, expecting the passer to bolt away, indicating his guilt.

Instead, the heavyset man wearing the spectacles turned to face the cops and presented an expression of mild curiosity. He watched the officers continue past him, relaxing their pace as they neared Le Brun.

"Are you the one who had a woman telephone the precinct?" the older of the two patrolmen called out in an overloud voice.

"I am," John replied. He nodded down the length of the guardrail. "That man needs to be escorted to the Eric Apfelbaum Print and Engravin' Shop on Thirty-seventh Street."

"The deuce I do!" the passer responded in an incredulous tone.

The younger policeman came up beside him and held up his hand. "This gentleman is accusing you of passing counterfeit money, sir."

"Balderdash!" the man shot back.

"Then you don't mind if I look in your purse?"

"Not at all, officer. Look to your heart's content. Then arrest this lunatic for making a false accusation."

John and the older policeman drew close to the other two. The oversized wallet was opened and its paper money brought into the daylight.

"Let's see. Five, ten, fifteen . . ." The younger cop continued his slow riffling process in silence. "Two hundred and seventy-five dollars, from at least a dozen banks, of three different denominations, and with many serial numbers."

"As I expected," Le Brun returned in a calm voice. "Those are the genuine bills he's returnin' to the printer, to pay for his next batch of counterfeit fives. Which are waitin' for him at the print shop. His trouser pockets are also bulgin' with—"

"Which bank do you believe was copied?" the older policeman interrupted, ignoring John's logic and casting a sweeping glance around the area, where curious bystanders were cautiously measuring just how close to the action they could advance.

"Vineland National," John said.

"I found not a single bill from Vineland," the young policeman said. "If he were passing—"

Through a toothy smile, the older cop said to the passer, "You can be on your way, sir."

While the inspection of the oversized wallet was taking place, Le Brun realized the error of having Lordis call the local police precinct. This was the Tenderloin, the most corrupt district of Manhattan, infamous for the venality of its lawmen. Clearly, printer Apfelbaum had been paying protection money to the police as part of the price of doing illegal business. His costs were being repaid before the detective's eyes. John berated himself for the mistake.

*Even though I gave a snap order, I should have remembered where the print shop lies,* he thought. *My mistake is not advancing age; it's spending too much time in retirement and not enough actively engaged in what I do best. The knife is still steel, but the edge has grown dull.* Yet even as he articulated the reason for his failure, he knew there was another cause: Lordis's mute anger at being rejected in favor of the agency manager had rattled him.

The call was made to board the train, which stopped in Newark, New Brunswick, Princeton, and Trenton, with a final destination of Philadelphia. Passengers crowded forward, eager not only to board but also to catch a bit of conversation from the tantalizing scene.

Le Brun produced his detective credentials. "Hold up!" he said in his best authoritative voice. "This license was given to me personally by Mayor George B. McClellan, Jr. . . . based upon the endorsement of Joseph Pulitzer, J. P. Morgan, and half a dozen other worthies of this city." He held the credentials high as a street theater maneuver to immobilize the policemen and the surrounding crowd. He was delighted to register the controlled panic in the expression of the older policemen. "I'm sure neither of you fine officers wants to be held accountable for lettin' a criminal slip through your fingers. I strongly suggest that we all walk up to—"

"I'm going to miss my train," the passer snapped, attempting to bull toward the stairs. John blocked his progress.

"Clear the way!" a deep male voice demanded from the outer edge of the crowd. "United States Secret Service. Good morning, Mr. Le Brun."

John had dealt with the square-jawed, imposing man on both of his visits to the New York office of the Secret Service. "*Excellent* mornin', Agent Wright."

Wright's narrowed eyes shifted from the older cop's badge number to that of the younger one. "Have these officers been of assistance?"

"As you can see, the suspect did not get away," John evaded.

Wright refocused on the passer, who offered a cocky sneer. "You are being held on suspicion of passing counterfeit money." Without retraining his gaze, he said to John, "The Service is grateful for your vigilance."

"Don't thank me, thank my agency manager."

First the older policeman, then his junior turned and used the task of dispersing the crowd as excuse to distance themselves from the arrest.

"I shall. And I'll see that your agency is compensated for your expenses," Wright promised.

John watched the Secret Service agent secure the criminal's

hands behind his back with a pair of handcuffs. "Not necessary. Riddin' the city of this gang is its own reward." *Along with the John Le Brun Detective Agency name that I will make sure articles in the city newspapers mention,* John thought to himself. *I'm going to need extra business to pay for our vacations to St. Lucia and Paris.*

Onlookers closest to the arrest burst into spontaneous applause. John indulged them with a theatrical bow. *Almost as good as being on the stage,* he thought.

# CHAPTER THREE

## June 19, 1910

THE PORT OF BRUNSWICK, Georgia, had boasted a cold storage warehouse for only the past four years. In that short time, however, the owner had needed to double its size. In 1877 the steamships *Le Frigorifique* and *Paraguay* were the first vessels to transport frozen cargo, bringing mutton from Argentina to France. The world-changing feat, however, had been adopted slowly. One commodity that encouraged and expanded refrigerated transport was the banana. Before 1900, few North Americans had eaten the tropical fruit. But, as John Le Brun was fond of saying whenever he offered the delicacy to a visitor, "I believe it was not an apple tree in the center of the Garden of Eden but a banana plant. A single bite and you're lost."

One cargo ship that brought bananas to Brunswick and thence by rail to markets as far north as Boston was the *Pindy*.

She had been launched in 1895 as a steam-driven refrigerated vessel, capable of plying the waves at a bit more than fifteen nautical miles per hour. A crusty skirt of barnacles had slowed her somewhat in recent years, and the relentless ravishments of tropical saltwater had rusted the gunwales and rivets and dulled the paint. She was the embodiment of the word "weather-beaten."

"Oh, my!" Lordis lamented, as Warfield Tidewell steered his new Model Thirty Cadillac up to the wharf where the *Pindy* floated low on the Brunswick River. Warfield had been John Le Brun's protégé a decade earlier and had succeeded as the city sheriff when John retired. He had grown exponentially richer when he secured a dealership that sold both Cadillacs and Buicks.

"It ain't the *La Provence*," John admitted, as he took Lordis's hand in his. For the past decade, the growing wealth of the U.S. upper classes had allowed many to vacation in Europe, and increasingly luxurious passenger ships were their means of crossing the Atlantic Ocean. *La Provence* was such a steamship, accommodating 358 first-class passengers, 339 second, and 898 third, running year-round between New York and La Havre, the port used by those intent on seeing Paris.

"It ain't even the *La Lorraine*," John continued, speaking of another liner that sailed between New York and La Havre that was six years older than *La Provence*. By his ready agreement with her dismay, he hoped to limit his wife's complaints. "But it's infinitely less expensive, and it is steamin' to paradise." Having seen the aging *Pindy* in port roughly every ten days for almost two years, John had anticipated the problem and, at every possible occasion, put the photographs of St. Lucia supplied by the ship's captain under his wife's nose.

"Besides," Warfield said to Lordis, "you'll be on it, looking out at the world's beauty. You'll quickly forget what its hull looks like." He flashed his handsome grin. "The same way John forgets how homely he is when he's looking at your beauty."

When the older couple had first discussed their honeymoon plans, Lordis had hoped aloud that they might spend a week in Paris, followed by another week roaming its environs. The honeymoon had been postponed due to Lordis's obligation to care for her best friend's children. More than a year before that obligation ended, John had announced to her that he had won a free round-trip cruise to St. Lucia by besting in a chess match Bobby Johnson, the captain of the *Pindy*. The photographs, which were not snapshots from a Brownie but professional images taken by a large-format camera, had convinced Lordis to defer the Paris trip for another year.

Lordis laughed at Warfield's waggish remark, and John knew that the day had been saved.

Two Negro draymen were in the process of unloading John's pair of oversized suitcases and Lordis's carpetbag, steamer trunk, and three hatboxes directly in front of the cargo ship's gangplank. Both men were at least as old as John. Their grunting could be heard from where the three white people stood.

John and Lordis thanked Warfield for his send-off, then walked up the gangplank to where the captain stood. Bobby Johnson's uniform was neither starched nor brilliantly white, as were those of the masters of grand passenger liners. Instead, he wore new, midnight-blue trousers, a well-worn navy-blue jacket, and a black-and-white captain's hat whose edges were lined with permanent sweat stains.

"Welcome aboard!" Johnson greeted. He was a thin, sinewy man with blond hair gone to silver, pale eyes partially hidden by tinted spectacles, and white teeth gleaming through a generous, open smile. He glanced momentarily at the afternoon sun hanging above distant trees. "We cast off in thirty minutes. Should be a smooth sea. Let me show you around the upper decks and introduce you to Mr. and Mrs. Van Fleet." He nodded toward a couple who stood on the mizzen deck peering in the direction of the Jekyl Island Club, the most exclusive winter resort in the country.

None of the passengers gave heed to the half-dozen men securing the forward cargo holds, their various shades of brown skin glistening from their labors.

---

NOT LONG AFTER he came to know John, Bobby Johnson had crowed that everyone on board his vessel, down to the boiler stokers, ate well on the *Pindy*. John had made certain of his boast by sampling the cook's skills when the ship had docked in Brunswick in February. In what was to become a routine, the Le Bruns began dinner with the captain and the ship's only other passengers promptly at eight bells. As with many other cargo vessels, the *Pindy* had been designed with a pair of extra cabins to accommodate guests. Beyond these, a larger-than-usual mess, and a mizzen area outfitted with deck chairs, no other luxuries were provided.

A Victrola cabinet was fixed to the deck in the far corner of the room. From its ornate bell cascaded sounds of a Beethoven string quartet.

Captain Johnson sat at the head of the dining table. Serving as sommelier, he reached into a silver ice bucket stand at his side and poured a French Chablis into five Irish cut-crystal glasses. When they had been distributed, he saluted his guests, who had already introduced themselves to each other.

"To a safe and serene voyage." Johnson took his first sip with the others and added, "It gets mighty lonely on the briny, so I thank you for your company." He grinned. "However, I stress that I am not lonesome to the point of desperation; I recruit only interesting souls of considerable accomplishments with *bon vivant* personalities."

"Recruit, you say? Shanghaied is more like it," returned Paul Van Fleet amiably. On the mizzen deck, the man had revealed himself to the Le Bruns to be a Wall Street financier with a pedigree that stretched back to the New Amsterdam days of settlement. His wife, Minerva, was the daughter of a Pennsylvania coal mine owner.

"Where did the captain find you?" Lordis asked the husband.

"At Delmonico's. It's one block from the New York Yacht Club and, of course, frequented by many of its members."

"You bein' one of them," John said, more statement than question.

"I am indeed," Van Fleet answered. In John's estimation, the man presented more than a passing resemblance to President William Taft, although his belt size was perhaps three inches smaller. "I'm a member as well of the Metropolitan Club, the Yale Club, Automobile, Trade, and Jockey Clubs."

"I hold honorary memberships in the Players and Sceptred Isles Clubs, as well as a payin' membership in the Manhattan Club," John announced. His agenda was to use his association with the Players' celebrated artistic members as his particular status symbol; to proclaim by the Sceptred Isle more than a passing acquaintance with London; and, via the Manhattan, to indicate that he aligned his attitudes with egalitarian Progressives rather than the exclusionary, staunchly conservative capitalist class. He knew that his list would obliquely telegraph to the Van Fleets what should and should not be discussed regarding politics, social issues, and the like to spare the guests from awkward moments. The *Pindy* was simply too small and the trip too long for inadvertent contretemps.

The tinny music ended, and the captain rose to exchange the platter for a too-well-played Victor recording of Adelina Patti singing "Le Serenata," "Comin' Thru the Rye," "Home, Sweet Home," and "La Calasera."

"I've never heard of the Sceptred Isle Club," Minerva Van Fleet admitted.

"It's in London," John said. He watched the elevating of two pairs of eyebrows and knew that his membership had impressed his new acquaintances.

"The *original* Clubland," Lordis added.

Paul smiled blandly at Lordis, then said to John, "I once heard your name mentioned at the Yacht Club, by no less than Commodore Morgan. Something about being a nonpareil sleuth. He did not mention that you hail from Brunswick. I had expected that you two would be sharing the same southbound train with us."

"I have one foot planted in my home town and the other in New York."

"A New World Colossus of Rhodes," Mr. Van Fleet proclaimed, showing off his knowledge of ancient history.

"That he is," Lordis interjected. "And although I grew up in North Carolina, we met a stone's throw from Central Park."

"We now travel back and forth roughly four times a year," John said. "Think of Lordis as Persephone and me as Hades, draggin' her each season to the underworld."

Lordis rolled her eyes at the mythical metaphor she had heard him use more than a dozen times.

"My image of you is that of a wicked cribbage player," Mr. Van Fleet disclosed.

The remark caught John completely off guard. "Me? Well, I played cribbage years ago for a spell, but I was never an expert."

Van Fleet stared at Captain Johnson, who returned an owlishly placid expression.

The New York Yacht Club member folded his arms over his pronounced belly. "Did you not also win this trip by superior gamesmanship, Mr. Le Brun?"

"Mr. Le Brun is an expert at chess," the captain supplied. "Never before have I lost bets to two such masters in one year. A clause in my contract allows me whatever fare I can charge for the ship's spare staterooms. When I can, I try to lure accomplished chess and cribbage players to travel the sea with me, but at their own cost. Clearly, I met my matches with you two. Unless I'm more careful, I shall never accrue enough money to retire."

The group laughed awkwardly at his remark. Even given the harshness of life at sea, the captain's face indicated that he had already reached the age when many men were already retired.

Lordis asked, "When you finally put down stakes, where do you think that will be?"

"St. Lucia," Johnson replied without hesitation. "On one of the hills overlooking Rodney Bay. Soon enough you'll know why."

Minerva had been sampling her shrimp appetizer with hesitant motions, offering no comments and looking as if she already regretted leaving a pampered life in New York City. To include her in the conversation, Lordis asked, "Do you play cribbage or chess, Mrs. Van Fleet?"

"No. I play hearts at my ladies' club. Otherwise, on the rare occasion when I have idle hours, I do embroidery. I'm currently reproducing sections of the Bayeux Tapestry."

"How ambitious!" Lordis exclaimed.

Minerva sighed. "I've also brought a stack of novels and periodicals with me, to compensate for the simple surroundings."

Lordis shot a glance at John, but he had shifted his attention to the captain. "Lordis plays chess as well. When you're not at the helm, you should give her a try."

Johnson hoisted one eyebrow and looked at Lordis with appraising eyes. "A woman who plays chess. Unusual, isn't it?"

Lordis reproduced the captain's expression but focused on her husband. "My skills have been underestimated before, Captain. You had best be on your guard."

# CHAPTER FOUR

## June 24, 1910

THE PATH OF THE *PINDY* took her past the eastern reaches of the Bahamas and the Turks and Caicos Islands. It had steamed between Puerto Rico and the Virgin Islands, although not close enough to view those islands as more than hazy gray-green rises above the increasingly crystalline, blue-green sea. From there on, she plied the Caribbean. Far off the starboard bow, St. Kitts and Nevis were succeeded by Montserrat, again too distant to appreciate. Finally, the ship angled closer to the archipelago that curved like a comma for almost 500 miles and ended at Tobago. The only outbound port of call had been Pointe-a-Pitre in Guadeloupe, where enormous pallets weighted down with crates of stockings, dresses, suits, and shoes from New England mills and furniture from the Carolinas were unloaded.

Because Guadeloupe is shaped like a bowtie, with its primary harbor on the south side of the knot, the *Pindy*'s detour allowed her passengers a long midday look at the island's western side. Pristine, white beaches stretched mile after mile, bordered by palm trees and backed by rugged mountains. From time to time, dark-skinned inhabitants wearing light colors moved along invisible roads. Everyone they spotted walked or drove horse-drawn carts. There was no sign of any motorized vehicle.

Toward the island's southern reach, the slopes of La Soufrière rose to an impressive 4,813 feet. The mountain was covered with short trees and other vegetation, but its conical shape indicated clearly that it was one of the scores of ancient volcanoes that had formed the Leeward and Windward Island chains. The Le Bruns and Van Fleets admired the views with excitement, wondering among themselves how St. Lucia would compare.

By the time the stars were bright in the night sky, the *Pindy* was back in open water, making for St. Lucia at full speed. While herds of fleecy clouds had been a daily sight, only one mid-afternoon squall had dampened the trip from Brunswick, stirring the ocean to waves high enough to send Minerva Van Fleet to her cabin with a touch of *mal de mer*. The water south of Guadeloupe was particularly calm, turning the reflected moonlight into an infinitely long, gently wavering obelisk.

John retired to bed early, determined to greet their vacation island with full energy. For three nights, Captain Johnson had fended off Lordis's challenge to play chess, using various excuses. Finally, after she had directly accused him at the dinner table of fearing to lose to a woman, he had picked up the verbal gauntlet. The Van Fleets and John had left them alone to do battle in the dining room cum music center/lounge/gaming area.

John performed what he called "my mornin' ablutions," and still Lordis slept. She finally roused when he sat on the edge of the bed to lace up his shoes.

"Hey, Sleepin' Beauty," he said. "How late did you come to bed?"

She yawned expansively. "Almost midnight."

"Do tell." He watched Lordis dig the sleep from the corner of her eye. Her thick wealth of hair was fanned wildly across her pillow. Her pale skin had not a trace of makeup. And yet, to him, she was as beautiful as the subject of Botticelli's *Birth of Venus.* "Who won the match?"

"He actually thought he needed to patronize me by giving up an early pawn," Lordis replied.

"I bet you made him regret it right quick."

"You are so good at winning bets, my love! Four moves later we were even on the captured pawn count, but I had one of his knights. From that point on, he fought like a lion."

"Who emerged triumphant?" John tried again.

Lordis sat up and stretched. "He had to take the helm at midnight, and I figured he would have won within another five or six moves. So I conceded. I was weary of his pace by then anyway."

"I understand. He takes an easy five times longer than we do." John finished tying his shoes and stood. "I had the feelin' he threw the game that won me this trip."

Lordis rose. "With all his free time, if he lures good chess players onto the ship, he should be a grand master by now. But if he makes the profit from this cabin and the other, why would he throw games?"

"To make a bigger profit?" John surmised.

"What bigger profit?"

"We'll know before we leave St. Lucia."

Lordis crossed to one of the room's portholes and looked out. "We're here!" she said, in her excited little-girl voice.

John stood behind his wife. "That's St. Lucia, all right. But the captain informs me that the ship will take on coal before we can disembark."

"Why would that be?" Lordis wondered.

"I would assume so as not to contaminate the products being loaded afterward. Nobody wants bananas covered in coal dust. The same with sugar, coffee, or whatever other produce comes on board."

Since 1886, the port of Castries had served as a central coaling station for the neighboring islands. Ships transported coal from distant parts of the New World, to be heaped into mountains that rose and shrank from day to day.

After the Van Fleets and Le Bruns packed their belongings, the four gathered at an upper deck rail and watched with voiced disbelief. More than sixty years into the industrial revolution, coal was being unloaded and loaded manually at St. Lucia instead of by a mechanized conveyor system. Bare-chested men hefted huge bamboo baskets onto the heads of women, who used nothing more than small pillow pads to cushion the weight. Walking ramrod straight, their skin shiny with coal dust, the women climbed ladders with perfect balance and were relieved of their burdens by another set of men, who dumped the coal into a hold. Farther down the dock, an equal number of workers reversed the process, unloading a North American coaler. All the men and women were of African heritage.

When the coaling operation ended, a pair of St. Lucian-style tugboats moved the *Pindy* through the inner bay and to a long wharf paralleled by a large shed built of galvanized, corrugated metal. The loading of bananas began mere minutes after thick hawsers secured the ship against the dock. While the Le Bruns and Van Fleets waited for their luggage to be taken down the gangplank, they watched the efficient but primitive process. Men appeared at large propped-up windows on the bay side of the wharf and passed the banana bunches outside. Each bunch was wrapped in banana straw for protection against bruising. The *Pindy*'s hull hatches were unbattened and raised, creating openings in her side large enough for the bunches to be passed through. As with the coal, women did the labor between the two teams of men, ferrying the bunches on their heads, stabilizing them with a cloth pad tied by lace under their chins.

As John watched the continuous choreography, he was reminded of ants carrying off crumbs of food from a picnic cloth.

"Logs," Captain Johnson said, as John slipped the leather strap of his Brownie No. 2 camera from his shoulder and folded open its pocket, causing the bellows to expand.

"Pardon?" he said.

"The whites down here call the black workers 'logs.' Doesn't make any sense to me, but that's their term."

The camera had been Lordis's main Christmas gift to her husband in anticipation of their trip to St. Lucia. He had exposed several test rolls of film with success before leaving. For their vacation he had bought twelve rolls of two-and-a-quarter-inch film at fifteen cents a roll. John put the viewfinder to his eye and took a shot of the dock. "Do you know the air temperature, Captain?"

"Feels like its climbing to eighty degrees. That's the average on St. Lucia pretty much year-round. With the breeze it's darned near perfect. A major contributor to making the island a paradise."

"The island, perhaps, is paradise, but its civilization needs much improvement," Lordis judged in a soft voice, as if in apology for her critical observation.

"Nothing that a good infusion of cash wouldn't fix," Johnson returned. "St. Lucia is the poorest of the Windward Islands. They have a bad imbalance of trade, which only worsens their circumstances."

John panned the camera clockwise from north to south along a plain interspersed with clumps of houses and vegetation, then through a rough horseshoe shape between high hills criss-crossed with narrow streets. Except for a pair of church spires, the tightly packed buildings rose no higher than three stories. Just below them were jumbles of warehouses and fabrication facilities. Behind Castries, in the middle distance, the hills were dotted with shanties. Across the bay, a tabletop mountain on the south also held structures. The buildings on the mountain looked sturdy and substantial. The better roads were covered in crushed shell, the worse formed of nothing more than rutted, hard-packed dirt. Everywhere, humanity teemed. There seemed not enough houses by half to shelter the masses working in and moving around the island's main town. He realized he had already shot half a roll of film.

John reflected that on Manhattan Island, dark-skinned people were a distinct minority south of Ninetieth Street. In Brunswick, perhaps a fifth of the faces were colored. In Castries, the overwhelming majority were of African origin.

Regarding the relatively primitive panorama in front of them, the four denizens of New York City moved unconsciously closer to each other. Captain Johnson returned from overseeing work on the main deck. He pointed to a man standing on the dock beside a horse-drawn wagon that contained the Le Bruns' and Van Fleets' belongings.

"Good people, it's time for you to begin your adventure," Johnson said in a merry tone. "That gentleman standing in front of the wagon is Monsieur Carlisle Thiery. As I explained, he will act as your factotum for your fortnight plus two days on St. Lucia." Unlike the usual ten-day cycle of the *Pindy* from St. Lucia to Brunswick and back, the upcoming trip would last six days longer. The reason was downtime for engine and shaft servicing and hull restoration.

"You pay him half the agreed-upon fee up front and half when you leave . . . plus whatever tip you feel is fitting for services rendered above and beyond. He's especially valuable if you should need a lawyer. Actually a solicitor, since he received his degree from Cambridge University's law school."

"Cambridge in England?" Minerva asked in an incredulous tone.

"I've seen his diploma," Johnson replied.

Minerva squinted to get a better look at the man under discussion. "Carlisle Thiery. Sounds English and French. Is he white?"

In 1906, John had lost the sight of one eye. The one that still worked, however, remained keen. He trained it on the dockside anomaly of a man dressed in a linen two-piece suit wearing a starched white shirt with a high celluloid collar, as opposed to the male wharf workers who wore what looked to be an informal uniform of brown trousers with cuffs turned up, white shirts with no collars, black unbuttoned vests, and no shoes.

A burgundy-colored handkerchief poked out of Thiery's upper jacket pocket. He wore a gray tie with a pattern indistinguishable from the distance. Gold glinted from his shirt cuffs, indicating links rather than buttons. The patent leather of his shoes already glistened in the morning sun, but he was in the process of rubbing the tips and vamps self-consciously against the backs of his trouser legs. He completed his attention-getting outfit with a Panama hat, so that Le Brun could see neither the exact shade nor the quality of his hair. From where John stood, Solicitor Thiery seemed to have a good tan. He guessed his age to be early thirties.

"Is he white?" the captain repeated. The corner of his mouth twisted into something less amiable than his usual smile. "You would do better to ask someone more intimately involved with St. Lucia. I venture you shall have a thousand questions answered by the next time we meet." He touched his forefinger to his cap and turned toward the top deck.

"I wonder how many other tourists, from all corners of the earth, are presently on St. Lucia," Paul Van Fleet said as the group started down the gangplank. "No one I know has ever been here. I must admit, one of my major motivations for accepting Johnson's prize was for bragging rights at my clubs."

Lordis said, "One would think more than a few Englishmen and women would be here, since it is a British colony. Here for both business and pure wanderlust. The British are certainly an adventurous people, gallivanting around the globe."

"Plantin' their flag on every shore and claimin' it for the Empire," John added.

Lordis, who walked just ahead of her husband, waggled her forefinger at his negative remark. "No, what I'm referring to is that book I read about the English ladies traipsing alone to places like Saudi Arabia and the Congo and sharing their adventures in diaries. I call them intrepid."

"Except for the ones who are never heard from again and end up in harems or cooking pots," Mrs. Van Fleet commented, raising her paisley-printed parasol.

The solicitor/greeter glanced quickly at a slip of paper in his hand, then tucked it into a trouser pocket as the foursome neared. "Mr. and Mrs. Le Brun?"

John half-hoisted his hand.

"And Mr. and Mrs. Van Fleet. I am Carlisle Thiery. Welcome to St. Lucia!"

From up close, John detected a pronounced angle of cheekbone, slightly wider nasal alar lobules than those of most pure Caucasians, and enough extra length to his fingers to betray a degree of African heritage. His hair was black and wavy nearly to the point of being kinky. The answer in John's mind to Mrs. Van Fleet's question was that Thiery was of mixed race, but that anyone's negative attitude developed upon observations such as he had made was ignorant. To Le Brun, what each man or woman believed and how that individual acted on those beliefs were what should be used to distinguish her or him from others.

As a consequence of his natural curiosity and his years as sheriff and detective, John knew that he constantly studied strangers far more intently than would the normal man. He had been motivated to concentrate his observational skills because Minerva Van Fleet had made it an issue and Captain Johnson had deflected her question. Up close, he also observed the singular difference between Thiery's high-class English accent and the symphony of a unique French patois coming from the dockside workers who moved past the wagon. *I wonder how long he lived in England,* John thought. *Could just a couple of years studying law wash away all traces of his native accent and cadence?*

"If you have no objections, we can walk to the New Bristol Hotel," said their facilitator. "It's only a few blocks inland. I'll point out shops of possible interest along the way." He jerked his thumb backward. "That man will bring your belongings to the hotel. He's trustworthy."

John looked at the brown-skinned driver. He was taller than John, and thinner. The ease with which he loaded Lordis's steamer trunk into the wagon spoke convincingly of his strength. John's attention was redirected to Paul Van Fleet. His fellow traveler's cheek twitched a bit at the prospect of moving his girth so far on foot, but he gamely held his tongue.

As the group walked briefly along Jeremie Street, then inland along Bourbon and onto Micoud Street, it became clear that Castries was a business city and not a tourist mecca. The only shops that offered a degree of interest to the ladies were those of a jeweler who sold the work of local artisans, an art gallery containing both local and European paintings and sculpture, and a narrow store that sold native-woven and -dyed cloth in bolts. The rest of the discretionary purchase shops sold items from Great Britain or the United States.

John noted that many of the buildings bore the French influence of balconies and latticework. He also noted that they were fashioned of wood rather than stone, brick, or concrete. *One errant match and this burg could go up like Chicago did,* he thought.

"The treasures of our island are not in Castries, which is our only town of size," said Thiery. "St. Lucia is special precisely because it is so unspoiled. I intend to expose you to its many beauties in the time you spend with us."

"We'll be riding most of that time, I trust," said Mr. Van Fleet, puffing before and after his sentence.

"Naturally. After you've approved of your rooms, I'll have hotel employees drive you out to a local beach to enjoy the afternoon. Then tomorrow, unless you wish to alter the agenda, I'd like to present personally some of our most spectacular beaches on the north end of our island."

No one objected. Thiery excused himself at the New Bristol's check-in desk, explaining that his lawyerly obligations demanded he leave them for the afternoon.

"You look a bit discomforted," John observed of his wife.

"It is my time of the month," Lordis replied, "and the concoction your apothecary mixed for me has failed to relieve any of my cramping." She glanced toward the hotel entrance. "I saw a good-sized drugstore across the street."

"Do you want me to—"

"I'm capable of making my needs known, even in a foreign country," Lordis said firmly but without sign of irritation. "I'll see you in the room."

The hotel's staff did its best to offer a pleasant experience for guests. However, their eagerness and efficiency could not negate an old, soft mattress and a Spartan bathroom, with low-pressure water that never became hot. The louvered doors leading to the veranda did little to shut out the noise filtering up from the street. John carried a gecko out of the shower and set it hurriedly on the outside wall so that Lordis might not be further depressed.

"It's not the Waldorf-Astoria," John said when Lordis came through the door, "but it's also not campin' in the elements."

"It's fine," Lordis assured him.

Lordis set down the bottle she had purchased at the apothecary shop.

"I hope that will make you feel better," John said.

"I shall see. I figure the shop is the best in Castries; Mr. Thiery was leaving it carrying a white paper sack as I entered."

John examined the blue tincture bottle with curiosity. "I reckon that dandy patronizes only the best."

---

THE DRIVER WHO had brought the vacationers' luggage from the docks to the hotel was part of the New Bristol staff. His name was Gilles Beaufort, and he had a brother and fellow employee named Anton, who looked much like him. Both were strongly built, with milk-chocolate skin. Each drove a two-passenger carriage to transport the Le Bruns and Van Fleets to Choc Beach. The spot lay about three miles north of Castries. Both couples were delighted by how much more beautiful and calm the water was than in New York and Georgia. Moreover, the honey-colored sand was pristine. Minerva, however, could not help expressing fleeting disappointment that there were no bathing machines, structures shaped like outhouses on wide wheels that were pushed into and out of the water by horses for the privacy of the bather. Ropes had been secured to coconut palms edging the beach so that the ladies could follow them out to where they were tied off on anchored buoys. Given the gentle lapping of the waves, however, the measure was not deemed necessary by either Minerva or Lordis.

Minerva, who the Le Bruns judged to be about forty, wore a white shirt-blouse with a sailor collar over bloomers trimmed with blue ribbons and bows. Her cap resembled a Puritan bonnet. Lordis's fashion was more daring, sporting a sleeveless black blouse with matching Knickerbockers and an oil-impregnated puff cap. Both ladies wore slippers with cork bottoms.

Fashionable seaside suits for men barely varied, made of cotton in two parts, with horizontal stripes alternating white with a sedate color. Shirts were half-sleeved, and trunks extended to just above the knees. Both couples had dared saltwater before their vacation, the Van Fleets becoming acquainted with it at Coney Island Beach. All their limbs except for John's arms were alabaster white.

The four ventured from the beach into the invitingly mild sea, playfully splashing each other like children and chasing the small fish that darted around them once they had entered to their waists. The delight on Lordis's face was a tonic to John. Hard, postwar circumstances had not allowed him to pamper and spoil his first wife, and then she had died of yellow fever far too young. He was daily grateful for a second chance to brighten the life of a woman. Even though Lordis had lived in luxury, she had been a perpetual servant to three ungrateful men unworthy of her devotion.

An unexpected pleasantry was added to the outing when music suddenly emanated from the direction of the carriages. Anton Beaufort had produced a violin as if by magic. He played an impromptu concert, not with great artistry but certainly with verve, first selecting popular English and American dance hall pieces, then choosing several Caribbean melodies, and finally ending with a few simple classical solos.

The four North Americans were surprised when more than an hour had passed and their skins glowed a soft pink. Containers of fresh water were provided by the brothers Beauchamp from large baskets stowed under their buggy seats, so that they could rinse away the ocean salt and change clothes in a cabana built by and reserved exclusively for the hotel. Everyone agreed that their vacation had begun well.

---

AT TEN MINUTES before seven, Carlisle Thiery appeared at the hotel with his wife Sibyl on his arm. The lawyer was clearly very proud of having wed her. When he introduced her, he said, "This is Sibyl. *Si belle, est-ce vrai?*" which was a French pun meaning "So beautiful, is it not true?" John agreed. He noted that while her doe eyes were as brown as her husband's and her hair brown and wavy, she looked Northern European with no trace of mixed blood. Sibyl's age appeared to be somewhere between her late twenties and early thirties. She was slender and delicate but still exuded an aura of health. She was a head shorter than Carlisle, doll-like in proportions, gestures, and porcelain skin. She, like Minerva Van Fleet, was not eager to initiate conversation. When she did, her voice was so softly childlike that listeners automatically bent toward her.

"Monsieur Thiery," the address every local worker gave him, had selected a restaurant on the western verge of Castries's harbor. It was called La Chatelaine and overlooked the street from the second story of a powder-blue painted building. Sturdy pink shutters were hoisted high to create an open front wall. The view faced due west, with the sun lowering toward the slight curve of the Caribbean Sea, framed on either side by the hillocks that guarded the harbor. Sunlight pierced a thin line of clouds, falling upon the glistening waters in golden, fan-like beams.

"Magnificent!" Lordis exclaimed.

Carlisle grinned at the success of his hosting. "We've come early enough that you should see clouds change from orange to salmon to red. Perhaps before you leave us, you'll even catch the elusive green flash just before the last rays of light disappear."

"'Red at night/sailors' delight,'" John recited. "I imagine when the rains come, these shutters must make the place quite dreary."

"You're asking me indirectly about what weather to expect for your vacation," Monsieur replied, as the gentlemen seated their ladies. "It is true that next week begins what we call the 'wet season.' However, that is not every day, and even on those days when it does rain, it's most often confined to between four and six in the afternoon and while you sleep."

John wanted more. "The hurricanes don't invade until August and September, if my readin' correctly informed me."

"True enough. St. Lucia is usually out of the path of most hurricanes. Starting next week, though, we can experience the occasional tropical storm. A period of considerable rain and wind, but not of hurricane force. This is necessary to make the island so lush and to supply our splendid waterfalls." As he sat and snapped open his linen napkin, Thiery added, "Our paradise is not perfect. The land lacks vital minerals, coal, or oil. Sometimes, too much rain. But the same rain that turns many roads to mud makes our trees and herbs grow, and these not only provide us fuel but also turn our lava into rich soil."

"Lava means volcanoes," Minerva worried aloud.

"Without volcanoes, there would be no islands here. Have no fear, friends. St. Lucia has one sleepy volcano that snores sulfur fumes, but nothing like the one that devastated Martinique. "

The vacationers' faces together looked as grim as a hanging jury. They all understood the reference. Only eight years earlier, on May 8 of 1902, Martinique's Mount Pelée erupted after two weeks of warnings that were almost totally ignored, causing the greatest natural disaster in the modern history of the region. The city of Saint-Pierre, known as the Paris of the Caribbean, was utterly destroyed. Sulfurous gases up to 2,000 degrees Fahrenheit raced through the streets. Tremendous blasts released enough ash to choke all thoroughfares. No structures survived. Reports claimed that all but three among 30,000 inhabitants died. Those who fled into the harbor were boiled alive. Fifteen of sixteen moored ships were capsized by the tsunami-like movement of the sea, killing everyone on board.

"I saw the plumes of smoke and ash easily from the Morne," Sibyl said in her soft, clipped British accent. When she registered the blank looks coming from across the table, she dipped her head to the left and added, "Morne Fortune, Good Luck Mountain, lies just to the south of Castries. I was up there in the wireless office, and I sent the news of the explosion all around the world."

"You work outside of the home?" Lordis asked, with tact.

"Yes, but only a short walk from our house. At that time I was an apprentice, but now I direct the office."

"It's an important position," Carlisle affirmed, smiling at his wife. "We have no underwater communication cable yet for the Windward Islands. We have added telephone wires on the poles that supply electricity, but few can afford the service. Most of St. Lucia's news travels by mouth."

"Do you have children?" Minerva asked Mrs. Thiery.

"I do. Two girls. Vicky and Lizzy. Eight and four years old."

"And who cares for them when you work?" the financier's wife continued to probe.

Sibyl weathered the woman's cobra-like stare without blinking. "Carlisle's mother lives with us. She is happy to care for the children when we go out at night as well."

"This is an interestin' menu," John declared, redirecting the conversation. "How does curried chicken come to be offered?"

"The influence of a host of East Indian immigrants," Carlisle supplied.

"Do you mean people from Malaysia or Indonesia?" John asked.

"No. I mean from the country of India . . . as opposed to the West Indies. Their presence is due to a changing economy. Our sugarcane planters find it increasingly difficult to compete with the rising beet sugar competition in Europe and your country and the sugarcane from Southeast Asia. In the last ten years, we've had some eight thousand native laborers leave the island."

"To where?" Lordis asked.

"Digging the Panama Canal. Working French gold mines. Difficult and dangerous as those jobs are, they command better pay than our cane field work."

"Ah, for the good old days of slave labor, eh?" Paul interjected in a tone that indicated he meant his words as a joke.

The long silence around the table caused him to blush slightly.

"I've seen no Indians," John said.

Thiery nodded. "They generally stick to their own little villages, mostly around the plantations. They don't make enough money to visit Castries often, and they're not welcome in the black settlements."

"Because they're willing to work for less," Paul said, changing to a deadly serious voice.

"Yes, they do drive the wages down. But also because they've willingly sold themselves into virtual slavery; the ancestors of our black citizens were brought here in chains. To our citizens of African heritage, it's an important distinction of pride." He shook his head ruefully. "Ironically, further animosity is caused between the two groups because the Indians regard all blacks as inferior to their race. Just one level higher than the Untouchables caste."

"Is blood shed over this?" Lordis asked.

"Very rarely. St. Lucia is a remarkably peaceful place. You ladies can walk alone in any populated area or on any beach with no fear of harm."

Minerva did not look convinced.

John raised his menu again. "Bouyon. Lambi."

"That's conch," Thiery supplied.

"Yes, I know. Strong French influence in your food."

"Indeed," the lawyer replied. "Until its ownership was finally settled in 1803, St. Lucia traded hands between the English and the French fourteen times. The French held it roughly four-and-a-half times longer than the British in those two hundred years, making their influence much stronger. Unfortunately, the constant warring and destruction kept the island from developing a stable infrastructure. You can see the evidence even today. Plus, the shifting control encouraged occupation by pirates and escaped slaves, both black and white, which discouraged honest, law-abiding immigrants. We St. Lucians have had a rough time of it. But things are rapidly improving."

Lordis said, "John read to me that your national dish is green figs and salt fish with green bananas. I see it here on—"

"It is, I'm afraid, an acquired taste," Carlisle discouraged. "Sure to make you thirsty, Mrs. Le Brun. La Chatelaine's specialties are stews. Either the bouyon or the pepper pot."

For a time, Carlisle controlled the conversation. He revealed that he had pestered most of the sea captains to provide him with all newspapers they carried out of their ports of call. He was eager to learn more than editions of the New York *Herald* and the New Orleans *Picayune* provided about the January Air Meet at Dominguez Field in Los Angeles, the first international aviation meet in the United States.

Among the visitors, Paul Van Fleet had amassed the most information, and he freely shared it.

"The design of airplanes advances at an astonishing pace," Thiery proclaimed. "I am certain that within no more than a decade, versions will be built that can transport a dozen civilians hundreds of miles."

John shook his head. "You're bein' a bit sanguine, Monsieur Thiery. It's largely a question of capitalist investment. I believe that only after some intrepid soul is able to fly across the Atlantic will the large infusions of cash become available for such craft as you imagine. Once they're proven truly safe, thousands of the well-heeled will gladly pay dearly to be able to leap the Pond in a day rather than steam across it for five days. Although far from rich, I would be one of them. I confess that oceans petrify me."

John's cautious prediction caused their host to lapse into mute musing, allowing a general conversation regarding the wines that should be served with the meal. Gradually, as the food was consumed and clinking salutes succeeded each other, the conversation became merrier and more random.

Growing suddenly serious, Carlisle Thiery said, "I do not wish to dictate your entire itinerary for you. Nor can excursions be planned too far out, given the vagaries of weather. However, tomorrow night you two gentlemen must prepare yourselves to be feted by the St. Lucia Island Club. It is our gentleman's home away from home, fashioned after the Planter's Club in London. Indeed, it is made up almost entirely of the island's planters."

"Are you a member?" Lordis asked.

Thiery constructed a smile. "Professional persons such as lawyers and doctors are not included."

"So, if it were the Foundation Digger's Club, the ditch diggers wouldn't be included," John said.

Caught off guard, Carlisle uttered a short convulsive laugh. "Just so, just so. Members travel to Castries from distant parts of the island every Saturday late afternoon. Depending on the season and the weather, there might only be four in attendance, or perhaps as many as twenty. I'm sorry to say, with the wet season just beginning, you're not likely to meet too many. There are four bedrooms on the second floor for those who choose to overnight here. Some stay on Friday and Sunday nights as well."

"And their wives?" Minerva wanted to know.

"They remain at the plantations as a rule and entertain each other in their splendid homes. I have arranged a diversion for you two ladies as well. The St. Lucia Ladies' Book Club meets once a month, and, as chance would have it, that meeting will also take place tomorrow night. Due to our distance from London, Boston, Paris, and New York, we receive the latest novels as much as a year after publication. Anything recent you ladies may have read that you can recommend and briefly describe would turn you into instant friends."

"Of the wives of the lawyers, doctors, and other professionals," John added.

This time, Carlisle's amusement merely curled the corner of his lip. He waited until the main course dishes were cleared before saying, "For Sunday, may I assume you all attend church services?"

Minerva's eyes darted to her husband's face. He said, "Of course. We are Dutch Reformed, but I doubt you have that denomination on St. Lucia."

"The Church of England is our Protestant faith here," Carlisle answered. He pivoted to address Lordis and John. "We have three Roman Catholic churches in this area. There's the new Cathedral of the Immaculate—"

"We're Anglican," Lordis interrupted.

The lawyer's head reared back slightly. "Ah. Pardon me. That's what comes from making an assumption based on a last name."

"And a Gallic nose," John added, amiably poking fun at his profile.

"Then all three couples at this table will worship at 'the red brick church,' as many call it. Although we're a British island, almost 80 percent of our population is Roman Catholic."

The Thierys continued to educate their guests to facts of history and religion until their waiter arrived with a chilled, uncorked bottle of wine, replacing the drained bottles in the silver-plated bucket.

"As our dessert wine, a La Tour Blanche Sauternes," Monsieur Thiery proclaimed. "Sauternes have good and bad years, and I was assured this vintage is one of the better crops."

John had known little about wines, foreign or domestic, before he became intimate with Lordis Goode. She had gained her broad knowledge from the father and two sons she served, all of whom were social climbers and snobs. John remembered that good Sauternes years depended on heavy mists rising from the two French rivers adjacent to the vineyards. The extra wetness allowed the growth of a fungus named *Botrytis cinerea*, which in turn caused rot infestation that made the harvest-time grapes delicious. Lordis declined to comment, so John also held his tongue. Looking at the Van Fleets' complaisant expressions, he was sure they had no knowledge of the cost of such a wine and the gesture the Thierys had made. *Rotten cheese, cultivating mushrooms on rotting organic material, encouraging rotting grapes,* John thought to himself. *I'm glad I'm only French American.*

"You are spoiling us far beyond what we have contracted to pay you, sir," Lordis said.

Carlisle shrugged. "If you believe that to be true, I'm sure you'll find a way to return the kindness." He punctuated his sentence with a dismissing laugh.

---

WHEN LORDIS EMERGED from the hotel bathroom wearing a light robe, she said to John, "I've been waiting for you to speak first, but since you haven't . . . Do you not get the distinct feeling that first you and Paul and now all of us are being manipulated like marionettes?"

"All the way back to Bobby Johnson rollin' over on that chess game bet," John replied as he fluffed his pillow. "Then tellin' us he intended to retire here. Never you mind, my darlin'. I brought a pair of scissors."

"Scissors?"

"Indeed. To be able to cut invisible puppet strings whenever we decide we've had enough of dancin' to their tune."

# CHAPTER FIVE

## June 25, 1910

THE "WHILE YOU SLEEP RAIN" that Carlisle Thiery spoke of lasted until ten o'clock on Saturday morning. Moments after the sun broke through the clouds, Anton and Gilles Beaufort sat waiting in their buggies in front of the New Bristol Hotel. The nattily dressed solicitor once again commanded his own carriage. He regretted not being able to carry any of the vacationers but expected he would need to return to Castries for an appointment before their tour was completed.

The drive along the rough road that led to the northern tip of St. Lucia was slowed by water-filled dips that sometimes equaled the dimensions of swimming pools. Except for Broadway, which cut diagonally across Manhattan Island, New York City streets and avenues above Fourteenth Street were laid out in strictly straight lines. Similarly, Brunswick, Georgia, had a rectilinear plan. The roads of St. Lucia, however, twisted around the bases and lower slopes of wandering hills and mountains. Six miles as the crow flew took more than eight on land. The Le Bruns were informed by Gilles that trips southward on the western part of the island would be even lengthier.

After more than an hour, the buggies pulled up to the edge of a spectacularly long beach of sugar sand. Small, brightly painted fishing canoes with knife-like stems bobbed on the aquamarine water. At the island's northern edge rose a peninsula with two bald, blunt, long-dead volcanoes at either extreme. Slate-blue clouds hung above a light haze. The vegetation was scattered and scrubby.

"Rodney Bay!" Thiery announced in a loud voice.

Everyone piled out of the carriages. John turned a slow, 360-degree circle, capturing snapshots as he did. "Not many people livin' here," he observed.

"True enough," Thiery replied. "Salt water just under the soil keeps crops and anything but the most hardy plants from growing. A few swampy ponds foster mosquitoes. But the ponds can be easily drained, and dirt can be mounded up to support more elegant bushes and trees. This beach is a rare thing, is it not?"

"Indeed," John agreed.

Carlisle surprised the Georgian by slipping off his patent-leather shoes, stripping down his stockings, and rolling up the cuffs of his trousers. In a powerful voice he called out, "Everyone! Let's walk along the edge of the water. You can look for shells and play catch with the crabs."

While the women followed Thiery's suggestions, he spoke to John and Paul, who had followed his lead and exposed their legs up to the knees.

The lawyer said, "I have heard that more and more of your citizens are spending parts of their summers at the Long Island and New Jersey beaches, Mr. Van Fleet."

"That's true."

Thiery turned to John. "Captain Johnson regaled me several months back regarding your involvement with a fabulous millionaire's beach resort called the Jekyl Island Club. That beach is supposed to be quite inviting."

"Also true," John said.

"But what are those beaches compared to this one?"

"Second-class, due to the difference of the water," John provided, waiting for the lawyer to set the hook. He was disappointed.

Carlisle Thiery would only go so far as to say, "So, in spite of all the power and wealth of your country, little St. Lucia wins gold for its beaches . . . and, I dare say, its pervasively mild climate." Not waiting for his guests' agreement, he dashed toward the edge of the water.

"Imagine if this scenic island were off the coast of Florida," Van Fleet said to Le Brun.

"The Bahamas are," John reminded him.

"They're little more than sand dunes."

"If this island were fifteen hundred miles closer to our shores, our capitalists would have covered over every flat inch of it with macadam, mansions, high-rises, restaurants, roller coasters, and Ferris wheels. It's fortunate it's so far from us."

"But that ocean trip wasn't so bad," Van Fleet persisted. "Heck, a passenger liner could probably cut an entire day off the time we spent on the water. And then there's the inevitable refinement of the airplane, as Thiery said."

"He and Captain Johnson have got you thinkin' exactly what they want you to think," John remarked. "Our country is indeed goin' resort crazy, so why not consider the perfect water and climate of the Caribbean. But so far south?"

Van Fleet gave no answer but satisfied himself with staring at the dozen two-man fishing boats anchored off shore.

---

WHEN THE LADIES TIRED of exploring the beach, the buggies moved eastward, toward a hilly ridge not far away. Thiery's stated goal was to show the group a sugar plantation. The particular sugarcane farm was the only working one in the area. The owner's name was Andrew Ashton. His family had owned the 300-acre plantation for almost one hundred years. The man's smooth hands and well-trimmed nails betrayed that he had never spent a full day hacking or hoeing in his cane fields. However, he had clearly spent years supervising his operation. His face was gullied with wrinkles and tan as a leather satchel. His brownish-yellow teeth indicated that he had chewed untold plugs of tobacco. John would not have been surprised if someone had vowed Ashton was only fifty; likewise, he would not have blinked if told the man was sixty-five.

John had read that sugarcane at maturity was an impressive plant, growing in multiple stalks from a single root, the stalks becoming up to two inches in diameter and the top of the plant reaching as high as twenty feet. Above sword-shaped leaves poked spear-like upper stalks that ended in delicate tassels. He had learned that various types of sugarcane were colored near-white, yellow, deep green, red, purple, and violet. Nothing like his images were visible. Instead, the stalks had been cut nearly to the ground. John expressed his disappointment to the plantation owner.

"Well, you've come after the last harvesting. But, with the onset of the rainy season, workers have returned to the fields by the scores," explained Ashton. "Now, this area is old growth, so they'll be planting cuttings from live stalks, each about a foot long, each with several joints that we call 'nodes.'"

"There are much larger plantations on the windward side of the island," Thiery added. "Cane prefers flat ground, with clay loam or muck."

Ashton remembered his manners and removed his broad-brimmed hat in the presence of the wives. "And wherever there is enough water to keep the plants happy without drowning them. The sunlight is a constant blessing, of course, and the only other things we need from Mother Nature are wind or falling water. We have both."

The owner led the group to a cone-shaped stone structure some twenty feet high and about fifteen feet in diameter at its base. The pinnacle of the cone had been omitted. It had been built at the edge of a decline. At one side, four wings covered in cloth rotated slowly in the breeze, the very image of the "dragon" windmill that Don Quixote tilted with. A single door had been designed in the sugar mill's top level. Inside the cone, grinding stones rolled round and round to crush hacked-up lengths of mature cane fed by menial South Asian laborers. From the crushed cane, raw sugar juice dripped down to be captured on the level below.

Ashton pointed to another stone structure abutted to the steep edge of the mountain that backed the plantation. "That's our other mill, run by falling water. Called an *ingenio*, from the Spanish." He pointed out a storage house, tool sheds, workers' hovels, and several other buildings.

"Running this place is an expensive proposition. Too expensive, given the falling prices of sugar around the world. Even using Indians, I can't compete with the Cuban and Brazilian slave forces." Ashton shook his head and continued in a peculiar combination accent that indicated he spent as much time speaking the native Creole as the King's English. He nodded directly west, toward Rodney Bay. "I own most of this area, and I'm looking to sell it. Sell it and make a permanent trip back to Jolly Olde England."

John pivoted to find Carlisle Thiery. The lawyer had silently distanced himself beyond earshot, as if his movement would prove that he had no involvement in what the plantation owner had begun pitching.

"Who would buy a failing sugarcane plantation?" Paul Van Fleet asked with one eyebrow cocked. Le Brun had long since realized this facial expression signaled that the financier's grinding stones were moving, crunching numbers and estimating the juice of profits.

Ashton answered, "Somebody smart enough to realize the sands of that beach are white gold. Look at how many passenger ships have been built in the last ten years. There's word aplenty that certain visionaries in your country, France, and England are planning ships to cruise the Caribbean. Some of them will be dropping their passengers off for extended stays. There's nothing in Martinique or Guadeloupe to compare with Rodney Bay." Van Fleet swung his right arm as if to swat such a preposterous thought away. "I imagine that a truly first-class development here would take the underwriting of a conglomerate," Ashton continued. "They should know that they'll get no cheaper labor on any island half so beautiful, both during the building phase and in the running of a resort."

"Where do we sign?" John said suddenly.

Andrew Ashton's eyes lit momentarily, until he realized he was being teased.

"It's not out of the realm of possibility," Van Fleet judged. "I can see several members of the New York Yacht Club wanting to sail down here on vacation. Talk about privacy!"

"But St. Lucia is part of the British Empire," John stated. "Puerto Rico is our possession now, and I hear tell it has magnificent beaches. Also, the Danish part of the Virgin Islands is not off the table. The Danish king rejected our offer of five million for St. Croix, St. Thomas, and St. John back in '02, but our military wants somethin' in that area for strategic reasons. Might could be another U.S. protectorate soon enough." He locked Ashton's eyes with his. "And those gems are a darned sight closer to our shores than the Windwards."

John realized that Lordis stood directly behind him. He wondered how much of the conversation she had captured, even as he continued.

"However, both Mr. Van Fleet and I are intimate with gentlemen who have piles of readily disposable cash. There's no harm in us layin' out the details."

"It would come down to cost versus benefit," Van Fleet joined in.

John spun slowly, so that Van Fleet and Ashton could follow his changed focus. "And, naturally, the Foreign Office in London and several other branches of His Majesty's government would need to stick in their two shillin's worth of concerns. Fortunately, there happens to be among us a solicitor who graduated from Cambridge."

---

AS HE PROMISED TO DO, Carlisle Thiery had driven away before the tour completed. Andrew Ashton rode behind the two hotel buggies on the return trip to Castries, his conveyance being a jaunting cart, so smartly shaped that it reminded John of a racing sulky. *In spite of bemoaning the imminent collapse of his plantation,* John thought, *Ashton's a member of the St. Lucia Island Club elite, riding and dressing like royalty. One man's definition of hard times is another's of living high on the hog.*

The high-angled, cloud-burning sun had evaporated the morning puddles and hardened the road, speeding the passage back to the port town. When the streets became well-traveled, Ashton called out a farewell, waved, and disappeared around a corner.

---

AMPLE TIME had been allowed for the vacationers to relax before heading out to the respective clubs. As Lordis lay resting in bed next to John under the rotating paddles of an electric ceiling fan, she said, "My suspicions were correct all along . . . about our merry sea captain and the fastidious solicitor."

"Correct indeed," John granted.

"You certainly aren't considering fronting for those two with your millionaire acquaintances," she declared.

John rolled on his side to watch her motile face. "Why not?"

"Why not? To shill for the same men who cheated you out of thousands of dollars when your own cousin fronted for them? The slimy lot grabbed your piece of Jekyll Island for next to nothing."

"The way of the world, my love," he replied. "Here's my opportunity to be on the winner's side in a land grab."

Lordis's rising indignation drew her upright. She glowered at her husband.

John burst out laughing. "I do declare, I married Carrie Nation and Susan Anthony combined. Relax, dear. My only mention of this schemin' once we get home will be for dinner table amusement."

"I'll hold you to that. That elegant Carlisle Thiery is nothing more than an ambulance chaser in sheep's clothing."

"'Ambulance chaser,'" John repeated. "Never heard that term before. It's very visual."

"It's all too common in New York," Lordis said with disdain. "No wonder Shakespeare had one of his characters say, 'The first thing we do, let's kill all the lawyers.'"

Among his numerous intellectual interests, John Le Brun was an avid devotee of William Shakespeare's works, both in print and in the performance of his plays. He knew that the speaker of the well-known line was one Dick the Butcher, a follower of the rebel Jack Cade, who wanted to overthrow King Henry VI and the status quo. Debates had appeared for years in print as to whether or not Shakespeare meant the line in defense of the profession or to malign it. John decided that, since he was already teasing his wife, annotating her comment was not a wise act.

"This lawyer seems harmless enough," John said instead. "He's certainly transparent in his desire to benefit from St. Lucia's improvement. Should we condemn him for wantin' what's good for all the people?"

"We should condemn him for standing first in line, with his elegant suit pockets spread wide to receive the wealth," Lordis countered. "And isn't he an enigma? We've already seen what we expected to see: The few whites dominate, and the black majority are slaves in all except for whatever scrap of paper gave them their legal freedom. Carlisle Thiery is both black and white. Obviously, he is a professional man. How free can a mulatto become in this country?"

John rolled over and closed his eyes. "We have fourteen more days on St. Lucia. I dare say, learnin' about its people will be as divertin' and educational as about its geography."

---

JUST AS HE HAD EXPLAINED the evening before, Carlisle Thiery was not welcome inside the Planter's Club. John and Paul Van Fleet had been told that they were expected between seven-thirty and eight o'clock on Saturday evening. The two vacationers sat in the hotel lobby, debating whether or not Thiery would show, if only to escort them to the club. At five minutes before eight, they agreed that finding the place was up to them. The desk clerk explained that the building lay only two blocks distant. John suggested that they take a horse-drawn cab, and the corpulent financier agreed with gratitude written on his face.

"We should gird ourselves against all sorts of pleas for infusions of American cash," Van Fleet said during the ride.

"I have put a combination lock on my wallet," John agreed.

Le Brun had not expected the clubhouse to be any grand edifice, such as the huge stone piles erected along New York's Fifth Avenue—the Union League, Metropolitan, Progress, Harvard, University and Union Clubs. He did, nonetheless, expect a grander structure than the typical Castries two-story building. The plantation owners, after all, dominated the island and possessed the majority of the wealth. The Planter's Club looked only a bit grander and larger than the building in which La Chatelaine was housed.

The two North Americans were greeted at the front door by Andrew Ashton, who immediately led them through the foyer and into a large sitting room on the left side of the clubhouse. It was furnished with leather easy chairs, tables, a trio of floor lamps, and two bookshelves overflowing with literature in English and French. Photographs of various plantations adorned the walls. John observed that a wide archway connected the sitting room to a dining room behind, with French doors at either end to coax errant breezes through. He noted that sitting and dining rooms of the most prominent Brunswick homes were almost as large.

Waiting in a wide circle, brandy snifters in hand, were six men. In the spacious room, their small number seemed to John, as his hometown friend Nicodemus had been fond of saying, “Rolling around like a few marbles in a tin can.” He suspected the reason for the low turnout was not only the beginning of the wet season but also the decline in the number of sugar plantations. He labored to connect the six names to their faces as they were introduced. They were Neville Wilcox, Nigel Harvey, Jack Mayberry, Raymond Scott, Algernon Brummel, and Howard Norcross. Paul and John were greeted with enthusiasm and immediately offered drinks.

“I’ve heard that you spent some time in Mayfair,” Neville Wilcox said to Le Brun, speaking of the district of London most densely populated by men’s clubs, which were the invention of English gentlemen. “I wonder if you passed the Planter’s Club.”

“I’m sorry. I can’t recall if I did or did not,” John replied. What he was certain of was that, if he had, that clubhouse had made no impression on him. More to the point, it had never come up in his conversations with Geoffrey Moore, his transcontinental businessman friend who had been turned rabid by the bite of club joining. Englishman Moore had been the man who had pestered Le Brun to visit London immediately after he retired. John had been squired to a half-dozen of his clubs and shown the edifices of a score more. Either by visit, by indirect introduction, or by walking tour, John was familiar with White's, Boodle's, Brook's, the Royal Thames Yacht, Lord's, Union, Guards, The Athenaeum, Garrick, Army and Navy, St. James, Naval and Military, Junior Carlton, Sceptred Isle, Authors', Royal Automobile, and more he could not readily remember. But the London Planter's Club he had never seen nor heard spoken of. The fact seemed curious to him, because a vast portion of the wealth of the British Empire depended on overseas plantations in India, Burma, Ceylon, South and East Africa, and around the Caribbean. He suspected that many of the enterprises' owners were absentee landlords, living in England and rarely visiting their holdings. Such a club should have had an enormously rich membership. *Perhaps it does,* John thought, *but it isn't a London club of prestige. The same men must fixate on the more exclusive home-country clubs. Here in St. Lucia, there is only one white man's club, and yet it is pedestrian in comparison. I imagine nothing can testify more starkly as to the relative poverty of this island than the place in which I stand.*

"I understand that you were a successful planter of sea cotton and indigo in your youth," said Howard Norcross.

"I can't claim great success," John returned. "In the days followin' our defeat at the hands of the Yankees, very few other than the carpetbaggers and scalawags made good money."

"Is that what inspired you to become an officer of the law and a detective?"

"Indeed. Both from my need to make money and to help satisfy local justice."

"Which eventually led you to solve an important murder case at London's Sceptred Isle Club," Norcross praised.

"Working with Sir Arthur Conan Doyle, the author of the Sherlock Holmes tales," Algernon Brummel added, showing off for his fellow members.

"Might any of you know Geoffrey Moore?" John asked. When no one recognized the name, he understood that Captain Bobby Johnson had been the free-flowing conduit recounting a good portion of John's life to at least the ears of planters Norcross and Brummel.

"Even more spectacular was your solving of the murders at the Jekyl Island Club," Norcross interjected.

"That club's members are associates of mine," Paul edged into the conversation. "I share membership with them through the Metropolitan and New York Yacht Clubs."

A man entered the foyer with haste and thrust his riding cape and hat into the hands of the butler. All heads turned in his direction. He glanced at the guests briefly, but his gaze fixed on Nigel Harvey. Harvey returned his stare, his eyes narrowing, jaw setting, and chin angling upward.

"Another member . . . Mr. Peter Palmer," Andrew Ashton imparted to John and Paul. Palmer appeared to be considerably younger than any of the other planters, still smooth-skinned and sleek-haired.

"I was told you weren't coming," Harvey said coolly to Palmer.

"I changed my mind," Palmer replied. "How often does one living on a remote island have the chance to meet a world-class detective?"

"I thought you'd still be talking to every laborer around my plantation," Harvey accused. His ruddy, lightly veined cheeks had turned a bit redder.

"You don't own them. Everyone is free on this island," said Palmer.

"Pour yourself a brandy, Peter," advised planter Brummel. "Then come meet our distinguished guests. We also have with us a world-class financier." Palmer moved past the group into the dining room.

"Give us your early impressions of our island," Raymond Scott, the oldest-looking among the group, invited the guests.

John allowed Paul Van Fleet to take the lead. Presently, the assembly was called to dinner. Callalou soup was the first course, followed by fried snapper.

"Paul and I have toured Mr. Ashton's plantation," John said as the group finished the main course, "but I'm sure y'all can enlighten us with fascinatin' stories about the life of the sugarcane planter."

"It's an increasingly difficult life," Nigel Harvey said with vehemence. "I expect Andrew has told you of our troubles with constantly falling prices for our products. Those of us who have survived to this point have learned the lesson of economies of scale. When a plantation close to yours fails, you need to buy it. The number of field workers cannot shrink much, but the mill operation can economize on labor, the number of white overseers be reduced. There are fewer redundant machines, fewer wagons, one warehouse in Castries. Size gives one the ability to own the whole chain of production. What your American tycoons call vertical integration."

"If you don't have at least one thousand acres under cultivation, you'll be out of business within the next few years," declared Neville Wilcox, whose words were slightly slurred from too many refills of St. Lucian rum punch.

"How much has the importation of Indians helped you?" Van Fleet asked.

Harvey shot a dark glance in Peter Palmer's direction. "They produce about 20 percent more than our native blacks over the same amount of time. Which is why some planters go to ridiculous lengths to attract them."

"My Lord, Mr. Harvey! I offer a mere two shillings a week more than you do," Palmer answered.

"You don't stop there. Last year you gave your workers netting to enclose their sleeping mats. This year, you've begun providing them with sandals."

"Acts that favor me as much as it does them," Peter countered.

He addressed the two guests. "Without netting, the workers are forced to burn green leaves in the huts to drive away the mosquitoes. Clearly, it's not effective. I've lost untold hours each year to yellow fever from those who take weeks to recover. If they die, I lose time replacing them."

"Netting seems a prudent outlay," Paul Van Fleet reasoned.

"The logs and the wogs alike have no respect for possessions," said Raymond Scott, coming to Nigel Harvey's defense. "Did you not complain to me, Peter, that many of them allowed rents in the weave, so that the mosquitoes got through anyway?"

"It's their children. They're just like ours, roughhousing without regard to delicate things."

"What about this sandal business?" Harvey asked. "Those are not cheap."

"Considering what they can accomplish, they are," Peter riposted. Again, he addressed the guests. "There's little we can do about poisonous snake bites and rat bites, ant invasions, or occasional lightning fires, but surely we can cut down on the endemic hookworm problem. None of us provides portable outhouses for the fields, so the workers just squat where they are. I showed my colleagues the scientific journal that proved hookworm larvae can live up to forty-eight hours on dry soil and three weeks in wet. They burrow through the soles of the workers' feet. Hookworm, not laziness, is what has slowed our black population down."

"More and more expense, even as we earn less and less," Harvey fumed. "The next thing I expect to hear is socialization of health care."

"Why is that a bad thing?" John asked, doing his best to conceal his consternation over the callousness of so many among the planters.

Algernon Brummel gave a complaisant shrug. "It is. First of all, because it would mean extending health care to almost forty-five thousand laborers who barely earn enough to keep themselves alive much less contribute to the running of the government. Secondly, it would be demoralizing to our Negroes, whose collective pride would be wounded by receiving something for nothing. No one on this island, the blacks included, wants to be a Marxian communist."

Nigel Harvey's grim expression indicated that he continued to smolder. John suspected that his mood came from more than fundamental disagreements on running a plantation; it arose as well from being embarrassed in front of foreign guests. Harvey cleared his throat loudly and jerked his head in Palmer's direction.

"He's even more indulgent than his father, and God knows how far that old curmudgeon could go the few times he came down with a fit of remorse. He sent young Peter to one of the more progressive universities in England, I'm afraid. Those idiot dons, who have never spent an hour working any soil nor spent one hour managing subordinates, so love inculcating 'bleeding heart of Jesus' socialism into their students."

"It's called good business sense," Peter countered.

"Call it what you will, it will ruin you, lad. Your father and I agreed on almost every aspect of running a plantation. It was a damnable shame when he died—what was it—eighteen months back."

"Piss off!" Peter shouted, clearly having enough of the older man's insults. "You and he argued all the time. Neither one of you had a new thought in your head about worker relations for the past twenty years."

Raymond Scott rose rapidly from his seat, his face reddening. "As president of the club, I forbid one more cross word between you two! If you cannot stop quarreling, confine it to the other side of the island. This club is meant to be a retreat from the cares of the day. It is simply dunderheaded that we must plan in advance which of you two will attend on a Saturday."

Neither of the men he addressed returned words. Each sat in a dark, brooding posture. Scott snatched his linen napkin from the table and retook his seat with all the dignity he could muster. "Next Saturday, we will settle this business. We have already embarrassed the club beyond apology in front of these worthy guests. In the meantime, one of you should excuse himself."

Immediately, Nigel Harvey leapt up. "I'll go. I have many dark-skinned people to talk to early tomorrow." He was allowed to exit the club without any response to his words.

After several moments of pregnant silence, Scott said to Van Fleet and Le Brun, "The start of a new season puts a great deal of pressure on all of us. Should we experiment with the burning technique being used elsewhere? Should our members have first choice of laborers within a certain distance from their plantations? How can we prepare in case there is not enough rainfall this year?" His face brightened as quickly as a light bulb being turned on. "But no cares should be brought to this dining table. What say we have dessert immediately? I understand it's fruits and marmalade cakes!"

---

JOHN FOUND LORDIS sitting on a cane chair just inside the hotel room's veranda, watching a line of raindrops splash the tile just beyond her toes.

"The rain is warm here," Lordis said without turning.

"I noticed. Remind me to purchase a couple of umbrellas," John said as he stripped off his suit jacket and shook off the water that had not already soaked into the fibers. "Otherwise, we and our duds will start to rot." When Lordis responded with only a nod of her head, he asked, "Enjoyin' the patter of the rain?"

"I am. As in St. Matthew's holy land, it falls on the upright and the evil doers alike."

John removed his tie. "I detect a less than perfect night at the book club."

"It was as white as the lilies of the field," Lordis replied. "And I thought segregation in Brunswick is strictly maintained. One of the first things the so-called ladies did was apologize for 'the black cloud that covers our island.' As if they could survive without their black and mulatto peons. For God's sake, their ancestors imported the blacks' ancestors!

"But you'll be glad to know that I held my tongue. And Minerva and I scored a bumper crop of points with them for contributing those novels and periodicals we finished on the *Pindy.* She and I are *personae magna grata,* if my old Latin lessons serve. What about your adventure at the St. Lucia Island Club?"

"Are you familiar with that Negro spiritual, 'All God's Chillun Got Wings?'"

"Yes, of course."

"One verse says, 'All God's chillun got shoes.' Well, not in St. Lucia. A goodly portion of the plantation workers suffer from hookworms—which thrive in the soil—but the owners won't buy them shoes or sandals."

"If we're to enjoy this vacation," Lordis said, "we had better put on horse blinders and concentrate on the scenery."

"And the mostly lovely weather," John added, as he removed his rain-soaked collar.

## CHAPTER SIX

# June 26, 1910

ANGLICAN CHURCH SERVICES began at 10 A.M. in Castries, owing to the extended distance some of its members traveled. The Van Fleets were neither in their hotel room nor in the lobby when the Le Bruns searched for them. They were also not inside the church when the organ prelude began.

"They're probably fifty-mile Christians," John whispered to his wife.

"What does that mean?" Lordis obliged.

"It means you only behave yourself within fifty miles of your church. When you're out of sight of it, anythin' goes."

As he cast his gaze around the congregation, John was surprised to note that the white and light-skinned, mixed-race attendees were interspersed. Twelve men, women, and children whose skin might be described as fawn, chocolate brown, or ebony sat as a group in the back two rows of pews. Carlisle Thiery, his wife, and two girls entered just before the service began, their outfits near-identical shades of white, gliding down the aisle in a tight bunch like a bride's nosegay of roses. They took their places in the first pew as if by habit, with the eyes of the congregation on them.

The sounds of the priest and the congregants were pointedly British in the intonations of speech. John imagined that, except for the church's humble architecture and more than two dozen congregants of mixed color, the scene around him would have fit comfortably in any outskirt of London. He had expected that the tempi of the hymns would be quicker than in Lordis's New York Anglican church and that the melodies would have a more joyous lilt, but each tune was sung as if it were a dirge. The homily examined the biblical passage "Am I my brother's keeper?" John noted that the definition of "brother" was left vague, with no specifics. He harbored a suspicion that the island priest's job as a sermonizer was difficult. Preaching Jesus's mandates to a privileged flock while not taking them to task for their less-than-Christian behavior toward needy neighbors was a delicate matter.

While the organ postlude vibrated the church, the worshippers fed with exaggerated politeness through the doors and into the sun. Lordis was within one person of shaking the priest's hand when a white man wearing a police uniform appeared in the street on horseback, moving at a fast trot. When he arrived in front of the building, he reined in so hard that the horse reared slightly. He hopped off, muttered a quick command to one of the colored men who had just finished worshipping, and handed him the reins. He scanned the crowd, found the face he was looking for, and hastened forward. The object of his search stepped away from the path. He was a tall, thin white man well into his fifties, dressed in what looked to be a tailor-made suit and sporting a handlebar moustache and mutton chop sideburns.

The tall man listened to a hastily delivered report, nodding gravely several times. Then his eyebrows furrowed.

"Le Brun? I know no one named Le Brun."

John stepped through the paralyzed parishioners and approached the two men. He felt his heart speed up and thump his sternum, anticipating some harrowing news from Brunswick or New York. "I am John Le Brun. What is the problem?"

The man's face grew slack at John's Georgia drawl. In a low voice he said, "I am Richard Tubble, the lieutenant governor of St. Lucia. This officer reports the burning of the Palmer mansion on the opposite side of the island."

A collective murmur of dismay arose from the congregants.

"The home of Peter Palmer?" John asked.

"Then you are acquainted with him. Mr. Nigel Harvey says that you are a detective of some renown. He would like to engage you to consult in this affair."

"I don't know what help I might be," John said. "I'm a stranger on vacation, with no tools of my profession."

"I understand. In fact, my first inclination is to dismiss the request, precisely because you are not a citizen. We suffer building fires several times a year. Some have burned down entire sections of our towns. However, since Mr. Harvey owns a plantation near to the Palmers' and was at the site, he must feel that this disaster was not a simple accident. We have no detective on our island, sir. Might you be inclined to indulge the man?"

Lordis had managed to drift close to the conversation, one ear cocked. John turned toward her. "They're askin' me to use my professional skills."

Lordis nodded. "Then they are wise."

"I need to get my camera from the New Bristol Hotel," John said, taking Lordis by the hand.

"You and your lady may ride with me," said Tubble. He looked at the priest, and in a strong voice added, "Father, please see that someone carries my wife home."

---

ST. LUCIA IS TWELVE MILES across at its widest. However, owing to the maze of mountains and valleys, the most direct west-to-east route in the country's center runs fifteen miles from Caribbean to Atlantic shores. The lieutenant governor's phaeton carriage was drawn by two powerful horses, yet the wending trip lasted nearly two hours. For the first forty minutes, the surrounding countryside was cultivated in various fields of crops, but as their route ascended and as sharply angled stone and lava walls closed in, the vegetation grew wild and thick, dominated by rainforest trees and vines. Signs of human activities vanished. Colorful birds winged above them. Those hidden in trees cackled and twittered, while unseen creatures whistled and whirred.

While they traveled, John remembered that the chief inspector in the Sceptred Isle Club case was a Mr. Tibble. He was glad he had not encountered that man in the same capacity on St. Lucia. *Talking to Tibble and Tubble would surely spell trouble*, he thought puckishly. He decided for several reasons not to share the coincidence with the lieutenant governor.

In spite of his dignified appearance, Richard Tubble was a garrulous character. He apologized for taking the North Americans away from their vacation and tried to compensate by acting as an impromptu guide, pointing out the more stunning variety of flora, including the flame-colored immortelle, ixora with its multicolored flowers, the jasmine, orchids, cassia, oleander, frangipani, bougainvillea, and hibiscus. He pointed out the hardwood mahogany trees, whose red and black seeds were favored for making necklaces; the giant and ancient ferns; and balsa, the world's lightest wood.

"It seems that a great percentage of the island can never be used for farming," Lordis observed.

"Pretty much every acre that can be is," Tubble replied. "The only means to 'make the rough places plain' would be to bring in huge earth-moving machines. But that cost is beyond us. The shovel, the hoe, and the pickaxe are still the primary tools here, just as they were three hundred years ago."

As the three drove close to the Palmer plantation, passing sloping, furrowed fields green with new life, the lieutenant governor swung his head left and right several times. "This must be a major disaster," he judged. "Saturdays and Sundays during the wet season is the only time the laborers can work on their own plots. Nothing less than a major calamity could get them away from tending their gardens."

Soon after, the first smells of the aftermath of fire invaded John Le Brun's nostrils. Then, beyond extensive fields of sugarcane stalks, came the sights of outbuildings in good condition, and finally tight groups of dark-skinned people, milling about as if by random impulses, all focusing on the ruined plantation house from a respectful distance. Three policemen faced the crowds, dressed in uniforms of black shoes and trousers, white high-collared jackets with brass buttons, black belts with prominent brass buckles, and white pith helmets. Their presence did not seem needed.

The house was a two-story structure that reminded John of the many low country, antebellum plantation homes of Georgia and South Carolina. A wide front veranda ran around three sides, elevated four steps above the ground. From the veranda's front rose six Corinthian columns that seemed to be made of granite. An upper walkway and what remained of the roof overhang were supported by the columns. The house's windows were overlarge. The outer walls had been painted a pastel yellow.

Except for smoke damage, the first story of the mansion looked sound. The second story and roof, however, were tortured hulks, with soot-blackened inner walls exposed in several places. Smoke rose in lazy plumes from the home's interior. Twisted masses of copper roof could be seen through window frames barren of glass and mullions, large patches of verdigris burned away, exposing the metal's original color.

A white man strode toward Richard Tubble's carriage.

"Mansfield," Tubble said to his passengers, to introduce the man. "The plantation's overseer."

Mansfield was a tall, burly fellow, walking slightly bow-legged, as if he spent most of his time in the saddle.

"Lieutenant Governor," Mansfield said, tipping his hat. "I can only tell you for sure what I've seen myself, but I collected stories from the blacks, what claim to have found the house in flames."

Tubble did not bother to introduce the people sitting behind him. "What time did you arrive?"

"A bit before four. The first ones who discovered the fire figure they were here almost an hour before that, attracted by tongues of flame shooting high above the house. They were so busy trying to put out the blaze and save the family belongings that, for a few minutes, they couldn't spare anyone to fetch me."

"How far away do you live?" John asked.

The foreman blinked at being addressed by the stranger but quickly decided that someone riding with the lieutenant governor had a right to ask questions.

"About a quarter mile, to the south."

The lieutenant governor scanned the area. "I had expected to see Nigel Harvey."

"He arrived maybe forty minutes after I did. The police officer on duty decided to ride to Castries to find you. That was when Mr. Harvey asked him to find a John Le Brun as well."

"That would be me," John said.

"Where is Harvey now?" asked Tubble.

"He left right after Sergeant Hume rode off. I assume he returned to Stratford."

Tubble nodded at the information, then refocused on the house. "The lower floor seems to have been saved."

"Mostly. The workers formed a bucket brigade. Nobody could get more than halfway up the main stairs. They swear the top floor was completely in flames when the first of them arrived. Then the night rain started—heavier than usual—and once the roof collapsed, the rain put out the blaze."

"What about the Palmer family?"

Mansfield shook his head. "All dead . . . except for Master Peter. Marie Colette as well, the children's nanny."

"How do you know Mr. Palmer is alive?" Tubble asked.

"Because he arrived from Castries at about ten o'clock. I guess he stayed overnight at the St. Lucia Club."

"Where is he now?"

Mansfield shifted his weight. He pulled a soot-besmirched handkerchief from a back trouser pocket and mopped at his sweat-drenched forehead. "He was carried to my place. He's being watched over by my wife. Peter is a man of great passion when he's aroused. He was half-insane when he rode up to the sight. I suppose Sergeant Hume told him the terrible news on the East-West Road. His horse was foaming at the mouth, half dead from having been driven so hard. Master Peter wouldn't let anyone hold him back. Charged up the stairs. He was the first one who saw the bodies." The overseer grimaced and shook his head.

"And Mr. Palmer came back down by himself?" questioned Tubble.

"No. He was screaming and coughing, screaming and coughing. And then he stopped. I sent two logs I trust inside to bring him down. He was unconscious. I had them bear him to my house in a wagon."

"Did those two workers see any cause for the fire?" John asked.

Mansfield lifted his large hands in an impotent gesture. "They found him in the upstairs hallway. I doubt they took any time to look around."

"Well, I will," John said, stepping out of the phaeton.

Tubble told the overseer, "Mr. Le Brun is a professional detective from the United States."

Mansfield looked duly impressed. He stepped back from the carriage.

John stretched his hand out for the items Lordis held in her lap. They were a small notepad, a fountain pen, two brown paper bags, and his Brownie No. 2 camera.

"Why don't I come with you?" Lordis suggested, as John had expected. While he gathered materials at the hotel, she had quickly changed into a cotton blouse, riding breeches, and low quarter shoes she had brought for hiking.

"The fewer people who move through an accident scene the better," he was glad to remind her.

Lordis signaled her disappointment with a sigh as she handed her husband his hastily assembled detective kit.

John pushed the notepad and writing instrument in one side pocket and the bags in another. He slung his camera strap over his shoulder. The camera made a muffled thump against the revolver in his hip holster. He had shown the weapon to no one, including Captain Bobby Johnson and the Van Fleets. He suspected the importation of a firearm would be frowned upon by the police of St. Lucia, but as a lawman of decades' experience and one who had found need for such a piece more than a few times in the past, he was never wholly comfortable without the weight on his back hip.

Tubble said, "You should find the bodies of the wife, the nanny, and a young girl and boy. Any other body would be a surprise."

"Do you wish someone to accompany me, Mr. Tubble?" John asked.

"Not so long as you're just looking and capturing images," the island's top official said. "Call out if you need help."

At the feet of one of the nearest onlookers stood a wooden bucket. John fetched his handkerchief, bent, and wet the cloth in the half-inch of water remaining in the bucket's bottom. As he approached the ruined plantation house, John studied the faces of the onlookers. Only four besides Mansfield were white, and two of these were policemen. The rest, at least one hundred souls, were all dark-skinned. The lawn looked like a gargantuan yard sale. Tables, chairs, mirrors, cabinets, lamps, china, silverware, knick-knacks, books, throw pillows, area carpets, paintings, an umbrella stand, and much more were heaped in disorderly piles. He reflected that the first floor of the home had held enough possessions to fill a normal second-hand goods shop.

John climbed the front steps, drew in a deep breath, and neared the double doors. He observed that the wood around the knobs and lock was split, indicating that someone had kicked the doors open. He trod through the stained puddles of water covering the two-story foyer's polished wooden floor and ventured a few steps to his left to the entrance of what had been designed as a library and study. A dozen or so of the easily reachable shelves stood empty. To his amazement, another dozen shelves were filled with more knick-knacks and books. One or more valiant rescuers had wisely thought to rip the curtains from the windows and carry them away. To the right of the foyer lay the formal dining room. John found that its curtains had also been removed. The room stood even more barren than the library had. The only piece of furniture not rescued was a gigantic walnut breakfront. It had been wrestled about a foot from the wall but then abandoned.

John walked to the foot of the double-wide staircase. He lifted his handkerchief to his mouth and pressed it lightly under his nose. Before transferring his weight fully, he tested each step. The smell of the smoke became stronger and more acrid. He raised his free hand and positioned it just above the railing, ready to grab it if a step proved weak.

Reaching the head of the stairs, he saw the evidence of

where Peter Palmer had collapsed. He noted as well the smeared shoe prints covering the top stairs and the hallway immediately beyond. Circling around the marks, John mounted to the hall and slowly pivoted. He counted five doors. Three doors stood open.

The hallway ran in an inverted capital U shape. The passage to Le Brun's left was blocked by a large portion of the fallen roof. He advanced cautiously on the open door farthest to the right. Ever since falling victim to the amateur photographer craze, John had wished that photos could be captured in the world's infinite pallet of hues. In this house of horror, however, only the color red would be found. Everything else was a shade of ash gray or soot black. John entered the master bedroom. The varnish and stain that had covered the tester bed had aided in turning the posts and rails to the quality of wood found at the bottom of an extinguished campfire. The canopy no longer existed. On the partly consumed mattress lay a human figure. At first, he could not discern its sex. He took two steps closer, counseling himself not to give in to shock but to maintain a detached mindset.

On only one other occasion, during his tenure as sheriff of Brunswick, had Le Brun been confronted by a human whose skin, hair, and outer layers of muscle had been consumed by flame. The corpse was blackened, but the scene's single lurid color made it even worse to behold. Red tissue showed wherever the skin had melted or split open. With the bedclothes completely burned away, he recognized that what he gazed on was a woman. Except for just above the nape of her neck, where her hair had been partly protected by a pillow, it no longer existed. Her cheek closest to where he stood had been burned away, exposing white teeth and black gums. All of her eyelids and the orbs of her eyes were gone, rimmed by black sockets. She lay on her back atop the exposed bedsprings, with her arms tight against her torso.

John came as close as he could without being overwhelmed by the stench of roasted meat. He slowly circled the bed. If Peter Palmer's wife had been murdered, along with his children and the nursemaid, and if a fire had been set to conceal the means, he could see no evidence of it within the damage.

Le Brun took two photos of the corpse, as well as two more covering photographs of the room. He then entered the other two bedrooms that were not blocked and photographed first the dead nursemaid and then the girl child, advancing the film until all twelve exposures had been taken. In the daughter's room he noted that an inside door stood partway open. It connected to a bedroom closer to the front of the house. In it, a small boy lay on his right side with his legs partially drawn up. From his size, John judged that he could not have been more than six years old.

In none of the rooms did Le Brun discover evidence of cause for the fire. The detective was sure of several things. Firstly, the night had been warm enough that no chimney would be lit or warming pan filled with coals and placed under bedcovers, if indeed such nighttime activities ever took place on St. Lucia. Secondly, the chances of all four occupants of the second story being overcome in their sleep was remote. Most often, a candle flame would catch something like a curtain blowing in the wind. Or a careless smoker would fall asleep in a bedroom with a cigarette held between a fore- and middle finger. By the time that room was aflame, smoke or the sound of the fire's hungry consumption would awaken sleepers in adjacent rooms. Others might die, if escape routes were blocked or if they feared jumping from upper-story windows, but dead children would be found hiding in closets and adults under a window rather than on their beds. Often, articles of cloth or clothing would be found shoved against the bottom of their door. None of these scenes was presented to Le Brun. Every bedroom had at least one window, and three of them opened to the upper veranda for easy escape. He retreated from the scenes of horror to the first floor.

Standing in the frame of the broken double doors, John paused to jot a page of notes with his pen. Then he retraced his route and walked to where Tubble, the overseer, and Lordis waited with obvious expectation. As he came close, he held up his camera.

"Does your island have a competent person who develops film?" he asked.

"There is one shop in Castries," the lieutenant governor replied.

"I think it best if you have one of your most trusted men standin' in the darkroom when the person does his work," John said.

"Why such caution?" Lordis asked.

"To be sure these photographs aren't ruined or lost on purpose."

Tubble looked doubtful. "But to mistrust a camera shop employee who lives clear across the island?"

"I know no one on St. Lucia well enough to trust them. When such is the case, blanket mistrust is the prudent attitude to take."

"Fair enough," the magistrate relented.

"What I saw up there doesn't make sense," John said, switching topics. He proceeded to tell exactly what he had witnessed. As he came to the end of his accounting, images from inside the mansion appeared in his mind's eye, side by side.

"I found the nanny and the boy curled up on their right flanks. The mother and daughter were each on their backs, with their arms at their sides. The fact that two lay in the same position on their flanks isn't strange. That they are each on their right side is a fifty-fifty chance. However, to have the other two lyin' full face up and with both arms close to their hips strains statistical odds."

"It does indeed," Tubble agreed. "But did you see signs of suffocation or knife wounds?"

"The work of a small knife or of suffocation can't be detected given the extent of the outer tissue damage. If somethin' untoward can be found, it will have to be under the layers of charred skin and muscle. The bodies were not shriveled. I suspect the lungs, heart, throats, and brains are intact. The most competent and thorough coroner available must be involved. Not a local physician who sometimes serves as a pathologist."

Tubble drummed his fingers on the edge of his carriage to keep his hand busy while his head considered John's words. "Humphrey Davies is the chief pathologist for all the Windward Islands. He served for years at the Hospital of St. Mary of Bethlehem."

"Yes, Bedlam, in London," John said.

"He's seen his share of bizarre deaths. But he lives on Grenada. It would take at least two days to get him here. He's not keen on travel."

John expelled a short, derisive sound. "If it's his job, I wouldn't care how keen or dull he is. This event surely demands his presence."

"I agree," Tubble said.

Le Brun turned to Mansfield, the overseer. "I would hunt up some impervious sheetin' such as rubberized mats and surround the corpses with ice."

"Ice," Tubble said in a dubious tone. "That needs to come from the plant in Castries. As to impervious material . . . ." Tubble lapsed into silence.

John looked with dismay at the trampled confusion of foot- and shoe prints in the earth near them. "These actions can't be helped. Now, I observed that the front doors were broken in."

"Yes, kicked in," confirmed Mansfield.

"So they were locked when the laborers arrived."

"They told me both those and the back door."

John grunted as he absorbed the answer. "Have you asked

if the doors appeared intact, that is, not tampered with before the workers kicked them in?"

"I can certainly ask about," said Mansfield.

"Also, how many entered the house. I would think the number was great to remove such an accumulation of belongin's so quickly." Mansfield nodded and started with a weary tread toward the nearest group of workers. "Ask as well if they found any windows open," John added.

"I am getting the impression that we are fortunate to have you visiting our island, sir," Tubble said to Le Brun in spite of his deflated posture.

"Save your praise until I've finished investigatin'. Would you mind gettin' your Sunday shoes dirty, Mr. Tubble?"

"No, sir. They can be cleaned."

"I'm dressed for investigating," Lordis volunteered brightly, champing at the bit to involve herself in the investigation. Her left hand brushed nervously back and forth against the material of her riding breeches.

John could think of no excuse to bar Lordis from participating in his next activity. "Yes, you are. Two and a half sets of eyes are better than one and a half. Let's begin."

John led the pair in an ever-widening spiral away from the mansion, past the cold storage and cook houses.

"Are we looking for footprints only?" Tubble asked.

"For anythin' out of place. But mostly for prints. Those doors might have been locked on somebody's way out."

Again, a dubious tone issued from Tubble's throat. "With so many poor working these plantations, the owners always lock their doors and first-story windows at night. The only way someone could get inside without forcing a door or window would be with a duplicate key."

"Beside Peter Palmer, how many others might have such a key?"

"Beyond Mrs. Palmer, I can't think of anyone. The Palmers have no cousins, uncles, or aunts on the island. Peter has a sister, but she left St. Lucia several years ago and, as I understand it, had no intention of ever returning."

The three walkers fanned out about ten feet from each other, advancing with heads lowered and arcing slowly back and forth. When they exited the covering of shade trees surrounding the rear of the mansion, they changed their search pattern to a broad sweep. They entered the verge of the vast sugarcane fields, which bordered a stream. The sunlight felt like glowing flatirons against their exposed skin.

"As you can see, when the sun shines, damp soil quickly becomes like rock," Tubble pointed out. "That's why we rely so heavily on frequent rains. One week without water and the crops are in grave danger."

The trio's search pattern put them well into the massive cane field and nearly to its hillside limit on the west side. Lordis was the first to step beyond the rows.

"This is interesting!" she called out.

John and Richard hurried to her side. She pointed.

"Barefoot prints," Lordis said. "One, two, three . . . There appear to be six sets in all, moving away from the house."

"All roughly the same size," Tubble noted. He squatted and stuck out his right hand.

"Don't touch them!" John cautioned. He slipped the camera from his shoulder and opened the back. "But why would they only head away from the house?"

"I expect they approached from another route," Tubble offered. "One more solid."

John produced a film packet from his pocket, opened it, fitted the end to the camera's sprockets, shut the cover, and advanced the unexposed roll. "What we need here is plaster to make castin's. In the meantime, I'll capture them on film."

Lordis looked from south to north, studying the paths of the footprints. "Didn't you tell me Peter Palmer is providing sandals for all his workers?"

"You saw them yourself," John replied. "Brand new. On nearly all the workers standin' in front of the house."

"Then who are these people?" she asked. "They're most likely men, from their size." The five-foot-seven-inch woman suspended her right foot just above one of the prints. The print impression was slightly wider and longer than her shoed foot.

Richard Tubble had picked up a discarded length of dry bamboo stalk and twisted it into the ground as the husband and wife conferred. He tied his white handkerchief to the upright stalk.

"Let's follow the tracks as far as we can," John said.

The distance between prints and the fact that they were deeper at the toe ends than at the heels indicated the trio had been moving at a jog or trot. The impressions continued alongside the stream for about a thousand feet, the water emanating from a valley between two high hills. Shrubs, weeds, and vines choked the area. In between, grasses had been trampled in the recent past. When the search team came close to about two up-tilted acres of felled, burned, and girdled trees, the stream flowed faster, exposing layers of rocks. Here, the trails of the barefooted men vanished.

"It seems as if they walked on the stone surfaces only," Tubble noted.

"As if to prevent us from tracking them farther," Lordis completed his thought.

John peered up the long narrow valley to where it curved northwest into the rainforest jungle and disappeared. When he turned to the government official, he found Tubble staring at the mountain even farther inland, its lower slopes cloaked in mist. Tubble looked seriously troubled.

"The *Neg Maron*," he said in a soft voice.

"Pardon?" Le Brun responded.

"*Neg Maron*," Tubble repeated. "Some call them the Maroons. The first of them date back to 1803. That was the year England regained control of St. Lucia, after the French had held it off and on for a long time. The French had abolished slavery and hired the Africans as freemen. The Crown still recognized slavery in spite of much opposition from abolitionist societies. Their soldiers went about rounding up the Africans and restoring them to chains. Many escaped into the rainforests you see directly before you. Quite a few were re-taken, but enough eluded capture to form communities. They had a few rifles and many machetes, and the rest fought with bows and arrows and spears. Pursuit became a matter of diminishing returns and was abandoned.

"The government in London abolished exporting African slaves in 1807. St. Lucia was secured permanently in 1814. The institution of slavery in the Empire didn't end until 1834. By that time, those living in these mountains had established subsistence living. Occasionally, they traded with collaborators. It continues unchanged until this very day. We know from the coloreds we arrest for consorting with them that there are about two hundred and fifty living in well-concealed villages up and down the Barre d'Isle."

"'Backbone of the Island,'" John translated for Lordis. He reached up unconsciously to the shoulder in which he had been wounded during the Civil War and massaged it lightly. High humidity invariably bothered it.

Tubble nodded. "The really rugged interior. '*Neg Maron*' means 'runaway black.' It has also come to mean 'ignorant' and 'savage' in St. Lucia's general vocabulary."

"That is fascinating . . . and frightening," Lordis decided.

From within the rainforest came a deep animal cry.

"What was that?" Lordis asked, taking an unconscious step backward.

"I don't know," said Tubble. "St. Lucia doesn't have any large predators. Then again, I once heard a rumor of a French planter who imported a pair of lion cubs as pets. But that was more than a century ago."

The surrounding vegetation had become noiseless, as if holding its breath in anticipation of a violent event.

"Do these *Neg Maron* carry out periodic raids on the plantations?" John asked as he peered into the dense undergrowth.

Tubble shrugged. "They haven't in decades." He pointed to the dead trees that had been chopped down, burned, or girdled. "But this could definitely set them off. The plantation owners are desperate to cultivate ever-larger fields. Only the biggest enterprises can survive with the falling price of sugar. Peter Palmer was evidently preparing this valley. Once the trees die and are removed, the undergrowth is burned with the husks of dried cane. The next season, cane cuttings will be planted. I wouldn't be surprised if this valley forms the border of one of the Maroon villages."

"But the mansion was locked," Le Brun argued. "How could they get inside?"

"The same way they climb coconut trees: one could shimmy up a column or one of the trellises at the rear of the house, gaining entrance through an open upstairs window."

John placed his hands behind the small of his back and rocked gently in place. "This gives us a motive if those unfortunate women and children were murdered. What doesn't feel right is that these *Neg Maron* have been so peaceful for so long. And, from what you've told us, Mr. Tubble, they only got violent when they were pursued."

"But with the planters cultivating every inch of usable land, what was done to this valley may have been a 'straw that broke the camel's back' situation to them."

"Where will we get plaster to make casts?" Lordis broke into the dialogue.

"Mr. Mansfield will know," Tubble answered.

John stopped rocking. "The casts should be made of right footprints only. The course of this investigation depends on the findin's of your Dr. Davies. For the rest of the day, you and Mr. Mansfield should interview as many of those involved as you can. Mr. Palmer will need special handlin'. He met me last evenin' at the St. Lucia Island Club and revealed himself to be a man of considerable passion. He might respond better to a concerned stranger than to an official at this time." Le Brun glanced at his wife. "The soft touch and voice of a gracious lady might also prove a balm to his ravaged soul."

---

LORDIS AND JOHN RODE on horses borrowed from the Palmer stable, navigating by the foreman's detailed directions. At the limit of the mansion grounds they came upon the Palmer family cemetery. John angled his steed close to the stone wall so that he might read the tombstones.

"Three French names. The oldest, Anton Jobin," he said.

The rest of the interred totaled fourteen persons with Anglo-Saxon names, all related to the Palmer family. Among those buried were James Palmer II, James III, and Henry, whose dates were April 19, 1842-December 29, 1908.

Toward the back of the enclosure was a raised grave made of white marble. It was backed by a towering angel with its hands pressed together in prayer and its head bowed.

"Must be somebody important," Lordis judged. "Makes the other graves look sad."

"All graves look sad to me," John responded. "Except the Great Pyramids of Egypt and the Taj Mahal."

"You know what I meant," Lordis said, peevishly.

John read the inscription. "Constance Palmer/Beloved Wife of Henry/1845 to 1872. So, Peter's mother was a second wife."

Lordis pointed from astride her horse. "She's over here. Anne. Just plain 'wife'—1846 to 1887."

"And an equally plain grave in comparison to that of the first Mrs. Henry Palmer," John noted.

"This plot is about to grow substantially," Lordis said in a sad tone.

---

THE OVERSEER'S HOME was not difficult to find. It was a modest, one-story structure, with a cook house and large shed close behind.

Mrs. Mansfield, who introduced herself as Maybelle, greeted the Le Bruns at the door. Like her husband, she was a stocky person. She was his mate in height as well, standing almost six feet tall.

"How has he been?" Lordis asked, speaking of the bereaved husband and father.

"Much quieter than when he arrived. Of course, he put a pint of rum down his throat since then. Fell asleep for about half an hour but woke with a scream."

"Who is it?" Peter called from the back of the dwelling. The shotgun house had a sitting area on the right and dining and pantry rooms behind it. On the left side were three modest bedrooms. Peter was in the farthest of them. Mrs. Mansfield led the way with an arthritic gait.

When Le Brun's form appeared in the door frame, Peter Palmer worked at focusing his drink-affected vision. "Mr. . . . Le Brun! Why . . . are you here?"

John stepped forward. "I was asked to visit you by Lieutenant Governor Tubble," he lied, thinking of the animosity between Palmer and Nigel Harvey. "This is my—"

Before John could introduce Lordis, Palmer struggled to slide his torso up the headboard. He reached for the sheet that covered him but failed in the attempt. "You were asked because you're a detective?"

"Because I've had considerable experience examinin' personal disasters," John evaded.

"They're all dead," Peter said through a sob. "Even my son . . ." He searched his besotted mind for several seconds. "Ewen."

Lordis rushed forward and took the griever's right hand in hers. "We're so sorry, Mr. Palmer. I'm John's wife."

Palmer labored a smile, which gave Lordis the courage to sit at the foot of the bed.

"I should have died with them," Palmer lamented. He looked at John. "Your visit to the club saved my life. Otherwise, I had intended to stay at home last night."

"We shall all be grateful for that providence," said Le Brun.

"What started the fire?" the owner of the plantation needed to know.

"That is not yet determined." John leaned back against the room's inner wall. "If you had died with the rest of your family, who would inherit the plantation?"

"My sister, Penelope. She lives in England and is married with a child." Peter shook his head. With starts and stops, he explained, "She hated living on St. Lucia. Couldn't wait to escape. She made a visit to London and Bath. She failed to return, as she had promised. My father expected that she would remain an old maid and be his servant until he died. He was livid at what he called 'her treachery.' Cut her out of his will. He was the major reason she hated living here." He sighed. "Our father was a bastard."

John took a moment to absorb the harsh statement. "Many children have ongoin' conflicts with their parents. Could you be specific about your opinion of him?"

"My father was selfish to the core. He thought of his own comforts and desires first, second, and third. Then, only if there was any time or money left did he think of his family. Or of those who worked for him. He drove my mother to an early grave with his antics. When he died, I determined to atone for his sins wherever I could. That meant that Penny should once again inherit in such a case as you suggest." The man's head jerked with a sudden, sharp movement, as if an invisible force had struck him in the back of the neck with a stout object.

"Why are you asking this question? Do you think I was meant to die, along with the rest of my family?"

"As a detective, I'm predisposed to ask such questions and to make sure accidents are exactly what they seem to be," John again dissembled. "For example, when a tragedy occurs inside a locked house, I always ask who held keys to outside doors. Do you have your house keys with you?"

Peter looked around the room and saw what he was looking for draped over a high-backed chair. He pointed in that direction. "In my jacket. The right side pocket."

John unbuttoned the pocket and withdrew a ring that contained seven keys. Two were especially large and ornate. John noted that their serrations ran at right angles to each other along the blade, so that the keys were more three-dimensional than the normal variety. He selected them out from the other five and held them up.

"These are the house keys?"

"That's right."

"Other than these, how many other sets of keys do you know of?"

Palmer looked as if he was sobering up quickly. His eyes blinked rapidly in thought. "There are three sets that I know of. The second is kept in a bottom kitchen drawer. It was used by my wife if I was out of the house and she needed to leave the plantation for one reason or the other. The third we kept in a lacquer box inside a drawer of the master bedroom dresser. We referred to it as 'the safety set.'"

"Three sets only," John said, to compel Peter to think harder.

"Wait a bit! When my father died, I came across a bill for two locks and four sets of keys. Eight in all. Yes. My father was very careful of all of them, because the locks are complex and we don't have a locksmith on St. Lucia who can duplicate them. Penny may have taken the fourth set with her to England . . . if only to convince my father that she intended to return."

"Accordin' to the workers who arrived first, both front and rear doors were locked tight. They had to break them open," John said. "Neither your wife nor your nanny smoked, did they?"

"Certainly not! Both were ladies."

"Do you keep tapers burnin' through the night?"

"Never. That's why this fire is such a terrible mishap," said Palmer, dropping his forehead onto his raised right hand. "The workers said there was no lightning. I don't understand how it could have happened."

"Pray for strength, Mr. Palmer," Lordis counseled, reaching out and squeezing the plantation owner's hand.

John returned the key ring to Palmer's jacket pocket. "In the comin' days, both I and your government will do our best to give you a definite answer as to the cause. In the meantime, you need to stay as calm as you can and rest."

Palmer shook his head. "How can I rest? I must see to the funeral and burial arrangements."

John hesitated for a moment but could think of no way around telling the man the truth. "I'm afraid the bodies won't be released to you until the governor-general's coroner arrives from Grenada and performs thorough autopsies. It's standard procedure in such cases," he added, even as he thought, *Or at least it damned well should be.*

The physiognomy of Peter Palmer's face transformed, from one dominated by grief to one of high suspicion. Le Brun guided his wife off the bed, uttering a few quick phrases restating their condolences and reaffirming support for the sole survivor of the Palmer family on St. Lucia. Before Peter Palmer could press him further, he had pulled Lordis into the hallway and out the front door.

---

ON THE WAY TO overseer Manfield's house, the Le Bruns passed a signpost pointing south that indicated the town of

Dennery and several more prosaic names such as Fond d'Or, Errard and Stratford, the last being the name Mansfield mentioned as Nigel Harvey's house and plantation.

"Since the man offered to pay for my services," John said to Lordis, pulling his horse's reins to the right, "I believe we are obliged to have a conversation with him."

The main road connecting the plantations, the town of Dennery, and several coast-hugging villages ran parallel with the Atlantic Ocean. Lordis and John saw that the water color was deep blue on the windward side of the island and the waves were choppy. The breeze was also brisker, which John surmised must suck the moisture from the ground much faster than on the Castries side. The roads and buildings on the east were primitive, the infrastructure along the Atlantic wild in comparison to the west side. Only the plantation houses lent an air of grandeur and gentility to the area.

"Even when you asked for specifics about his father," Lordis suddenly said as they trotted along the dirt road, "Mr. Palmer was vague. I wonder what the man's exact sins were."

"I don't imagine we'll ever know," John returned. "They could be exaggerated in the son's mind. I know from readin' biographies and novels that some devastatin' conflicts can arise. All the way back to Oedipus and his father. In my experience, people either become unconscious tintypes of their dominant parent or consciously the polar opposite. Peter Palmer at least claims to be the latter."

"I hope those barefoot prints I found will help with your case," Lordis said, redirecting the conversation to fish for a compliment.

"We shall see. But, with my one bad eye, havin' the aid of your two sharp ones has already proven of invaluable help." John made an unhappy noise low in his throat. "I am doubtful of my ultimate usefulness here."

"Why is that?"

"I don't have ready access to those who can type blood; that microscope I bought sits back in Brunswick. No fingerprintin' kit, no lockpickin' tools. No support from friendly lawmen or wealthy friends who can exert pressure on my behalf. I have no idea of the internal politics, the secret alliances, any harbored animosities beyond those of Palmer and Harvey. As I told Mr. Tubble, there is no one I can trust. Unless this is quickly proven to be no more than an accident, I expect an uphill struggle all the way."

"You will triumph," Lordis said with confidence. "You always do. I shall help see that you do."

"That's very kind of you, dear, but I also refuse to devote our entire honeymoon to professional work."

Lordis leaned forward in her saddle. She rode astride rather than the affected, sidesaddle manner that many New York City women of wealth still used. "The coroner won't be able to conduct his investigation for two more days. Let's make the most of touring tomorrow." She glanced to her left. "This road is well rutted. I wonder if it leads to a Stratford workers' village."

"I suppose we could detour for a few minutes," John allowed.

Behind the cane fields, surrounded by small private agricultural plots, stood two lines of structures. On one side, four were fashioned of wood, with wooden floors. Other than the fact that they were elevated above the ground, they were barren of any amenities. The doorways had threadbare curtains; the window frames held no glass or mullions. The roofs were covered with dried, thatched vegetation. These four small houses, however, were considerably advanced in comparison to the dozens of huts across a muddy courtyard that were built of bamboo. Their roofs were also thatched with less durable coconut branches. Both types of shelters were no bigger than ten by twelve feet.

The workers and their children, all natives of the Indian subcontinent, were engaged in tending to their gardens. They paused with curiosity as Lordis and John dismounted. None dared question the presence of the white strangers. Lordis was bolder than John, peeking inside two of the bamboo dwellings. When she returned, her expression was aghast.

"The floors are dirt," she told John. "The first one has one bed, barely large enough for two, with a mattress that must be home fashioned. It also had a couple rugs made of woven palm leaves. The second had no bed at all. Both had fruit crates for storing a few articles of clothing. I thought slavery was abolished here more than a hundred years ago."

"In name only," John replied. "These people are just as much slaves now, but economic ones. No wonder the natives are fleein' the island. I note that not a one of these East Indians is wearin' shoes or sandals."

"Let's go, John," Lordis said, moving toward her borrowed horse. "If I stay a moment longer, I shall burst into tears."

---

STRATFORD PLANTATION HOUSE was made known by a large wooden sign affixed to a tree that stood near the road. The lettering was in Dutch blue, on a pastel yellow background. The house sat back from the main road some three hundred feet. Two mulatto guards armed with shotguns stood in the opening of the front fence. A pair of saddled horses were tied up nearby. John announced himself.

"Mr. Harvey said you might visit," the older guard declared. The two men stood back, allowing the Le Bruns to take the crushed-shell path to the house.

A male servant with tea-with-cream skin escorted the Le Bruns into the plantation house, which was similar in layout to that of Peter Palmer. A few moments after they sat on the parlor couch, a light-complexioned mulatto female servant with fetching features and figure entered with iced tea and tea cakes. "Please make yourself at home. The master will be with you soon," she said. Her English betrayed a hint of the Creole lilt.

Within moments, Nigel Harvey entered from the foyer. John introduced the man to Lordis.

Harvey gestured to the refreshments. "I doubt that you've eaten since breakfast." While his guests sampled the food, he said to John, "I gleaned after only a minute or so of listening to you speak last night that you are a man of high intelligence. That being the case, I'm sure you understand that I wish to hire you because of the bad blood between the Palmer family and me."

"Bad enough to have two guards at your front gate?" John remarked.

"For the time being. If I pay you and you prove the cause of the fire and the deaths, then Peter will not only see that I am innocent of any part, but he will also be beholden to me. He feels nothing by half. If he's moved to sympathy, he'll bankrupt himself buying mosquito nets and sandals. If he's moved to anger, he can be very dangerous. Everyone knows that about him. He beat a man senseless in Castries last year because the fellow maligned his family. Even though Peter knew the man was right."

"You have more confidence in me than I have in myself in this case," John warned.

"Peter's father and I were indeed competitors. That old rapscallion tried to put something over on me at least once a year. Rarely succeeded. But I must admit that, after he keeled over, his son has been like St. Paul's thorn in my flesh."

"Buyin' mosquito nettin' and sandals for the workers," John remembered.

"Exactly. And paying higher wages." Harvey's thick eyebrows rose. "By the by, what do you charge for your services?"

John had his reply ready. "Ordinarily, I charge nine U.S. dollars an hour, plus expenses." He watched with not a little pleasure as Harvey struggled to swallow the figure. He patted Lordis's hand. "But since this is my honeymoon, and I will owe Mrs. Le Brun several extra days of vacation, in this instance my fee is ten an hour."

Harvey's eyes bulged. "If this investigation lasts a week, that's more than we pay our school teachers in a year."

"What a shame!" Lordis exclaimed. "You should be paying your teachers twice that!"

The owner's lips pursed.

"Are you married, Mr. Harvey?" Lordis asked.

"I am. With two sons and a daughter. My wife and daughter are on an extended visit to Martinique, staying with relatives," the lord of the manor supplied.

Lordis turned her gaze on the pretty serving maid, who stood just outside the room.

John leaned forward to cut off his wife's view. He said, "I require a five-hour retainer." Before Harvey could complain, he added, "Have you and Peter Palmer ever come to blows over your differences?"

"Never. We are not, despite the shouting, hot-blooded Africans."

John sat back theatrically. "Hot-blooded you say? I was told that there is almost no violence on St. Lucia."

"Only because the logs and the wogs know their place. But it simmers just under the surface, Mr. Le Brun." At last Harvey sat, after drawing an upholstered leather chair up close to the tea table. "I heard a rumor that you and Mr. Van Fleet had been lured to St. Lucia to talk it up as a vacation paradise to your rich acquaintances. Naturally, everyone has gone out of their way to be forgetful of our recent dark past."

John set down the cake he had just started eating. "What past is that?"

"Just three years ago our coal carriers went on strike over working conditions. They destroyed provision shops and looted the Castries market. The police force of Castries only has twenty-two men. It took every Man Jack of them plus some extra constabulary from Barbados and St. Vincent to stop the mayhem. At the Cul-de-Sac sugar factory, it came to a head. Four killed and twenty-three wounded. But even that didn't stop the unrest.

The *H.M.S. Indefatigable* had to sail into the harbor to finally put an end to the trouble. I take it this news did not make it into your newspapers."

"I read nothing of it," John said.

Nigel Harvey rolled his eyes. "Please don't let on that I told you about it. Goes to show you just how unimportant St. Lucia is to the rest of the world. Especially our sugar."

"Tell us about that," Lordis encouraged.

Harvey looked pleased to be able to unload his tale of woe. "Raising sugarcane and getting the sugar to market is a grueling business, Mrs. Le Brun. Add to that the growth of world competition and the exodus of workers from the island for better-paying jobs. I'm barely staying afloat, and we'll grind forty to fifty cartloads and extract from eleven hundred pounds to a ton of raw sugar a day. Sugar used to be king on St. Lucia, even though the islands to the north of us are better suited due to their weather and soil. Now, sugar is down to only 45 percent of our export. Those of us who survive know that only economies of scale can preserve us. I'm afraid that young Palmer would think that I might stoop to murder in order to grab his lands."

"There must be relatives who you would need to negotiate with anyway," John said, hoping to learn what Harvey knew of the Palmer line of inheritance.

"I have no idea who there is," Harvey fumed. "Old Henry had a daughter, but she moved to England. When he was drunk—which was often—he used to bellow at the club about cutting her out of his will. I have no idea whether he did or not. Even if that is true, the family must have relatives in England."

"But none here on the island?" John asked.

Nigel thrust out his lower lip and shook his head. "I know pretty much every white soul of quality on St. Lucia, and none of them is related to the Palmers."

The slamming of a door and tromping of multiple boots brought the conversation to an abrupt hiatus. The noises grew louder, and then a young male voice called out with an urgent sharpness.

"Dad! Dad!"

"In here," the elder Harvey directed, rising from his chair.

Two men, dressed similarly in boots, riding breeches, collarless shirts, and patterned vests, entered the parlor in tandem, both taking a hitch in their strides at the sight of strangers. They were younger, thinner versions of Nigel Harvey, both in their twenties. The older-looking one's hair was curly and reddish, and his eyes were an arresting tint of green. His brother was slightly shorter, with slate-blue eyes. The hair of the second son's crown was a dirty blonde shade and already thinning. He sported a moustache that was not full enough to be impressive.

"Hello," the older son said to the Le Bruns, in a volume half of what he had used a moment earlier.

"These are my boys . . . Pierce and Michael," Nigel introduced. His face darkened into a frown. "What is so important that you track mud through the house?"

"Yellow fever. Down at Camp Two," Pierce reported.

The plantation owner thrust out his hands in supplication toward his guests. "You see what I mean? At the start of the planting season." He redirected his attention to his older son. "How many?"

"Six so far. From the two huts closest to the pond. But three are children."

"Then only three sets of hands out of commission," Nigel calculated. He sighed. "See that they rest and get plenty of sugar water. And stay the hell away from Camp Two. Why did it take two of you to tell me?"

"One of the carts also broke an axle," Michael said.

"So? Summon the wheelwright!"

The son's shoulders slumped. He looked guiltily at the two guests, then back to his father. "Don't you remember what he said last time?"

Nigel reached inside his jacket pocket, withdrew his billfold, and pulled out a bank note. He held it out for Michael. "You remind him of the time of year. Get to it!"

The brothers returned sharp nods and disappeared through the mansion's front door.

"If it's not one thing, it's another," Harvey lamented as he collapsed into his chair.

"How many total souls—of quality or otherwise—are there in all?" Lordis asked, recapturing the thread of their interrupted conversation.

Harvey whirled around. "What's that?"

"White souls," Lordis said.

Harvey calculated. "Ah. If I recall correctly, it's between three thousand and four thousand. As I said, I don't know a one who's related to the Palmers."

"Because you're hirin' me," John continued, "you must suspect that someone murdered the Palmer family."

Harvey sighed. "I don't want to believe it. I truly hope it's not so. However, there might be a blighter among the planters who would like to take advantage of the bad blood between me and young Peter. It's to my advantage for you to flush out such a person." He took a moment to calculate. "But I can only afford twenty hours of your expertise. I hope that will be enough."

"As do I," Le Brun returned.

Harvey rose from the chair. "Then I'll return to the burdens of the day. You will be sure to inform me of any event that would seem to tie me to this unfortunate accident."

John rose as well and held out his hand, palm up. "Certainly. Payin' my retainer will guarantee that."

---

UPON THE RETURN from Stratford to the Palmer plantation, Lordis and John passed the two-story structure that sheltered the house servants. Again, John noted that the people in the immediate area were all of lighter skin than those working in the fields. Lieutenant Governor Tubble was still engaged in the aftermath of the fire. The masses of house contents had been moved out of the elements to a nearby storage barn. Tubble informed the detective that plaster of Paris had been found and, by using a light muslin core, a local craftsman had cast detailed molds of the six right footprints found at the edge of the fields.

"Did you find other door keys?" John inquired.

Richard Tubble confirmed the securing of the keys in the kitchen and within a lacquer box in the half-burned master bedroom dresser.

"But not a fourth set?"

"No. Should there be?"

"Accordin' to Peter Palmer. And no overt sign of break-in?" Le Brun sought to reaffirm.

Tubble looked at his dirt-covered Sunday shoes with dismay. "Nothing overt. However, if someone did climb to the second story, most of the windows were destroyed. You'd never be able to prove entry there." The island's top official asked about Peter Palmer's condition. After John reported it, he added a brief accounting of the meeting with Nigel Harvey.

A small porcelain figurine had been dropped next to the path running up to the burned-out mansion. Tubble kicked at it, then decided not to bend for it. He looked at the Le Bruns. "I imagine you have had more than enough for today. I certainly have. Allow me to carry you back to Castries before night closes in. We'll wait until the coroner arrives and return then. These next few days will allow me time to assemble a party to venture up that valley and seek out *Neg Maron*. Don't neglect to give me those rolls of film for processing when we get back to Castries." Tubble moved toward his carriage with a sigh and a heavy tread.

John bent to the ignored figurine. He saw that it was the female half of a pair. He realized this because its shape was contorted so that it could not stand by itself. It obviously relied on being intertwined with a partner piece for mutual support. A fresh break just below its left shoulder indicated that it had recently been stepped on. The arm that survived was raised as if caressing a face. John slipped it into his jacket pocket, with the intent of protecting it until some semblance of order was restored among the mansion's many saved items.

# CHAPTER SEVEN

## June 27, 1910

THE NEW DAY DAWNED in perfect paradise splendor for vacation exploration. In order that the Le Bruns would not be imposed upon by the Van Fleets, Carlisle Thiery, any members of the St. Lucia Island Club, or even Lieutenant Governor Tubble, John personally rented a jaunting cart at a Castries stable. At the same time, Lordis visited the open food market and purchased a papaya turning from green to yellow. Through gestures and by demonstration, the Creole-speaking seller taught her that if she could press her thumb with a little difficulty into the flesh, it was ripe for eating. She bought as well a wheel of bread and a jar of Chivers Breakfast Orange Marmalade, imported from England. To carry her picnic provisions, she purchased a locally woven basket. The pair were off at a little past nine o'clock, with Lordis clutching the only island map John could find with details of the various roads.

The route south necessitated an immediate climb up the mountain called Morne Fortune that Sibyl Thiery had spoken of in the La Chatelaine Restaurant. When they reached the summit, they paused to enjoy the view of the entire city of Castries, its well-protected harbor, and the shoreline as far north as the high hills beyond Choc Beach. All around them at the top were grand buildings, some residences and others looking governmental. At the western point, they drove past a fort with a sizable gun battery, but they did not stop. Their goal was to travel south as far as the village of Canaries.

After they wound down the mountain, they entered an immense alluvial plain blanketed by farms. The area was appropriately named Cul-de-Sac. Among the crops John could identify were cocoa, guava, and banana plants and, on the higher prominences, lines of coconut palms. They realized after a time that every person they encountered seemed to be of pure African heritage. By ten o'clock, the sun beat down hard enough to convince Lordis to unfurl her parasol.

They bypassed Marigot Bay. In spite of the crude map, their suspicion was that unknown hindrances might prevent them from reaching the day's final destination with enough time to explore before heading back. They came upon a fork in the Castries-to-Soufrière Road, where a wooden sign indicated the town of Anse-la-Raye to the right and Roseau to the left. The latter route promised a hillside view of the surrounding area. The horse had shown spirit, so they took the high road.

"This don't merit a name," John judged as the road wound through a scattering of rude shacks. "They could have one sign readin' 'You are enterin' Roseau' on one side and 'You are leavin' Roseau' on the other."

"Keep your disappointment to yourself," Lordis counseled. "The local folk don't look exactly overjoyed at seeing us."

Lordis, however, had seen what she expected to see. The faces on the settlement's inhabitants were studiously neutral.

A woman or child might turn to watch the cart's passing for several seconds, then turn back to whatever task she had been engaged in.

"I suppose they build their roads at the crest of these hills to keep them from guttering," Lordis guessed. "With all the rainfall, the erosion must be something terrible on open soil."

John stopped the cart and turned toward the valley to his right. "Whatever the reason, such byways do offer spectacular views."

Husband and wife looked down on a broad, lushly verdant valley cut by a river. At the far end of the land, where the Caribbean lapped against it, sat the small town of Anse-la-Raye. Filling the entire valley behind it, divided by gliricidia trees into plots averaging about two acres, were fields of banana plants.

Just ahead of where the Le Bruns had stopped, a man sat at the edge of the road on a canvas camp chair. He wore a colorful print short-sleeved shirt, beige cotton pants, and open-toed sandals. Under the shadow of his broad-brimmed Panama hat, he ate a banana. At his feet were gathered a number of the fruits, each individual finger yellow. The man's profile was to the road. His attention fixed on four other men who labored among the banana plants, which John estimated to reach about fifteen feet above the earth. The four were extremely dark-skinned, darker even than their deep-brown-stained A-type undershirts. Two of the men worked with hoes, ripping weeds away from the areas that were not shaded by the immense rosette canopies of elliptical leaves that crowned the false trunks. The other two hacked at selected banana plants with machetes. The group appeared to range from their early twenties into their late thirties. The man sitting on the folding chair John estimated to be at least in his fifties. His skin, at pronounced variance with the other men, was fawn in shade. He called down to one of the workers in the island patois and pointed a bony forefinger at him.

John encouraged the horse a dozen paces farther. The man on the chair swiveled his head. For a moment, he seemed like a wax mannequin. Then he smiled broadly. What remained of his teeth gleamed white. He pointed to the fruit at his feet.

"*Plé, manjè!*"

"He's invitin' us to try his bananas," John said.

The pair dismounted. They approached the man, who bent and picked up the rest of the yellow bananas. "*Un pat. Konmsi lanmen.*" He raised his free hand and wiggled his fingers.

"Like a hand," John understood.

The fellow nodded. "*Toubonnmankon kon sa.*"

"*Je parle français,*" John told him. He had learned that the dominant language of St. Lucia was a unique mixture of several African tongues and French and called Kwéyòl.

The man regarded the sun, almost at its zenith, and said, "*Bonnapwémidi.*"

"*Et un bon après-midi a vous.*"

The fellow doffed his hat. "*Bon après-midi, Monsieur!*" He emphasized the last word. "*Je suis Monsieur Abel.*"

"The bananas are pointing up," Lordis marveled, gazing at the crop. "I always thought they hung down. And they're quite green."

John considered taking a photograph of the plant and its fascinating fruit, but he realized how much of its splendor was in the colors and rejected the idea.

"*Gween fig,*" Abel said. "Green gold."

"You speak English as well," John noted.

"English. French. Kwéyòl."

John began peeling the finger he had selected. "We know very little about bananas. Can you tell us about them?"

Abel offered his gap-toothed smile and, like Diogenes the Cynic, gestured for Lordis to block his seated body from the sun with her umbrella. "*Vous avais de Anméwik.* So I try to speak American." His accent shifted to sounds that could be understood in the Deep South.

Using a pidgin mish-mosh of the three languages, the overseer explained that bananas are herbs and not trees. When asked about the bamboo poles surrounding each mature central stalk, he told them that the herb had no tap root and needed propping. Periodic hoeing was necessary to prevent the weeds from stealing the ground nutrients. By flexing his fingers, Abel indicated that a bunch, which was five to ten feet long, contained fifty to one hundred-fifty fingers, grouped in circular hands of ten to twenty. Once the plants fruited, they died and were replaced by suckers from the underground stem. Abel took them close to the workers and showed them the planting process. The suckers were cut off, trimmed, cleaned of nematodes and borer weevils, and the holes were sprinkled with a grandular nematicide. Only then were the suckers planted. Three or four times a year fertilizer was spread in a circle around each plant, not close enough to burn it but rather at the limits of the spread of the roots.

Without being told, John observed that the soil was loose and that virtually all of the planted acreage sloped slightly downward toward the river, so that rain would not stand in puddles but rather slowly drain off during the wet season.

The last fact offered by Abel was that the two men swinging the machetes were pruning to remove surplus growth and prevent crowding in the clump, or mat.

"Very interestin'. *Très intéressant!*" John exclaimed. During their host's lecture, he had noted that, although Abel had seen many years, the man sat up especially straight. His movements were deliberate and with a studied elegance. Further, whenever his explanations demanded, he lapsed without difficulty into fluent English. *The old fellow has been having us on*, John felt sure. *Nobody has such a good English accent without having more skill than he's willing to show.*

"The white people in Castries don't want to talk to us about people like you," John said, pointedly avoiding French. "Do you say 'mulattoes'?"

"*Milat* for men; *miyatwès* for women," Abel answered.

"We would like to understand the relationships among those fully African, those fully white and those who are mixed," Lordis jumped in, apparently also having come to the same conclusion as her husband regarding the overseer's command of English.

"How much you want to know?" Abel shot back. "*Combien? Ki kontité?*" He rubbed his thumb back and forth over his fingers.

John dug into his trouser pocket and produced seven shillings and five pence. "This much."

Abel shook his head. "I offer the truth. No *quick-quack* stories. The truth costs one pound."

John whistled at the high figure and shook his head.

"And I give you all the bananas," the man countered, then laughed. "Do you go to Anse-la-Raye?"

"We wish to go there."

"I ride with you. Make sure you do not get lost. Tell you all you want to know."

After calling out a few commands to the field workers, Abel put himself, his chair, and his bananas on the back board of the cart. He twisted around so that his face addressed John more than Lordis. John set the horse moving at a slow pace, not wanting to reach the town too quickly.

Abel said, "Been trouble on all the islands since the first white man. They say when he discovered the New World he fell on his knees and thanked God. Then he fell upon the natives. Killed many with white man diseases, many with rifle and sword, then more by working them as slaves. When he needed more slaves, he went to Africa. Only after many centuries were they made free."

"In 1838, we understand," Lordis said.

"On paper it is true. Some left the plantations for logging, making charcoal for fires, fishing, shop-keeping. But many others had no other work except what they knew. Went from slaves by chains to slaves by starvation. It is still like that."

"You don't starve; you're a boss," John challenged.

Abel laughed heartily. "I am a boss, but I am not free."

"Because you're part African."

"You have said 'mulatto.' To the white man, color mean everything. Our white men have names for every amount of black. Sacatra, griffe, quadroon, octaroon." Abel made a sound of disdain deep in his throat. "To him, these mean more or less good. But he is the only reason people like me are so. The masters—" the man shot a quick glance at Lordis. "—*couché avec les belles négwès . . .* "

"I understand," John told him.

"So do I," Lordis said.

"They keep them as house servants. Or hide them in a town apartment. *Ipokwit* all."

"Hypocrites indeed," Lordis echoed.

"And then they sleep with the daughter of the *mattresse.* But no matter how *chabin*, how white the skin, the person can never be the equal of the white."

"You can sit beside the whites in the churches. You can own land," John probed.

"If you have money to buy the land. The law says a black man can vote, if he has land and pays taxes." He held up the remainder of the hand of bananas. "I know only this many such black men on St. Lucia."

"But you say you are 'Monsieur,'" John continued. "You demand a better title."

Monsieur Abel shrugged. "The white man gives everyone his attitude. Like a *maladi.* The mulatto will not marry even a *belle* black woman. Instead, he will marry a *lèd* white woman." He scrunched up his face and drew back his lips into a hideous expression.

"Did you marry an ugly woman?" Lordis asked.

Abel shooed the question away. "I marry no woman. When I was young I worked in the government. I was more smart than many whites. But I could go no higher than a clerk. So I leave Castries. Better life in Anse-la-Raye."

"We know a mulatto man in Castries," John said. "Carlisle Thiery."

Abel's smile slipped. "I know *Avokat* Thiery. Very grand. He votes." He pointed back where the cart had passed. "He owns acres, *là-haut*. A clever one, Monsieur Thiery. He wants to become more rich, bringing many more whites to St. Lucia, *en vacances*."

"We've learned," John said. "But apparently after everyone livin' on St. Lucia."

"People such as me and many *nègs* do not want people like you. We do not wish to be treated like your *nègs* on our own island."

A vision of scores of American blacks and mulattoes who had touched his life, their second-rate citizen existences and crushing tribulations, rushed through John's mind like a great torrent. "I can understand."

The group came to the outskirts of the village. Abel pointed. "Go that way."

"Monsieur Thiery's wife is white," Lordis stated.

"Yes. From England. That story I do not know, but it must be interesting." Abel's eyebrows furrowed. "Life for blacks and mulattoes is not so good as ours where you live. If a man or woman has even one drop of black blood, then he or she is black."

"Not every white person in the United States believes that," John countered. "My wife and I try to judge people by their actions rather than the color of their skin."

Abel did not look convinced. "You have laws that keep black and white *sépawé*."

"Yes. The law says 'separate but equal.'"

The overseer shook his head. "Never equal. The white man is rich. His homes, his restaurants, his schools will always be better."

The cart came to the river and crossed a well-worn wooden bridge. The river bed was only half filled, exposing uneven courses of enormous stones. On its banks, barefooted black women wearing colorful scarves and long skirts knotted up at their waists beat wash against the wet rocks. Items they had already tended to dried on more elevated boulders. One of the women had a wracking, tubercular cough that echoed up from the ravine. Two goats cavorted upstream, sampling the newly grown grasses.

"Will you go to Soufrière?" Abel asked.

"We hope to . . . tomorrow."

"In Soufrière, when la Révolution happened in France, they made their own guillotine. Some French masters' heads rolled across the sand then," he said with an evil grin. "The poor are rich in one thing only: they are many more than the wealthy." Before either of the Le Bruns could respond to his provocative words, Abel pointed to the narrow fishing boats that had been pulled onto the beach.

"We make our boats from the gommier tree," Abel said. "Bring the trunks down from the forest and burn out the insides."

John grabbed his camera and took a snapshot of three boats. He captured another image, of fishermen tending to nets, spreading them out or mending them.

"This is terrible," Lordis said, looking at the scene. "Look at the rags those men are wearing. They can't even afford clothes for their backs."

Abel broke into his hearty laugh. "No, Mrs. They are *superstitieux.* They believe the fish will only give their lives to feed poor men. So they dress in rags when they work. I go now." He grabbed his camp chair. "Must not forget my *chèz;* my *chèz* and my hat are what make me the boss."

*How could you omit your lighter complexion?* John thought.

Abel held out his right hand. "And your pound sterling makes me rich this week."

As he dug into his pocket for his wallet, John said, "Carlisle Thiery went to Cambridge University to become a lawyer. That cost a great deal of money. Do you know who paid his bills?"

Abel shrugged. "Many mulattoes live in shame. Keep secrets of their birth. I would think he is the child of a quadroon or octaroon woman and a government official *embarras*. But not my business." He turned away and began walking toward the center of the village. "*Au revoir*, Americans!"

---

WHEN THE COUPLE was back on the road and heading to Canaries, Lordis said, "What a sad state of affairs. The light-coloreds here hate the whites but covet what they have. At the same time, they look down their noses at those who are fully black."

John snapped the reins to encourage the horse to a quicker pace. "You spent your youth in the South. You know the same kind of prejudice runs through our black communities. The 'high yellows' consider themselves a better social class than people with darker skin. Georgia and South Carolina mulattoes also won't marry anyone darker than they are."

Lordis patted her forehead with her handkerchief. "I had hoped it would be better in a place that bills itself as paradise. Like Abel said, superiority and intolerance are diseases spread by whites."

"And he is definitely infected. Our country's golden doors are indeed open to the 'homeless, tempest-tost' of foreign shores, even though every new group gets their turn in the barrel. But it's never gotten better for Negroes because the black slave/white master memories die hard. The answer is to educate the ignorant masses and make as many of us as possible intolerant toward intolerance."

---

CANARIES WAS ANOTHER fishing village, little different from Anse-la-Raye. The majority of houses were crowded against each other, small and simple, fashioned from wood, with thatched roofs. Most were gaily painted in pastel colors. A few buildings were two stories high. The more elaborate structures were mixtures of Victorian and French architecture; the commercial ones being made of stone, covered with stucco, and whitewashed. A modest Roman Catholic church occupied a central location. In the center of the village, the road was crowned and constructed of flat stones, but before the village limits were reached it returned to dirt.

When Lordis and John stopped to picnic on the beach, they realized that they had neglected to pack anything to drink. A single village store sold sundry foreign items, almost all from the British Isles, Canada, or the United States. Carbonated ginger beer sealed inside glass bottles and capped by the recent Crown Cork Bottle Seal method were kept slightly cool in a bucket of water. The vacationers carried the bottles and their picnic basket down to the beach and sat under the shadow of a coconut palm. Two minutes later, a male villager passed by, pointed up, and made it known by gestures and sound effects that falling coconuts could kill the ignorant unwary. They retreated to the aromatic shade of a wild bougainvillea bush.

John pointed south. "There's the top of the first Piton, beyond that hill."

"Can we reach it?" Lordis asked.

John pushed the remains of their meal into the basket. "It's farther than it looks. We'll be comin' south again real soon."

A little after two o'clock John and Lordis turned the carriage around and headed back toward Castries. A look at the same scenery from the opposite direction offered new discoveries. For a time, a flight of pelicans circled curiously above them. An iguana dashed with a crooked gait in front of their path, so low to the dirt that no shadow could be seen under it. For a time, Lordis thought that John had lapsed into silence to better absorb their surroundings. When his reverie grew too protracted, she knew he was thinking about a subject important enough to turn his senses inward.

"The burned plantation?" Lordis asked.

John cocked his head to one side. "The use of fire to try to hide murder is not an uncommon act. The facts that no one escaped and that two were lyin' on their backs are compellin' enough, but when those footprints are added, the whole thing stinks of careful plannin'. I need to be there when that coroner does his grim work."

"You shall be," his wife affirmed.

---

AS LORDIS AND JOHN entered the New Bristol Hotel, they were rushed upon by a man with a British accent so proper it made John purse his lips.

"Hello, hello, hello!" the bald-headed man greeted, smiling with such exaggeration that his eyes became slits. His forehead had a sheen of perspiration, and he wiggled his raised forefinger as if he had ague. "You are Mr. and Mrs. Le Brun, are you not?"

"We are," John answered.

"I'm Leslie Lyons, the proprietor of the hotel. So sorry not to have been here to greet you or to catch you subsequently."

"Be that as it may," John said, trying to cut short the obsequious posturing. "You wish to ask us somethin'?"

Lyons dipped his head so far to the left and shook it so vigorously that he seemed to be shaking water from his ear. "Yes, well, we have a vexing problem that requires resolution. It seems that the governor-general wishes to have the inspector-general from Barbados and the coroner from Grenada stay with us. However, we are currently completely booked."

"Surely, you're not thinking of throwing us out onto the street," Lordis objected in a loud voice.

The clerk threw up his hands. "Certainly not! Monsieur Thiery placed your reservation and, I understand, has been acting as your guide and facilitator. I contacted him regarding this problem, and he has offered a wonderful accommodation for you." He swung his hand with affected elegance into the waiting area.

As if responding to a stage cue, Carlisle Thiery rose from a chair that faced away from the hotel's front door. He turned, looked directly at the Le Bruns, and executed a bow from the waist.

"An improvement, in my estimation," the lawyer spoke, simultaneously gliding toward them and taking in the elements of the hotel lobby with a critical expression. "There is a vacant house next to ours on the Morne. I've taken the liberty of speaking with the realtor, and he is willing—on my say-so—to allow you to rent it for the same price as you are paying for your rooms at the hotel. Magnificent view. Cooler breezes. My family at your beck and call."

"But it's so isolated," John noted, "and we have no means of transport."

"Not at all. We have a telephone. Whenever you wish a hackney to pick you up, you need only call the hotel here, and a carriage and driver will be at your front door within fifteen minutes."

John scanned the face of the desk clerk for information. "What about Paul and Minerva Van Fleet?"

"They've become the happy guests of Andrew Ashton, sir. Up at Rodney Bay."

"I see." John swung around to address their self-appointed host. "Your proposition sounds agreeable."

"Oh, wonderful," gushed proprietor Lyons from behind him.

"I have my carriage outside," said Thiery. "I'll deliver you personally, as soon as you can pack."

---

THE MOMENT JOHN SHUT their hotel room door, Lordis said, "Ordinarily, I'd be offended not to have you confer with me on such a decision, but I know you must have a reason for agreeing."

John stroked his wife's cheek tenderly. "My reason, dear heart, is the unsettlin' feelin' that overcame me today on our ride: maybe it wasn't the plantation fire at all. Maybe it was my anger at bein' played by Captain Johnson, Carlisle Thiery, and Andrew Ashton."

Lordis emptied the room's armoire of her dresses. "Then you should be angrier. Ashton has got his mitts on the Van Fleets. Thiery has been chosen—or volunteered—to manipulate you."

"Which is why I want the opportunity to peel back all the layers of that gentleman." John opened the balcony doors and looked down at Carlisle Thiery, who stood patiently beside his carriage, a lit cigarette glowing between his fingers. "I also admit to a personal curiosity that might could be solved by stayin' close to him: I dearly want to know how a man of color got his hands on the money to attend Cambridge."

---

WHEN JOHN AND LORDIS had made themselves comfortable in the rear of Carlisle's elegant extension top, cut-under carriage, the lawyer snapped the reins smartly and set his matched pair of horses trotting through Castries.

Thiery cast a quick glance back at his passengers. "Because you two left the hotel this morning without saying where you were going, I was contacted as your representative. I hope I wasn't too forward in trying to accommodate both you and the hotel in the best manner possible."

"Not at all," John told him.

"I've also taken the liberty of preparing places for you and Mrs. Le Brun at our dinner table tonight."

The Thiery property was about a quarter acre, with only the area around the house on flat ground. The rest was terraced and beautifully landscaped, with the sharp rise of the mountain directly behind. On the opposite side of the road, treetops alternated with views of the city.

Thiery drove past his own home to the property directly next door. As he brought the horses to a halt, he said, "This is where you will be staying. It is very much like ours in size and layout." He handed John a key, sprang from the driver's seat, and began struggling with the steamer trunk.

"Mr. Lyons is so embarrassed at needing to ask you to vacate," he said in a voice strained by the tightening of his upper muscles, "that he has promised to lend the services of the hotel drivers free of charge whenever you require them."

"That's right kind," John allowed. "I think two of us heftin' Mrs. Le Brun's mobile clothing store will be more successful."

Immediately after setting down his half of the burden at the house's front door, Carlisle grabbed his golden watch chain and fished his watch out of its pocket. "We're well behind the time I estimated for delivering you. After we finish unloading, you two should wash up and come right over for dinner."

In rapid order, the house was opened and all of the vacationers' belongings temporarily stored in the entry.

"Washing up is not enough," Lordis declared. "Late or not, I refuse to dine in clothes that smell of sweat and smoke."

---

THE THIERY HOUSE was grand in comparison to most other homes around Castries but not to some of its immediate neighbors. It was a two-story Victorian, painted lime green and white, with a living room, private study, kitchen, and dining rooms downstairs and a bathroom and three bedrooms above. Water ran in the kitchen and bathroom via an enclosed basin supplied by rain runoff from the tile roof. The house was retro-electrified. The floors were also made of tile, with areas covered by throw rugs. A large mirror graced the foyer, and several primitive landscape paintings of St. Lucia hung on the living room walls. The Victorian age furniture was too ornate and large for its surroundings.

The Thiery children had already been fed and excused to their room. Waiting for the Le Bruns were Sibyl and a woman whose beauty was not diminished by middle age. Her skin was the color of the throat of a fawn, which served to accent a full set of straight white teeth. Her carriage resembled that of a woman of substance, her neck long, her chin slightly raised. Her eyes were an arresting amber-brown. Her wavy reddish-brown hair was drawn back so that her ears showed. From each lobe dangled iridescent ovals of mother of pearl. Both she and Sibyl wore flower-print dresses of an identical pattern, leading John to guess that one of them was an accomplished seamstress. While the lawyer's wife and mother were both thin, his mother stood about two inches taller.

"Lordis and John Le Brun," Carlisle said in a formal tone, "you've met *Si belle*, of course. This is my mother, Emeline."

John stepped forward, took the woman's right hand, executed a continental bow, and brushed her fingertips with his lips. "*Enchanté*, Madame Thiery."

Emeline smiled, raising the flesh on her prominent cheekbones. "It is a pleasure to have you visit the home of my son and daughter-in-law." She dipped her head in acknowledgement of Lordis.

With the formalities dispensed, the five took seats at the dining table. A black maid appeared from the kitchen with a dish made from christophene, a Caribbean squash. While she ladled the first course into porcelain bowls, the lawyer inquired of his guests' day. John gushed about their jaunt, but he made no mention of Monsieur Abel for fear that the Anse-la-Raye man had a checkered past in Castries that might have touched the Thierys badly.

"And tomorrow?" Sibyl asked the pair.

"We have decided to rest," Lordis answered. "Nothing beyond exploring Castries. John wishes to be present the following day when the coroner performs the autopsies on the Palmer family."

Emeline made a tsking noise. "Such a calamity. I understand that some of the *Neg Maron* were on the plantation when the fire occurred."

"Ah, you've heard that," John returned. "The evidence isn't conclusive. And even if the footprints are somehow matched to the forest people, that does not necessarily indicate that they set the fire."

"No, of course not." Emeline half-filled her soup spoon and raised it to her lips with great care.

"Were you acquainted with the Palmer family?" Lordis asked the older woman.

"She's from Castries. The west of our island and the east are separated by more than rough mountains," Carlisle replied for his mother.

"But information certainly flies through those mazelike mountains," John said, to no one in particular.

"On a small island, such a big tragedy becomes the general talk for some time," said Carlisle. "I expect that a line of carriages will travel out to the Palmer plantation starting early the day after tomorrow."

"Will your carriage be among them?" Lordis asked.

"No, Mrs. Le Brun, it will not. My sympathies go out to those lost, but I have several critical appointments on my calendar. I would appreciate hearing what happened from you and your husband."

The main course consisted of seafood jambalaya containing chunks of lobster, shrimp, and ham, served over a bed of braised seasoned rice. When most of it had been consumed, Carlisle's mother asked about John's detective exploits and was particularly interested in the history of the Jekyl Island Club. John indulged her for a quarter hour and then turned the conversation. He fixed his gaze on the son's chest.

"That's the same tie you wore when we first met you."

Carlisle lifted the starched linen napkin from where it covered his tie. The silk material had a light gray background and lines of small shields at the diagonal. "Excellent observation. It's the official one from Cambridge."

"Do tell. Enlighten Mrs. Le Brun and me about the heraldry, if you would," John invited.

"You know, I'm not totally sure of the significance of the color red here. I believe it stands for the fact that one must to be willing to shed blood for a cause. At any rate, each shield is divided into four by a white ermine cross. Each of the red panels contains a golden rampant lion, which represents fierce bravery. At the center of the cross is an open Bible."

John turned to Carlisle's mother. "You must be very proud that your son earned a degree from Cambridge."

"I am indeed."

"We have seen that your family are churchgoers," John probed. "If Cambridge is noted for anything more than its school of law it is its college of divinity. Why did you choose law instead of theology, Monsieur Thiery?"

Carlisle tucked his tie self-consciously between the buttons of his white shirt. "I suppose because no matter how skilled the priest becomes at arguing the cause of living justly, he cannot be sure his flock will behave that way. The skilled lawyer, however, gains the tools to argue decisively for the punishment of the unjust and the vindication of the just."

"But that doesn't always happen," Lordis jumped in.

"True," Carlisle said, "but the greater his skills, the more likely justice will be done in this unfair world."

John said, "If . . . the skilled one represents the just side. I was asked at the St. Lucia Island Club why I became a lawman, and I replied very much as you have."

The lawyer thumped the tabletop three times. "Of course you did."

"But I was elected to my position of sheriff. For your law degree," John said, "you traveled a great distance and paid a great amount of money, I'm sure."

"Each year, two scholarships to study in the British Isles are awarded on St. Lucia," Emeline explained. "Carlisle graduated at the top of his class here in Castries. The scholarship was well spent; he's the only person on this island who ever earned a law degree from Cambridge."

"Is there a stipulation to the awards that the recipients return to St. Lucia?" John asked.

"There is an expectation but no contract," Carlisle answered. "I love St. Lucia. There was never any question that I would remain in England. Even if I had wanted to stay, it would have been nigh unto impossible to earn a living."

"Are you speaking about prejudice?" Lordis asked.

"I am indeed. The British pride themselves on broadmindedness, but it's almost always in theory, not practice. You know the Rudyard Kipling poem written for Queen Victoria's Diamond Jubilee?"

"About the white man's burden?" John said.

"The same. Most people think it was the poet's jingoistic rationalization in favor of imperialism and a paean to the superiority of the Englishman over other races."

John glanced briefly at the black maid standing ready in the doorway. "I certainly did."

"Actually, the poem is subtitled 'The United States and the Philippine Islands.' Following your Spanish-American War, you fought to wrest away Spain's hold in the Pacific, to give your warships a place from which to intimidate the Far East and protect American interests. Kipling intended the poem to be a warning to your country . . . of the wages of imperialist sins:

Take up the White Man's burden, Send forth the best ye breed
Go bind your sons to exile, to serve your captives' need;
To wait in heavy harness, On fluttered folk and wild—
Your new-caught, sullen peoples, Half-devil and half-child."

As John listened, he thought with some amusement, *Who would have supposed two middle-class Americans on vacation would be lectured by two St. Lucian mulatto males in the same day?*

Without missing a beat after his recitation, their host asked, “Did you happen to see the cricket field in Anse-la-Raye? No matter how small the village, they will clear a flat area for cricket.”

“Bizarre sport if you ask me,” Emeline Thiery declared. “But there are cricket fields all around the world, thanks to British imperialism.”

Conversation touching on cricket, English football, American football, and baseball continued through the coconut cheesecake.

“Do you keep yourself fit by playin’ any sport?” John asked of the thinly built lawyer.

“I have no time for sport.”

John thought about Bobby Johnson and wondered how he had met Carlisle Thiery. “Then what about competitions of the mind? Do you play chess, cribbage, whist, or auction bridge?”

The lawyer leveled his gaze on the detective. “The same holds true. Leisure pursuits are the recreation of the poor and the rich. Those in between cannot afford the time.”

Looking at the quality of the dishes, utensils, and glasses on the table, John thought, *His point is not at all about time but about being a mulatto, stuck smack-dab between whites and blacks.*

While her husband reflected, Lordis broke up the get-together, using the excuse of needing to unpack.

---

ONCE LORDIS AND JOHN were alone in the rented house and Lordis had found the switch for the electric parlor light, she said, “I must congratulate you on your self-control tonight, Mr. Le Brun. Railing against imperialism is, after all, one of your favorite preoccupations.”

Since meeting John, Lordis had heard him orate on imperialism and, in particular, American imperialism at least a dozen times. If allowed enough time, he laid out the history of economic/political/military empire-building strategies as far back as the ancient Greeks and Phoenicians colonizing the Mediterranean. When he arrived at the subject of "Johnny-come-lately America," as he put it, he started with British settlers inexorably stealing land from the native Americans, then quoted Thomas Jefferson's expectation that the loosening of Spanish control in the New World would allow the expansion of U.S. interests, and followed up with President Polk's encouragement of the Mexican-American War and the takeover of California. John's main anger was directed at the propaganda employed to influence American citizen attitudes by a plutocracy-directed press in order to justify intervention in Cuba and the annexation of the Philippines, the latter after killing several hundred thousand unwilling Filipinos. Once he had a head of steam up, the self-taught scholar would quote verbatim from a *Monthly Review* editorial that stated "in Britain, empire was justified as a benevolent 'white man's burden.' In the United States, empire does not even exist; 'we' are merely protecting the causes of freedom, democracy, and justice worldwide." He often cited the work of U.S. Navy Admiral Alfred Thayer Mahan in his 1890 masterwork *The Influence of Sea Power Upon History*. The book had influenced virtually every world power, causing a build up of fleets that had not been seen since the Spanish Armada took on the navy of Elizabeth I. John's well-rehearsed peroration concluded grimly by predicting that the arms race among the United States, Great Britain, Germany, France, and Japan would result inevitably in a global war on a scale never before seen.

"When I'm talkin' I can't be learnin'," John replied to Lordis's dig, walking to the center of the parlor and giving the spare remaining pieces of furniture the once-over. "The Thierys have been on the receivin' end of colonial exploitation; I have not. I thought if I held my tongue I might hear about their thoughts concernin' the U.S. of A. annexin' the Windward Islands."

"Positive or negative thoughts?" asked Lordis.

"I can see them playin' the—"

Lordis had ventured past the dining room, which was totally devoid of furniture, and had turned to enter the kitchen when John's sudden silence brought her to a halt. "Yes?"

"I was goin' to say, 'I can see the Thierys playin' the black side or the white, dependin' on how many powerful pieces they think they can control for their personal ends.' But black and white down here has a much greater meanin' than mere chessmen."

"Neither Carlisle nor his mother divulged that much," Lordis pointed out.

John approached her. "As I expected. They are careful and calculatin'."

Lordis opened several drawers and cupboard cabinets, finding precious little beyond a few pots and pans and a smattering of cleaning materials, bowls, plates, and utensils. "When Mr. Thiery mentioned his mother the other night at the restaurant, I pictured a silent little woman wearing an apron. This one carries herself like a queen."

"And directs the course of the conversation," John added. "A formidable woman."

"She steered clear of promoting St. Lucia for increased tourism," Lordis observed, "but she picked your brain for the names of the wealthy whom you know." She moved on to the small room that served triple duty as laundry, pantry, and utility space and found soap flakes, a bottle of bleach, and a bag of clothespins. At the same time, John walked into the cramped room opposite.

"Probably used as a study," he judged. "Bare as a newborn babe."

Lordis grabbed her three hatboxes and started up the stairs to the second floor. "I get the feeling that we have been neatly turned into prisoners in a cage with a better view."

"We can beg off on future dinner invitations," John called

from the parlor, where he was scratching his head at the prospect of hauling Lordis's steamer trunk upstairs. "Avoid bein' squeezed for more information."

The two rear bedrooms were broom clean, but the master bedroom had a large canopy bed and a dresser. Lordis pushed aside the mosquito netting tucked under the mattress all around the four-poster and set her nightgown on the cover sheet. After noisily bumping the trunk up twelve steps, John paused with it outside in the upper hallway, his chest heaving from the effort. Without commenting, Lordis grabbed the trunk by one of its handles and roughhoused it into the room.

"Do you really believe we can avoid them?" she asked. "We have twelve days before Captain Bobby Johnson, the Freebooter of the Caribbean, sails back into Castries with his skull and crossbones flying. With Emeline and Sibyl backing Carlisle, we're bound to have a tough time resisting their agendas."

John removed his belt and gun holster and set them on the antiquated dresser. "Your words are so melodramatic, there ought to be an organ playin' in the next room."

"You think so? I know the capabilities of women far better than you do, John Le Brun. My mother always said, 'The reason women allow men to wage war is that if the women did it, there wouldn't be a single soul left standing.'"

# CHAPTER EIGHT

## June 29, 1910

ANTON BEAUFORT ARRIVED at the rented house at precisely nine o'clock on the morning of the Palmer autopsies. Either by careful planning or pure coincidence, the buggy that carried Lordis and John fell behind those of Lieutenant Governor Tubble and Castries Chief of Police James Dautry, who had with him Chief Coroner of the Windward Islands Reginald Brooks. Introductions were called back and forth between the conveyances. The abbreviated column moved at a brisk pace along the East-West Road. The Le Bruns' driver was as taciturn as he had been during the outing at Choc Beach. Unlike Richard Tubble, as he drove through the rainforest he made no comments, even when a splendidly plumed parrot flew directly in front of him. He was finally compelled to speak, however, when John noted a decayed wooden sign nailed to a tree and half obscured by foliage.

"I missed seein' that sign the first time we came this way. Was the word carved into it '*Tristesse,*' Mr. Beaufort?" John asked.

"Yes, sir, it was indeed," the man replied with a Kwèyole lilt in a plummy bass baritone. "It means 'sadness.'"

"Yes. Why is it there?"

"The Frenchman who briefly took the plantation from the Palmer family put it up there before he and his family left. During the French Revolution."

"Ah."

"Some people still call the plantation 'Tristesse' thinking that's its name. But it isn't."

"What is the name?" Lordis asked.

"Don't have one."

"Well, that should be the name now," she judged, "after all the recent sorrow it's seen."

Waiting in front of the ruined house was Peter Palmer, standing close beside the parish priest from the nearby town of Dennery. Also in the gathering were Palmer's three surviving house servants, Dennery Chief of Police Brendan Riley, and one of his officers, a mulatto man in his late fifties with a semi-bald head whose remaining hair resembled bolls of cotton. From his bent knees and sagging shoulders, he looked like he was having trouble staying awake.

As soon as Peter Palmer spotted the three buggies, he started walking around the side of the house toward the horse stable tailed by the trio of servants. The priest and policemen hung back.

The priest put himself among the three buggies and introduced himself as Father Gauthier. He carried a Bible in his left hand, balanced on the left side of his chest as if it were a dueling weapon.

"Mr. Palmer has had the graves dug already. He wants the burials as soon as possible."

"He can have whatever he wants after I'm finished," Coroner Brooks declared.

"I'm glad you're finally here," Chief Riley told the group. "The last of the ice melted during the night."

"Do you have an examining table set up?" asked Brooks.

"Behind the barn, in the shade of a tree. We used a pair of sawhorses and some wide planks."

Brooks did not look happy with the answer. "Lead on!"

Only a few steps distant from the table were four empty coffins and lids with nails half hammered into them, not fashioned by a professional casket maker but painted with several coats of black lacquer. The interiors were raw wood.

When the coroner watched Palmer and the servants take up positions near the barn, the coroner announced in a loud voice, "I require only two witnesses and an assistant. Mr. Le Brun and Lieutenant Governor Tubble." Then he pointed at the larger of the two male house servants. "And you. Everyone else, find a place to rest. Perhaps at the front of the house."

The coroner had pulled a doctor's satchel and a duffel bag from the wagon he arrived in. He waited until the remainder of the group had moved out of eyesight before untying the bag.

The first corpse had already been laid out on the makeshift examining table, still wrapped in a water-repellant tarpaulin. Dr. Brooks carefully lifted the covering away. His grimace as he uncovered the burnt-black body assured Le Brun that his own revulsion on Sunday had not been an overreaction.

Brooks said to Richard Tubble, "When you handed me those photographs yesterday evening, I understood why you didn't move the bodies to Castries. Too delicate indeed."

The lieutenant governor dipped his head in John's direction. "Mr. Le Brun took the photos and recommended you perform the autopsies."

Brooks opened the duffel bag and extracted two rubberized aprons and two cloth masks. He tossed one set to the mulatto house servant. "You're an American detective of far-flung fame," he said, without looking at John.

"So I'm told," John replied. From where he stood he could smell the camphor impregnated in the masks, meant to negate the odors of decay.

"Have you assisted in any such examinations?" Brooks asked.

"I've watched but never touched."

"Good enough. Watch once again."

"I don't feel I can do this," the house servant confessed.

John glanced around, trying to locate Anton Beaufort, the driver from the hotel. By John's estimation, the man stood about an inch taller than six foot and, although on the thin side, had a palpably powerful physique. And, although he played his violin with a good degree of feeling, he seemed fully capable of mastering his emotions. Before he could suggest Beaufort as a candidate, however, the coroner spoke.

"Of course you can do it. We're not dealing with voodoo or zombies. These are just the shells of souls that have departed." He studied the corpse on the table. "You will immobilize each body when I cut and also help me when I turn or lift it." Brooks took a step backward as he yanked his fingers tightly in his gloves. "It's bad enough they're in such states, but to have no autopsy table, no scale, no hooks, straps, hoist, or pulleys to assist . . . . I don't mind saying it's vexing."

"I understand," John said, as he thought of the tools of his profession sitting uselessly in Brunswick, Georgia.

Brooks lowered his mask. From his satchel he extracted a number of instruments and laid them on the bench above the corpse's head. They included two sizes of scalpels, a bone saw, rib cutters, skull chisel, hammer, several clamps, and a large syringe with a long, thick needle.

"Which one am I looking at?" he asked, staring at the missing cheek and the teeth beyond.

"The woman lyin' on what was left of the master bed," John said. "It should be Mrs. Palmer."

Brooks pointed to his satchel. "You obviously know how to

work a camera. You'll find mine in there. I will open the lower jaw, and you photograph the teeth for me."

Doing his best to ignore the crackling noise, John focused the bellows camera and captured several shots.

Brooks eased the head down and walked slowly around the supine corpse. "Your photographs captured her in this position, correct?"

"Almost exactly," John agreed. "Arms at her sides."

The doctor picked up a large scalpel and plunged it into the dead woman's throat. He worked until he had the air passages opened.

"There is virtually no soot in the trachea. She was not breathing when the fire started. I will examine the primary and secondary bronchi just to be certain."

Tubble locked eyes with Le Brun. "Dead beforehand? That means she was murdered."

"Let's wait and let the good doctor tell us," John counseled. He returned his attention to the coroner, who labored through the charred flesh and tight muscles to make the classic "Y" incision in the torso, the two upper parts of the cut running from the shoulders to the mid-point between the nipples and the long cut over the sternum and across the abdomen to just above the pubis.

Sobs emerged from the male house servant, a mulatto man who John guessed to be in his middle thirties. Tears traveled down his cheeks.

Without acknowledging the noises, Brooks went to work with his rib cutters until he had the internal chest organs exposed. He bent close to the body, turning his head this way and that. Then he used his syringe to draw a generous sample of blood from the heart.

Once again employing his scalpels, the coroner cut into the left and right primary bronchi.

"Also clear of soot. She was definitely dead before the fire began."

"Any sign of a wound?" John asked, as he captured the torso interior on film.

"No gross insult. With all this burned and cracked skin, something subtle like a needle prick or even a dagger wound is likely impossible to find." Brooks stepped back for a few moments, removed his mask, breathed fresh air, and then returned to the examination. He nodded at the servant.

"Hold her head against the table. That's it."

First, Brooks did a careful visual examination of the entire skull. Then, cursing under his breath at the brittle, cracking skin, he made an incision in the scalp, starting behind one ear at the mastoid region, continuing up and extending down to the back of the opposite ear. John averted his good eye when the doctor began to laboriously peel the scalp forward and away from bone and muscle exposing the skull cap. Using his hammer, scalpel chisel, and saw, the doctor removed the skull bone, exposing the brain to the daylight.

"Much more to see on the inside," Brooks remarked. He worked his scalpels down along the brain case until he was able to lift the organ out.

"Oh, my!" the coroner exclaimed, holding the brain in both hands.

"What is it?" Tubble asked anxiously.

The left surface of the organ was smeared with blood. "This woman was stabbed through her left ear. By something slender." Brooks picked up his syringe and used the needle to gently explore the size and depth of the wound. "Something on the order of an ice pick."

"How bizarre!" Tubble exclaimed.

After John took another photograph, Brooks replaced the brain halfway into the skull cavity, fitting it in at an angle. "I wonder if it doesn't make more sense to suspend her examination and get the other woman's body up here."

The children's nanny had been found on her side. The

rigidity of her burned muscles made the corpse more difficult to balance on the table, compelling John to don a pair of gloves and grasp her ankles.

After a swift examination of the exterior of the second woman's body, the coroner went directly to work removing the brain. It had the same wound as the first.

"I know from Mr. Le Brun's photographs that she was found lying on her right side," Brooks said to the house servant. "That would insure that little blood would seep from the ear."

The coroner bothered only to examine the tracheae and brains of the final two corpses. As everyone near the table expected by that time, the windpipes were clear of soot and the brains had been pierced deeply through the left ear canals.

"God in heaven!" Richard Tubble exhaled. "A quadruple murder."

"No doubt when all four were sleepin'," John contributed. "Most likely done by not one but two men. One would throw himself on each victim and clap his hand over the mouth to prevent screamin'. The other was right-handed, so he approached from the corpse's left side and thrust some sharp implement through the ear."

Tubble argued, "It could conceivably be only one man."

Le Brun scrunched his face up into an expression of deep doubt. "It could, but that would be takin' a big risk. Holdin' down a person who fears for her life is difficult enough without also needin' to immobilize her head, clamp her mouth shut and aim the murder weapon cleanly into her ear in darkness."

"Perhaps a torch was used if there were two people," Brooks speculated, which John had learned in London was the British term for flashlight. "Since I brought no torch with me I would never have seen a wound in the outer ear canal."

"Infamous! Unspeakably evil!" Tubble declared. "And the house set afire to cover these crimes. What manner of brutes would do such a thing?"

John squeezed the bridge of his nose with his thumb and forefinger. "I know who Peter Palmer will suspect: Nigel Harvey. Not him directly, but a pair of hired killers."

"Palmer might well think that way," Tubble allowed, "so we must be prepared to stop him from behaving rashly. I believe, given the evidence of the sets of footprints we found, that our primary suspects must be members of the *Neg Maron.*"

"But we cannot fixate on the prints to the exclusion of other possibilities," John warned. "Their appearance may be purely coincidental."

"However," Tubble shot back, "I personally observed that every other set of tracks in that area was made by either boots or sandals. Thanks to Peter Palmer's beneficence, barefoot prints are now unusual on this plantation."

"You two may continue to argue on, but I've finished what I was called here to do," the coroner said. "I will close up these bodies now. When I return to Castries I shall write up my reports and require you gentleman to sign as corroborating witnesses. This infamy demands precise documentation to back up the photographs."

Feeling as if he had been cued, John returned the coroner's camera to his satchel.

Richard Tubble stepped back from the table and looked upon the grisly panorama of burned half-corpses. The sun had shifted during the examinations so that three of the bodies lay exposed to direct light. Several flies circled and lighted on the unflinching figures.

"Let's make haste to put these unfortunate souls into their coffins," Tubble said. "No one else should have to see this. Naturally, the nanny won't be buried in the family plot; she'll have to be seen to later."

---

JOHN HURRIED ACROSS the lawns to address Peter Palmer before the others involved in the autopsies could speak. "I am very sorry to tell you, sir, that your family and the nursemaid were all murdered." Almost before Palmer had digested the findings, in spite of his argument with the lieutenant governor, he hastened to add, "The evidence of the many footprints leadin' into the rainforest point to the *Neg Maron* as the culprits." John knew that if Nigel Harvey turned out to be the instigator of the murders, there was ample time to reorient the grieving man in that direction.

The muscles of Palmer's lower jaw bulged and the tendons in his neck stood out prominently. His eyelids widened, making his eyes look enormous. His breathing had become shallow and rapid.

"Those creatures have been left alone for far too long," he declared. "It is past time that the vermin be exterminated."

"Not today," Lieutenant Governor Tubble said firmly. "We haven't the manpower to do the job."

"When?" Palmer asked in the tone of a demand. "When then?"

"Patience," Tubble counseled. "It will take a while to recruit and plan a strategy. The day after tomorrow."

"No later than that," the plantation owner responded. "My loved ones cry out for justice."

"They should do their cryin' from sanctified graves," John said softly. The persons encircling Palmer nodded as a body.

"This man is right," Father Gauthier said, setting his hand lightly on the bereaved husband and father's shoulder. "Let us commend their souls properly to the Lord."

Le Brun fixed his attention on the Dennery chief of police and his underling. Neither looked happy, which John assumed came from thinking about an imminent confrontation with the fierce, little-known *Neg Maron.*

As the gathering moved across the road toward the cemetery, John collared the plantation's overseer. "Y'know, no one bothered to inform me of your first name, Mr. Mansfield."

"It's Jacob."

"I would be pleased if you'd call me John. I wonder if I might call you Jacob."

The overseer smiled. "Certainly."

"I know you want to attend the burial ceremony, but it will take a bit longer to seal the coffins and set them above the graves. I wonder if you might bring out those plaster casts of the footprints you made."

Jacob followed a step behind John's beeline movement back toward the rear of the mansion. "I didn't make the casts. A man from Mandele who works often with plaster did it. An excellent job to my way of thinking."

"Let's see."

The six sets of right footprints were nestled in packing material inside six shallow wooden crates. They had been stacked in a far corner of the horse stable. Le Brun and Mansfield carried them out to the examining table. For a long while, John studied the prints, moving away from one and coming right back to it or hurrying from one end of the table to the other. He reordered the positions of the boxes and studied them again.

"Mind you, I'm good at readin' shoeprints," Le Brun told his companion. "But bare feet are somethin' else. However, it seems to me that all of these lower surfaces—what do they call them—plantar I think—are too smooth for men who walk around without shoes all the time. Imagine all the cuts and scrapes you'd get from stones, sharp twigs, and the like. Especially if you lived full-time in the rainforest."

"You have a good point," Mansfield said.

"Somethin' else." John pulled from his inside jacket pocket a doubled-up twelve-inch ruler that was fashioned from stiff paper. He used it to measure each of the sets of prints. "Notice how two sets are ten and a quarter, two sets nine and three quarters, and two exactly nine. As if only three men had made the six sets of prints by joggin' that path twice."

"That makes no sense at all," Mansfield decided.

"Not in an everyday situation," John agreed. "But neither do the smooth bottoms on all the prints. I wonder if you would do this investigation an enormous favor and quietly recruit three of your men who have worked barefoot on the plantation for at least several years. Soak an area of exposed soil as if it had rained, let it half dry, and have the men jog through it. Then have your expert plaster person make another set of right foot castin's and mark them numbers seven, eight, and nine."

The overseer's eyes burned with excitement. "I have an idea of what you're looking for, John, and I certainly will do what I can to serve your investigation and Master Peter."

"You will truly serve both if . . ." John admonished, holding his forefinger aloft to emphasize his tone of voice, "you keep the reason for this exercise completely to yourself."

"I shall indeed," Mansfield promised.

John held out his right hand to seal the pledge. "Let's get these castin's back in the stable and pay our respects."

---

VIRTUALLY THE ENTIRE POPULATION of the plantation, as well as neighbors and the unrelated curious, had gathered in and around the small cemetery, surrounding both the inner and outer sides of its stone wall. John elected to stand at the back of the throng. He caught Lordis's eye and indicated by gesture that she should maintain her place between Lieutenant Governor Tubble and Anton Beaufort. The Dennery parish priest, unaccustomed to but pleased at having the undivided attention of so big a congregation, had waited until the milling stopped. He handed his Bible to Peter Palmer, produced a missal, and began the Mass for the Dead. It became swiftly clear that he was not about to omit one paragraph.

*I would think the Palmers were Anglican,* John reflected. *Perhaps they weren't religious in any way. Or, with only a few thousand white folk on St. Lucia, probably the only church that can stay viable on the unpopulated side of the island is a Roman Catholic one. But we all worship the same God. And if there is a heaven, it won't have dividing walls.*

As the Requiem Mass droned on and John grew restive, he looked idly behind him. Off in the distance, near to what was called the Dennery-Micoud Road, stood Nigel Harvey and about a dozen more people flanking him. John recognized the two gate guards. He also recognized the two young white men as Harvey's sons. The rest were men and women of mixed race, including the female servant John and Lordis had met inside the Harvey plantation house.

John surreptitiously backed from the crowd as the *Dies Irae* ended and the Tract began. When he had retreated some fifty feet, he pivoted and walked slowly toward Harvey.

"Terrible. Just terrible," Nigel whispered to John when the detective was by his side. A moment later he said, "What was the coroner's finding?"

"Murder," John said as softly as he could.

"Truly? And who is the culprit?"

"Not yet determined." Le Brun was certain that Harvey's concern went beyond justice for the dead. "So I'm still on the case . . . unless you tell me otherwise."

"No, no," Harvey hastened to say. "I want Peter Palmer to know unequivocally that I am willing to pay you to expose the truth of this infamy. By the way, the St. Lucia Island Club will be open tonight. Ordinarily, its doors are closed from Monday mid-morning until Friday afternoon. We're all supervising our plantations during the week. But everyone around the island wants to know what has happened here today. You should give them a report."

"Why don't you?" John asked.

"Because Peter Palmer is most likely to go to Castries after the burials." Harvey jerked his head in the direction of the cemetery. "He's got no decent place to stay on this side of the island. The best that Dennery has to offer is third-rate."

"I'll try to get over to the club," John said.

Harvey nodded with a look of satisfaction, and silence resumed within his contingent.

When the Gospel began, Nigel again broke into a strong whisper. "How do you plan to run down the murderer?"

"Somethin' unusual on this plantation suggests an invasion by a number of *Neg Maron.* The—"

"*Neg Maron?* Why would they attack the Palmers?"

"Peter seems to have been girdlin' and burnin' trees up a long valley into the rainforest."

Nigel broke into a tight-lipped smile, even as he shook his head. "Desperation to increase his acreage. So it's retribution, then. What an unexpected conclusion."

"Possible conclusion," Le Brun corrected. "We won't know until we can interrogate some of the forest people."

"Well, count me in on the hunt. Me, my sons, and maybe I can recruit one or two others. When does it happen?"

"I have heard the plan is for the day after tomorrow."

"I'll check with Sheriff Riley. Will you be in attendance?"

"Unless I am banned." Having said all he wished to, Le Brun nodded a farewell and strode back toward the ongoing Requiem Mass.

---

ACCORDING TO LIEUTENANT GOVERNOR TUBBLE, funerals on St. Lucia were generally followed by a meal or buffet. The burning of the house, the smoke damage to its upholstered chairs, and the stark horror of the mass burial all precluded the opportunity for happy reminiscences and a ritualized return to normalcy. Richard Tubble was the first to leave, followed soon after by Chief of Police Dautry and Chief Coroner Brooks. John asked Anton Beaufort to stay out of his buggy until Peter Palmer's trotter was hitched to his smart sulky with overlarge wheels. The new widower moved out of his horse barn with speed and accelerated as he reached the East-West Road, never looking back.

Soon after, the carriage bearing Lordis and John climbed into the rainforest on a deserted road. The mountains shouldered in, creating the illusion that they could close up the man-made cut in a matter of moments.

Lordis touched John's arm at the elbow. "I saw you walk back to Nigel Harvey's group during the service."

"I did indeed."

"What did you two have to say to each other?"

"Not very much." John tilted his head in the direction of their driver and, from the partial concealment of his lap, waggled a warning finger at his wife. "He told me that the St. Lucia Island Club would be opened tonight so that the planters around the rest of the island could hear the news."

"I'm content to stay up at the house," Lordis said. "If there's some women's meeting, I want no part of reliving today. Living it was quite enough."

John adjusted his position on the upholstered carriage seat to prevent his holster from digging into his lower back. "Doubly so because this is still our vacation."

"Do you think you'll have any reason to return to this side of the island?"

"I do. Two days hence, actually," John replied. "Based on those footprints, a force will be recruited to find the forest dwellers who live closest to the Palmer plantation."

"Don't think you'll be part of that hunt," Lordis said in an authoritative voice.

"I assume the chief of police and the lieutenant governor will not allow vacationers to wander into harm's way. I'll merely be at the tail end to offer my expertise concernin' whether or not I believe the crime has been solved."

Lordis smoothed the folds of her dress over her thighs. "I will accompany you."

As he had on the trip out from Castries, Anton volunteered nothing as he guided the carriage around a turn in the road. Lordis leaned forward and angled her face upward to address him.

"Mr. Beaufort, will you be free to drive us back to the plantation two mornings from today?"

"I have been told to make myself available to you whenever you require, Madam," he replied.

"In that case, let us not waste tomorrow," John broke in. "We got as far south as Canaries the other day. We would very much like to see the volcano and the Pitons tomorrow. Would an eight-thirty start be too early?"

"No, sir," said the black driver, who then lapsed into another protracted silence.

---

DIRECTLY AFTER THE HOTEL DRIVER dropped the Le Bruns off at the rented house atop Morne Fortune and the pair were inside the front door, Lordis said, "Why don't you trust Mr. Beaufort?"

"I trust Jacob Mansfield slightly, based on his words and behavior concernin' the Palmer family. But I trust no one completely. Neither you nor I truly know a single soul in the strictest sense of the word. Mr. Beaufort may be as innocent as a lamb, but if we speak in front of him he may happen to repeat our thoughts to a number of people . . . perhaps to a murderer or to the one who hired him."

Lordis made a grand flourish closing the front door. "We're alone now, Mr. Le Brun. Tell me who killed those women."

John peeled off his jacket with relief. "I doubt it was one or more women. Nor was it a solitary man." He related the information of the identical wounds through the left ears and his theory of how two men had accomplished the serial executions without arousing the rest of the sleepers.

"Diabolical!" Lordis pronounced. "And probably too complicated for men from the forest."

"I agree. If there were indeed six men, they would more likely divide their efforts and set the house, the barns, and many other structures aflame. Their primary goal should be to drive the owner out of business, not commit murder."

"And to give an indirect warning to any other planter who would dare to annex Tristesse and develop that wild valley," Lordis added.

John began unbuttoning his shirt with haste. "Woo-wee, I am warm! I would dearly like to find an open rainwater tank to throw myself into."

"Thank the Lord for the breezes and the cool nights." Lordis grabbed a paper Japanese fan from the freestanding table in the foyer and snapped it open. "So, this business of tramping through the mountains looking for six *Neg Maron* is nothing more than a wild goose chase."

"I believe."

"And yet you want to return to Tristesse."

"I do." John walked toward the kitchen area, where an ice locker held pitchers of tea and lemonade. As the two indulged in cool refreshment, John spoke of his directive to have plaster footprint casts made of longtime plantation workers and of his need to compare them with the original casts. "To me, the six that were made a couple days back are of men who ordinarily wear shoes."

"How strange," Lordis commented.

"Further, that there were only three men, who duplicated their jogs in order to make it seem as if a sizable number of mountain primitives had visited the plantation. You know the adage: the criminal always returns to the scene of the crime?"

"Yes, but you've told me that's—using your word – 'hogwash.'"

"The 'always' is hogwash. But when the crime goes unsolved for more than a couple days, it seems that a goodly number of the guilty do hang around to see how their luck is holdin' out."

Lordis sat on one of the dining chairs. "And you believe it might be the case here."

"I believe that there will be many police, more than a few other planters, and men in their employ who one might have paid to commit this crime." John sat beside his wife. "If and when the supposed nearby village of *Neg Maron* is not found, then I will bring out the original plaster casts and strongly suggest that every man present remove shoes and socks and press his feet against those casts for comparison. Now, I have no idea if the bottoms of feet have the same unique line patterns as do hand palms and fingers. But even if they're only half as accurate, the authorities can focus on the whereabouts of the likeliest suspects on the night of the murders and burnin'."

John expected praise for his plan. Instead, Lordis's eyebrows furrowed, and a pair of creases appeared on her forehead.

"What other strategies have you developed?" she asked.

John collapsed backward. "Lordis, I told you a few days ago that I am at a significant disadvantage here. I have none of my tools—"

"I know. No leverage with the local authorities. No familiarity with bad blood." Lordis took her time sipping her lemonade. "Then I suggest that your next strategy is to pray."

Caught off guard, John uttered an involuntary laugh. "You know I believe in the power of prayer. But I sincerely doubt that if God allowed those four innocent creatures to be slaughtered, He will drop the answer to this crime in my lap."

"I doubt that as well," Lordis replied with composure. "What I suggest is that you pray for Him to sharpen all the considerable talents He's given you and all the skills you have amassed over the decades in solving crimes. Pray that your celebrated gut instinct works at full capacity." Lordis stood and moved with no haste toward the master bedroom. "If you think that such action is useless, I will do your praying for you."

---

THE WINDOWS OF THE St. Lucia Island Club clubhouse blazed with light as John approached. Every hitching post up and down the length of the street was in use, both for saddle and carriage horses. Several men stood chatting in small groups on the narrow veranda that ran the width of the clubhouse.

Le Brun had learned on his initial visit that the membership consisted of eight planters from the Atlantic Ocean side, Andrew Ashton alone on the north end, twenty men from the Cul-de-Sac valley south to Vieux Fort on the Caribbean Sea side, plus the owners of the Cul-de-Sac sugar refinery and the largest perishable warehouse in Castries. Thirteen were in attendance at the special gathering when John arrived. He was clearly once again the center of attention. Every man found a place in either the sitting or dining room to listen to him expound on the investigation to date and to press him afterward to reveal his thoughts on the crime's solution. While he spoke, two more members insinuated themselves into the crowded sitting room.

John refused to mention a murder instrument or the creation of a second set of plaster castings. To cut off badgering about specifics, he said in a loud voice, "I am not the coroner. He is the one to give you specifics about the murders. The mornin' after next, a hunt will be conducted in the forest immediately north of the Palmer plantation. Your police will, naturally, have a presence, but I don't need to tell you how much rugged territory will need to be explored. How many of you have already pledged your services and the services of those in your employ?"

Three of the planters raised their hands.

"It's just too far to travel from Vieux Fort," one said.

"And it's still planting season," another called out. "This should be a job for the law."

"What would you say to such excuses if your entire family had died and your house was burned down?" Andrew Ashton challenged, first to the two objectors and then sweeping his gaze to take in the two rooms.

Eyes shifted back and forth.

"Your plantation might be next if they get away with this," Neville Wilcox asserted. "It's high time we cleaned out these nests of savages anyway."

"Who has contacted the military for assistance?" asked an owner who had not been at the previous Saturday-night dinner.

"A token guard is stationed here but not authorized for civil action," Algernon Brummel stated.

"The hell you say!" another man unfamiliar to Le Brun shot back. "They quelled the coal rioters."

"Only after the deaths and woundings and when their naval stores were threatened," Brummel returned.

"Gentlemen!" club president Raymond Scott broke in, waving his hands in the air. "I think it best to call out the names of all in attendance and poll—"

Scott's eyes focused on the foyer. The crowd parted. Peter Palmer entered the sitting room. Hands thrust out to his hand or to rub him solicitously on the shoulders.

"Welcome, Peter," Scott said. "As you can see, your friends deeply sympathize with your losses and are anxious to provide you any support we can."

"I thank you all," the youngest planter replied, his eyes welling with tears. "My lawyer sent an inquiry to Lloyd's of London, and the wireless reply confirmed that my house can be restored."

A collective murmur of relief rose from the rooms.

"I would ask you and your families to pray for the eternal salvation of my loved ones and for Marie Colette, our nursemaid. However, what I most crave from all of you is your support in the pursuit of two-legged beasts living in the mountains northwest of my plantation."

"Yes, how many will be at the Palmer plantation no later than ten o'clock on Friday morning, the first of July?" Scott asked with a pat air of expectation. To abet his question, he thrust his hand up.

The hands of the original three volunteers likewise shot up. After slight pauses, two more, then three others rose. As Peter surveyed the group, two more raised their hands to half-mast.

"Nigel Harvey has pledged himself, his sons, and at least one other," John added, having earlier assured himself that the owner of Stratford plantation, as he had indicated, was not in attendance.

"All right," Peter said after a sharp nod. "With a force of police from both sides of St. Lucia that should be enough."

*If they all keep their promises,* John thought skeptically.

---

AFTER THE CLUBHOUSE MEETING, John looked in vain for Anton Beaufort and his carriage. The man had suggested that Le Brun walk the short distance to the New Bristol Hotel and request a ride up Morne Fortune after the session at the St. Lucia Island Club broke up. One of the windward-side planters, however, asked at the front steps of the club where he was headed and declared that John's destination was on his way home. He traveled behind another planter's carriage headed toward Micoud. John saw that both men had shotguns stowed in their conveyances. The specter of the *Neg Maron*, lately transformed into something like a dread legend, had suddenly loomed real and large.

The night was glorious. Once the carriages turned away from the lights of Castries, the sky became nearly black. Even the haze of the Milky Way was visible beyond the twinkling stars. As they climbed the mountain, the evening breeze carried several floral scents to John's nose. He reflected that nature was oblivious to the sorrows of mankind.

John thanked the club member and tried to appear spry as he descended from the carriage. He waited until the vehicles had passed, then walked up the rising path to the rented house. His hand brushed against an object inside his left suit jacket pocket. He lifted it from its forgotten place of concealment. He found the door locked and used the brass knocker.

Lordis threw back the deadbolt and opened the door. She wore the only house dress she had brought with her. A single lamp burned in the living room, creating an aura behind her.

John held up the object to the light. "A memento for you, love."

Lordis studied the porcelain figure of the young woman. "Where did you get that?"

"I picked it up from the ground in front of the Palmer plantation. I was goin' to return it, but somebody had broken it."

Lordis accepted the piece and studied it. "It's missing its mate as well."

"Probably buried in the ground by many passin' shoes," John surmised.

"I suppose, with all the other loss, it won't be missed. Yes, it will make an interesting, if sad, memento," Lorids agreed.

"I'm glad you took the trouble to lock up, " John said as he entered the house.

The side of Lordis's mouth curled down as she shut the door. "If only I had taken the trouble not to turn on any of the lights."

"What do you mean?" John asked.

"You remember I said that I was perfectly content not having to relive today for anyone else's benefit?"

"I do. What happened?"

Lordis threw herself down on a Victorian sofa that had been created at least thirty years earlier. "I was forced to, against my will. About half an hour after you left for the club, there was a knock on the door. I had several lights on, so I couldn't pretend not to be here."

"Let me guess," John said. "Carlisle Thiery."

"No. He stayed next door, to mind the children. Instead, I got the two women."

"Sibyl and Emeline."

"Which we now know are the mythical Harpies' proper names. They are the English and mulatto versions of grand inquisitors from the age of Ferdinand and Isabella. They said they had seen through a window that you alone were carted down the hill, so they brought me the leftovers from their dinner."

"Were they good?"

"Excellent. Land crab meat sauteed with breadcrumbs and seasoning and served in their shells. Hearts of palm. And for dessert, guava jelly cookies. And *still* not worth the grilling they put me through."

John sat beside his wife and gently stroked her hand. "I'm sorry to have left you. You, of course, said nothin' about the exact nature of the lethal wounds?"

"I said the coroner would not divulge that information."

"Nor my havin' more plaster casts made."

"No. But they said that Carlisle was quite distressed at having ignored us yesterday and today and insisted that I tell them what we plan to do for the next two days." Lordis drew in a quick breath. "Which is how I learned that Paul and Minerva Van Fleet will be touring the same parts of St. Lucia that we will tomorrow. They will be conducted by Anton's brother, Gilles. Anton's services for the day are free as part of the ongoing debt of the New Bristol Hotel. Sibyl reminded me."

"Free is good."

"I suppose," Lordis allowed. "I also mentioned what I knew of the plans to venture into the rainforest and track down the descendents of the runaways day after next. I said that you and I would serve as witnesses and then asked if Carlisle knew about the plan."

John let go of Lordis's hand. "Did he?"

"They said yes. For a lawyer, that man seems to have developed the information network of a spy."

"Indeed."

Lordis smiled so wickedly that half her teeth showed. "I asked Sibyl if her husband planned to accompany the police and planters into the forest with a weapon."

"And the answer was no," John supplied. "Imagine him in his elegant suit, Cambridge tie, and patent leather shoes pickin' his way over streams and through brambles!"

"I also asked if he is Peter Palmer's lawyer. The answer is again no. Palmer's lawyer was born in Brighton, England. Lewis Newton or Norton. I assume he's as white as the driven snow."

"Sadly, I'm not surprised by this news, given the superior attitudes I've heard at the St. Lucia Island Club." John touched his forefinger lightly to the tip of Lordis's nose. "For a woman who complains about how much she was forced to reveal, I believe you got as good as you gave. I'm proud of you."

Lordis captured the offending digit and gave it a little twist. "Thank you. They also volunteered that when the chief coroner and inspector general return to Grenada, the Van Fleets will once again take up residence at the New Bristol Hotel."

"The schemers!" John said, irked in spite of his jesting tone. "Then I shall insist that we—"

"No," Lordis interrupted. "Remember the saggy mattress, the still air, and the tepid water. Except for its remoteness from downtown, this accommodation is considerably better." Lordis placed her open palms on her temples and shook her head back and forth. "Besides, I was helpless in the face of full-force histrionics. Emeline took the initiative and let me know that she, Sibyl, and Carlisle would be crushed if we elected to return. Actually wringing her hands like they do in bad plays, she said they promised the owners of this house that we would be paying ten days' rent. It seems that the owners are having a hard time selling the place and find themselves strapped for cash."

John thought for a moment. "I shall simply make sure that you are not left alone to their less-than-tender mercies anymore."

Lordis rose and took a few gliding steps from the sofa. “Let us retreat to the bedroom. You need to tell me what transpired at the club.” She stopped suddenly, drew in her stomach, pushed out her chest and offered John a beguiling look. “Unless you find that the night breeze and the smell of bougainvillea turn your thoughts to something else.”

# CHAPTER NINE

## June 30, 1910

IN SPITE OF ANTON BEAUFORT'S promise that he would arrive at the top of Morne Fortune at eight-thirty, his carriage did not pull up in front of the rented house until five minutes after nine. The reasons were Minerva and Paul Van Fleet, who had not emerged from the hotel until quarter to nine, well breakfasted and loaded with fans, parasol, bathing suits, and a snack basket. They were carried in a separate carriage by Gilles Beaufort.

"Good morning one; good morning all!" Paul greeted. He pointed to John. "We hear you have been engaged in the pursuit of your profession rather than vacation."

"Not of his own volition," Lordis answered as she stepped up into the second carriage. "He was asked by no one less than the lieutenant governor of St. Lucia."

While his mate's words were not true in the purest sense, John was pleased by her offensive response.

"I'm at least glad that you could take this beautiful day to explore the island with us," Paul continued. "We've done nothing but laze around on the beaches, eat, and drink."

The evidence of the financier's words was manifest on the Van Fleets' skins. What had not tanned was pink. Both their noses were peeling. They also both looked a bit plumper.

"Where to first, Mr. Beaufort?" John asked.

Both brothers turned to him. Anton said, "To the volcano. Then a forest path to King Louis's mineral baths and a waterfall."

"Followed by a drive up to what I am told will be a spectacular view of the Pitons," Paul broke in.

"With a late lunch and touring through the town of Soufrière," Minerva joined in with the chorus.

"Enough said," Lordis said. "Let's go."

---

THE DAY WAS INDEED beautiful, with gusty breezes strong enough to cause hands to fly periodically to hats. Mile after mile, the landscape was dominated by agriculture and horticulture. Black workers by the dozens toiled among the crops, few of them bothering to stop to watch the carriages roll by. The horses were fresh and ate up the miles with their hooves. By eleven-fifteen, the group reached the rough road that led to the volcano.

"We were assured that this volcano is safe," Paul Van Fleet called out, loudly enough that the Le Bruns could hear him.

Gilles slowed his carriage and turned. "No volcano is completely safe. This one, called Qualibou, made noises and gave off steam a few times between 1760 and 1780, but it did not explode. The geologists tell us that the center blew apart about forty thousand years ago. Much of it landed in the sea."

Gilles, like his brother, was a man of few words. He spoke only of major points of interest, and, when he did, his facts were distilled into as few syllables as possible.

The carriages entered the enormous ring of ancient lava walls. Inside, the center of the blown-out volcano looked like a sand quarry, dark yellow in color, with virtually no vegetation. The smell of sulfur was unpleasantly strong.

The four tourists left the buggies, with Anton leading the way and Gilles staying behind to mind the horses.

"The long-ago explosion was beyond even the one in Martinique," the guide began. He pointed in several directions. "The bottom of the volcano was twelve kilometers in diameter. Now, the edges are covered with native plants and crops, where the lava has mixed with soil brought in by the wind. Some farmers live inside the ring."

The four Americans voiced their amazement as the guide brought them within safe viewing distance of about two dozen bodies of bubbling brown material spread out among a number of acres.

"These are called cauldrons," Anton lectured. "They are very hot, from steam that rises through the earth. What you look at is boiling mud. The steam contains sulfur."

"Like hell itself," Minerva interjected.

"They look like rising soufflés," Paul observed. "I suppose that's how the village we sped past got the name Soufrière."

"No, sir," Anton replied. "In French, *soufre* means 'sulfur.'"

"I would have guessed the town was named for *souffrir*, the verb that means 'to suffer, to tolerate, to endure.'" John commented. "It seems to me that the vast majority of the citizens of this island paradise suffer, tolerate, and endure far more than they should have to."

Anton regarded the visitor with an appraising look that John had not seen before. He seemed to want to respond to John's observation but thought better of it and swallowed his words. A moment later, he said, "We have much more to see today." He turned and walked down the path toward the carriages without asking if anyone wished to linger.

The next promised stop was at the mineral baths commissioned by Louis XIV for the benefit of Windward Island soldiers. The baths had not been repaired in years and were no longer in use. They were accessed by a quarter-mile trail that took the party via an overgrown path through trees, shrubs, ferns, and flowering foliage. Again, Anton led the way, hacking with a machete whenever the plant growth blocked progress. Gilles once again stayed with the carriages.

The way to the baths was a shallow but steady incline. Consequently, Paul Van Fleet needed to rest every two hundred feet or so. Other challenges to the trail were water runoffs that scoured out dirt and left behind moss-covered rocks. Lordis slipped on one, windmilled briefly, but caught herself before falling.

"That won't do," John said, looking around. He spotted a dead branch with a fork at one end lying within a clump of ferns. He took a single step toward it, then hesitated. He raised his booted right foot and used it to part the slender fronds.

"What are you doing?" Lordis asked.

John advanced another step and repeated his boot maneuver. "I want to make a walkin' stick for you, but I don't want to get bit."

"Bit?" Minerva echoed with alarm. "Bit by what?"

"From what I've read, there are few dangerous critters on St. Lucia," John answered, "but one of them is very deadly. It's a snake called a fer-de-lance. It's a pit viper, and it don't mind bein' around humans."

"Can it kill you?" Minerva asked.

John snatched up the stick and retreated to the path. "It surely can, so stay on the path, Mrs. Van Fleet." He measured the stick's length with his good eye. "The reason I was so cautious is that once I thought I saw a huge cottonmouth—"

"A what?" Paul broke in.

John bent the branch against a rock and mashed down on it, breaking it at the near-perfect length to fashion a walking stick for Lordis. "A water moccasin. Big poisonous snake in my part of the country. I picked up a long branch to whack it to death. But what I thought was a snake turned out to be another branch."

"That was lucky," Minerva said

"Not really. The branch I picked up was a water moccasin." He handed his smirking wife the stick. Le Brun allowed the New Yorkers' eyes to grow enormous before bursting into laughter. "I'm just havin' you on. It's a joke."

"Not funny," Paul said.

"It is, inside a Park Avenue mansion," John countered. "Shall we continue?"

The trail ascended through a narrow natural gorge carved out by eons of falling water. Not far past the abandoned buildings of the mineral baths stretched a wide but shallow pond whose water looked like someone had recently disturbed the muddy bottom. Beyond it, tumbling about fifty feet in John's judgment, was a waterfall.

"Diamond Waterfall," Anton announced. "It is made by water coming up from inside the ground. That is what makes its dark color and the yellow, green, and purple stains on the rocks around it." The guide dipped his head toward the baths. "Surely someone has told you that Napoleon's empress, Josephine, lived when she was very young on the north side of St. Lucia and later came to live in Soufrière."

"Zatso?" Paul exclaimed. "Who would have thought!"

"She bathed here as a girl. The main bathhouse was destroyed by the common people after the French Revolution." Anton looked directly at John. "Unfortunately, they failed to finish their part of the revolution."

"Are any of the flowers poisonous?" Minerva worried.

"Not here. There is a tree that grows near our beaches. It is called the manchineel. It has tiny poison dots on its leaf and stalk; its fruit looks like little apples but they are poison; the sap from broken leaves and branches causes blisters."

"Not all is heavenly in paradise," Lordis told her appalled companion.

"Anything bad in the water if I bathed my feet in it?" Paul asked.

"Not a good idea," Anton replied. "Let us continue to the most famous sights in all of St. Lucia: the Pitons. Since Mr. and Mrs. Van Fleet are more fearful of our plants and animals, perhaps Mr. and Mrs. Le Brun would lead the way."

"Happy to," Lordis said, enjoying her status as intrepid explorer. She pivoted smartly, planted her walking stick, and took a long first stride.

The path was more open on the return trip, with much of the overhanging vegetation either hacked away by Beaufort's machete, snapped off by the walking stick, or trampled by five pairs of shoes.

Lordis was in an ebullient mood, chatting away as she walked, turning every now and then to speak directly to John. About three quarters of the way to the carriages, John looked down the path, grabbed her hard by the wrist, and yanked her back in his direction.

"Ow!" she complained. "What's—"

"Snake!" John cried out. "Speak of the devil. It's a fer-de-lance."

"My God!" Minerva screamed. "I shall faint."

"Don't you dare!" Paul told her sternly. "I do not wish to catch you."

The snake sunned itself on a wide space of the path. It was loosely curled, with its back end invisible in the encroaching vegetation. Its broad, flat head had been initially turned away from the group, but it had clearly sensed the vibrations of Lordis's footsteps. It swung around with astonishing speed and looked up at the woman.

"Lordis got too close to it," John said in a calm voice. "That's a striking position." He took the walking stick from his wife's trembling hand. "Mr. Beaufort, I wonder if you have ever dealt personally with one of these creatures?"

"No, sir."

John raised the stick slowly. "Then trade weapons with me."

When he held the machete, John said without turning from the irritated-looking snake, "Snap off the tops of that fork so that just a little remains." When he heard the noises of breaking wood, he instructed, "Now, come forward and turn the stick upside down. I will distract the snake, and you pin its head. Do you understand?"

"I do."

John studied the dense gathering of greenery to his left. He raised the machete and swung it slowly back and forth, causing the snake to fix on the shiny movements. Then he moved slowly off the path. The fer-de-lance's head followed him. John lifted his booted foot to take another step into the undergrowth. He stopped with his leg lifted and pushed the leaves aside.

"God Almighty!" John exclaimed as he spun quickly counterclockwise. He swung the machete down with speed and force, then jumped back.

The fer-de-lance in the path sprang into an attack, launching itself at John's exposed right leg. The long white fangs flashed in the sunlight. The snake struck John's boot an inch below the top and immediately retreated into a tighter coil, more of its great length slithering from beneath a gathering of green leaves.

Lordis and the two Van Fleets screamed at the sight, shrinking in a tight group back up the trail.

Anton Beaufort was frozen in place, holding the pinning stick aloft. John plucked it from his grasp with his left hand and stabbed down backhanded into the mass of serpentine muscle. The snake followed its path and launched out again, rising to meet the place above where the wood forked.

The machete blade arced down again, severing the viper's head and continuing through it to break the stick. John took a quick step backward. With wary motions, he poked and prodded the plant life to his left.

"You gotta be smarter than I was," John declared, his breath coming in short, clavicular jerks. "They sometimes move in pairs." He used the stick to coax out of the undergrowth a dead fer-de-lance that was about four feet long. It had been deeply cut about six inches behind its head. The women moaned at the sight. Paul thrust out his arms for balance, decided that was not enough, and collapsed on his posterior onto the path.

Anton rushed to support the overweight Van Fleet. His brother, Gilles, ran up the path carrying a buggy whip.

"What—" Before he could finish his question, Gilles saw the bodies of the two snakes lying on the path. The body of the one closer to him was completely severed from its head. Showing no sign of fear, he grasped the snake near the tail end and walked backward until the reptile was stretched out fully.

"Five feet," Gilles announced. "Maybe ten pounds."

"Saints preserve us," Lordis exhaled, turning in a tight circle in an effort to spy more snakes.

"That one is a female," John said with assurance. "Much bigger head and fangs."

Helped back to his feet but leaning forward with his hands on his knees, Paul managed to say, "You're probably wrong. The male of each species is the bigger and more powerful one."

"A common misconception," John responded, studying the light- and dark-brown-colored reptile nearer to him. He ran the stick along the camouflage patterns of muted colors on its back, then flipped it partway over to expose its yellow underside. "Human males and most other mammals are. But the opposite is true with the majority of reptiles, except lizards and crocodiles. Same with fish and insects."

"Really?" Paul said, looking dubious. "How would you know that?"

"My husband reads," Lordis said with pride. "We both do, but he devours books by the dozens."

"We both read," Minerva said defensively.

"This sort of information rarely appears in financial periodicals," Lordis said flatly. "Nor in romances and ladies' journals."

Minerva bristled. "Who cares what size—"

Lordis looked up into the overhanging verdure and spoke without waiting for Minerva to finish. "John also informed me of twenty-foot-long boa constrictors that drop out of trees, squeeze you to death, and then swallow you whole."

Paul put a sheltering hand around his wife's shoulder. "From now on, we do not venture onto jungle paths. Beaches and carriage rides will suffice."

John handed the machete back to Anton. "You know, only a few weeks ago I was tellin' someone in New York City that 'If you want to kill a snake, cut off its head.' It would be fun to bring these monsters back to Castries if you have a closed container to carry them."

Anton nodded and picked up the male snake's corpse. His brother collected the two parts of the female. They resumed the short walk back to the carriages, with the Le Bruns behind them and the Van Fleets taking up the rear very close behind.

While Paul relieved his bladder behind a clump of trees surrounded by bare ground, Anton pulled a reed basket from under the buckboard of his buggy. Inside it was another container, whose shape immediately identified it as a violin case. Anton set the smaller, black case atop the driver's seat. His brother arranged the two snakes inside the basket and secured the wooden clasp.

John glanced at the carriage Gilles drove. "I noted those baskets way back when we went to Choc Beach. You have an identical one under your seat," he noted, speaking to the shorter brother. "Let me guess: you play a musical instrument as well."

"No, sir," Gilles replied. "The hotel provides the baskets for the use of the guests." He leaned in toward Le Brun. "You want the snakes, so your buggy should carry them. Our other guests . . . ."

"I agree." John moved to lift the container with the dead snakes, but Anton stepped in the way and grabbed the burden.

"I have had more than enough adventure for one day," Minerva declared from her place in the exact middle of the open area.

"I as well," Paul seconded, securing the top button of his trousers. "We'll drive through Soufrière and then head back to Castries."

"But you'll miss the Pitons," Lordis said.

Paul helped his wife into the carriage driven by Gilles Beaufort. "Another day. We have plenty of time."

As Anton turned from storing the snake carcasses under the carriage seat, John asked in a half voice, "Have you ever seen dangerous snakes in this area before?"

"Not I. But I have heard stories."

Neither of the Van Fleets wished the Le Bruns a continued good day.

"I believe you insulted them about their lack of serious readin'," John commented to Lordis.

"Will that prove a hardship for us?" she countered. "By the time we're forced together again on the *Pindy*, they'll have forgotten all about it. Or perhaps they'll take my words to heart and strive to become a bit more interesting."

"Five/four, favor you," John said, as he did every time he entered into an unimportant debate with Lordis.

---

THE PITONS ARE the most spectacular and famous of St. Lucia's natural wonders. The pair of steep cones, mantled in scrubby vegetation that desperately clings to their gray rock sides, rise out of the Caribbean Sea at the edge of the island's eastern coastline. Petit Piton is 160 feet lower than Gros Piton, but because it is most often viewed from the Soufrière side, perspective makes the two remnants of ancient volcanoes look like a perfect match. At about 2,500 feet high, they dominate the local area and seem adjacent, even though the considerable beach of Anse des Pitons lies in between.

A steep carriage ride up a nearby hill rewarded the Le Bruns with a remarkable, photogenic view of both peaks. A humble restaurant, clinging to the hill, provided an adequate luncheon. Lordis and John invited Anton to dine with them, but he declined politely and retreated to engage in conversation with the mulatto staff.

Also dining were two sets of well-heeled English travelers who had crossed the Atlantic on an extended vacation among the Windward Islands. For a time, they traded polite conversation with the Le Bruns, but they quickly reverted to their tight circle, leaving behind little more information than that they hailed from the village of Wimbledon and owned factories on the south side of London.

After lunch, Anton drove the Americans into the town of Soufrière. In his laconic style, the guide informed them that Soufrière had once been the capital of the island. Although it was twice the size of nearby villages, it nonetheless maintained a rustic feel. Some of the larger buildings in the town center spoke silently of the days of French occupation, with whitewashed two-story homes ornate with dormers, filigreed verandas, and abundant French doors. The Roman Catholic church still bore evidence of the damage from an 1839 earthquake. Most other structures were of wood, varying from proper houses in the town center to fisherman hovels just beyond the high tide mark on the south side of the bay.

On the back and side streets, gaily colored walls and roofs crammed together along the narrow valley, giving the illusion to John of a Pointillist painting surrounded by the green frame of the encroaching hills. A few of the walls featured amateur art depicting scenes of island life. Anton relaxed in the shade of a tall building, softly scratching out the hymn "Blessed Assurance" on his violin as John and Lordis strolled across the river that divided the town and explored a large cemetery with raised crypts, some dating back to the middle of the eighteenth century.

Less than an hour was required to explore most of Soufrière's streets. It quickly became manifest to the Le Bruns that it was almost wholly a black town. As they strolled, they were met with quick but assessing looks. A few of the locals acknowledged them with a nod or a half-smile, but the fact was clear that they were a pair of the occasional white people who visited out of curiosity and then returned to their privileged ways.

The ride back to Castries was unhurried and pleasant. The Le Bruns quit the carriage at the summit of Morne Fortune, giving Anton a generous tip. John grabbed the basket.

"Can you either wait for us or return in half an hour?" he asked. "We wish to shower and then go into Castries for dinner."

"They will smell badly soon," Anton warned, pointing down at the basket.

"I understand," John replied. "I won't keep them long."

"I'll wait. Where do you want the basket?"

---

CARLISLE THIERY DROPPED BY the Le Bruns' rented house at nine in the evening to invite the tourists over for an aperitif.

"That's very kind of you," John said, "but Lordis and I finished a bottle of wine between us, and I'm of an age where too much liquor will upset my stomach at best or ruin my night's sleep at worst." He held up his index finger. "However, before you leave, I have somethin' to show you."

John led the lawyer to the back edge of the property, where Anton had placed the basket. As he bent to open it, he detected the distinctive odor of rot. He threw the lid back and silently invited Thiery to inspect.

The only lights falling into the basket were weak rays through the living room window and soft moonbeams. Thiery's nose caught the scent. He inhaled instinctively. Then his eyes discerned the frozen coils of snake. He sprang back.

"Not one but two fer-de-lances," John confirmed. "Right beside the trail to the volcano waterfall. One of us could easily have been killed. If you're determined to promote your island for the creation of an exclusive resort, y'all had better hire people to police the underbrush around the attractions. It won't be one of my most glowin' accounts of this visit, I'll tell you."

Thiery shut the basket. "You're right in your advice, Mr. Le Brun. I'll have them disposed of tomorrow morning." He placed his hands on his hips and regarded John with an inscrutable expression. "Let me be brutally frank with you. I have indeed been engaged by several persons—Andrew Ashton being one, as you know—to facilitate the process of bringing tourist money to St. Lucia. However, I am definitely of two minds about the scheme. We desperately need the money. We constantly import more products than we export. Our foreign debt is piling up. But this little paradise will be destroyed if there is too much commercialization. What we assuredly do not need is to submit year-round to white Americans' negative attitudes toward persons of color."

"I understand," John said. "Often, it's the devil if you do and the devil if you don't. Aside from what you've already done, perhaps you should leave the rest to Providence."

"I leave nothing to Providence," Thiery assured the visitor.

# CHAPTER TEN

## July 1, 1910

"I PREDICT A DEBACLE," John told Lordis as they assembled the soft leather bag for the latest sojourn to the opposite side of St. Lucia. "At least from the islanders' attempt to solve the murders."

"But not from ours," Lordis said with confidence, taking care to include herself with the plural possessive. Then her eyebrows knit and her mouth turned down into a pout. "However, I wish you'd share every detail with me instead of playing the man of mystery."

"If I did that," John said, checking the bedroom of the rented house atop Morne Fortune for possibly needed items, "then how could you be free to develop your own theories and methods to prove them? Why should I deny myself your unique perspectives?"

"Fine. The Maroons are a diversion," Lordis said with assurance. "And yet you're hell bent on being on site when the snipe hunt takes place." John left the bedroom carrying his hastily assembled version of an investigation bag, with Lordis following three steps behind him. "Because somebody deliberately encouraged a hunt with those footprints. You're thinking whoever's responsible will probably be there today to see how successful this fool's errand is. Nine chances out of ten, the real killers of the Palmer family will be rubbing shoulders with us."

"And leavin' boot prints," John said, smiling. He peered out one of the living room windows down the terraced front yard to the road. "And here is our carriage, precisely on time."

"Wait a second!" Lordis exclaimed, grasping John's elbow. "Boot prints are not footprints. I assume you mean to compare the two, but that's like comparing apples and oranges."

"Not necessarily so," John countered. "More like apples and grapefruit. An apple might fit snugly into a grapefruit rind, but no mature grapefruit will fit into an apple peel."

"You, John Le Brun, are maddening!"

John threw open the front door. "I prefer to think of myself as an intriguin' challenge." He glanced down at the road, turned to usher his wife down the narrow path, then did a double-take.

"It's not Anton," John told Lordis. "It's his brother, what's his name?"

"Gilles," she supplied.

"Right." To the black hotel employee he called out, "We're ready, Mr. Beaufort!" To Lordis, in little more than a whisper, he said, "Remember to say nothin' at all about the investigation in front of anyone . . . includin' our driver."

---

WITHIN A FEW PACES after quitting their carriage, the vacationers and their driver were inside a replanted section of the Palmer plantation sugarcane. A large crew of workers, all originally from India, could be seen through the immature growth. At the sight of white faces, they redoubled their efforts. John was able to spy sandals on the feet of the two laborers closest to them. He unconsciously nodded his approval of Peter Palmer's simultaneously selfish and charitable act. The planter's stratagem seemed even wiser when John caught sight of a third worker, farther off, squatting with legs splayed to the limit of his lowered pants. Human feces was the main broadcasting and breeding material for the endemic hookworm that so devastated the worker population.

The trio walked to the open area where the barefoot prints had been left during the night of the murders and mansion burning. They reached the mouth of the valley within minutes. Those already gathered resembled, in John Le Brun's estimation, not so much a military campaign as a lynch mob. The participants wore all manner of dress and carried a mixed array of firearms. Shotguns, which were woefully ineffective for long-range combat, dominated. The rifles, with only a few exceptions, were of the single shot variety. One eager planter sported a bandolier, but half its ammunition loops were empty.

From a conversation he was able to eavesdrop on, John realized that the lieutenant governor had revealed the facts that the four people inside the mansion had been murdered and how the murders had been accomplished. The tone of the dialogue was one of outrage.

No one followed in the vacationers' wake, suggesting that they were the last who would arrive. Lordis stood out as the only female, wearing her "rough it" outfit and hoisting her umbrella. Rain had fallen through the last half-hour of their journey on the East-West Road. From the look of the scudding clouds, it promised to let up but still fell lightly, making those gathered huddle in their protective gear. Impatiently pacing like thoroughbred horses anxious to begin a race, they looked dangerous in spite of their amateur weaponry, motley dress, and lack of organization.

John scanned the assemblage. As he had expected, in spite of the rallying exhortations at the St. Lucia Island Club, only half of the members who had attended that meeting and pledged their support had shown. Struggling to create order were Lieutenant Governor Richard Tubble and James Dautry, the Castries chief of police. Dautry had brought with him five officers, who stood behind him at a rough equivalent of attention. The spanking white jackets and helmets they wore in the capital were conspicuous by their absence. To their side stood Sergeant Hume, the deputy chief of police for the town of Dennery, accompanied by two of his under-officers. Across a stretch of trampled ground stood the planters and their minions: Peter Palmer and his overseer, Jacob Mansfield; Neville Wilcox and another white man; president of the St. Lucia Island Club Raymond Scott, with two towering, fear-inspiring companions; one man John had not seen before, who held a lever-action repeating rifle; four more white men, two of which John remembered as Charles Black and Jack Mayberry, large land owners from Cul-de-Sac and Anse-le-Raye, respectively; and, standing off in their own group, Nigel Harvey, his two sons, and one of the mulatto guards who had greeted the Le Bruns at the entrance to Stratford.

Richard Tubble called for attention, then announced, "That seems to be all the volunteers we're getting, so let's commence. This valley runs west by northwest. At about one thousand feet in, it divides. Chief of Police Dautry and his force will head one group; Sergeant Hume heads the other." He walked among the planters and assigned men to one team or the other, as would a sports coach. When he was finished, he looked directly at Gilles Beaufort.

"You go with Hume's group," Tubble ordered.

"I am here only to drive our visitors," Beaufort said.

"I understand. However, right now Mr. and Mrs. Le Brun are perfectly capable of taking care of themselves." Tubble held what John recognized to be an Enfield rifle. With its smooth bolt action and its ten round magazine, it was the standard issue of the British military. The lieutenant governor set the butt down against the top of his boot, unbuttoned his jacket, and withdrew a Webley revolver. "You're a citizen of this island, and I am empowered to recruit you to duty." He walked up to the hotel employee and handed over the revolver. "You will act as the rear guard. See that none of these *Neg Maron* gets behind us."

Gilles did not look happy but accepted the weapon and fell into the gathering, standing alongside Raymond Scott's two black employees.

"That's a mercy," John said to Lordis, under his breath.

"Why?" Lordis asked.

"You'll see."

Tubble barked out his search strategy, along with admonitions toward discretion.

John's lips moved without sound as he counted participants. "Only twenty-seven in all."

"Lethal-looking nonetheless," Lordis judged.

Peter Palmer walked up to John and Lordis. He offered his hand and a wan smile. "Thank you for coming today. If we're lucky enough, we'll bring back some of these savages for you to question. Naturally, you mustn't follow us into the jungle."

"No, we'll wait right here," John assured, shoving his right hand into his pocket. He nodded toward the man he had not recognized. "Who's that fellow?"

"Him? That's George Turner," Palmer answered. "Owns the plantation just north of ours. Rarely attends St. Lucia Island Club gatherings. Very private. I'm pleased to see him here."

"George Turner," John repeated. "Just bein' a good neighbor, I suppose."

"He evidently didn't tell anyone he was coming. Anyway, thanks again."

"You take care," Lordis advised.

"I will." Palmer hurried back to the head of the little army. "Let's go!" he urged.

The assemblage ventured up the valley in an elongated column, moving hardly faster than an amble. John lowered his gaze and took half a dozen steps forward.

"You promised we wouldn't follow," Lordis said with a bit of anxiety in her voice. "Even if this is a snipe—"

"Hush, Missus!" John hissed. "I'm concentratin'."

As if John's words had reached him, Gilles Beaufort spun halfway around, fixed his focus on the two non-islanders, then pivoted and slowly brought up the rear of the troop.

John waited until a pair of felled trees blocked the sight line between himself and Beaufort. Then, from his trouser pocket, he pulled a handful of change. With his other hand, he reached into his jacket and produced his notebook and a pencil. He handed the latter items to his wife.

"Write these down, please—with space in between each: Beaufort/sixpence." He dropped a coin into a depression made by Gilles Beaufort's shoe, then moved forward. "Pierce Harvey/old shillin'." Dividing his attention between the vanishing posse and the boot prints made in the rain-softened earth, John weaved a slow pattern, left, forward, then right, and dropping coins. "Michael Harvey/florin. George . . ."

"Turner," Lordis supplied.

"Thank you. For some reason I'm bad at rememberin' names this mornin'."

"Now I understand why you said 'That's a mercy'; you didn't want Mr. Beaufort to see what you're doing."

"Exactly. George Turner/new shillin'. Raymond Scott assistant/half a crown." John flipped his last coin into the air and caught it. He walked quickly to where the leaders had faced the gathering. "Was this the place where Sergeant Hume stood?"

Lordis's eyebrows knit. "Either him or his officer."

"One's as likely as the other." John dropped the last coin. "So, write down: Hume/penny."

"This is the real reason we're out here," Lordis understood.

From his opposite inside jacket pocket, John produced his stiff-paper ruler and unfolded it to its full length. Reversing his advance, he re-pocketed each coin, dictating the length and width of the corresponding boot print to Lordis. When he was finished and standing over the print made by Gilles Beaufort, he said, "I didn't need Jacob Mansfield's. He's the biggest man in the whole lot. I've seen his print already, and it's far too large to be any of those six sets that we have plaster castin's of. Likewise, Police Chief Dautry. That's his boot print over yonder. His feet must be narrow to the point of peculiarity, or else his feet are stuffed like sausage innards in his boots."

"And Nigel Harvey?"

"His guard kept walkin' over his prints. Didn't seem like on purpose. Just bad luck for me. But that can be fixed in due course."

"What about those planters and their workers from the west side of St. Lucia?" Lordis asked.

John shook his head. "Don't make any sense. At the club, I heard tell nothin' about any animus against the Palmer family. And if they coveted land, they would have much better targets than Tristesse. The Palmers have been tryin' to keep from goin' under in the sugarcane business. The west side plantation owners have switched to raisin' bananas, and I heard no complaints from them. As to their workers . . . they have nothin' to gain. No access to horses either. Therefore, no motive and no opportunity. Strike out the lot of them. However, as you've seen in Manhattan, the law in uniform can be bought by anyone with enough coin. And since they're the ones appointed to catch criminals, who is to catch them?"

"So they stay on your list," said Lordis, stretching her free hand beyond the limits of her umbrella and satisfying herself that the rain had stopped.

"Then you agree with my process of reasonin'."

Lordis lowered the umbrella and furled it. "I do. I was playing devil's advocate."

"In masterly fashion," John said.

"Don't patronize me," Lordis warned.

"Take a compliment at face value," John riposted.

Lordis smirked, then pointed to the notebook in her husband's hand. "So, which prints could conform to the plaster castings?"

Le Brun studied the jotted measurements. "Gilles Beaufort. Pierce Harvey. Michael Harvey. And this fellow George Turner."

"All reasonable candidates, except for Mr. Beaufort," Lordis said, staring up the now-vacant valley. She looked with expectation for a continuation of John's analysis. "Am I wrong?"

"The forest is quiet," he observed, surprising her with his refusal to reassure her.

"I'm sure all that noise frightened the birds and beasts away."

For a time, the two listened to the silence. The sun had climbed nearly to its zenith, and its power to pull the recently fallen rain from the earth and the surfaces of millions of leaves was palpable. Tendrils of faint fog stole like furtive fingers from the cool shadows of rocky ledges, wending down the slopes toward the stream.

"Let's wander a piece in the direction they went. I'm sure it will be safe," John said.

"All right. I'm tired of just standing here."

The dozen or so trees that had been felled for clearing compelled a zig-zag course up the mouth of the valley. The stark memory of the pair of poisonous snakes also caused the vacationers to move with deliberation, ever vigilant of what lay ahead of them on the ground.

"I'm sorry," John said suddenly.

Lordis stopped walking. "About what?"

"We should have gone to Paris instead."

"Nonsense! I'm enjoying our honeymoon immensely," Lordis insisted.

John came to the edge of the stream and began choosing flat stepping stones to aid their progress inland. "Spoken like a supportive wife."

"No. St. Lucia is truly beautiful. I also feel as Paul Van Fleet does: I can boast of visiting a place few among those in the States can. Boatloads of people have been to Paris. And, besides, we'll get there next year." She squeezed John's hand. "Then I'll boast of having had two honeymoons."

John maintained his grip on her, guiding Lordis upward against the softly-burbling flow of the stream. When they came to the shade of an overhanging branch, he stopped. "I do believe the water is risin' already from that rain." He turned and watched the sparkling constant flow of liquid cascade around boulders, over stones, and atop pebbles.

The Le Bruns stood for an extended space of time staring downstream, John behind Lordis, steadying her with his hands placed lightly around her waist.

"We should have brought our picnic basket from the wagon," Lordis said. "Who knows how long they'll be gone."

"We can always—"

John paused in mid-sentence as the report of a rifle echoed out of the rainforest. Then, swiftly, three distant sharp cracks pierced the valley air.

The pair turned about face, scanning the dense greenery as far as it would allow. Lordis looked at John with alarm. "I thought they'd find no one."

"I would have bet on it. Maybe we should retreat."

Taking the lead, John retraced their route downward. When they arrived at the edge of the sugarcane plantings, they stopped and observed the length of the valley.

"That wasn't much of a melee," Lordis said.

"Not at all," John agreed.

Lordis blinked with a sudden recollection and abruptly inhaled a noisy breath. "You had Mr. Mansfield recruit some veteran field hands to help create more plaster casts."

"I did. As I've said, given his bereaved behavior on the mornin' of the house burnin' and his long association with the Palmer family, Mr. Mansfield is about as trustworthy a character as a stranger like me could find. For sure, his bare feet didn't create any of the original prints."

"Right. I would assume he's had those castings made. But you didn't ask him about them this morning." Lordis raised her umbrella against the intense rays of the sun that evaded the forest canopy. "Was that because he was surrounded by all the others?"

"It was. I'll take him aside when he returns."

From far up the valley came the strident sounds of men's voices.

"That wasn't long," John said. "Let's see what happened."

Gilles Beaufort, who had been assigned to protect the rear, appeared first, followed half a minute later by Raymond Scott and his two black employees. Scott and one man supported the third by means of a four-handed seat carry. A blood-soaked strip of white cloth had been tied around the wounded one's thigh as tourniquet and bandage. Behind them, at some fifty yards' distance, came the Palmer and Harvey groups, as well as their plantation neighbor to the north, George Turner.

"What happened?" John called out, grabbing his soft bag from the top of a stone.

Between grunts, Scott said, "One of Chief Dautry's idiot officers saw a black face through the vegetation and shot without even a challenge. He hit my man here."

John continued to close the distance between himself and the returning groups. "Bad wound?"

"Bad enough. Bullet went through the flesh. Didn't hit bone or artery, thank the Lord. The rest of them stayed on to—"

Sharp exclamations, first of surprise and then of anger, bellowed out of Peter Palmer. Jacob Mansfield held something in his right hand that had enraged the survivor of the Palmer mansion murders.

"Bastard!" Palmer screamed, looking directly at Nigel Harvey. He raised his rifle and pointed it at his neighbor.

Michael Harvey, who stood closest to his father, threw himself headlong into Nigel's middle, driving him to the ground. A fraction of a second later, Palmer's rifle went off, kicking slightly as the report filled the air.

The Harveys' mulatto guard had already swung his shotgun upward. Before Peter Palmer could eject the spent shell from his rifle, the guard let loose both barrels of his weapon. Palmer sprang backward from the force of the double impact, blood spraying through the undergrowth and onto the trunk of a barren tree. Palmer fell heavily. Jacob Mansfield pointed his shotgun in the general direction of the Harvey group.

John had started into a trot before the first missile was fired. "Stop!" he cried out in his most commanding voice. "Put up your weapons!"

Everyone but Le Brun froze in place, allowing him to round the dead tree and look on the scene of carnage. He saw that the guard's aim had been true, the two explosions of shot ripping out half of Peter Palmer's chest. The man was already dead.

Pierce and Michael Harvey helped their father to his feet.

"What set him off?" John demanded, speaking of the dead man.

In answer, Tristesse overseer Mansfield picked up the item he had displayed but then dropped during the deadly confrontation. He held it up for all to see.

"It's an awl," Mansfield said, his voice quivering with rage. "Exactly the right shape for piercing the brains of four innocent sleepers. The handle looks like it's been sanded, but if you look closely you can see tiny bits of paint in the grain. Paint the colors of Stratford plantation."

John remembered the color combination of the plantation's front sign: sky blue against a field of sunflower yellow.

"It may be close to our colors, but we never had an awl on our property," Nigel vowed vehemently.

"Makes sense. Awls are for makin' shoes," John could not help saying.

John took his Kodak camera from the soft bag, opened and focused it, and took a shot of the awl. From the vast store of esoteric knowledge he had amassed over the decades, John saw in his mind's eye an array of awls. The one he photographed was specialized for leatherworking, its handle shaped like an urn, with a neck halfway up to ease the grip of fingers and thumb. Pierce Harvey advanced and pointed at the tool. "That was planted there. Deliberately planted to lay the blame for the Palmer murders on my family."

"One thing is certain," John said, lowering his voice in an effort to calm the very agitated group. "That wasn't dropped by your *Neg Maron.* That's almost new. Lyin' here in this damp area for more than five days, it would most likely have the start of some rust on it. And the sanded surface would have darkened. It could have been dropped this very mornin'." He walked up close to Jacob Mansfield's outstretched, open palm. "By handlin' it, you've covered over other fingerprints." John studied the awl but did not touch it. "I assume the rest of the parties continued into the forest."

"They did," said Raymond Scott, who rested his backside against the trunk of the fallen tree on which his wounded worker lay.

"Well, somebody should trek up there and tell them to call it a day. This awl changes the situation," Le Brun said to the group. Immediately, Gilles Beaufort started back up the valley. John trained his camera on the dead man and captured images from two angles.

Glowering at the Harvey group, Mansfield removed his hunting vest and draped it over Peter Palmer's corpse.

John sighed deeply, turned toward Lordis, who had advanced within a few steps of her husband, and signaled that she should take the camera and bag from him.

"I'm carrying Nillen back to Castries straightaway," Raymond announced to the group in general. He waved a warning finger. "By this time tomorrow, I'd better know which stupid bastard fired at him."

No one said a word. The club president and his healthy employee carried the wounded one down the valley toward the seemingly endless rows of sugarcane.

Jacob Mansfield forcefully pulled Le Brun out of earshot of the other men. John could sense the intense rage still coursing through the big man's body.

"You thought this business with the barefoot prints and the *Neg Maron* was a ruse," Mansfield said. He opened his fist. "What should we think of this awl?"

Instead of answering directly, John softly said, "Nothin' rash. I know you've just been through another tremendous shock, but I need your assistance in gettin' to the bottom of this mess. Do you think you are strong enough to help me?"

"If it means justice for the poor Palmer family, of course I am. How?"

"We can't let the people here scatter all over the island until after I examine several men's feet."

Mansfield looked in the direction of his employer's semi-shrouded body. "Do you want to see those new plaster castings?"

"I do." John took the awl from the overseer's hand. "Don't move from this spot."

John approached Lordis, put his arm around her waist, and guided her closer to the remaining gathering of men. "You have a critically important job to do, my dear."

"Name it," she said.

"Once everyone is fully assembled here, explain what we saw of the discovery of this awl. Give it to the lieutenant governor.

Then recount the altercation that resulted in Mr. Palmer's death. Ask loudly if any of the other witnesses disagrees with the facts. If this occurs, take down his testimony word for word and see that he signs it."

"I've sat at your proverbial knee long enough to know how you would do it, John," Lordis assured.

"Good." He pressed the awl into her open palm. "Now, Mr. Mansfield is takin' me to the estate grounds. He'll be sendin' some kind of cart back here to transport Mr. Palmer. A goodly number of the group will want to be gone from this debacle posthaste. Don't let that happen. Assure Lieutenant Governor Tubble that I have a very good reason for this. He must see that no one else leaves this plantation before comin' to the barn behind the burned mansion."

Lordis's face glowed with excitement. "It will be done to the letter."

The detective planted a small kiss on her cheek and hurried back to Jacob Mansfield.

---

ONCE AGAIN, a makeshift table was rigged in front of the mansion's horse stable. This time, however, instead of a series of charred corpses, six sets of right footprint molds lay atop the boards, numbered four, five, six, seven, eight and nine. John gazed down at the last three.

"As I'm sure you suspected," Mansfield said, "these prints are much rougher. I selected men of medium height who had worked our fields for at least the last ten years."

"Well before Master Peter distributed sandals," John said.

"Correct."

John compared the three with the molds seven through nine. "Much rougher. Quite a few scars and splits on the worker prints."

"And the castings don't tell the whole story. They don't show the thickness of the calluses and the dryness of the skin of the workers' feet. Doesn't this prove that the murders and burning couldn't have been done by workers?"

"Prove?" John echoed. "I wouldn't make such a pat statement, but it does strongly suggest that the dirty work was done by men who ordinarily wear shoes or boots." John pulled out his paper ruler and once more measured the dimensions of the first six mold prints.

"Here they are," Mansfield announced.

"Quickly!" John ordered. "I want no one to see the last three molds you had made."

"I'll hide them," the overseer said, scooping up the three flat boxes in his huge hands.

In a rough double file behind the field wagon that carried Peter Palmer's corpse came the remainder of the posse, looking even more unhappy than when they had ascended the valley. Lordis walked near the front. By the subtle shaking of her head, raising of her eyebrows, and thrusting out of her lower lip, she indicated that she had had no trouble with the task John had assigned her.

"We determined who shot Scott's loading boss," Richard Tubble called out. Without turning or pointing at the culprit, he said, "One of Chief Dautry's officers. A mistake. However, he will be cited for his recklessness."

John was able to pick out the guilty policeman from his hangdog expression and from the distance that his fellow officers gave him. He knew at least one contributing factor to the "mistake"; the white policeman had seen one of the few black faces from among the hunting party and had rashly assumed it belonged to a forest descendent of runaway slaves. In spite of John's indignation on behalf of the wounded man, he held his tongue.

"We clearly need better organization the next time," Tubble said.

Jacob Mansfield emerged from the barn, his hands free.

John understood that the lieutenant governor did not look

upon the discovery of the awl in the same manner as he did. He held up his hand. "Before you discuss a next time, I wish to conduct research. I realize this will seem like a bizarre request, but I need every man who went into that valley to sit on the grass, unlace his right boot, and strip off his sock."

Sets of eyes darted back and forth, asking without words what the others around them thought. Two men muttered. Several others shrugged. Most obeyed without hesitation.

As each man completed the task, John knelt at his feet and took measurements. About a minute into the process, planter George Turner asked, "What is this for anyway?"

"Footprints were left behind on the night the house behind you burned," John replied. A general remonstrance rose from the group. John was unfazed. "Listen well, gentlemen! I know that the great majority of you—perhaps all—are intent on seein' that justice is done here. Otherwise you wouldn't have volunteered to spend your day trompin' through nasty jungle. Indulge me for just a few more minutes."

The group noise settled quickly. As he moved among them with his ruler, John immediately thanked more than half the men and told them they could stand to the side. The others, including Sergeant Hume and his assistant chief, two of the Castries policemen, Nigel Harvey and his two sons, George Turner, the man accompanying planter Charles Black, Jack Mayberry and his assistant, and Gilles Beaufort, he asked to sit where they were. Each was asked to slide his right leg backward, drawing up his knee. Then John guided the man's foot into each of the boxes. Some were asked to place their foot in a box more than one time.

When John finished, he washed his hands at a nearby water pump and waited for all the men to finish replacing their footwear. He pulled his handkerchief from his pocket and theatrically gained the group's focus by drying his hands in deliberately slow motion.

"Based on my observations, the footprints that most closely match those barefoot castin's taken followin' the murders of the Palmer family and maid are those of George Turner . . ."

The planter neighbor to the north stood stock still in disbelief for two seconds, then exploded. "Poppycock! I was at home with my family that entire night. No fewer than—"

". . . Jack Mayberry," John bulled on.

"Ridiculous as well!" Mayberry called out. "I was at the St. Lucia Island Club until all hours. How could I—"

"He was," Charles Black vouched.

"I believe you both," John replied calmly. "And Nigel, Pierce, and Michael Harvey."

"An outrage!" Nigel Harvey shouted. "I'm the one who hired you to do this investigating!"

John held up his hands and maintained his silence until he could be heard without shouting. "What y'all see in these boxes is not an exact science. However, we can tell that the prints were made by the feet of men who ordinarily wear shoes or boots. If the footprints leadin' from the Tristesse mansion belonged to savage blacks of the rainforest, they would be much rougher."

"But we can't all have committed the crime," Jack Mayberry argued. "Many men who wear shoes on St. Lucia must have right feet that closely fit into those molds."

"Right you are!" John snapped back. "However, the vast preponderance of those same many men can be eliminated because we who investigate crimes focus on means, motive, and opportunity. I know personally that Mr. Mayberry was on the opposite side of your island when the crimes were committed. Which reduces the list to Pierce, Michael, and Nigel Harvey, and George Turner."

Turner started toward Le Brun. "I—"

"Be silent and hold your ground, Mr. Turner!" Richard Tubble ordered, wresting the lever-action rifle from the man's grasp.

John clasped his hands behind his lower back and lightly rocked back and forth between his toes and heels. "As a visitor to St. Lucia, I have been told numerous times how difficult it has become to make a profit at the sugar business. That the only way to survive is by economies of scale and vertical integration. Therefore, the plantation owners directly to the north and south of Tristesse have a definite motivation in addin' its holdin's to their own. The Harveys and Mr. Turner, bein' on this side of the island that night and all men of vigor, with the capability of recruitin' underlings to their efforts, also had the means. With Mr. Peter Palmer away, they had the opportunity."

Le Brun looked at Lieutenant Governor Tubble and Castries Chief of Police Dautry. "Even given that this is an island, I recommend placin' these men where they will present no risk to flight."

Several seconds of violent outbursts ensued, until Tubble shot a bullet from his Enfield into the ground.

"Mr. Le Brun makes a valid point. Everyone here is to understand that these men are right now being held under suspicion, given the facts of the footprints, the discovered awl, and the motive, et cetera, that he outlined. They are not being immediately charged."

"And how am I to run a plantation that is already wanting effective supervisors?" Nigel Harvey asked in a quivering voice.

"I as well!" George Turner echoed.

"Your point is valid," Tubble allowed, "and the judicial system of our island will labor without rest to uncover the truth. Until then, your plantations will have to muddle along as best they can."

A mixed ruckus of ranting, threats, vows, assurances, and the like immediately ensued, but eventually enough calm was restored that those not accused began to disperse and those suspected were gathered together under the supervision of multiple officers.

As he mounted one of the eastbound carriages, Nigel Harvey shook his fist at Le Brun. "You're not half as smart as that sea captain says you are! You're fired! And don't try to collect any more from me, you foreign bastard!"

"I want those molds loaded into Chief Dautry's carriage," Tubble directed. Mansfield loped into the barn and returned with a galvanized tin basin half-filled with hay. He set the three molds into the basin and packed the empty areas tightly with the hay. Dautry and the policeman who had shot plantation owner Scott's employee set off for Castries.

Shaking his head, John retreated to the barn that stored the Palmer family belongings, gathering Lordis as he went. Jacob Mansfield followed them a minute later.

"The police don't have enough to get a conviction on either the Harveys or George Turner," Mansfield said through a scowling mouth.

"True enough," John replied, as he thought about the overseer obliterating any fingerprints that might have been on the awl. "Perhaps, if you wrack your brain, you'll be able to remember or find somethin' else that will provide conclusive proof."

Mansfield spit into the dirt. "I doubt it. And here am I needing to run this place by myself. If I hold it together, what will my reward be?"

"Peter had a sister," Lordis said. "Perhaps she'll return, put you in charge, and give you a good bump-up in salary."

"Knowing what I know about Penny, she'll hire an agent to sell this land, never leave England, and never give me a thought."

"She married in England and has a child," John prompted.

"That's right. Gone seven years. Maybe has more than one child by now. Did Peter talk to you about her?"

"Briefly."

"She fell in love with a man who lives in Bath. If memory serves, he runs a tea shop. That's been a tourist town since the

Roman times. I imagine the shop does well, and she's infinitely happier than she was here."

"Because of the tyranny of her father?"

"Exactly."

"There must be an address somewhere to reach her," Lordis pressed.

Mansfield looked doubtful. "When she failed to return to St. Lucia, Penny was dead to the old man. I highly doubt he would keep an address. Besides, if it existed it would have been kept with family correspondence. All of that went up in flame."

The breeze that had been blowing in from the Atlantic suddenly began gusting. John locked eyes with Jacob Mansfield, as if to hypnotize him into remembering. "Think! Either Peter or his father must have mentioned the husband's name."

The overseer shook his head glumly.

"Or at least the name of the tea shop."

"I'll try to recall," Mansfield said. "I know it's important."

"And we shall press on with the investigation," Lordis promised.

"One last thing," John said. "I can't be sure that no one in the Castries police is in on this crime. In case the molds carted away are lost or shattered, I want to have the other set ready for presentation."

"The first three," Jacob clarified.

"Yes. If you have a large basket such as many of the Castries carriages include, place them in it and push it under our driver's seat."

The overseer moved off, to fetch the molds and disassemble the table.

John saw that Gilles Beaufort had placed himself under a shade tree to wait for his charges. John smiled and waved at him. Gilles nodded in response.

"Let's be gone from here as soon as possible," John said to Lordis.

"You know, we had our eyes fixed on the ground back there," Lordis said, speaking of the entrance to the valley. "And we walked where the awl was found, both up and back. I don't see how the both of us could have missed something as large and out of place as a sanded oak awl handle."

"Don't forget that fact," John admonished. "Meanwhile, there are things to be done on the Castries side."

"But surely there must be more to explore on this side," she argued. "As long as we've come all the way across the island, shouldn't we at least visit that town—Dennery—and ask around about Penelope Palmer? Perhaps we can find a confidante whom she still writes to."

John gestured for Lordis to lead the way back to Beaufort's buggy. "Not today. We'll come back soon."

Lordis looked deeply doubtful. "I don't understand, John. Why not explore here if you've narrowed the suspects down to Turner and the Harveys?"

"I've done nothin' of the sort," John said under his breath, hardly moving his lips. "What I said on the way out about talkin' in front of no one goes double from here on. When we return to this side, we will not be driven by anyone."

Lordis turned her back to the gusting wind. "I understand. But surely Mr. Beaufort will think that something is amiss if we don't talk about today's events. It just isn't natural."

"True enough. What I mean is that we discuss nothing but what has transpired in public. No new theories of who might be guilty. No mention of Miss Penelope. As far as you and I are concerned, the primary suspects are the Harveys and Mr. Turner."

Lordis snatched John's equipment bag from the ground. "I know!" she said brightly. "I'll use the time we're traveling back to Castries to press Mr. Beaufort for his impressions."

Gilles rose from his place under the tree in time to see Jacob Mansfield heft the basket with the three molds onto the floor of the carriage, his face red and cheeks puffed out from the effort.

"It's got a few items that might have fingerprints on them from inside the mansion," John explained to the clearly curious Gilles Beaufort. "I'm doin' the chief a favor and bringin' them back for him."

The driver gave the slightest of nods and mounted to his seat.

---

I THANK YOU KINDLY for all your efforts today, Mr. Beaufort," John said, pressing several pieces of the change he had used in the footprints into the hotel driver's palm. John and Lordis stood on the brick pavement in front of the government offices that faced the north end of Castries harbor. The basket with the hidden molds lay at their feet.

"When you finish your tasks," Gilles said, "come to the hotel. I'll bring you back up the mountain."

John noted that this was the longest string of words the man had uttered since leaving the Palmer plantation. Cleverly and relentlessly as Lordis had examined him for his observations and opinions on what had transpired in the morning, he rarely replied with more than a "yes," "no," or "I don't know."

"Pshaw!" he said to the driver. "We can get other transport. You've had quite a day already. I'm glad you weren't at the front of that huntin' party; you might have been the one shot."

Beaufort nodded as if he understood fully John's implication. He snapped the reins and guided his carriage up the street and around the corner.

"He's very polite," Lordis commented, "and heaven knows he says too little to get himself in trouble. But still there is something about him that makes my skin crawl."

"And it should," John replied.

Lordis touched her husband's shoulder. "Whatever do you mean?"

John lifted the basket. "Damn me but these molds are heavy. Let's get our errands done before you and I have a long chat," John suggested. "I want to get to the wireless radio station before it closes."

---

LIEUTENANT GOVERNOR TUBBLE was in his office when the Le Bruns entered the building. Even as he extended his hand, he shook his head ponderously back and forth. "Terrible, terrible morning. Please sit."

"Terrible indeed." John pulled back one of the chairs for his wife. "I need to turn over two things to your care. The first is the roll of film I exposed." While he rummaged through his bag, Tubble went behind his desk, opened the top drawer, and took two five-pound notes from a lock box.

"To help reimburse you," the official explained. "Especially since the man who hired you has reneged on payment."

"We appreciate it," Lordis said quickly, knowing her husband's propensity to wave off unexpected money. She leaned forward and took the bills from a slightly surprised Tubble.

John sat and set the film on the official's desk.

"And what is that burden you wrestled into my office?" Tubble asked, pointing to the basket.

"You were with us when Lordis discovered the barefoot prints. I'm sure you recall that there were six sets in all. The shape of the various right feet strongly suggested that three men had run through the area twice . . . probably to make us think it was a substantial number of *Neg Maron.*"

"And these are half of the casts that were made?"

"They are. Probably duplicates of the three I sent off with Chief Dautry. Too many people saw those loaded. I don't know how safe your evidence holdin' area is, but we have too little evidence as it is to risk someone pulverizin' them."

Tubble nodded. "So you want me to store this set."

"Without tellin' another soul," John said.

"I'll leave them in that basket right where you put them until this entire business is settled."

"Good. One final piece of business: all of the Palmer family is now dead and, accordin' to Jacob Mansfield, there are no relatives on St. Lucia. The estranged sister of Peter is the apparent heiress. Her first name is Penelope. She also goes by Penny. She married in England and is said to live in Bath, with a husband and at least one child."

"Her married name?" Tubble asked.

"The Palmer plantation overseer claims he doesn't know it, but I intend to ask around more."

"She does need to be informed immediately," said the lieutenant governor. "I should get a telegram off to the Bath police."

"The overseer believes the husband owns a tea shop. You might also suggest that the department of records for Bath or whatever its county seat is be checked for the maiden name of Palmer on marriage certificates issued within the last seven years. Mrs. Le Brun and I will be sendin' a personal telegram this afternoon. We might could deliver yours as well."

Tubble extracted a sheet of official letterhead stationery from his top drawer and began writing. The Americans waited patiently for him to finish. When he had, John said, "I wonder if I might trouble you as well for somethin' else. Might you give me the power, with another sheet of your official paper and your signature, to investigate the murders . . . me bein' an obvious foreigner."

"Yes, good idea." Tubble jotted two lines down, read what he had written, crumpled up the paper, and began again.

"I also collected your handgun from Gilles Beaufort," John said as Tubble reviewed his amended words and blotted the paper.

"Ah, right! Thanks for remembering."

John did not reach again into the bag. "However, I'd like to ask a favor in not returnin' it to you just yet. I believe my investigatin' has placed the two of us in potential danger."

"Even with the most likely suspects in custody?"

"Even so."

Tubble jerked his head toward Le Brun's waist. "Isn't that gun you've been hiding behind your back defense enough?"

"For me it is. But my wife also needs to carry one. Not long ago in New York City, she had no defense when a criminal I was pursuin' kidnapped her."

Lordis read the look of misgiving on the magistrate's face. "I assure you, Lieutenant Governor, that—unlike some of your police—I am cool-headed under stress. My husband has also taught me well how to handle pistols and revolvers."

"Very well," Tubble relented. "But this is most unusual."

"This whole series of events is most unusual," John pointed out. "So much so that you can expect us to continue our investigation, although more quietly. We will, of course, keep you apprised at every step."

"See that you do," Tubble said, passing over the two documents he had prepared. A knock on the jamb of his open door diverted his attention. A mulatto man dressed in a light-colored suit held up several sheets of paper.

"One last thing," John said. "You have that awl, do you not?"

"The chief of police has it."

"It is definitely of the shoemakin' variety."

"What would Turner or Harvey be doing with a shoemaking awl?" Tubble asked.

"Exactly. Do you happen to know how many shops on St. Lucia make or mend footwear?"

"Not offhand. But I should think it can't be more than a handful." Tubble grabbed a piece of paper and dipped his nib pen into the open inkwell. "I see where you're driving."

"Good. Then we'll be goin'," John said. "But we'll see you soon enough."

---

WHILE LORDIS SHOPPED for ingredients for a few home-cooked meals, John visited the only hardware store they had seen. The business was fairly well stocked. He purchased several small files, a medium-sized hammer with a ball peen, a chisel, a spool of hard wire, and three lengths of piano wire of varying thickness. As he laid the items on the clerk's counter, he asked if the store had awls for sale. The clerk declared that the tool had little demand and vowed that no one had inquired of or purchased one in more than a year. As proof, he led John down a back aisle, bent to a cubbyhole, and removed a cardboard box layered in dust. Inside lay one awl, but it was of the woodworking variety, with a wooden handle shaped like a rifle cartridge.

With his shopping list only half-completed, John sought out a ship's chandlery adjacent to the docks. To his delight, he found and purchased a crude set of seven dental picks that he supposed might be used by a ship's doctor. When he asked to buy an awl as well, the only types the shop sold were the stitching variety. The slight hooks at the end of their needles were made to pierce varying thicknesses of canvas.

Rather than seek out either Anton or Gilles Beaufort and their carriages, the Le Bruns engaged another hackney and returned to their rented home. The moment that driver had driven out of earshot, Lordis turned on her husband like a lioness ready to pounce on a meal.

"Enough temporizing, John Le Brun! Tell me why I should feel as I do about Gilles Beaufort."

John pushed his burdens into the crook of his left arm and dug into his pocket for the house key. "Because his foot conforms best of anyone tested to one of the molds."

"And yet you didn't include him among the suspects."

"If he is one of our culprits, I want him to think he's gotten away with murder. He may lead us to the other two." John opened the front door and stepped back to allow Lordis inside.

"And wasn't he perfectly positioned to drop that awl? The last to move up the valley and the first to descend," Lordis remembered.

"I assume he dropped it on the way back down. Otherwise, as you already observed—my able assistant—one of us would have spied it."

Lordis's eyelids batted from John's unexpected praise. "Why do you say his foot conformed best?"

"First of all, his sole is smoother than that of any field worker or *Neg Maron.*"

"But so were all the men in the huntin' party."

"Second, it's the same length and width as mold four."

Lordis crossed into the kitchen and set down the two woven baskets she had purchased. One was filled with fruits, vegetables, nuts, and small wrapped packages of chicken and fish. The other held a block of ice. "Again, a half-dozen of the men were more or less that length and width. Certainly, George Turner and the Harvey boys."

"Beaufort fit perfectly, not 'more or less,'" John said. "But here is the first dead giveaway: two of the six molds cast showed only a faint impression of the pinkie toe. Gilles's littlest right toe had clearly been broken at some former time. It mended crooked, to the degree that it sits partway over the fourth toe."

"Amazing," Lordis granted. "I understand how the lines and whorls of fingers and palms can be so useful in identifying criminals, but feet seem so much less complex."

"And yet, as early as 1888, a criminal by the name of LeDru was identified and convicted based on the analysis of his barefoot prints. Those tracks were created at a jog, but ones made at a walk speak silent volumes. Foot pressure indirectly talks about weight. A bad hip may affect a gait pattern."

Lordis stopped storing the food in the icebox, fascinated by her husband's ability to astonish her with his knowledge of detection, even after years of knowing him.

"The other dead giveaway," John said, "is that molds three and four suggest from lack of impression in the middle that the runner has a high arch. The act of runnin' lessens the accuracy of the barefoot print, but of all the men suspected, Gilles's arch is the highest."

Lordis's face grew slack. She straightened up and seemed to be looking through the wall.

"Exactly," John said. "If Gilles is one of the murderers, then Anton is most likely the second. Think back to our day with both Anton and Gilles down at the volcano and that waterfall. Both their carriages have big baskets. Big enough for one to hold two fer-de-lances."

"My God! But wouldn't the snakes have hissed and shook the basket, trying to get out?"

"No. I've caught plenty of snakes in my time. Soon as we drop 'em in a gunny sack, they go quiet. I don't know why, but they do."

"Anton suggested that you lead the way down the path from the waterfall," Lordis remembered. "I decided to take the lead, but that probably wasn't what he intended. Why would they want you dead?"

"Or even too sick to continue investigatin'. Whoever's hired those brothers must respect me. At least more than their local police. Who, I must say at the risk of soundin' superior, are apparently no threat to even a halfway accomplished murderer and arsonist."

"I wonder if there's a third brother we don't know about."

"There was definitely a third man," John said.

"Or maybe four," Lordis countered. "What motivation can three black men from Castries have?" Her eyes brightened.

"Carlisle Thiery might be involved. He certainly seems intent on controlling tracts of St. Lucian land."

"But only on the west side. What could he possibly gain from the slaughter of a plantation family on the east?"

"And yet the answer to your question may be the answer to the murders."

"Of a family with a survivin' daughter who lives in England?" John handed Lordis a package of crushed tea leaves. "Accordin' to Mansfield, she has no interest in returnin' to manage the plantation. He thinks she'll sell it via an agent on St. Lucia."

"Or a lawyer, like Thiery."

"Farfetched, Mrs. Le Brun. To risk hangin' for an agent's percentage?"

"Hey, Le Brun," Lordis shot back. "Any idea is allowed whilst brainstorming. So it's back to Turner or the Harveys being the most interested parties," she posited. "It's not as if the Beauforts work for Lawyer Thiery. They drive for the hotel, which must allow them to travel all over the island. Anyone can hire them—even foreigners who might be interested in gobbling up pieces of St. Lucia on the cheap. Foreigners like the two English couples we dined next to near the Pitons."

"There's a reason why the expression is 'idle speculation,'" John said, again reining in his wife's eager suggestions. "Let's focus on the ex-Miss Penelope Palmer right now."

---

THE ST. LUCIA WIRELESS radio office sat in the middle of a three-building government complex at the apex of Morne Fortune. To the side of the structure, surrounded by a white lawn formed of small rocks, rose an antenna about twenty-five feet high, braced by six guy wires.

"Probably can't rise any higher due to the high winds in hurricane season," John guessed, as he held open the building's front door for Lordis.

The large room that served as the wireless office lay directly to the right of the foyer. Sibyl Thiery stood behind a long counter, her petite height allowing only the top half of her torso, her neck, and her head to show. A mulatto man sat at the back of the room typing on a keyboard. Sibyl smiled in recognition at the Le Bruns.

"Hello! How nice to have you visit," Sibyl said in her usual soft voice.

"Both a visit and for business, Mrs. Thiery," John said. He set two pieces of paper on the counter. "The first is to communicate with my detective agency in New York City. There is the address and the telephone number. I want to let them know how to get in touch with me in case of an emergency." As Sibyl studied the information on the paper, he added, "We've had telephones for so long in the States that I probably don't know how you manage wireless telegraphy now."

Sibyl said, "It does continue to change. We have had telegraph writers—much like typewriters—since before I worked here. The one Louis is using is three years old. He can type almost as quickly as you can talk. The keys transmit bursts of code, much more quickly than anyone could do using a single key."

"I understand that the Italian Marconi revolutionized this communication method," John said.

"Yes. Rather than wires, he used radio waves, which move at nearly the speed of light and can travel great distances." As she spoke, Sibyl entered data into a ledger book on the counter. Among the columns were the names and addresses of the sender and intended receiver, the charge for the service, the time and date the request was delivered, the worker keying the message, the time of its transmission, and its confirmation of receipt. Already printed at the far left of each page were sequential numbers, indicating the total number of telegrams sent.

"You said you have a second message?" Sibyl asked.

"Indeed." John produced the official St. Lucia government letterhead with Lieutenant Governor Tubble's message to the chief of police of Bath, England. "We're carryin' this as a favor."

Sibyl read the message. "Oh, gracious God!" she exclaimed. "Peter Palmer has been killed?"

"Unfortunately so," Lordis said.

"By whom?"

"By an employee of the Harvey plantation. He was defending his boss."

Sibyl inhaled as deeply as her small lungs could manage, then expelled her breath in a quick, sharp motion. "One tragedy upon another. Which leaves only his sister to inherit the plantation, I would guess from this telegram."

"As far as we know," John said.

"Were you there?" Sibyl asked John.

"We both were," Lordis answered.

"Well, you must relate everything to me, Carlisle, and Mother Thiery this evening. I can cook more—"

"We've shopped to make our own dinner, thank you," Lordis interrupted.

"Then afterward, for drinks on the veranda," Sibyl persisted.

---

THE THIERY VERANDA was on the second floor, requiring the Le Bruns to walk through the master bedroom. The other bedroom that opened on the upstairs open-air space belonged to Emeline. John observed that, in spite of Carlisle's expensive clothing, his gold watch, and his impressive carriage, the furnishings of both bedrooms were modest and not of the best quality. More money by far had been expended on the kitchen, dining and living rooms, which informed John that an earnest front was maintained by the family. The lawyer was definitely the member who dealt most with the public, and likely he sometimes entertained at home as well. John understood that

Carlisle's ambitions were far from fulfilled. The man, abetted by his wife and mother, had constructed, through his dress and the look of his home's first floor, the illusion of genteel affluence in order to get more of the real thing.

"My congratulations on your investigation," Carlisle said, as he poured rum punch into five balloon glasses.

"My investigation so far," John corrected. "More needs to be looked into."

"What might that be?" Emeline asked from her rattan chair.

"Seein' if either Mr. Turner or the Harveys can substantiate that they couldn't have been on the Palmer plantation that night. Askin' up and down the east coast road if anyone out late happened to see any of them. Communicatin' with Peter Palmer's sister. Perhaps the guilty party has lately pressed her for her attitudes toward the plantation in the last few months." John smiled at Carlisle. "Just as I and Mr. Van Fleet have been pressed about our opinions toward sellin' St. Lucia as a vacation paradise."

The solicitor had just finished pouring his own drink. He saluted John with his glass. "Since that is now fully in the open, you could reap a five percent finder's fee on every dollar you help bring in."

"This isn't the time to discuss money or resorts," Emeline said. "Or even what happens to the Palmer estate. How will justice be served?"

"Sometimes it isn't," Carlisle said to his mother. "Our esteemed visitor will tell you that as both detective and former sheriff. And who would be crazy enough to take over such a large sugarcane plantation, with the price of sugar dropping every year? Even if Turner and the Harveys cannot be found guilty beyond a reasonable doubt and are crazy enough to make bids, would the sister want to sell to them?"

"I assure you: someone will want that land," Emeline declared. "Why can't bananas be grown on the east side as well as the west?" She focused on her son. "You should be able to tell us. You own a few acres down in Anse-la-Raye."

"As an absentee owner," said Thiery. "I was offered that field in exchange for many hours of my professional services. As far as knowing enough about cultivating bananas, the buyer would need to consult a true expert. I suppose—if the purchaser wasn't too greedy—a profit could be made from a variety of plantings. Too many of our owners depend on a single crop, and then drought or storm or rot wipes them out."

"Another reason for dropping sugarcane as a crop," Sibyl weighed in, "is that those plantations are only in full operation for about thirty-six weeks a year. The other sixteen weeks, the workers get no pay and must survive on the little they have saved and whatever they've grown in their own small plots."

"Goodness! We had no idea," Lordis revealed.

Carlisle said, "Even worse, most of the private worker plots aren't varied enough to provide a balanced diet. There's general malnutrition all over St. Lucia. Which worsens the workers' ability to combat tuberculosis and several venereal diseases. That is why part of me is in favor of a constant influx of foreign money. Something other than crops must be introduced to improve the general welfare."

"I understand from Nigel Harvey that your teachers are paid very little," Lordis said.

"So true. They're paid about the same as dock workers. I don't know what we'd do if all the children who are mandated to attend school by law actually showed up. We'd need to double the number of teachers."

"Which those who vote would never approve of anyway," John assumed.

"Because they would need to double their education tax rates." Carlisle threw out his hands. "In a way, our laws are fair. Only those who earn $300 a year above the table and who own land get to vote. If everyone had the right, the poor would be voting themselves benefits that they have no ability to pay for."

"But it also neatly insures that the few maintain control," John observed.

"Just as in the United States. In spite of half a century of militating, your women still do not have the right to vote."

"Amen," Lordis said, raising her glass.

"And your blacks suffer from those 'Jim Crow' laws." Carlisle offered his guests a skeptical glare. "'Separate but equal' railroad cars, lunch counters, bathrooms. Separate for certain; equal in words only."

"You are far better informed of our history than we are of yours," John praised. "So, tell me, what is the makeup of your upper government?"

"We have an executive and legislative council. The legislative branch is composed of a chief justice and five principal plantation owners."

"Which means the complexion of both branches is pure white," John said.

Carlisle threw half the contents of his drink down his throat, then replied, "Look at the color of my skin. Just how fair do you suppose I think that is?"

## CHAPTER ELEVEN

# July 2, 1910

IN ORDER TO AVOID the inquisitive family next door, Lordis and John did not ask to use the Thiery telephone to call for a hackney. Fortunately, their walk to a carriage rental agency in Castries was all downhill and in good weather. They brought with them John's camera and the basket Lordis had bought days before, half-loaded with previously purchased perishables. They stopped briefly at the open market to complete their lunch, and by nine o'clock on the sunny Saturday morning, they were off to the east side of St. Lucia.

To call Dennery a town was a compliment. It only deserved the name in relation to the other even smaller gatherings of structures such as Praslin, Mamika and Micoud that the islanders referred to as villages. The few streets of Dennery, however, had orderly and well-built houses and some shops, all painted in a similar rainbow of pastels as the villages along the west coast. A quick drive up one street and down the other revealed that the town survived on fishing in the Atlantic and to serve the large plantations along a nine-mile stretch.

John secured the buggy to a post in the center of town, and he and Lordis began ambling. The plan was to politely stop every person they met and ask about the night of the Palmer mansion burning. John was not surprised in the slightest that no one had seen or knew of any unusual activity in that area or even on the roads leading to Tristesse that night. As people—white, mulatto, and black—told them, the population on the east side of St. Lucia was almost exclusively laborers. Sleep happened soon after dusk. The coastal roads were unlit, making their rutted lengths treacherous to travel. Except in the villages, houses were unlit and generally stood well back from the roads.

In truth, John's initial question was an excuse to open up a broader line of inquiry. His hope was to learn more about the history of the Palmer family and its relationships with its neighbors and thus expose a previously unknown motive for murder. The detective's experience assured him that the vast majority of people approached would be averse to speaking with a nosy stranger. However, if he persisted, there were always one or two "old fishwives" who were more than happy to prattle on and on about the lives of others, laying dirty secrets bare whenever they could.

Gold was struck when the couple ducked their heads into a barn close by where they had tied their horse. Woodworking projects in varying stages of completion filled the floor. Just outside the barn's sliding doors sat an elegant bench that had clearly been intended only for indoor use but which had seen better days and was now bare of varnish and cracking in various places from the effects of the sun and the nearby sea. Inside, a lanky man who John guessed from his skin color to be a quadroon worked at stripping a cabinet of its layers of varnish and stain just beyond the hard fall of sunlight. He smiled from his first moment of laying eyes on the unknown couple.

"How are you?" he wanted to know, wiping his dusty hands on his apron.

"We're excellent!" Lordis returned. "And how are you this lovely day?"

"I'm above ground, so that's good enough for me. My name's Jessie." What made Jessie's lilting reply more than just a stock witticism was the fact that he could not have been a day under sixty-five and possibly significantly older. He moved past his sanding project with an arthritic motion. "We don't usually get strangers in Dennery."

"I would expect," John returned. "I'm John Le Brun, and this is my wife, Lordis. We're visitin' St. Lucia from the United States."

"So I hear, from your accent. On vacation?"

"That's right."

Jessie advanced to the entrance of the barn. He gestured to the old bench. "Then you're likely in no hurry. Why not have a seat?"

"Thank you, we will," Lordis accepted.

The elderly man stepped out of view for a moment and returned dragging a well-worn rocking chair. He brought it into the shade that also covered the bench and eased himself down. His eyelids narrowed in an assessing expression.

"Would you happen to be that detective couple I heard tell of?"

John laughed and glanced at Lordis. She could not have grinned any wider at being included in the question. "We are. We were told correctly: there may be few telephones, but news travels around this island quickly nevertheless."

"Not news of the world or famous people. Not news about changes in our government, mind you, but of island people and their crazy ways, of course," Jessie agreed.

"Excuse me." Lordis rose abruptly, and without explanation, walked to the rented buggy.

Knowing that his wife was keenly attuned to his plan, John made no comment about her sudden movement. "Have you lived in Dennery for a long time?" he asked.

"In the town for about twenty years. On this side of the island all my life."

John lifted his camera from his lap. "You're a handsome-lookin' gentleman. Would you mind if I captured your image?"

"Not at all," said Jessie. "I'll even stop rocking for you."

John focused the camera and took a snapshot of the Dennery man from the waist up. If the longtime local provided information that seemed valuable, he wanted to be able to show the man's face to the authorities on the opposite side of St. Lucia to get their input as to his reliability.

"I imagine you know a great deal about the Palmer family," John dug more deeply.

"You imagine well," the woodworker replied, resuming his rocking. "I grew up there and learned carpentry under the eye of an old artist. Ben Bemba."

"So you worked there when Peter's father, Henry, was the master of Tristesse."

Jessie nodded soberly. "I was born at that plantation two years before Henry was. I left in 1887, the year his second wife died. Couldn't stand being there no more."

Lordis returned carrying the luncheon basket. She set it on the bench as Jessie spoke his last words and threw back the gingham cloth that covered the meal. "We have too much food for just myself and my husband, Jessie," she offered. "Will you do us the favor of eating with us?"

"I don't mind at all, thank you," he said, showing obvious delight at the invitation.

"You say you couldn't stand bein' on the Palmer plantation anymore," John reviewed. "I heard from Jacob Mansfield that

Henry was a harsh man but that he sometimes regretted his actions and became rather soft and indulgent."

"He was spoiled by his mother and indulged by his father, so his personality came natural to him," Jessie said, rocking forward to inspect the contents of the basket.

"When we spoke with Peter, he seemed to hate his father," Lordis said.

"I was only there for the first eight years of Peter's life, but Henry was the exact opposite toward him that James had been toward Henry. Mean, demanding, critical. Even went so far as to call poor Peter a disappointment. Is that banana chicken?"

"It is. Here's a plate for you. John and I will share the other plate. And a fork. In that jar is cold hearts of palm. That's a coconut loaf cake. And those bottles are filled with ginger beer. Please don't be shy."

Jessie's eyes grew saucer wide. "One thing I ain't is shy." He took generous portions as he continued talking. "Yes, Henry could be indulgent, too. Especially to his first wife."

"Constance," said Lordis. "Beloved wife."

"You must have read her tombstone."

Lordis nodded.

"He loved her something fierce. It was easy. She was beautiful and charming and smart. Had a smile like the sun rising. But she was also delicate. Lost one baby with a miscarriage, and the other one died the same day it was born. She always had bad lungs. She died of tuberculosis when she was only twenty-seven. It near-killed Henry. Made him really mean for a time. He softened a bit when he married again, to a woman who had some money. From Martinique. Name of Anne Baxter."

"She was the mother of Peter and Penelope," John checked.

"That's right." Jessie's attention was diverted by the appearance of a heavyset black woman who walked down the street with difficulty. She carried a silk fan in her right hand and waved it in front of her round face without stopping.

"Good day, Madame Lucille," Jessie greeted.

"And to you, Mr. Jessie," the woman said through gasps of breath. "And who are these?"

"Customers."

"Ah."

"Stay out of the sun," Jessie advised her. Lucille looked like she was searching her brain for an excuse to include herself in the conversation. After a few moments of awkward silence, she gave up the effort, sighed, and moved on.

When Lucille was out of the range of hearing, Jessie leaned forward and said in a conspiratorial tone, "You don't want to get any history from her. If she was telling the story of the three blind mice, they'd become six, and the farmer's wife would use a sword. Just to impress you. Not only that, half the things that happen around here she accounts to magic or the supernatural. She actually believes that a woman who opens up an umbrella inside a house will never be married. Or the same fate if she wears a new ring on her left ring finger. She owns nothing but black underwear, to keep the evil spirits away." He took a big bite out of his portion of chicken.

Eager to return the woodworker's attention to the subjects of his investigation, John said, "Henry was good to Peter's mother but—"

"No. Not very good. He needed the woman's money, but he never loved her." The old carpenter's eyebrows shot up. "This is not to say he didn't love. Just not Anne Baxter."

"'Where there is marriage without love, there will be love without marriage,'" Lordis said softly, quoting Benjamin Franklin.

Jessie smiled slyly and nodded. "Yes. Love outside marriage. The second wife brought several servants with her. One was her cook, named Jetia. She was very good at preparing food, and she loved her own cooking." He jerked his thumb in the direction of the woman in the street he had spoken to. "Looked like Madame Lucille. But she had a daughter who was thin.

Thin and beautiful. Beautiful and smart, like Henry's first wife. When Innocente arrived at Tristesse, she was only eleven. But she blossomed like a hibiscus over the next few years."

"Was Jetia black?" John asked.

Jessie finished his chicken and licked his fingers. "No. A griffe. Like me."

"And her daughter?"

"One-half white." Jessie took on a wistful look. "The best features from both worlds."

"How old was she when Henry took her to his bed?" Lordis asked.

Without any hesitation, Jessie said, "Fourteen. Henry was thirty-five." He shrugged. "The worst feature of this world."

Lordis made a judgmental sound deep in her throat. "And how did Mrs. Palmer react to this?"

"She was unhappy. But she was not a handsome woman, and she was no longer on Martinique. She knew she was far from unique. Just like most of the other planters' wives. "

"Betrayed," Lordis said.

"Compromised," Jessie replied.

"How long did the affair last?" John wanted to know.

"Until after the baby was born."

"Boy or girl?"

"Boy. Healthy. Handsome. Alert."

"What happened to mother and son?"

"Actually, the cook, her daughter, and her grandson. They vanished one night," Jessie said. His eyes drifted down and to the left, in reverie. He looked sad. "One Friday night, actually. Friday, they were on the plantation; Saturday, they were gone. No one dared ask where."

"Where do you think?" John asked.

Jessie shrugged. "Most thought to another plantation. One on the west side of St. Lucia. But I have visited many plantations in the past twenty-some years, doing my work. No one admitted to knowing anything. They disappeared as if they had been shot and dumped in the Barre d'Isle."

"The deep rainforests," John said.

"Yes. What I hope is that they were sent back to Martinique. The second wife could not stand to look at them and made Henry send them away."

"From then on, was Peter's father faithful?" Lordis asked.

Jessie laughed. "Not a bit. He took at least three other daughters of workers. Nothing long-time. They were plain girls. Neither looks nor brains enough to make Henry love. Each time he finished with one of them, he bought Anne expensive clothing and perfumes. So he could feel all right to sin again whenever the opportunity came. Who knows what he did in Castries, when he said he was going to the St. Lucia Island Club. Anne began drinking night and day while Innocente was pregnant. Never stopped. In 1887, when she was forty-one, she fell down the stairs and broke her neck. That was when I left Tristesse."

"Peter called his father a bastard," John said, hoping to stir up more passions in the embittered man, compelling him to reveal other secrets.

Lips pursed, Jessie ladled out a helping of hearts of palm. When he had finished, he said, "Peter was right. Did you come to know him well?"

"No."

"He was a good fellow. Hot-headed sometimes, but at the bottom he was good. Not real smart. He read and read to make up for it. No matter how hard he worked to please his father, though, Henry was disappointed."

"What about Penelope?"

"She also hated her father. Got away from him as soon as she could. She lives in England."

John finished his helping of chicken and cleaned his fingers with a scrap of old newspaper. "Yes, we have heard. Do you know precisely where she is?"

"I have no idea."

"We heard she married there. Would you know her married name?"

"No, sir. I know nothing after she left."

"And did this hatred of Henry Palmer extend to the Harvey family?"

Jessie paused to give Le Brun a hard stare. "You wish to know if you have accused the right men."

"Absolutely."

"The Harveys are not good to those who work for them. They're all tight with their purses. But if you would try to convince me that any of those men is a murderer, I would laugh in your face."

"We have footprint molds that match the sizes of their feet, and a tool painted with the Stratford colors," John challenged.

"Give me half an hour, and I will find you three men who also fit those molds. The blue and yellow paint you can take off my shelves. And, I'm sure, three or four other shelves right here in Dennery."

Lordis offered Jessie another ginger beer to replace the one he had drained. "If not the Harveys, then Mr. Turner?"

"Not him either. To be honest, I don't believe either Turner or the Harveys are interested in buying the Palmer plantation. They have more than enough problems with their own lands. I never heard one word about either of them threatening the Palmers. Especially Peter. And you can ask all around Dennery: I hear everything."

---

SOON AFTER LUNCH, John and Lordis quit Dennery and turned north to take the East-West Road back to Castries. They had not reached the town limit before Lordis blurted out her thoughts.

"It is Carlisle Thiery after all! Him and his supercilious mother. Emeline must be right around the age that

Innocente would be. And Carlisle is definitely the age of the illegitimate boy."

John kept the horse moving at the same pace. "So, Innocente changed her name to Emeline."

"With good reason," Lordis replied, losing none of her enthusiasm. "Probably her cook mother changed her name as well, to start over. Jessie looked for them at the various plantations, but they were in Castries. We could ask around about a heavy-set female cook who worked in the city thirty years ago."

"Don't you imagine every good-looking mulatto woman on this island—in fact, on all the islands in this chain—was seduced or just plain taken by white men?"

"Yes, but—"

"Here, it's the natural order of things," John bulled on. "Their version of the *droit du seigneur*. Have you heard the term?"

"No."

"In medieval Europe, the lord of a realm had the right to sleep with any bride on her weddin' night, even before the groom had her."

"How barbaric," Lordis fumed. "It's a wonder we ever came out of the Middle Ages."

"Then books and posters educated the smarter common people. If only those lords had thought ahead, they would have murdered Gutenberg and destroyed his printin' press before the first book was sold. Let's say your hunch is right."

"My educated hunch," Lordis corrected.

"What's the motivation? Revenge after all these years? It's not as if this wronged child-woman or her son could get anythin' valuable out of mass murder. Certainly not the plantation. Peter Palmer told us that he had reinstated his sister in his will. If Carlisle is Henry's son, how could he prove it? There wouldn't be a birth certificate. Even if he could and Penny Palmer didn't exist, I doubt that this colony's laws allow a mixed-race bastard to inherit land."

"But we've been informed that everyone on St. Lucia is equal—at least in the eyes of the law."

"I'll grant you that if Carlisle is Henry's son, he and his mother would have a motive for revenge. But that's too weak a motive for such calculatin' people."

"We've already agreed that he knows Anton and Gilles Beaufort," Lordis asserted. "That's three men. And you said that the right little toe on Gilles's foot matched the mold."

John laughed. "Now there's a picture! The piss-elegant Carlisle Thiery runnin' barefoot—twice—at the edge of fields filled with hookworms. He looked scared to dip his toes in the sea."

Lordis bounced lightly on the buggy seat. "Maybe he hired three murderers. This explains why that avaricious young lawyer was so intent on getting us up to the house next to theirs. He quickly realized how clever you are. Once Nigel Harvey hired you to investigate, he needed to know what you're thinking at every moment."

"Now, that's an excellent observation," John granted.

"So, we will investigate the three to a fare-thee-well . . . won't we?" Lordis latched onto John's wrist to make sure he would reply.

"Not to the point of excludin' everyone else," he said. "But investigate them we will."

# CHAPTER TWELVE

## July 3, 1910

THE LE BRUNS ATTENDED the Castries Anglican church a second time. Again, the Van Fleets did not appear. Lieutenant Governor Richard Tubble and his wife were there, as was the entire Thiery family, including Emeline. The five wore pure white, as on the previous Sunday, arrived with only one minute to spare, and sat in the front row, directly under the pulpit.

Once again, the singing was nothing like the high-tempo, highly rhythmic melodies the Le Bruns had heard sung by children in a St. Lucian village street or from unseen workers laboring in fields of banana plants. "Onward, Christian Soldiers" sounded as if defeated crusaders were limping back to England. The sermon dealt with the mystery of the Communion wafer and wine being the actual body and blood of Jesus, which always strained John's relationship with dogma.

When the service ended, Tubble moved swiftly to where Lordis and John minced forward on the center aisle. He had his wife in tow, a woman with ash-gray elegantly coiffed hair, an aquiline nose, and lower teeth that looked like an extra pair of incisors had been squeezed in. She was only a bit shorter than her husband and equally thin. In their Sunday finery the two looked like minor British royalty.

"Mr. John Le Brun, Mrs. Lordis Le Brun, this is my wife, Gweneth," Tubble introduced. Greetings and pleasantries were exchanged. "I have information to share," he continued in a subdued voice. "I wonder if you would care to partake of Elevenses with us at the Government House."

"We would be delighted," John replied.

The four climbed into the grand phaeton carriage, which was pulled by matched dappled horses. As they rode away from the church, John noted the hawk-like stares of the three Thiery adults.

---

THE GOVERNMENT HOUSE is the residence of St. Lucia's chief official. It sits high up on Morne Fortune. Once through the property's iron gateway, the road curves gracefully up to a porte cochere fronting a rambling structure designed in late Victorian style. As John suspected, even on a Sunday there was a groomsman to care for the horses and carriage and a grounds man at work manicuring the beds of flowers planted beneath broadleaf and palm trees. Within the brick walls, a butler stood ready to take hats, a waiter bustled in the dining room, and a maid polished silverware in a preparation passage.

Le Brun marveled at the contrast to his home. Except for his several filled bookcases, John's approach to living was simplicity. A visitor to his home might have thought that his lack of mirrors, etageres, porcelain figurine collections, photographs in frames, mass-produced wall hangings, nested storage boxes, stuffed and mounted animal trophy heads, and the like was due to lack of money or space. Such was not the case. Inside Government House, however, the accumulation of an acquisitive age resembled an unpacked warehouse. *It's the same in New York and Brunswick in this age of mass production,* John thought. *Affluence demands display.*

Elevenses, an imported ritual from Great Britain, usually featured tea or coffee and a light snack. The Government House, like the White House in Washington, was ever ready to ramp up for an unexpected visitation. The Le Bruns had eaten a filling breakfast at the New Bristol Hotel before walking to church. The array of cakes, cookies, and pudding set before them guaranteed that they would only require a light, late dinner to satisfy their stomachs for the remainder of the day.

Once the Tubbles and Le Bruns were seated, Richard said, "I have informed Mrs. Tubble of the events of the Palmer murders." Gweneth smiled benignly. "Let me bring you two up to date on official activities of the past two days. Firstly, Chief Dautry himself carried the awl to the two most popular shoe shops in Castries. He was prepared to journey to two general leatherworking shops in town and three more in outlying villages, but that was unnecessary. The owner of the second shop checked and learned from an employee that one of their awls was indeed missing. The employee recognized the awl but stated that it had not been previously painted nor later sanded. Obviously, it's a common tool of the trade, so they had others. The worker who noted its absence figured it had merely been misplaced and resolved to keep the loss in mind until it appeared."

"Could anyone in the shop set a date when it was missed?" John asked.

"The first realization was last Monday. The employee allowed that it might have been missing for as long as two weeks before that."

"Is the owner a mulatto?" John asked.

"As a matter of fact, he is," Richard replied.

"Well," Mrs. Tubble said, "that goes a way toward exonerating the Harvey family."

"Any special reason why you say that, Mrs. Tubble?" John asked.

"First, that the tool did not come from their plantation, in spite of the colors on the handle. Secondly, I would expect that the Harveys have their shoes and boots made by Winston Mills, on High Street. The same as Richard and other members of the government do."

John took a moment to infer the woman's meaning. "Mr. Mills is a white man."

"Indeed. The owner of the shop from which the awl was stolen is Mr. Boulton."

Le Brun struggled within himself to maintain an unreadable exterior. "We should not indulge in such an assumption. I should think a Harvey male crosses the island at least once a week, since Castries is so vital. That one may, in fact, have gone to the shop they don't frequent expressly not to be recognized if the business with the awl came back to haunt his family." He pulled his notebook from his inside jacket pocket. He used his ever-present fountain pen to begin writing names. The rest of the group waited in patient silence. When he finished, he tore out the page and handed it to the lieutenant governor.

"I understand that your time is precious, Governor Tubble," John said, "but I would ask that you perform this task yourself. Go to the mulatto shoe shop owner, present him with this list, and ask him to check his accounts and his memory. I think it will be necessary for him to go back three weeks. Require him to tell you if any of the men on that list have done business in his shop or merely wandered in durin' that time. Pull him aside, so that only he hears your request. Also inform him that if he fails to do a thorough review or if he talks to a single soul about this task, he may be held as an accessory to a capital crime. In other words, put the fear of God into him."

"I have used that phrase on more than one occasion," Tubble assured, as his eyes swept the list. They stopped moving about halfway down. "I can understand George Turner and all of the Harvey men, but why is Carlisle Thiery on the list?"

"For good reason."

"And both Beaufort brothers?"

"For the same good reason, which I will divulge if what I suspect turns out to be true."

"Should I open investigations on these three men?"

John crossed his arms over his chest. "You may be forced to, seventy-two hours from now. Until that time, I would like to probe their backgrounds on my own. I believe I have a source that will not arouse nearly as much suspicion as would I or any members of your police force."

"If you are confident, then I'll grant your request," said Tubble. "But if you believe that Turner and the Harveys are innocent, they should not languish in jail for any longer than is necessary."

"I completely agree."

Gweneth Tubble touched her husband's hand lightly. "If I may be so bold, Richard, I second the notion of delaying any police act that suggests Carlisle Thiery is less than a paragon of virtue."

Tubble nodded. "Gweneth is right. He is a highly respected champion of rights for people of color—especially those of mixed race. Every time it seems that a mulatto is treated unfairly by our government, he is right there in defense. Really knows how to use handbills and posters and certain loudmouth rabble rousers as his mouthpieces."

"By 'our government' I assume you mean the one hundred percent white men who control both branches," John said.

"That's true," Tubble admitted.

"Are those of mixed race treated unfairly on a regular basis?" John persisted.

Tubble sucked in his cheeks and settled back into his chair. "That depends on who is asked. Both sides view issues with predisposition and prejudice. Are our menial workers paid miserable wages? Yes, they are. Do they have a right to be unhappy about this? Yes. Is such treatment unique to St. Lucia? No. Do our laborers have the right to riot and loot, as happened two years ago? They say yes. The business owners who had shops and warehouses destroyed say no. The law says no. Is St. Lucia the poorest island in this part of the Caribbean? Again, yes." Tubble's speech picked up speed. It was clearly something rehearsed over and over in his mind, even if seldom spoken aloud. "Are there untapped resources such as oil or minerals to exploit to change the current conditions? No. Are the white men in charge making larger profits on St. Lucia than their peers on neighboring islands? No. Are they nevertheless living many degrees better than the blacks? Yes. Is education a fundamental key to improving the island? Definitely. Is education poorly taught and for too few years on St. Lucia? Yes. Are we able to pay to improve it? No. It's all a vicious cycle."

"Those who were put down at the Cul-de-Sac sugar factory are still licking their wounds," Gweneth said, in a warning voice, looking hard at John. "You say you've fixed your sights on Carlisle Thiery and the Beauforts, which is to say a prominent and respected mulatto and two black men whom many believe were falsely arrested."

"Probably a third black man," John said, "with the lawyer directin' their actions."

"A dangerous line of pursuit," the lady of Government House declared.

"What do you mean by falsely arrested?" Lordis asked the Tubbles.

Richard said, "On several occasions, Anton and Gilles Beaufort have been suspected of theft. Not enough proof could be assembled against them. However, three years ago, they were caught red-handed making off with two large wagons filled with lumber, mortar, and bricks from a construction site. Their barrister was Carlisle Thiery."

John turned to Lordis. "Didn't he tell us he's a solicitor?"

"He did," Lordis confirmed.

John redirected his gaze to Tubble. "Am I mistaken, or aren't lawyers who are solicitors forbidden to act as barristers?"

"In a number of countries they are. The Windward Islands, however, have evolved their own peculiar set of laws. Our Bar Standards Board, for example, can allow a solicitor to conduct litigation also, provided he has the schooling to satisfy the requirements."

"And, obviously, Carlisle Thiery does."

Tubble shrugged. "He's the only lawyer on our island who earned his credentials from the Cambridge School of Law. That goes a long way with the Bar Standards Board."

"Was he able to help the Beauforts?" Lordis asked.

Tubble laughed. "I should say so. His cocky defense became something of minor legend around the government offices. You see, Anton and Gilles were the two who had delivered the materials in the first place. They worked for a well-off cousin who runs a construction supply yard at the edge of the docks. Thiery's assertion was that the original deliveries were of inferior material. In order to avoid a later lawsuit for supplying lower-grade lumber and bricks than were specified in the contract, the cousin and brothers conspired to substitute the proper grades in the dead of night. They first needed to clear the space of the original materials. Then they ostensibly planned to return a second time with the substitutes, and no one would be the wiser."

"You're havin' us on," John said.

"I am not," Tubble asserted. "Sufficient wood and bricks of better grade existed in the yard so that their tale might have been true. Thiery pleaded them down to serving only two months in prison for breaking and entering. He was nearly held in contempt by Judge Montague for asserting that no time should be served. Turned himself into something of a martyr for the downtrodden black people. If those same downtrodden masses would take the time to look at how he dresses, who he associates with, and where he lives, they'd realize nothing is farther from the truth."

"So, Anton and Gilles Beaufort owe Carlisle Thiery a considerable debt," Lordis filled in.

The lieutenant governor lifted his coffee cup toward his lips but paused. "If they have not already squared him."

"And the Beauforts have a cousin," John said.

"Yes. Name of Emmanuel Beaufort."

"What about a third brother?"

"I have no idea. I can check on that. Something so minor shouldn't arouse suspicion." Tubble took the proffered pen from John's fingers and scribbled a note on the piece of paper the detective had given him.

"I don't understand," Gweneth said. "How could these three possibly have anything to do with murders and a fire on the opposite side of St. Lucia?" And then, in a rush, "For that matter, what could two black men and a mulatto have to gain?"

"Excellent questions, Mrs. Tubble," said John. "Especially since there is a sister in the picture, a sister Peter Palmer told us is in his will to inherit the plantation if everyone in his family died."

John set down his coffee cup and dabbed his mouth with a linen napkin. "Lordis and I are, of course, visitors to your island. I've been asked to solve a crime that may have social implications. We have seen the deplorable livin' conditions among the plantation field workers. Would you agree that, since they were granted their freedom, the blacks merely traded iron chains for economic ones?"

Color rose on Tubble's cheeks. "As I have said, if we had the resources to improve the lots of the poor on our island, we would quickly see to it."

"The Beaufort brothers are employed at a place where they constantly see and hear the advantages that all manner of white folk, foreign and domestic, have," John continued, keeping his voice as neutrally conversational as he could manage. "I can easily imagine resentment on their side. Can you give us an idea of how the island's mulattoes feel?"

Richard Tubble tugged forcefully on his left earlobe, as if an itch was suddenly tormenting him. "As children of primarily white men and black or mixed-race mothers, they belong in neither world. Often, out of guilt or fondness, the fathers have seen that they have advantages. They set them up in shops or see that they are trained as artisans. They use their influence to secure low- and middle-level government positions for their unclaimed offspring. A few of the children are sent overseas to become ministers or doctors or lawyers—like Carlisle Thiery."

"But, at least for the public eye, the white fathers must be very interested in keeping these people's paternity secret," Lordis interjected.

Gweneth answered, "All of them are. They succeed at different levels. The word almost always gets out, but polite society only speaks of these indiscretions behind closed doors."

"Do either of you know of a man named Thiery whose name Carlisle has claimed?"

Gweneth shook her head.

"I know no one of that name," Richard said. "However, even though St. Lucia has a small white population, I can't know everyone."

"This belongin' in neither world," John delved. "How do the mulattoes cope?"

Richard Tubble seemed strangely amused by the question. "They associate with each other in private. However, not as a unified class. The more white blood courses through their veins, the more selective they become. My impression—which has been formed by dozens of observations—is that they hate the planters and those of us in upper government. The former lords of this island, the French, had a saying: 'Color is wedded to slavery. Nothing can render the slave the equal of the master.' That attitude has never left this island. So the mulattoes deplore the whites because of their maintenance of class structure, but they'll be damned if they'll associate with pure blacks. They dress, choose their church, and speak proper English specifically to maintain a gulf separating them from those below."

From another room a telephone jangled. John used it as a cue. "You've been most kind in invitin' us into your home, and we'll not take any more of your precious Sunday."

Richard Tubble began to rise.

"However . . ." John hastened to add.

Tubble sat, affecting a wan smile.

". . . you haven't mentioned any return news from England regardin' the findin' of Penelope née Palmer."

Tubble stood. "Simply because there has been no news."

John helped Lordis rise, then said to the lieutenant governor, "I would recommend that you send another message. This time ask for an immediate receipt confirmation."

---

FROM THE FRONT GATE of Government House, the Le Bruns walked up to the commanding summit of Morne Fortune. The reason for the positioning of a fort at the edge of the mountain became manifest when they looked down on Castries's harbor and the Caribbean Sea beyond. The fort had not been active since 1905, but an honor guard of uniformed men patrolled the area. They learned from one of the guards that the original stronghold had been built by the French in 1768. A large-scale battle was fought over its control in 1796 and eventually taken by the Twenty-seventh Foot Royal Inniskilling Fusiliers. Renamed Fort Charlotte, it had belonged to the British without interruption since 1803.

Between 1888 and 1890, four ten-inch guns were installed and christened Apostle's Battery.

"This will serve well to defend Castries when the next war comes," John declared, causing their uniformed guide to raise his eyebrows. The man led them on a brief tour of the lower level of the fort and of several cells and carved-out caves, where ammunition and powder had been stored.

On their return walk, the Le Bruns passed the Thiery home. The sounds of a piano escaped from inside and filled the local area. They paused to listen. Moments later, Carlisle appeared.

"Come see the new piano!" he called down to the road. "It was delivered yesterday afternoon."

The Thiery living room furniture had been rearranged so that the upright could fit against the wall facing the entry. John noted that although the piano was new to the home, it was not a new instrument. He knew that the ages of pianos were difficult to judge from their exteriors alone, but the dullness and crazing of the walnut varnish betrayed at least two decades of wear. Nevertheless, the strings were in tune. It had already been covered with a machine-manufactured mantilla of lace, atop which sat a porcelain, wood, and glass collection of miniature elephants and four framed photographs—a modest echo of the clutter of the lieutenant governor's home.

Sitting on the padded bench with a ramrod-straight posture and curved fingers was the eight-year-old daughter. Her sister stood at her left side, ready to turn musical pages. John reflected, *When their names were first mentioned, I paid their significance no heed. Vicky and Lizzy are short for Victoria and Elizabeth. Now I realize that Carlisle and Sybil paid homage to England's two greatest queens. White queens.*

Victoria played "Twinkle, Twinkle, Little Star" with good accuracy. When she finished and Lordis praised her, Sibyl said, in the tone of a proud mother, "She's been taking lessons from Madame Wells, who once played at Royal Albert Hall. Now that Vicky's proven herself, we've gotten her this piano for her birthday."

"Happy birthday," John wished the beaming child, even as he wondered if he would soon be exploding her comfortable world.

"Do you play the piano as well?" Lordis asked Elizabeth.

The younger child shook her head and put on a sad face.

"Do you want to?" Lordis continued.

Elizabeth altered her movement by ninety degrees.

Her mother said, "She can try it if it pleases her, but Carlisle and I would prefer she play a stringed instrument such as violin or viola."

John looked around for the Thiery matriarch but failed to find her.

"Can we get you some refreshment?" Carlisle asked the North Americans.

"No, thank you," John declined. "We've just come from your Government House."

"Yes, we saw you ride off with the lieutenant governor and his wife." The lawyer pushed his hands into his trouser pockets, affecting a casual pose. "Anything interesting going on?"

John moved a bit closer to his wife. "Not really. Lordis and I nosed around the east side of St. Lucia yesterday, hopin' to pick up a good motivation for either Turner or Harvey to attack the Palmers."

"Came up dry, did you?"

"Indeed. The hope of buyin' the estate seems to be the one and only reason. But the attack is what we in the Deep South call 'ham handed.'"

"Poorly thought out and executed?" Carlisle guessed.

"Precisely. Points the guilty finger right at a neighbor. Especially one with a tool once painted yellow and blue."

"I heard about the attempt to sand the color off. Such information flies around, even on weekends."

Lordis tugged on John's elbow.

John said, "We'll not interrupt any further." He smiled at

the older daughter. "If you leave your windows open, we'll enjoy the rest of your concert."

---

"THIS LIVING ON the side of a mountain is getting old," Lordis complained as she surveyed the few leftovers in the rented home's icebox. "In New York, I need to walk no farther than five blocks to get virtually anything I want."

"Pretend you're shipwrecked on this paradise island. There's always that banana plant in the back corner of the Thierys' place," John teased her.

"We've pretty well painted ourselves into a culinary corner," Lordis continued, ignoring her husband. "Every restaurant we surveyed this week is closed on Sunday evening. Besides, I don't want to knock on the lawyer's door yet again to use their telephone. His fish eyes under that phony smile are more unsettling to me than ever."

John rummaged through his soft bag and produced two crumpled packets. "If you don't want to cook, it's mixed nuts and candied fruit in hard honey."

"Do you want to cook?" Lordis challenged.

"No indeed. I'm still fairly filled with cookies and cakes."

"Then I'll have to make do with what's in here." Lordis set out the contents of the icebox on the counter and began picking. "You indirectly asked Tubble for permission to give you seventy-two hours before he turns the investigation over to the police."

"Which is now sixty-six hours," John rejoined.

"So, tell me your plan of action to break this case open," Lordis said, using the jargon she had heard John exchange with his confederates in his detective agency.

"I am hopin' that Monsieur Abel is as able is he professes to be."

"How? As someone who worked in the Castries government?"

John shook his head. "As someone who must have lived in Castries at the same time as Innocente and her child."

Lordis swallowed what she was eating. "You are an excellent reader of what's going on behind the words people speak and the smiles they present. So, you must know this: even though we're not St. Lucian whites, we're whites nonetheless, and there is no love lost between Monsieur Abel and anyone with skin lighter than his."

John sampled a handful of nuts from one of the badly wrinkled bags. "True enough. But we both know he's an avaricious character. What did he say? 'Your pound *sterling* makes me rich this week.' Rich is like his chair and his hat; all three help separate him from the common workers. In that regard he's no better than the people he loathes. Maybe even worse." He popped a few nuts into his mouth, gave them several chews, and added, "I could also tell from his sneer and his remarks about Carlisle Thiery bein' 'grand' and wantin' to spoil the island with white vacationers that the almost-white lawyer is high on his hate list. I'm thinkin' that the lure of money, combined with his history, will turn him into a particularly effective apprentice detective."

"If we can find him."

John plucked a single piece from the candy bag. "He's bound to be somewhere around Anse-la-Raye. We'll get a buggy and hie on down there early tomorrow. But before that, I'm gonna do a bit more detective work myself."

---

THE SMALL STABLE at the back of the Thiery residence had barely enough room for its horse and carriage. A shallow shed connected to the wall farthest from the house, built with a pair of wide doors that were secured by a padlock. John stood in the darkness, listening to the muffled movements of the Thierys' horse. In his hands he held one of the dental picks he had purchased and a second tool he had fashioned from piano wire. To his relief, the sliver of moon was hidden by the hill and trees to his side. Although he carried in a trouser pocket the torchlight he had purchased in Castries, he did not need it. As with all locks, the workings were out of view, requiring the use of his mind's eye to imagine the placement and number of the actuating pins. John breathed a sigh of relief when his touch told him the padlock was not one of the new variety that used revolving actuators.

After several minutes of patient manipulation, John felt the padlock release. He carefully replaced his lock picking tools in a small case he had purchased, then brought out the flashlight and readied it. With the opposite hand, he lifted the padlock off its hinge and nudged one of the doors back. It groaned like a castle drawbridge rising.

John winced at the noise. For all his lock-picking preparation, he had neglected to purchase a small can of machine oil to silence hinges that were sure to have at least some rust from the humid climate. He opened both doors halfway and shone the flashlight inside.

The shed was divided in two. Half was open from top to bottom, allowing the storage of a wheelbarrow and long-handled gardening tools. The other half had been divided into four shelves. What John hoped to find were cans of yellow and blue paint and perhaps a brush or two not completely cleaned of evidence. Although the light found a spool of electrical wire, a few boxes and jars of nails and screws, a mini tool chest with hammer, screwdrivers, and the like, not a single can of paint had been stored there.

A broad wash of illumination suddenly fell across the far side of the Thiery back yard.

John shut off the flashlight, swung the doors shut, which again produced a groaning noise, and snapped the padlock shut on the metal gear. He turned and loped away from the brightness that threatened to expose him. Within a few steps, he had come to the edge of the Thiery property, necessitating pressing himself through two barely yielding bushes in the neighboring property. He continued on until he came to the edge of the dark house. There, he caught his breath and listened for clues to what was happening around the Thiery stable. He thought he heard the padlock being tested. Half a minute later, he heard a door being closed.

Unfortunately, the Thiery stable and shed lay on the opposite side of the property from the house that the Le Bruns had rented. John knew he could not risk retracing his original route. Nor could he walk out into the road, where his figure could easily be spotted from the Thiery front door or veranda, backlit by the lights of Castries.

Sighing at his predicament, John realized the only prudent route to regain the rented house was the long, circuitous route up Morne Fortune and then down an old and precarious set of wooden steps to the winding road below. He waited another minute, standing like a garden statue, then walked into the near-total darkness.

As he trudged along dark La Toc Road, he realized that he would soon pass the wireless radio station where Sibyl Thiery worked. He reflected on the telegrams he had sent, which started him thinking about telegrams in general. His pace slowed involuntarily, until he had almost stopped moving.

Uttering a sharp grunt, John resumed his pace. As he moved, he fished his makeshift lock picking case from his pocket.

The government building that housed the wireless office had evidently not been deemed a great risk to breaking and entering. The front lock was simplicity itself for John to pick. He was inside within a minute. The door to the wireless office was similarly easy to open. What the detective sought was nothing of face value, but his hope was that information inside would be priceless to the solution of the crime.

From a lower shelf of the counter that had been created to separate customers from employees, John took the logbook. His knees creaked as he sat cross-legged on the floor. He placed his back against the counter and then set the logbook on his lap. He shone his flashlight close to the open pages so that the room would stay as dark as possible. He recalled that the arrival date of the *Pindy* had been June 24, ten days earlier. He saw that the office handled roughly one hundred incoming and outgoing messages each working day. The background information for such traffic took up about two pages in the log. John began with July 2 and worked backwards. He carefully perused the columns of sender and receiver names, the time and date the request was delivered, the worker keying the message, the time of outgoing transmissions, and confirmation of receipt. Both the information of his transmitted message to Mary McMahon in New York and to police headquarters in Bath, England, were neatly penned in on one of the July 1 pages. His left forefinger kept his place as the task grew more and more tedious.

Not surprisingly, many of the messages came and went to the British Isles since it was the parent home of the colony and since so much of the import and export traveled on British ships from and to British or Irish ports. What Le Brun hoped to see, however, escaped his good eye. And then he came to June 23. On that day, a message had been logged in Sibyl Thiery's handwriting as being sent to Carlisle Thiery. The place of origin was Bethnal Green. The long name took up the entire space of the row so that there was no indication it was a district of London. And yet John knew of the place since he had visited the great city. While he had not walked the streets of the lower-class neighborhood, he had seen the name on a detailed map that had been his constant companion during the visit. The entry had stood out slightly. Among all the other fastidiously penned lines, a single letter had clearly been written over. It was the tiny correction of one vowel for another, a mark that would have gone unnoticed even by the detective had he not been primed to see it.

John smiled broadly, closed the logbook, and returned it to its proper place.

---

JOHN UNLOCKED THE DOOR to the rented house. He had been certain that, even though he had taken more than an hour to return, Lordis would be waiting up for him. His only surprise was that not one light burned. Before he could set his second foot inside the front door, his wife's voice came to him out of the darkness.

"My God, you've had me worried," she said, although in a calm, soft voice.

"I nearly got caught." John closed the door. "No paint cans. Why the total darkness?"

"So none of our nosy neighbors could play Peeping Tom or require me to open the door and check to see if you were here as well." A shadow moved on the living room couch. "Give yourself a few more moments. Then let's feel our way into the bedroom. I figured if no one answered the door, they couldn't be sure if we were in or out."

"Good for you," John said, moving a single step into the entry. "As you figured, Carlisle would be too smart to save any can of yellow or blue paint. But I did learn somethin' more damnin'."

"In their stable?"

"No. At the office Sibyl is in charge of." John told of breaking in and studying the telegram office logbook. He concluded with, "If you think back, we arrived on St. Lucia on June 24. The day before, a message came from England. Here's what I envision happened. Sibyl received it and wrote down the place of origin, which was Bath. Then she saw that it was addressed to Peter Palmer, so she stopped enterin' information. The message said that his sister had somehow met her end. Not just in terms of her weddin' vows is Sibyl Thiery tied to her husband. If this white Tudor rose was willin' to marry a mulatto, she must have been sympathetic to his mistreatment by her countrymen. Perhaps she was a liberal, ready to do her part for the cause of true racial equality, even before meetin' Carlisle. At some point before or after they were wed he must have told her about his parentage."

"So Emeline was indeed Innocente and the son was Carlisle," Lordis understood.

"This telegram strongly suggests it." John leaned back against the door. "Mind you, I have no idea how an illegitimate mulatto could hope to benefit from exterminatin' the Palmer family, but whatever the message was, the gears meshed rapidly."

"One thing that would need to happen is for Carlisle to be ostensibly unaware that sister Penny was gone," Lordis said.

"Exactly! Sibyl knows this. She changes one of the letters she has already written down from an 'a' to an 'e.' Bath becomes Bethnal Green. She's also smart enough to realize that if Carlisle lays some claim to the Palmer estate that he will be suspected of the massacres. She can't fill in the name of someone else on the island, because that person would deny havin' received a telegram on June 23. So she writes down her husband's name and gives him the task of fabricatin' the reason for a telegram from a district in London."

John stood for long moments awaiting his wife's reply. "What are you thinkin'?" he asked her.

"This set of crimes is still very messy," Lordis said. "We don't have a motive nearly strong enough for murder on lawyer Thiery's part."

"We'll need to learn much more about his past and the laws of this island. That can be supplied by one or more other mulattoes and by Lieutenant Governor Tubble."

"We don't know the content of the telegram," Lordis added.

"That compounds the mess," John granted. "Sibyl is in charge of the telegram office and undoubtedly watchin' every transmission to and from England. The machine that automatically converts the code generates a tape that can be consulted in case verification is required. But evidently, from what I found, the tapes must be thrown away after three days. Even without the actual message, however, we now have a date to zero in on and a specific question about a death to pose to the Bath police."

"We also don't know who stole the awl," Lordis said.

"But we may soon."

"And we can't connect Carlisle directly to the crime. He was shepherding us around fairly late on Saturday and in church on Sunday. Narrow opportunity for murder clear across a Stygian-dark island."

John moved forward. "But not impossible, given the right motivation. Let us to bed, my love."

"Not until we finish this discussion."

"We know that, although he will never be admitted to the St. Lucia Island Club, that Carlisle knows a great deal about it. In fact, he makes it his business to know all sorts of goin's-on around the island. He surely knew that Peter Palmer was not on the list of members signed up for the night that I and Paul Van Fleet were guests. But Peter changed his mind at the last minute, unknown to Carlisle. When the Palmer mansion was entered by the murderers, Peter was not found. A very loose end indeed. The awl then was planted durin' the *Neg Maron* hunt, to drive Peter Palmer mad enough to shoot at and maybe kill Nigel Harvey. As both Harvey and Jacob Mansfield related, the young planter was quite hot-headed when aroused. I'm sure the death of his whole family had him tight as a violin string. A man like Carlisle would count on that. Especially if he's obsessed with Tristesse plantation."

Lordis said, "And then there's the matter of the third murderer. You're not suggesting that elegant Carlisle Thiery was one of the those who left those footprints, are you?"

"I suppose the Beaufort brothers could have enlisted a third person." John captured Lordis's hand and guided her up from the couch. "But if he is anythin', the lawyer is a very careful man. He surely believes the motto of the pirates of this part of the world: dead men tell no tales. If he included someone who did not owe him what the Beauforts do, the only way he could insure that the man did not later blackmail him or confess to the police would be to kill him. Dependin' on who that might be, such a murder could easily lead right back to him or the Beauforts. Big mess. But none of it solvable tonight. And so to bed, my love."

Lordis allowed herself to be led toward the bedroom, but not without a sound of disagreement in her throat. "I flatly refuse to believe that Monsieur Thiery would ever go barefoot on a plantation, where hookworms abound."

"Perhaps a great reward would merit a small risk," John responded. "One thing is certain: Carlisle Thiery did not count on me and you gettin' involved in solvin' this crime." John felt his wife's hand tighten around his and something like an electric pulse pass from her to him. "If he did indeed create two of those phony *Neg Maron* prints, he will not want to face a 'Cinderella and the glass slipper' situation. Whatever the truth, I bet the man will not sleep well tonight."

Lordis entered the bedroom without any further resistance. Under her breath, however, she said, "The question is, will we?"

# CHAPTER THIRTEEN

## July 4, 1910

DIRECTLY AFTER BREAKING their evening fast at a Castries café, John and Lordis filled their picnic basket at the open market, concentrating on baked goods. They had been given a ride down the mountain by Carlisle Thiery, who, not surprisingly, pumped them for information about their intentions for the day. John announced that they had been told the most beautiful beach on St. Lucia was at Marigot Bay, a treasure within paradise hidden from sight of the South Coast Road. They planned to laze in the shade, eat, and dash periodically in and out of the Caribbean for most of the day. Thiery allowed that their plan was a good one. He wondered aloud if their day signaled that John was satisfied with the result of his investigation.

"If I weren't, what more could I do?" John evaded. "I'm just a vacationer."

"A vacationer known in two major cities of the world for his ability to solve crimes," Carlisle countered.

John answered, "Be that as it may. I only became involved because I was hired by Nigel Harvey, and he's now in jail. I doubt that I'll be paid for the time I spent from my vacation, much less puttin' in more time."

"And how do you think I feel about my honeymoon being so interrupted?" Lordis added.

The lawyer nodded. "Well, I continue to be your designated host. Please don't hesitate to call on me with any question or for any need."

Once again, John rented a one-horse buggy to make the trip. He and Lordis indeed planned to visit Marigot Bay, but only after they had located Monsieur Abel. Duplicating their first drive, they detoured up the hill to Roseau. Neither Abel nor the men he oversaw were among the dense stands of banana plants. Looping around the valley, they continued into Anse-la-Raye.

To one inhabitant after the other, John called out, "*Avez-vous vu Monsieur Abel?*" The first man acted as if he had no experience with French. The second person, a woman, replied that she had no idea where he was. The second man indicated that he was in a bar facing the beach.

When Lordis and John entered the open-walled bar, they found the old man seated across from a crony, drinking rum with a half-depleted bottle in front of them. John knew the hour was not yet eleven o'clock. Abel recognized the pair and offered them a casual salute.

"I am spending your money for the good of St. Lucia," he said loudly as they came nearer. "Have you returned to give me more money?"

"Actually, we have," John said. Without uttering another word, he placed his hand on the small of Lordis's back and guided her away from the quasi-al fresco enterprise.

"He's still sitting there," Lordis worried after half a minute of alternately staring at the cove and its activities and glancing over her shoulder.

"Don't worry," John replied. "The man prides himself on his ability to make an easy shilling."

A moment later Abel sauntered from the bar, adjusting his Panama hat. He crooked his finger and indicated that the wife and husband should join him for a stroll along the beach.

"How can I become rich for more than a few days?" Abel asked.

John allowed Lordis to walk at the man's side, presenting her alluring profile and figure. He spoke to the native mulatto from directly behind. "We're tryin' to help the police solve a crime that happened on the other side of St. Lucia."

Abel twisted around to regard Le Brun with wiser eyes. He failed and stopped kicking through the soft sand. "You are the detective so many are talking about." He looked John up and down as if he had not seen him until that moment. "You don't look like a detective."

"And you don't look like the king of Anse-la-Raye and the former prince of Castries . . . but you are."

Abel laughed, showing several spaces where teeth were missing. "True. Very true."

"It is your former princely self that I wish to hire, to use your many connections in Castries to learn old secrets."

"What secrets?"

"The last time we talked to you, you said that you knew Carlisle Thiery. Or do you only know of him?"

Monsieur Abel stirred the sand with his foot. "He says he is of St. Lucia, but I know him only after he returned from England and began to practice the law. For all his peacock strutting, he seems to be pure St. Lucian. No one I know has ever thought any different."

John thought wryly, *It's incredible how much better your English has gotten in a few days. The prospect of real money can produce miracles.*

Aloud, he said, "I need to know about the man when he was a boy. As far back as you can learn. To his cradle, if that is possible."

The meshing gears of the mulatto's brain could almost be heard. "Perhaps I will get lucky with people I know and trust. I have never asked any of them for such information. But I think, soon enough I will also need to ask people who might then talk with the solicitor. He is not a good man to have as an enemy."

John reached for his billfold. "What do you care? You live in Anse-la-Raye." He opened the pocket where he kept his banknotes and pulled out three pounds.

Abel shook his head soberly. "Not enough."

"If you need to ask those who are not your friends, I will pay another three pounds."

"No. Six pounds now," Abel bargained. "And six more when I give you answers."

"I may never find you again," John said. "And then I will need to call myself a fool for paying so much up front. Four."

"No, six."

John placed his hand in the small of Lordis's back. "That other man was willin' for three. Let's go back to him." He turned Lordis around and walked several steps. Abel said nothing.

Lordis stopped short, playing the perfect accomplice in John's ploy. "But I believe Monsieur Abel is smarter, even though they both worked in Castries and for the government. Go as high as five."

John regarded the feline-eyed man under the Panama hat. "At the advice of my wife, I will go as high as five but not a penny more."

Abel grinned and held out his hand. "Not a penny more . . . unless I can speak of Monsieur Thiery in his cradle. Then you will pay me another five pounds."

John shook the thin, prominently veined hand. "It's a deal."

"Yes. I know this word. A deal."

"Ahoy! Lordis and John Le Brun!"

The trio on the beach looked out on the water. A heavy-set figure moved with some effort to lower the foresail on a twenty-foot Bermudan-type sloop. His companion worked at the headsail. Their spirited activity denied in John's mind for several seconds that he looked upon the Van Fleets. Then he waved back.

"We're taking advantage of my skills at sailing!" Paul called out. "Why don't you two join us on the return trip?"

"We have a jaunting cart," Lordis replied.

"You want this information as quickly as possible?" Abel asked. "Then let me return your carriage to Castries, and you sail back with your friends."

John counted the five pounds into Abel's eager hand. "Where will we find you in Castries?"

"I use a little hotel at the top of St. Louis Street. It is not a place for you two to visit. I will meet you after three o'clock tomorrow in the park at the side of the cathedral."

"We know it," John affirmed. He then told his new confederate which stable they had used to rent the two-wheeled buggy. Abel doffed his hat at the pair and hastened to the only buggy in the area.

The Van Fleets allowed the rented sloop to ease its nose into the shallow limit of the Caribbean water. "Haven't seen you two in a donkey's years," Paul said. "Are you still involved in that sensational set of murders everyone in Castries is talking about?"

"A little," John replied.

"Did you solve it?"

John shrugged. "The evidence is circumstantial. Best to let the police sort the rest out."

From near the buggy came a shrill whistle. Abel pointed to the ground, where he had left the Le Brun's picnic basket.

"Is he taking your buggy back to town?" Minerva asked.

"He is. As you know well, money can get you just about anythin'."

"True, true," Paul said. "So then, you've decided to sail back with us. That's good, because the island looks so much lovelier from the water."

"So much lovelier without snakes," Minerva added. "We've been up since the crack of dawn. Sailed down to look at the Pitons and thought we'd stop here since we hadn't on previous trips."

Paul surveyed what he could see of Anse-la-Raye, smirked, and sighed. "Looks about as bland and poor as Soufrière. The natural wonders and the climate are what recommend this place. Two weeks will have been more than enough for Minerva and me."

"So, you won't be recommendin' it to your cronies at the Metropolitan and New York Yacht Clubs?"

"I'll tell them about it, but, as you noted long ago, it's quite far from the U.S. of A. And then there's the issue of grinding poverty. If some of them want to come down, explore, and buy up land, that'll be their business. Meantime, there are far too many ways of making fortunes in our own country."

"Did you stop at Marigot Bay?" Lordis wanted to know.

"We saw it on the map, but we passed it before the sun had risen over the hills. And we didn't want to miss sailing to the Pitons."

"That's our main goal today," John said.

"Then give us a quick tour of this quaint hole in the wall, and we'll weigh anchor."

---

MARIGOT BAY WAS, in the estimation of all four vacationers, the best stretch of scenery on all of St. Lucia. It was what Paul called "a perfect hurricane hole," meaning that it was an ideal place to shelter boats during foul weather. Unlike several of the other harbors on the southwestern stretch of St. Lucia, the bay cut back deeply for hundreds of feet. It was surrounded on three sides by steep hills crowded with trees. Two of the hills shouldered up against the relatively narrow entrance to the bay. At the water's edge grew lines of coconut palms. The verticality of the hills discouraged dwellings, of which there were only four.

Paul spoke of an incident in the constant wars between the French and English naval and military forces in the Windward Islands and wondered aloud if Marigot Bay had been the place where one ingenious captain had sailed in with his outgunned ship and had it covered with branches and fronds to disguise its presence from the open sea.

On the last leg of the sail, which was less than three and a half nautical miles to the mouth of Castries's harbor, Minerva took the helm. John and Lordis served as mates, and Paul ate what had not been consumed of the combined lunches.

"I read two books on sailing before I set foot on a sailboat," Minerva told Lordis directly after she had been complimented on her feel for the stiff westerly breeze. Without exchanging so much as a swift look between them, John and Lordis knew that the Wall Street financier's grand wife had taken to heart the lowly rebel detective wife's admonition about reading.

The sail ended at a bit before four o'clock. As John and Lordis walked toward the New Bristol Hotel to rest in the lobby before having an early evening meal, they encountered Jacob Mansfield in the street.

"I'm coming from Lewis Norton's office," he shared, "regarding the particulars of what should and shouldn't be done to restore the mansion now that Peter is dead. Everything is on hold until Penelope is located."

"That's proving more difficult than one would think, don't you agree?" John asked.

"Perhaps not," the estate overseer said. "I don't think she cares a whit what happens to the plantation, even given the money she stands to make from it."

John set his hands lightly on Lordis's shoulders. "Stay right there, dear heart." He then placed himself facing the nearest building, compelling Mansfield to adjust his place on the sidewalk. "Are you returnin' to Tristesse today?"

"Immediately," Mansfield answered, the space above the bridge of his nose furrowed with his anticipation.

"Good. You had best be alert to the possibility that someone may try to break into the barn that held the molds."

"Why? They're all gone."

"Not everyone knows that."

"So, you're hoping someone breaks into the barn?"

"It might complete the case," John said.

Mansfield drew himself up to his six-foot-two height. "If I'm not in the loft, someone I trust implicitly will be."

"Whoever's in there should be well-armed and prepared to shoot."

"I wouldn't mind shooting a bastard or two. Is there anything else I can do to see that the Palmers are avenged?"

Le Brun considered the offer for several moments. "Just stay vigilant. I needn't remind you that you've already had two horrendous incidents on the plantation."

---

AS SOON AS THE Le Bruns were dropped off on Morne Fortune, they walked to the Thiery home. The sounds of the piano filtered down once more through the front garden, slightly more secure in their tempo and note choice than the day the instrument had arrived.

Emeline answered the door and looked mildly pleased to see the detective and his wife.

"Considering all the kindnesses your son has shown toward us," Lordis said, after their initial greeting, "Mr. Le Brun and I would very much like to invite you all to dinner in Castries."

"How lovely," the household's still-young dowager declared. "However, I have prepared the dinner for Victoria, Elizabeth, and myself. I'm sure that my son and daughter-in-law would be pleased to accept."

"Is seven too early?" Lordis asked.

"Perhaps seven-thirty," Emeline countered. "Monsieur Thiery has been dreadfully busy with his practice of late. The extra half-hour will give him time to shower and change clothes. Have you eaten at La Croix?"

"We have not."

"Excellent food at reasonable prices," Emeline said with placid certainty.

---

THE TWO COUPLES traveled down the mountain in the Thiery carriage. The restaurant was close enough to the harbor to smell the tang of the salt water, clean, and gaily lit but far from up-scale. The greeter and waiter both addressed Carlisle as merely "Monsieur," and he accepted the title as a deserved sign of respect.

As the men seated their ladies, John observed that Carlisle wore an ecru suit, slightly darker than his normal choice. He also wore a different tie.

"Are those the scales of Lady Justice?" John asked.

Carlisle fished the tie out from between his lapels and looked down. "Absolutely. I purchased this in the same shop as my Cambridge University tie. Many of the students wear this reminder of equality under the law."

"No blindfolded-woman-holdin'-a-sword ties?" John quipped.

"No."

"Perhaps because Justice rarely is blind. It ought to be. But, even in courts, life is not completely fair."

"I work to see that it is," Carlisle rebutted, even as he sat and picked up his menu.

"Minus the sword, of course," John said, doing his best to make his smile look natural. "Have you spoken with the Van Fleets recently?"

"Not yesterday or today."

"We were with them most of the day," John said, to suggest further that he had abandoned the Palmer murders investigation. "Sailin'."

"How lovely," Sibyl enthused.

John leaned toward the lawyer in a conspiratorial manner and dropped his voice level. "You'll want to know that his intent is to act like he's not that interested in the resort idea. Would the word be 'indifferent'?"

"Perhaps 'diffident,'" Carlisle said.

John snapped his fingers. "An impressive sound there. Is that a legal term?"

"No. Just a little-used word."

"In short, he'll try to depress the whole lot of you owners, front men and so forth. But he's hot on the idea."

Lordis contributed a sharp nod as her part of the lie.

"And why would you tell me this?" Thiery asked.

"Because I'm not one of the rich inner circle. All I'll get for bringin' home a glowin' report will be a hearty pat on the back and an 'attaboy.' You, on the other hand, are a fair man and much more likely to give pecuniary reward where it's due."

From behind his raised menu, Carlisle said, "Pecuniary? It's a wonder you know that term and not 'diffident.'"

"Because it's a money term. Like lucre, legal tender, currency, cabbage, mazuma, moolah." John stopped when he had succeeded in raising both the Thierys' sets of eyebrows. "It's true that I won't stoop to increasin' our wealth by illegal means," he said, setting his hand on Lordis's, "but I am always on the lookout for well-thought-out plans and good partners. My observations of your dress and your home shout, Monsieur and Madame Thiery, that you two are of the same mind. More importantly, as a man highly knowledgeable of the law, you know precisely how to make things happen in St. Lucia. I believe alignin' with you is the smart move."

"You are correct on all counts, Mr. Le Brun. The highest-paid real estate or corporate lawyer from New York or London would be at sixes and sevens on our island."

"Why is that?" Lordis asked.

"Because of St. Lucia's checkered history. Years as a French colony, then a few as a British colony, then French, then British. What has survived is a legal system unlike any other island in the Caribbean. Unless I am mistaken, it is unlike any other country in the world." Thiery's face had slowly transformed to a mask of supreme self-satisfaction. "Our common law is English, and our civil code is French."

"Astonishin'! Do go on," John encouraged.

"Ah, no. It is a subject much too tedious for dinner conversation," Carlisle declared. "And much too premature. Plenty of time to explain the interesting possibilities this . . . mixed marriage can produce if American cash begins to flow into St. Lucia." He set down his menu. "I suggest their fresh fish steaks cooked in onion, garlic, and tomato sauce and served with rice and plantains."

# CHAPTER FOURTEEN

## July 5, 1910

AS LORDIS HAD PREDICTED for the previous night's sleep, John was unable to find oblivion until well toward morning. He had reviewed several times all apparently pertinent events he had experienced since landing on St. Lucia. Later into the small hours, he had gone over every sentence that he could recall uttered by anyone who might have hatched the plan to murder the Palmers. Again and again, the events, the words, the motivations pointed to Carlisle Thiery. And yet, in spite of the accruing evidence, he was equally certain that a man as smart as "Monsieur," a man armed with all the knowledge of a Cambridge Law School education, could triumph in a court by using the fundamental demand of "found guilty beyond a reasonable doubt." He wondered if the lawyer was so clever that he was purposely inviting a trial. Under English and French law, once he was found innocent he could not be tried again for the same crimes under the "double jeopardy" defense and the plea of *autrefois acquit,* translated as "already been acquitted." In John's mind, the strategy would virtually be required if Thiery laid claim to the Palmer plantation as the bastard son of Henry. Combined with the amassed evidence, such a claim made before a trial would be sufficient motivation for a white or even mixed-white-and-mulatto jury to convict Thiery. If John's vacation had enlightened him in only one matter, it was that mulattoes were directly and indirectly indoctrinated to hate everyone, their own kind included, and to begrudge the sudden fortune of any other citizen with so-called mixed blood.

The more Le Brun thought about Carlisle Thiery beating the law because of lack of hard evidence, the more desperate he became to find it. The element of motivation was not enough. The equivalent of taking his opponent's queen piece would be to prove that the lawyer was on the Palmer plantation on the night of the murders. One of the molds might indeed conform to "Monsieur's" bare foot, but John felt it was not enough. The many people on St. Lucia who knew Thiery would burst into laughter at the idea that the sartorially perfect lawyer would ever take off his shoes and run with exposed soles through tainted plantation soil.

John finally found sleep after he assembled his list of all positive actions for the day that had already begun.

When he awoke, John saw that Lordis had risen and left the bedroom. He found her dusting the rented living room. The woman who had done more than half the menial work in a mansion for many years was incapable of abiding dirt or untidiness anywhere around her. When she thought she was alone in other people's houses, she fluffed bolsters and straightened crooked paintings.

John crept up behind Lordis and wrapped his arms around her waist. She jolted slightly at the unanticipated hug.

"Lazy lie-a-bed," she scolded good-naturedly.

"You smell extra fresh," he said.

"I washed this dress and hung it out yesterday. That's the island air."

"What time is it?" John asked.

"After eight. I walked over to the Thierys' and asked the grande dame if she would call the hotel and have a carriage sent up for us."

"I see." John looked through the gauzy front curtain. "I also see that the sky is not very blue today."

"No. And when you go outside, you'll also feel the high humidity. There's a weather change happening. Gray clouds, drop in temperature. Definitely need to carry our umbrellas."

John released his hold. "Then I had better shake a leg."

"Shake them both," Lordis said.

---

JOHN HAD SEVERAL ITEMS on his list to be attended to before meeting Monsieur Abel at three o'clock in Castries's main park. He wanted to visit the Boulton shoemaking shop, followed by Lieutenant Governor Tubble's office. He also wanted to ask Lewis Norton, the Palmer lawyer, a few questions.

While breakfasting at the Dolphin Café, John found a discarded copy of the *Illustrated London News.* On the third page was a column detailing the run up to a conference that would create a Japan-Korea unity. Japan would formally annex Korea, which had already become a protectorate and then been deprived of its own administration of internal affairs by earlier treaties. The legality of the formal land grab was being disputed by the provisional government of the Republic of Korea, as well as branches of the governments of the United States, Canada, the United Kingdom, and Germany.

"Closer and closer to world war," John declared, after reading parts of the report to Lordis.

"I keep praying you're wrong," she replied.

"While the major powers keep preyin' on the rest of the world," John returned. He threw the newspaper down on a vacant chair. "I'm not sayin' it will come tomorrow, but every indicator points to its inevitability. What if Ben Jr. is eighteen when it breaks out?" he asked, speaking of one of Lordis's beloved former wards.

"What can ordinary citizens do?" Lordis asked, her face showing that John had awakened her fears with his last question.

"You can work for the cause of women's suffrage," John said. "History has proven that men are all too ready to go to war. Or to send foolish or powerless young men. Particularly the foreign market dealers, the men who make even bigger profits openin' overseas factories, the industrialists who control our politicians. A sudden rebalance with voters who have husbands and sons they don't want marchin' to war might prevent at least our country from enterin' into such folly."

Lordis looked at her husband in silence. She knew how often he had tried to reason with politicians, friends, newspapermen, and acquaintances with influence, and how often he had failed.

"Do you want another cup of coffee?" she asked.

John dug into his pocket for his billfold. "No. I'd only waste more time huntin' out bathrooms."

---

JOHN AND LORDIS entered the shoe shop of Edgar Boulton. It was a dusty and unkempt place, except in the cubbyholes where repaired and gleaming pairs of men's and women's shoes sat awaiting their owners' returns. No one watched the front of the shop, which was less than six feet deep. Somewhere behind a flimsy wall of unpainted composite board a machine whirred metallically. John pressed the counter bell several times.

The man who appeared was mulatto, the fawn-colored skin of his hands stained with boot black. He smiled broadly at his assumed customers.

"May I help you?"

"Mr. Boulton?" John said.

"Yes."

"My name is John Le Brun. I'm assistin' in the investigation of the murders at the Palmer plantation."

The man's smile slipped. "Assisting? Are you a St. Lucia policeman?"

"No, but–"

"I'll have you know that Lieutenant Governor Tubble came in here himself–"

"And asked you questions," John broke in. "When he was finished he told you to speak with no one else about the matter."

The shoe repairman blinked with surprise. "Exactly."

John produced the official letterhead signed by Richard Tubble empowering him to pursue the case. He opened it and held it up in front of Boulton's face. While the man's eyes scanned from line to line, he said, "I shall inform the lieutenant governor that you have faithfully obeyed those instructions. I have a few new questions, because we believe we have come closer to revealin' the persons behind the crime."

Boulton looked at Lordis, clearly wondering how the woman figured in the discussion.

"I'm with him," she said, nodding toward her husband.

"She's my assistant," John amplified. "Here is what I need to know: sometime between the day of the crime and the Wednesday after, did you have either of the followin' two mulatto women enter your premises?" John described first Sibyl and then Emeline Thiery in painstaking detail, including the sounds of their voices and their bearings. The description of Carlisle's wife produced no reaction, but the more John spoke of her mother-in-law, the more animated became the proprietor's face.

"Yes, the second one. You got her down to a 't.' She dressed very proper and waltzed in here like she was a duchess. It was almost exactly a week ago. Monday, as I recall."

"What did she say?"

"Nothing." Boulton held up his forefinger to halt interruption. "She came in right behind a black man who caused a major fuss. He said his name was Carter and that his father had left a pair of shoes here for repair more than three months ago. Had his story ready. His words came at me like a swarm of bees. Said the father was very forgetful, and when he—the son—had asked him where his black shoes were, he said he had dropped them off here but then forgot about them. This Carter said the shoes were expensive, which made me quite suspicious, since half the blacks on St. Lucia don't have a cheap pair of shoes much less dear ones. Anyway, I check my register back three, four, and five months and see no name of Carter. With that, the fellow says he can identify them and rushes past me into the shop. The back of the shop, where neither repaired shoes nor shoes to be worked on are stored."

"And what was the very proper lady doin' all this time?" John asked.

"Waiting patiently. I thought patiently, at least. It took me at least three more minutes to calm this Carter man down and get him out of my shop. By that time she had vanished. I assumed she was tired of waiting."

John angled to get a better view of the hinter area via an opening in the flimsy wall. "How many people work in your shop?"

"Sometimes my nephew helps. When he can't find better work. The rest of the time it's just me."

"And where is your bench?"

Boulton turned. "Right behind this wall. So I don't have far to walk when the bell rings."

"You never saw either the lady or the man who called himself Carter before that day?"

"Never. Nor since." The shoe repairman suddenly lost his patience. "Anything else?"

John checked with Lordis, whose smile lit her entire face. She said nothing.

Having folded up his document from the lieutenant governor, John pushed it back into his pocket. "You have been most helpful, but there is one more thing: as you were commanded by the police and Lieutenant Governor Tubble, continue to speak about this matter to no one. Even someone who presents an official-lookin' piece of paper."

Mr. Boulton's eyes went wide at the words. John winked and gestured for Lordis to precede him out of the shop.

"So, I'm at last your official assistant," Lordis said in a happy voice. "I need you to write that down on Le Brun Detective Agency letterhead."

---

LORDIS AND JOHN took the same seats they had on the previous visit to Richard Tubble's office. The lieutenant governor had looked harried on their entrance.

"I'm glad you're here. This holding of both Mr. Turner and the Harveys on suspicion of murder is a tricky thing. Especially if it's—as you believe—only to convince the real killers to let down their guards. The planters have gotten their friends to put a great deal of pressure on the police. Time is running out anyway, and my hands are tied in this."

"I understand," John said. "Let's see if we can't locate the final pieces."

Tubble's mood lightened slightly when he was told about Emeline Thiery's presence in the Boulton shoe repair shop.

"You do keep stitching together events," Tubble said, apparently unaware of the pun he had made. "But there still is no—as I heard a Londoner recently say—smoking gun."

"A very visual phrase. I've heard it used in public as well," John shared. "I first read it in my friend Arthur Conan Doyle's story, 'The Adventure of the Gloria Scott.'"

Tubble reacted as if he had been smacked. "You know Sir Arthur personally?"

"We worked together in London on a case," John said, unwilling to elevate himself further with the fact that the creator of Sherlock Holmes had served as his real-life Dr. Watson. John consulted his notebook. "Another interestin' fact to throw in the soup is that Lordis and I were almost bitten by two fer-de-lances on the path to Diamond Waterfall. We believe they were planted in our way by Gilles Beaufort, who had transported the snakes by means of a carriage basket."

"How awful! When do you two leave St. Lucia?" Tubble asked.

"In six days," Lordis jumped in.

Tubble folded his arms across his chest. "We'll need to take depositions from you two soon. Anything else?"

"Do you know or know of a *milat* named Abel? About fifty-five, with about half his teeth missin'. Probably a quadroon. Lives in Anse-la-Raye. Says he once worked here in Castries as a clerk in the government?"

Tubble shook his head to each fact. "Can't say as I do. If he's not lying, we can certainly find someone in this building who would know. Why?"

"We engaged him yesterday morning as our private eyes and ears. We arranged to meet with him in the park between Micoud and Brasil Streets this afternoon at three to get a report."

"Capital idea!" the lieutenant governor praised. "I'd like to come along with you."

"Is that wise?" Lordis asked John.

"It will be no louder a trumpet than you and me sittin' with him." To Tubble he said, "Is there any news about a third Beaufort brother?"

"Three sisters," the official replied, "but no other brother.

Some asking around has revealed that their cousin, Emmanuel, couldn't have abetted them. He was in Barbados the day before the murders and only got back last Thursday." Tubble unfolded his arms, placed his elbows on his desk, and set his chin on his hands in a posture as undignified as any the Le Bruns had witnessed. "Which suggests that Carlisle Thiery is the one who created the third set of footprints. Which seriously strains credulity."

"We know," John said. "Neither Lordis nor I can feature him runnin' through plantation mud . . . twice."

"We can put his foot in the molds, but even a good fit won't be enough. If he's guilty, we'll have to get him another way."

"What about your telegrams to Bath?" John asked.

"We received one saying the tea shops in Bath and the neighboring towns have all been visited, and none knows of a young wife originally from St. Lucia."

The pendulum clock on the back wall of the office chimed the third quarter-hour before three o'clock.

Lordis leaned forward. "Of course, if the Thierys are players in this case, the telegram you received could have been forged by Carlisle's wife. She is in charge of that office."

Tubble straightened up and tugged both of his jacket sleeves down. "I have thought of that. If Carlisle is formally accused, she will have to be pulled out of there and another telegram sent off."

"It's almost three," John said. "We should make our way to that park."

"Indeed," said Tubble.

---

THREE-THIRTY CAME and went, and Monsieur Abel failed to appear.

"There goes our five pounds," Lordis said glumly.

"I am quite surprised," John replied. He rose from the park

bench, scanning the area. "I pride myself on bein' an excellent judge of character. While that man is somethin' of a scoundrel, I believe he's also the kind who would not allow himself to break his word. He returned our jauntin' cart to the rental stable, as he promised to do." He turned to Richard Tubble. "He said he would be stayin' at a 'little hotel at the top of St. Louis Street.' Intimated that it's a bit sleazy."

"That would be the Fancy." Tubble said. "Named for a famous pirate ship, but a true irony when you see the place."

The trio walked the six blocks to the dilapidated rooming house. An elderly black man sitting on the front stoop and whittling a piece of wood into a fertility doll figure affirmed that Abel had taken a room the previous evening. He knew the mulatto well enough to supply the last name "Greenhut" to John's temporary employee.

"Second floor, way to da back," the informal clerk said.

Richard Tubble led the group up the stairs. The second floor had five doors, two on each side and one capping the hallway. Tubble stepped back so that John might knock. There was no response.

"Monsieur Abel?" John called out. "Mr. Greenhut?"

When he received no reply, Le Brun tried the doorknob. It turned easily. He pushed the door back, looked inside, and turned toward his companions.

"I want you to wait outside," he told Lordis.

She nodded and took a step backward, allowing the island's top official to move past her.

Abel Greenhut lay on his back atop the narrow bed, one foot on the floor, arms above his head. The frozen horror of his face indicated that his last moments had been terrible. He wore the same print shirt, cotton pants, and open-toed sandals he had worn when Lordis and John had first encountered him. The pockets of his trousers were turned out.

John surveyed the floor directly ahead of him before moving forward. "No sign of blood. Looks like he was strangled." He pointed to the bed. "Long depressions on either side of him. I'd say somebody fairly heavy kneeled over him. And the arms suggest somebody else pinned his arms to the mattress. Similar modus operandi to that of the Palmer clan murders."

"The Beaufort brothers at work again?" Tubble asked.

"I wouldn't doubt it." John gently touched the dead man's forehead, measuring his temperature. "This was done maybe an hour ago." He looked at Lordis. "You have Mr. Tubble's revolver on you?"

Lordis patted her soft purse. "Right in here."

"Good. Do us a favor, dear; hurry down to the New Bristol Hotel. Say that you'd like either Anton or Gilles to carry you up to the rented house to fetch somethin'. If they're there, say that you had looked for them at two o'clock and not found them. See what excuse is given. Then go through with the charade and come back to Castries." To Tubble he asked, "Where is the office of Lewis Norton?"

"Close by mine."

"Very well. Lordis, have whichever Beaufort chauffeurs you return to the main government office buildin'."

Lordis left without a word, carrying the pair of umbrellas she had been minding since the shoe shop, the striking of her heels making a minor racket on the desiccated wooden planking of the hotel hallway.

John took a handkerchief from his pocket. "You want answers in a hurry, and studyin' crime scenes is what I'm noted for. I'll disturb the place as little as possible. Please fetch the police and come back up as soon as you can."

"Very well," Tubble said. The hallway boards creaked again.

John stood over the corpse and spoke softly to it. "I know my apology is about as useful as tits on a bull, Monsieur Abel, but I promise to bring your killers to justice."

On the floor lay Abel's wallet. It had been cleaned out. John crossed to the open window, where a strong breeze blew the dingy curtains back and forth in a pendulum pattern. He looked outside and saw that a rusty iron fire escape led up to the third floor and had a counterweighted ladder that stretched down farther than the designer had intended toward the alley below. The wind, forced from a semi-wide street into a narrow alleyway, made a plaintive, moaning sound.

"Easy enough to reach by standin' on the seat of a buggy," John said to himself.

A wavering strand of thin off-white material caught his eye. It had been trapped by a weathered split in the outer frame of the window. John bent close to it and examined its length, color, thickness, and degree of roughness with his good eye. He made a sound of pleasure deep in his throat.

John stepped back and regarded the little room. To say that it had been ransacked would have been an overstatement since there was barely enough to toss. An ancient armoire lay open and empty. The surface of the tiny writing desk was barren but for a pencil, badly in need of sharpening, and Abel's Panama hat. John lifted the hat and found nothing under it. The desk had no drawers.

Next to the desk, an empty wastebasket lay on its side on the floor. The detective knelt down and peered under the bed. Other than a squadron of dust balls, the area was clear. The bottom of the mattress rested on four wooden slats. Nothing had been hidden there.

Le Brun stood. His mouth screwed up with an expression of vexation. "If there's anythin' under you," he said to the corpse, "which I sincerely doubt, it will have to be found by the police."

John wrestled the armoire out from the wall and peeked behind it. The rough back held nothing. Likewise, when he slid his hand back and forth under the bottom, he felt nothing. From his low position, he looked at the undersides of the writing desk and chair. Yet again, he was disappointed. He looked up at the ceiling and saw only the single electric light and fan combination that had been installed decades after the Fancy had been built. He stood on the chair and looked at the tops of the fan blades. Aside from layers of grime-cemented dust, nothing was attached to them.

In frustration, John dropped his bottom onto the chair and resigned himself to wait for the police. He used his handkerchief to blow his nose, which threatened to sneeze from the roomful of disturbed dust. He folded the cloth neatly and returned it to his pocket. He drummed his knuckles impatiently along the edge of the writing desk. His gaze fell on the Panama hat. Its image fetched from his memory an incident when he had saved his life and that of Lordis by hiding a Derringer under his derby. Whenever he traveled distances or expected danger, he brought along the small weapon and concealed it under his left shirt sleeve secured with rubber bands.

John lifted the hat from the desk and peeked under it. Shaped into a U, with edges fitted into either extreme of the inside sweatband, was a legal-size envelope.

"You sly fox," John said softly, as he wriggled the envelope out from inside the crown. He read the jottings:

*Carlisle mother Emeline grandmother Jetia arrive Castries 1879 work as cook daughter seamstress baby boy house halfway up Morne Doudon weekly visits for several years by white man maybe forty son good student well liked*

John tucked the envelope into his pocket, not content with turning it over to anyone but Richard Tubble.

Police Chief Dautry arrived fifteen minutes later with two subalterns. Richard Tubble was reported to have returned to his office. John emphasized that his fingers had touched nothing but the corpse's forehead and the Panama hat. He offered his observations and invited the policemen to verify his findings. When the policeman with corporal stripes began to take photographs, John pointed outside the open window.

"You should take at least one shot of the piece of horsehair stuck in this window frame. Then collect it."

Dautry laughed. "Did a horse kill the man?"

"No. But I think a man who plays a violin did."

All three policemen looked at Le Brun as if he were insane.

"Anton Beaufort is a violinist. The bow that moves across his strings has stretched hair taken from a horse's tail. One of those hairs probably stuck to his clothing and came off when he squeezed through the window frame."

"How can that be useful?" Dautry asked. "There are thousands of horses on St. Lucia."

"Not the kind that musical bows need," John replied. "The hair must be extra coarse and strong. The types of tail hairs that are used belong to Siberian, Mongolian, and Polish horses."

"Why?"

"Because the earth's orbit around the sun is not a perfect circle, and because its axis of spin is tilted. Which makes for colder, harsher winters in Siberia, Mongolia, and Poland than just about any other inhabited places between the polar circles. Which make for thicker, coarser, stronger tail hairs."

"Jesus!" one of the under-officers exclaimed, gazing at John with awed respect.

"The use of an ordinary microscope by a skilled veterinarian or zoologist will confirm that the hair comes from one of the horses I named. Then you need only determine if it matches the hairs on Anton Beaufort's bow."

"Take the damned photograph, Hutchinson!" Dautry ordered. "Then take the hair!"

"I'll leave you to do the dirty work," John said as he moved toward the door. "I'm scheduled to meet with Lieutenant Governor Tubble."

Dautry merely nodded.

To save time, John hailed a hack and directed the driver

to the government headquarters. He studied the sky as they maneuvered through Castries's streets.

"Clouds are gettin' lower and thicker," he commented to the black driver.

"Storm surely coming," the man shared. "Not a hurricane. But some tropical storms can be plenty bad as well."

Errant drops of rain were falling by the time the for-hire carriage stopped in front of the large white building. Lordis stood at the entrance, one of their umbrellas raised. John paid the driver and hurried to her side.

"Both the Beauforts took off at noon and told the clerk that they were working for their cousin the rest of the day," Lordis reported.

"Opportunity confirmed." John consulted his pocket watch. "Quarter to five. If we don't hurry, lawyer Norton is sure to close his office for the day."

"No, he won't." Lordis pointed down the street. "It's right there, next to the courthouse. Mr. Tubble went inside just before you arrived and left me here to bring you."

---

A MALE SECRETARY ushered the Le Bruns into Lewis Norton's inner sanctum. The lawyer was hoary old, with shocks of wild white hair poking out from the few places where he was not bald. He offered a smile that rearranged ranks of wrinkles and showed a row of top teeth too straight and white not to be false. Norton had never been a tall man, but the shrinkage of old age and arthritis made him almost gnome-like in appearance. His blue eyes, however, glowed with intelligence. He shook John's hand and touched Lordis's fingertips with a perfunctory kiss.

"Welcome, welcome! So, you want information that might help solve your investigation."

"We do," John affirmed. "I understand that the formal procedure allowin' you to make the contents of Peter Palmer's will available has been completed."

"It has." Norton tapped his forefinger on the white pages contained within an outer protective manila folder. "In the event of the death of all members of Peter Palmer's family on St. Lucia, the sole inheritor is his sister, named as Penelope Anne Palmer."

"Who we have heard is married and livin' in England," John said.

"But which has yet to be proven," Richard Tubble added immediately.

"That is my understanding . . . from you, in fact," Norton said to the lieutenant governor.

"What should happen if this sister cannot be found?" John asked.

The old lawyer paused to form his words. "We have never had such an instance concerning a large estate on St. Lucia. However, I have checked the laws of neighboring islands and of the United Kingdom. The unanimous precedent is that, in the case of a failed gift, the estate should be held custodial for a period of no less than seven years while a legitimate next of kin is assiduously searched out. Failing success, the land would lapse to the general weal."

"Meanin' if Penelope or all other relatives are never found or dead, St. Lucia would own the land and its assets and sell it," John translated, having years before tired of the jargon such as "failed gift" and "general weal" that lawyers used to make themselves indispensable to the average person.

"Correct," Norton replied.

"Can a bastard son inherit the estate if no one else can be found?" John continued.

The question caused the lawyer to blink rapidly, open his mouth, and blink some more. Finally, he said, "Do you ask this out of direct knowledge of St. Lucia's laws?"

"No. I ask because of the evidence of this case."

"A bastard son, you say?" Norton sought to verify.

"More to the point, a mulatto bastard son of the father."

"I am very much interested in hearing as well," Richard Tubble broke in.

Lewis Norton inhaled deeply and set his hands firmly against the edge of his impressive mahogany desk. "Let me preface my answer to you, Mr. Le Brun. St. Lucia is unique in the Caribbean for the number of times it changed flags. Fourteen times between the French and the English. To say that the island's history and evolution has been chaotic is an understatement. The legal result is a system that, as far as I know, is unique in all the world. Our system combines English common law with French civil law. The upshot is that an illegitimate mulatto son of a plantation owner in the scenario you pose can indeed petition to inherit the estate. I assure you that it has never happened. I can also assure you that if it did occur, this island would be thrown into legal turmoil."

"Because no one who was not completely white has ever owned a plantation," Lordis stated, the accusatory tone in her voice unmistakable.

Richard Tubble said, "Lewis, these good folk are—as you know—strangers to our island. It's clear that they are not sufficiently educated to this little world as it truly exists."

"They're some of those American Progressives we hear about," Norton interpreted, his voice imparting his antipathy to such creatures.

"According to our Declaration of Independence," Lordis said evenly, "'We hold these truths to be self-evident, that all men are created equal, that they are endowed by their Creator with certain unalienable rights, that among these are Life, Liberty, and the pursuit of Happiness.'"

The lawyer shook his head slowly. "But my ear tells me that you two grew up in your South. The blacks who lived there, in spite of your Declaration, were not equal but slaves until the armies of the North freed them many decades after that proclamation was written."

"Nevertheless—"

"And even now, they are—as are our black citizens—unequal in spite of the laws. Similarly, your plantation owners deemed slaves to be property and, as such, felt the right to take desirable women to their beds. You have mulattoes as well . . . quadroons, octaroons. Favored mulatto offspring were freed to form their own middle class. Freedmen, who often became craftspeople." The judge settled back in his well-upholstered chair. "Now, I don't know how it is in your country, but our mulattoes look down on all blacks. They side with the whites and inform on the blacks. When a mulatto of very light skin argues with one of a darker shade, the usual parting shot, to put the darker one in his or her place, is the phrase 'Go home and look at your grandmother.' I can only imagine the tempest that a mulatto inheriting a plantation would create amongst all permutations of skin color." He looked out one of the windows of his office. "Far greater than what is blowing up outside, I predict."

"Perhaps it would be good to find out," Lordis said.

John placed a restraining hand atop his wife's wrist.

"And who is this man of color?" Lewis Norton wanted to know.

"I believe you'll find out in due course," John answered. "Although I highly doubt he will ever be in a position to lay claim to the Palmer plantation."

---

AS THE LIEUTENANT GOVERNOR and the two North Americans exited the lawyer's offices, the lights went off behind them. The rain had begun to fall with more intensity.

"A great deal needs to happen tomorrow," Tubble said. "Turner and the Harveys must be formally charged or released. Or at least one or the other will have to be let go."

"They're both innocent," John declared. "They can be

released, but it will alert the guilty parties that the investigation has focused in another direction."

"Which they will rightly assume is in their direction. Then Chief Dautry will have to determine the timing for arresting the Beauforts and Thiery." Tubble counted off points on his fingers. "We have the footprints. We have Emeline Thiery in the leather shop. We have Anton alone where the awl was dropped on the ground. We can throw in those snakes for what they're worth. We can use the afternoon disappearance of the Beauforts in conjunction with Abel Greenhut's death. If we're lucky, one of them might have left behind a fingerprint."

"You may also have a hair Anton left behind," John said. The lieutenant governor was obviously confused, but John only added, "Ask Chief Dautry."

Tubble said, "I shall indeed. In the next few days we can also scour Castries for people who knew the Thierys years ago."

"We have the chronology offered by the carpenter in Dennery," Lordis threw in.

John took Abel's envelope from the protection of his jacket pocket and passed it quickly to Tubble. "You know the expression 'Keep it under your hat?'"

"Yes. It means to keep a secret."

"It turns out Abel Greenhut did just that. It's intelligence he gathered concernin' the Thierys' early years in Castries. Which calls to mind another expression: 'This adds another nail to your coffin.' Your police will want to use it to do thorough canvassin' through your city's older population and get sworn depositions."

"In your estimation, Mr. Le Brun, will all of this be enough?" Tubble solicited.

John shrugged in answer. "I believe 'enough' will prove to be the condition of Penelope Palmer. Once you get Sibyl Thiery out of the wireless office and re-contact the Bath police, you may obtain that elusive critical item. I also think Carlisle's knowledge of St. Lucian law must also count."

The intensity of the rain increased. Tubble lowered the hand that held his open umbrella, so that it almost touched the top of his head. "My mind is like cottage cheese; I'm no good for anything more today. I'm retiring to Government House if you need to contact me. Please stay safe."

The lieutenant governor dashed off toward the government headquarters.

"This town is a long way from New York City," John said, "but I'm sure it's just as hard to find a cab in the pour-down rain. Let's head toward the New Bristol Hotel and see who they can scare up to carry us up the mountain."

While they walked, John related his search of Abel's hotel room and repeated verbatim the notes the man had made on the envelope. As he had predicted, no unengaged cab could be found along their route. Even with umbrellas canted toward the direction of the rain, the Le Bruns were soaked by the time the hotel came into view.

"Let's sprint the rest of the way," John suggested.

Instead, Lordis came to a halt. "Wait!"

"What?"

"That doctored wireless message from Bath arrived the day before we did."

John shook the rain off his face. "It did. What are you thinkin'?"

"If Penelope has indeed died, there would have been the possibility beyond a wireless message that the news could arrive on St. Lucia another way soon after. Say, by letter. In that case, Peter would immediately amend his will. He would probably name a more distant relative. For Carlisle Thiery to be absolutely sure of getting what he wants, all the Palmers needed to die quickly. That notwithstanding, a careful man like him would still take a day to evolve and refine a solid plan."

As Lordis spoke her thoughts with slow deliberation, John looked longingly toward the protection of the hotel veranda. At the same time, he knew his mate was not the sort of woman too simple to first seek shelter before speaking unless there was a good reason. "I agree. But what does that have to do with us standin' out here?"

Lordis pivoted her head dramatically in the direction of the apothecary shop that stood across the street from the hotel. "Do you recall me visiting that place for cramping medicine?"

"Yes, of course."

"Who did I say I saw leaving it carrying a white paper sack?"

John felt the kindling of a warm glow in the pit of his stomach. He thought, *The Palmers weren't poisoned. It's highly unlikely Carlisle could have arranged to drug them to sleep. And yet the visit was made between the receipt of the telegram and the murders.* "Carlisle Thiery," he answered his wife. "But what was inside the sack?"

"We must find out," Lordis countered. "He certainly wasn't acting that day as if he were ailing in any way."

"It is indeed worth an inquiry." John nodded in the direction of the hotel. "Why don't you dry off a bit in the comfort of the New Bristol while I do a bit of snoopin'?"

At her husband's suggestion, Lordis wilted slightly.

"The druggist might be a good friend of Carlisle's," John argued. "If we go in there together, he could peg us for the gadfly couple tormentin' his longtime customer and clam up."

"You're right," Lordis acceded. "I'll wait for you on tenterhooks."

The pair separated. John determined to disguise his place of origin. Among his varied pursuits, he had several times taken roles in theatrical events. His favorite playwright was William Shakespeare. Once, at the Player's Club, he had been goaded into reciting the lines of the Bloody Sergeant from the Bard's *Macbeth* and been rewarded with a robust cheer from the gathered professionals.

"'Doubtful it stood,'" he recited, toning up his English accent, "'As two spent swimmers that do cling together/And choke their art.'"

Reassured by what he heard, John walked into the shop. A bell attached to the door jamb jingled as he entered. A middle-aged man dressed in a white smock stood behind the back counter grinding a mixture of powders with mortar and pestle. He stared at his work through pince-nez spectacles.

"Frightful night, what?" John complained, doing his level best to approximate the accents and language he had heard in the London clubs.

"True enough. Our first tropical storm of the season," the pale-skinned apothecary replied. "May I help you?"

John took a step closer. "I'm here at the recommendation of Monsieur Carlisle Thiery."

"I see."

"I would like you to fill for me the same order he placed two Fridays past. Do you recall it?"

The man's eyebrows shot up. "I certainly do. Are you worried about hookworms as well?"

John struggled to maintain his façade of composure. "I am."

"Were you with him when he stepped out of his shoes?"

"No. In fact, he neglected to tell me the circumstances of his possible exposure."

The druggist pushed the mixing bowl and masher to one side. "As I recall, he was inspecting his plots of bananas."

"Down at Anse-la-Raye," John was delighted to remark.

"Exactly. The ground was muddier than he expected, and he happened to step out of both shoes at nearly the same moment. I admitted that hookworm larvae might possibly wriggle up through stockings, but that the possibility was remote."

"However, being who he is, Carlisle would not take the risk," John supplied.

The druggist smiled as if he and John were sharing a great joke. Then he said, "And what circumstances have caused you to worry?"

"I'm from England, as I'm sure you've gathered. Here on business. I had no idea your island had this endemic problem.

I actually took off my boots at a plantation and soaked my hot and tired feet in a pool of water."

The apothecary winced. "Yes, your apprehension is more founded than Monsieur Thiery's."

"So, what precisely is it that you supplied him?"

"How long ago were you exposed?"

"Only a few hours."

The man nodded. "Then there is a great chance it will work, even if you have been exposed. I make up a mixture of Epsom salts, to dissolve the mucus membrane around the worm, and an extract of thyme oil as a biocide. Thyme is an amazing herb. It kills bacteria, worms, and fungus. In fact, it was used in ancient eras to prevent mummies from decaying."

"You don't say. How long will this take?"

The druggist spun around and began searching the shelves behind him. "I can mix it immediately. Fortunately for you, I have thyme oil left over from Monsieur Thiery's request."

---

JOHN LINGERED INSIDE the shop for ten minutes until the formulation was completed. While John had no use for it, he did not want the druggist to become suspicious about a man with an urgent story but no real interest in the purchase of the cure. In that short span of time, however, the rain increased from shower to sheets. Westward-blowing gusts of wind drove it downward at almost a forty-five-degree angle. Umbrellas were useless.

John dashed across the street and into the New Bristol Hotel.

"Luck?" Lordis asked from her place at one of the front windows.

"Better than that. You are a genius," John praised.

Lordis grinned her pleasure for only a moment, then returned her gaze to the street with knit eyebrows. "Tell me when we're safe and warm. There's not a carriage for hire out here."

John wiped the accumulated raindrops from his face. "We may be stuck here in Castries for the night. That might be better than bravin' this blow on the top of a mountain."

"If we don't get pneumonia for lack of a change of clothes," Lordis rejoined.

John pointed down the street. "Hold on. A possible savior."

When he saw the Le Bruns exit the hotel, Raymond Scott angled his carriage toward them, letting one hand slip from the reins just long enough to wave. The president of the St. Lucia Island Club wore the sort of rubberized gear used by deep sea fishermen. Behind him, the carriage interior was protected by isinglass curtains, which John had not seen before but knew were a semi-transparent material fashioned from the bladders of such large fish as sturgeon and cod.

Scott slowed his buggy. "Why are you two out here?"

"We can't find a hackney to take us up to our rented house on Morne Fortune."

Scott pulled hard on the reins. "I dare not say this is your lucky day, but I can bring you up there. I'm heading back to my plantation as quickly as I can. Do you feel the low pressure?"

"Yes. Around my eyes," Lordis replied.

Scott pushed one of the curtains aside. "Come on, get in! We're very attuned to air pressure in the islands. I can tell you this will become even worse."

The Le Bruns hastened into the carriage.

"Is there any news about whether Turner or Harvey is the guilty party?" the club president called loudly, to pierce the whistling wind.

"Not right now, but there should be soon."

"I hope so. Word of our tragedy has reached other islands in the chain," Scott imparted. "I came here today to negotiate an export contract, and that's all the agent wanted to talk about. Put me a good fifteen minutes behind my time."

John said. "I want to thank you most kindly for pickin' us up, Mr. Scott."

Scott's horses clip-clopped apace through the back streets of Castries. "Thank me when you're inside, safe and sound. I'm quite leery of the hairpin turns ahead of us; the climb up the Morne in such weather is devilishly slippery."

John looked at Lordis, whose eyes were wide with apprehension. She leaned close to her husband's ear and softly said, "If anyone creates a resort down here, they had better shut it down from July to October. This is more like perdition than paradise."

The trip up the mountain was as treacherous as the plantation owner had warned. The road was made slippery by numerous rivulets wending down it. Given the blinding rain, yielding roadbed, and unnatural darkness of the hour, the horses grew increasingly skittish and resisted the snapping of their reins to keep up the carriage's momentum. As the driver urged them around one of the switchback turns, a bolt of lightning pierced the thick clouds. Five seconds later, the crashing sound of the superheated atmosphere reached the carriage. The horse on the inner side of the turn reared to the limit of its traces. Both animals whinnied in fright. To his credit, Scott kept them under control, but John came within a breath of asking him to stop so that he and Lordis could walk the rest of the way.

"Are you sure you shouldn't tie up your horses at the house and stay with us until this passes?" John yelled to Scott.

"Is there a stable on the property?" the man returned.

"A small one. But I don't have the key."

"Then I'll push on. My horses are high-strung. If I leave them outside, they'll snap the reins, destroy the rig, and gallop over a cliff."

At last, the rented house appeared through the curtains of rain. John called out to Scott, who halted the carriage in the middle of a stretch of road that people in John's home region called a "thank-you-ma'am." John helped Lordis down onto the briefly level lane with its right-angled dip that encouraged water runoff. Both he and Lordis called out their immense gratitude.

A second later, Scott, his team, and the carriage were moving again, climbing into the force of the rain.

"Hurry, John!" Lordis exclaimed. She started running up the incline of the road. Before John could warn her, her right shoe landed in a mass of mud and never settled on solid ground. Her leg flew backward, counter to the momentum of the rest of her body. Uttering a cry of dismay, she landed first on her hands, then her upper chest, with her legs splayed into an awkward approximation of an athletic split.

John dropped his paper sack with the druggist's prescription and moved as fast as he dared toward his wife. "Are you all right?"

Lordis turned over onto her backside, holding her hands palm-up to allow the pelting rain to remove the mud. "No. Ow! I pulled something in my upper leg. But nothing is broken. Ow! Blast!"

"I'll carry you," John volunteered as he knelt beside her.

"Absolutely not! Then we'd both go down. Just help me up and give me your shoulder for my right arm."

The pair made their way carefully onto the rented property, up the stairs, and onto the small front porch. The slanting rain beat against their sides and backs as John found the front door key and fitted it into the lock. He stepped back and shepherded Lordis inside, then swung through the space and shut the door with force.

"Can you stand by yourself?" he asked.

"Barely. But my leg doesn't want to move. Help me over to the couch."

Once he had Lordis down and had positioned the coffee table so that she could elevate her leg, John returned to the room's front wall. He found the light switch and rotated it on. Electricity had been added to the home less than a decade earlier. The work had been done via metal channels attached to the walls, baseboards, and ceiling. What there was of it had been deemed sorely wanting in the estimation of both the Le Bruns. A single clear bulb shone from a utilitarian fixture in the middle of the parlor. It came on with an orange-yellow glow, indicating that the source of its power was being overtaxed.

A fleeting wash of light, softened by masses of dense clouds, came through the front windows. Lordis and John counted in silence. At nine seconds they heard the roll of thunder, like a flourish from a kettle drum.

As quickly as John could manage, he informed her of the excellent news concerning the druggist's formulation of a medicine to kill hookworms. "Far as I'm concerned, that's the final nail for Thiery's coffin."

"But we're the only ones who know it," Lordis worried.

"Unfortunately. This storm is most inopportune," John said, as he gently positioned a throw pillow under her heel and ankle. "For a minute, I played with the idea of askin' Mr. Scott if he would carry us over to Government House. But we already imposed on him too much."

"Because the lieutenant governor has a telephone," Lordis understood, as she hitched up her soaked dress and began massaging her leg.

"Correct. The minute this storm lets up, there need to be several men with guns bangin' on Monsieur Carlisle's door."

Lordis tugged her dress upward, which clung tenaciously to her wet skin and resisted removal. "Well, that will have to wait until this storm passes. Would you fetch me a towel, my hairbrush, and my nightdress, John? And my purse?"

A light went on in the upper hallway and went off a minute later. John returned and set the requested items next to Lordis on the couch. "I'm goin' on foot."

"Where?"

"First up to the top, where that little military outpost is. You know, the one with the honor guard for the fort."

"Don't be ridiculous," Lordis snapped.

"Why not? I can't get any wetter than I already am. And I don't like the idea of the Thierys bein' left at large. Not after Monsieur Abel was murdered."

"The Beaufort brothers no doubt did that," Lordis argued. "And probably without consulting the man who hired them."

"Nevertheless. The ante is way up. I can roust those soldiers and get them to come with me back down to Government House. Then—under Mr. Tubble's orders—they can arrest Carlisle and lock him in one of those cells we saw in the bowels of the fort."

"And, meantime, I'm left here with only one good leg."

Jagged fingers of lightning tore down from the sky striking tall objects not more than a few hundred feet from the house. Instantly, the room became black and formless. A sharp clap of thunder shook the walls and window panes.

John crossed the space with caution, turned the light switch to its off position, and secured the door lock. "Actually, this storm is a bit of good luck. It will discourage the Thierys from leavin' home. Their girls are probably screamin' their lungs out right about now. Even if the power comes back on, stay in the darkness."

"I'm not moving from this couch."

"Fine. If I were Monsieur Thiery, I would reason that we were most likely stuck in Castries. Even if someone knocks, don't answer. I'll take the key with me. Locked door. No lights. You safe and warm as a bug in a rug."

Lordis finished toweling herself off. She reached for her soft purse. "I can take care of myself. I'll just sit in the dark and say my prayers like a good girl."

John returned to the couch, bent over, and pressed a kiss against Lordis's lips. "For luck."

"I don't need luck," she protested.

"No, for me. I'm goin' out the back way in case Mother Thiery is glued to one of the front windows. I'll return in two shakes of a lamb's tail."

Lordis listened to John exit through the back door. She removed her waterlogged bust bodice and wriggled out of her panties. Shivering, she tugged down her nightdress and arranged the hem around her legs. For a time, she did as she said she would, reciting several prayers. Then, hearing the sound of the Thiery's piano inside her head, she began to hum softly the melody to "Twinkle, Twinkle, Little Star." As she moved on to "Jeannie with the Light Brown Hair," the second stanza stuck in her throat. The sound of a squeaking door came from the back of the property. She twisted around as far as her sprained thigh would allow and looked through the parlor back window. She saw a long shaft of light playing through the strings of rain, slowly sweeping the rear of the house.

"Steady, girl," Lordis counseled herself in a tiny voice. Her hand stole into her purse.

About a minute later, the same beam of light appeared on the front porch. The hard rain disguised all other outside sounds. She could discern nothing until another bolt of lightning illuminated the land to the north, where Castries lay. In the window, not one but two figures stood on the porch.

Lordis gasped and opened her eyelids as wide as possible, straining to gather any faint image. She expected a knock at the door. Instead, she heard a key being inserted. She watched as the door swung slowly open. A distant lightning strike threw off enough brilliance to allow Lordis to see the shapes of a medium-tall man and woman.

The torch light angled into the room. Initially, it played around the floor. Then its beam raised. Within moments, its throw blinded her.

"Mrs. Le Brun, where is your husband?" the lawyer asked.

"Whatever happened to knocking?" Lordis answered, unable to keep her voice completely steady. "What has happened to your impeccable manners, Monsieur Thiery?" She listened to the light switch being turned to no success.

"I need the set of footprint molds that Jacob Mansfield loaded onto Gilles Beaufort's carriage on July the first."

"Those? Oh, we gave them to Lieutenant Governor Tubble, and he moved them up to Government House for safekeeping. You've already determined that they're not in this house's stable."

"Where I found fresh footprints," Carlisle said. "In the mud and the grass."

"Footprints? How ironic. No need to measure them; they belong to my husband. He's at Government House by now."

"Why would he go there? There's nobody but the lieutenant governor's family and a few of the staff."

"I know!" Emeline crowed triumphantly. "He's headed all the way up, to fetch the fort guards. His movement isn't only about the molds."

Carlisle laughed. "Isn't it good that our guests are foreigners?" His torchlight swung in his mother's direction. He carefully placed a metal ring holding two keys in her skirt pocket.

Emeline nodded as she thumbed on the flashlight in her left hand. "Those footprints. . . . If they were deep, it means he's carrying the molds."

"No. They were about as deep as mine."

"Which you will need to wipe out," Emeline said. "But his ignorant plan allows you some time. Make sure he didn't move the molds into this house since last we searched."

Using the light of his torch, Carlisle hurried into the house's back rooms.

"How smoothly you managed to move us up here," Lordis praised. "Unlike you two, we don't lie. We honestly gave the second set to the lieutenant governor for safekeeping."

"Pardon me if I don't believe you."

"Why not?" Lordis asked.

"Your husband is like me and my son; he needs to be in control."

"I don't understand," Lordis said.

"No, you wouldn't."

Lordis listened to the sounds of Carlisle's footsteps ascending the stairs. "Why don't you give yourselves up to the police?"

"When you two have uncovered so little hard evidence?"

Lordis adjusted her bad leg slightly. "Do you think so?"

For long seconds, the two women stared at each other in silence.

"Nothing," Carlisle reported as he came hurriedly down the staircase.

"Then go and stop him!" Emeline Thiery ordered. The throw of her torchlight caught her son's torso. His rain slicker was unbuttoned, revealing the identical outfit he had worn to greet the Le Bruns at the dock. The raw linen suit, white shirt, and light-colored Cambridge tie stood out boldly in the darkness.

The lawyer dashed through the open door and vanished into the night.

"I watched you take that nasty fall from up on my veranda," Emeline said. She closed the door and raised her flashlight to the level of Lordis's face. Her hand brushed against her pocket, and the keys jingled inside.

"You're the keeper of the keys," Lordis said, counting on the woman's vanity and her need to show just how clever she was in spite of her constrained life, wanting Emeline to brag on and on until John returned with help.

"Literally and figuratively. From that pillow and your raised leg, I assume you did yourself considerable damage."

"Nothing you need to sew up," Lordis answered.

"Yes, I'm also a seamstress."

"A professional seamstress," Lordis expanded. "I know it, because we employed an amateur detective, an old St. Lucian who has worn many hats in his lifetime."

"What else have you learned about me?"

"You were born to a cook for a white family on Martinique."

Lordis thought she heard a soft quick intake of air. "That you came over with one of the family daughters—the woman who was the second wife of Henry Palmer. That you were taken as his mistress at a shamefully young age and eventually became pregnant. And then the wife had you, your mother, and your baby boy thrown out." Lordis slowed her delivery, both to expend more time and to let the depth of what had been uncovered about the Thierys sink in. "But Henry loved you, Innocente."

Lordis's words caused Emeline to lower her flashlight so that the cast of light fell on the coffee table. It caught the female half of the paired porcelain figurines that John had taken from his suit pocket.

"How did you get that?" Emeline demanded.

"It was carried out of the Palmer plantation house during the fire. My husband found it on the ground."

"And took it as a souvenir?" the woman accused.

"Not at all," Lordis replied calmly. "My husband saved it from being trampled underfoot. It had already lost an arm. Look for yourself!"

Emeline took a step toward the figurine, then decided to maintain her distance.

"You have the male figure, don't you?" Lordis asked. "I'm sure it was given to you years ago by Henry."

A sob escaped the mulatto woman's throat. "Yes, Henry loved me. More than his wife. More even than Constance."

"Constance, who was beloved."

"I was adored. He told me so, over and over."

"But you weren't white. So he did the best by you that he could. He supported you in Castries, continued to visit you as often as possible," Lordis said in a hypnotic tone. "Paid for much of Carlisle's schooling."

"He loved Carlisle more than Peter."

"I don't doubt it. Your son is very smart."

This time, Emeline was silent. Lordis paused for several

seconds, then pushed on. "You also kept the fourth set of house keys. Those strangely shaped brass keys to the front and back doors of the Palmer mansion."

"That's what you meant about me keeping keys. But now they're gone, where no one will ever find them. They served their purpose. Nothing beyond that is important." Emeline's last sentence had a mocking delivery.

"They served their purpose on the night those two women and two children were slaughtered," Lordis said. "Because of your desire for vengeance."

"You don't know anything about my desires," Emeline shot back.

"First those four, then Peter Palmer maneuvered into creating his own death. Then Monsieur Abel."

"Abel?" Emeline shot back, shining her torchlight directly at Lordis's face.

In spite of her pervading fear, Lordis exalted at learning the accuracy of the solution she and John had determined. "Murdered just a few hours ago. Choked to death. Undoubtedly by the Beaufort brothers."

"Those mindless beasts!" Emeline blurted out. "Nothing he gathered could prove us guilty. Jesus!"

"Jesus indeed. It's time for you to confess your sins."

"No," Emeline said with hard firmness. "No. My son will reason us through this."

"Really? With those molds fitting the Beaufort brothers' feet so perfectly?"

"The one set was destroyed this afternoon at police headquarters," Emeline revealed. "An accident that cost fifty pounds. Carlisle will soon learn the truth about where you two hid the other molds, and that will be the end of that."

To Lordis, it felt as if the mulatto woman had been standing in the parlor for hours. She began to despair that John would return soon. "That alone won't be enough. There's more going against you."

Emeline swung the torchlight across her body and raised her right hand. For the first time, Lordis became aware that the woman had been holding a machete behind her back. Its blade threw off a menacing gleam in the light.

"Tell me. If you refuse, I can separate you from the foot you have resting on that pillow."

"Deeper and deeper and deeper," Lordis said, even as she felt her heart pummeling her rib cage.

"You're foreigners, isolated on a mountain, with no power, in the middle of a howling storm. Who knows what trouble you got yourselves into. If you refuse to cooperate, we can arrange it so your bodies are never found. But we don't want that. Carlisle, Sibyl, and I can't understand why you two aren't helping us. Again and again, you express your sympathy for our mistreatment. Are you a mother, Mrs. Le Brun?"

"No."

"Then you can't possibly understand the sacrifices I've made for my son. He is not merely smart; he is the smartest man on this island. He has so many hopes and plans to improve St. Lucia. He bought land. He collaborated with white men to speculate on other land. From those profits, he plans to lend out money so others like us can own land as well. And then they will lend money so that finally enough people with color in their skins can pay the taxes and own the land required to vote. To vote as a bloc and pressure those in charge to give us the rights we were supposedly granted more than sixty years ago. My son was willing to be patient. He understood that he would be an old man by that time. But then a means to speed up the process a hundredfold came to us in a telegram. Carlisle is a Palmer. He deserves Tristesse more than any other child of Henry's."

Lordis paused as long as she dared, then said, "If you go out on the road in front of this house, a white paper sack is probably still lying near where I fell. John dropped it running to me. It contains the prescription for a mixture of Epsom salts and thyme oil. To kill hookworms."

The torchlight beam swung toward the floor. Emeline took several seconds to digest the news. Finally, in a voice disturbingly calm, she asked, "What else?"

Lordis's right hand stole imperceptibly into the tight space between the couch seat cushions. "Your son should have stopped with just the footprints. Planting the awl was too much. Mr. Boulton, the man who owns the shoe repair shop, remembers seeing you just before his awl disappeared. Will you murder him as well?"

Emeline swung the flashlight up. "Damn you two for coming to our island! Do you call the Frenchmen who carted their heartless lords to the guillotine murderers?"

"I do."

"You are wrong!" Emeline barked. "Not by their own hands but by their callousness and greed the French nobles allowed millions to die of disease, cold, and starvation. You have been among the St. Lucia Island Club. Surely you've heard their callousness and seen the evidence of their greed. They're all murderers to one degree or another. We had a guillotine in Soufrière during the same revolution. Our mistake was in only executing some of the white oppressors."

"Executing?" Lordis echoed. "Execution assumes a trial."

"Shut up. Shut up!" Pushed beyond endurance by Lordis's revelations and accusations, Emeline expelled an inarticulate shriek. The next instant she rushed forward, raising her machete blade above her head.

Lightning lit the sky beyond the front windows.

Lordis rocked backward involuntarily even as she lifted the cocked revolver she had borrowed from Richard Tubble and fired two shots directly at the hurtling figure.

---

OUT OF EARSHOT of his wife, John cursed a continuous streak. He slipped and slid up the Morne Fortune Road, which sent a torrent of water sluicing in his direction. Powerful gusts of wind blew from the east, pelting his left flank with stinging droplets of rain. Pieces of dislodged plants occasionally slapped against him.

Lightning strikes at the top of the tallest mountain in the area kept him in perpetual fear for his life. When he came close to the summit and passed the government building that held the wireless radio office, one bolt hit the lightning rod attached to the antenna. It created a sphere of energy that shoved John sideways. His nostrils filled with acrid, burning ozone. The momentary flash turned the mountaintop to daylight, and he saw with dismay that he had missed the turn to the west. The fort and battery lay off to his right. In the same instant, he spotted a dirt footpath that would save him long minutes. Somewhere behind him, close to the road, a tree limb snapped with a tremendous noise and fell onto the roadbed, shattering in pieces.

As he moved, John turned his flashlight off for brief periods, daring as many steps as he had memorized. He could see that the instrument had lost some of its power and was damned if he would have it fail entirely.

Swift as he moved, the trek westward took many minutes. Eventually, however, he reached the outlying area of Fort Charlotte and the Apostle's Battery. Two structures that looked as if they might be barracks loomed ahead of him. He saw no light but was not daunted since he knew all power had been lost on the mountain. John jogged to the nearer building and pounded on the front door. Receiving no response, he worked his way around its walls and banged on every window as well as a door that served the back. Still, no one answered.

Uttering a fresh vocabulary of curses, John ran to the second building. This one had only one door and two windows near the front, both of which were barred. Frustrated almost beyond endurance, he switched off his flashlight and pounded and pounded. No one opened the door. He shouted as loudly as he could.

John blinked as a piece of the door splintered, leaving a deep hole. A split-second later, from out of the darkness and above the howling wind, came the report of a small arms weapon. Instinctively, John went into a crouch and rushed around the corner of the structure. His first thought was that he had somehow been tracked by the Beaufort brothers, but he quickly rejected the idea. They were up-close murderers who used their hands. Carlisle Thiery lived on the mountain and was many times more likely to use a killing method that did not involve his hands.

While his back was bent, John felt the presence of the revolver on his hip. He unsnapped the Smith & Wesson Model 1899 .38 from its holster and took it in his hand. Being right-handed, he was at a disadvantage at the corner of the wall, needing to expose much of his length before firing. He elected to drop into a squat and peek at the panorama from where he had just come. His risk yielded him a fleeting look at a shape barely darker than its surroundings, dashing to the shelter of the first building. Escape down the mountain was cut off. His best means of concealment and safety lay in the angles of the old defense works.

Fort Charlotte was a product of numerous expansions and redesigns. It had rounded cannon turrets, sloping walls at the flanks and on the side that faced the Caribbean, and a honeycomb of chambers beneath ground level. Far below, the section of Castries adjoining the docks still had electric power. The reflection of lights off the low-hanging clouds provided just enough illumination to make the whitewashed fort stand out from its black surroundings.

Keeping the second building between him and the shooter, John dashed for the fort, running in a random, zig-zag pattern. Halfway to his goal he aimed wildly behind him and squeezed the trigger. When he had almost reached the outer wall, an answering shot rang out. John rounded a concrete corner that fed into a set of stairs. Keeping low, he descended a half-dozen steps. Then he stopped, poked his head up, and saw through the curtains of rain the faint shape of his pursuer crossing the open ground. Steadying the heel of his shooting hand on the top of the wall, he fired two shots. Neither hit their mark. The night was so dark and the rain so thick that he had no idea if they had even come close. What they accomplished, however, was to make the figure redouble its speed, racing to the protection of a half-buried storage bunker.

John backed down the remaining steps, training his revolver at the top of the entrance to the belly of the fort. When he reached the bottom, he put all but his head and right arm behind the ninety-degree turn. He waited patiently but in vain for his pursuer to appear.

From far away, John heard a clatter, which was followed by the echoing report of a gun, and finally by a torrent of curses. The total back length of the fort was about four hundred feet. He had entered the lower level at the southern extreme. His adversary had anticipated his ambush and taken the stairs that lay about three-quarters of the way along the wall, close to the northern extreme.

John pulled the flashlight from his coat pocket, retreated farther into the subterranean segment of the fort, and surveyed his surroundings with the beam. He memorized the way ahead of him, shut off the light, and sprinted down a long corridor, each of his footfalls slapping the floor stones with wet leather, creating a succession of noises.

A bullet ricocheted off the wall to John's right. The corridor reverberated with the report, followed by the noise of the bullet's glancing impact. John pointed his revolver at the location of the muzzle blast and fired his fourth bullet. Holding his flashlight directly upward, he used the knuckles of his left hand to guide him along the invisible wall until he found an opening he had spied. He entered a virtual maze of paths and rooms. As he thumbed on the flashlight and swung it quickly back and forth, he wished he had paid more attention to the guard who had led him and Lordis on their impromptu tour.

"I saw where you went," Carlisle Thiery's hollow-sounding voice called out. "It's a dead end. Unless you drop your weapon and take me to those molds, it's aptly named."

Every door John tried had been locked or sealed. He came to a widening in the hallway, which provided access to four doors. Two were set in the wall at the end of the hall; the other two were inset on the left and right walls. Only one of the back doors yielded to John's forceful tug. In the room beyond were numerous kegs, stacked two high and marked with the legend "Gunpowder" and, below the word, three Xs. John lifted one, then set it quickly back down. He left the door open and dodged back into the square that capped the hallway just in time to avoid Thiery's fifth bullet. He pressed his back into the niche of the side wall, effectively hiding him from any shot not taken within fifteen feet of where he stood.

"I know why you're up here," Carlisle said. "You thought you'd find the honor guard. What you didn't know was that when storms blow they're assigned to Castries. To bolster the small police force."

"But you assured me the people of St. Lucia are peaceful."

"They are . . . considering how poor most of them are. Rarely do they loot, but the white man thinks it's because he fills the streets with police and soldiers. That's because it's how he would behave if the situation were reversed."

"You really do hate white folk, don't you?" John said.

"Not all. I certainly don't hate my wife. Just the ones who think their skin entitles them to more than anyone else. Which is almost every white person on St. Lucia. For you to have walked up here in this weather, you must have learned something that made you think you could arrest me. What was it?"

While he spoke, Carlisle divided his attention. John did not recognize until too late the sounds of a pistol's magazine clip being ejected and a new clip being shoved into the grip. His opportunity to catch the lawyer holding an empty pistol had passed.

John told Thiery about the information they had learned from Jessie the carpenter and from the envelope inside Abel Greenhut's hat. He spoke of breaking into the wireless radio office and finding the doctored telegram information. He let the lawyer know that his mother had been identified in the shoe repair shop just before the awl disappeared. He ended with the unwitting testimony of the apothecary concerning the mixture to prevent a barefoot man running around on plantation soil from becoming infected with hookworm.

The deep rumbling of thunder penetrated to the deepest recesses of the fort.

"Who would have thought that a simple plan to lure you to St. Lucia and make you one of our front men could have gone so far astray," Carlisle remarked, with clear anger in his voice. "You were on vacation, man. And yet you stuck your nose into a tragedy that happened on the other side of the island."

"I didn't volunteer," John said. "I was paid to investigate, by Nigel Harvey."

Carlisle made a sound of disgust. "You could easily have said no. You accepted because you can never retire. You're a little man with one great skill: detective work. You're a nothing without it."

John had never been given such a frank analysis. He granted that the perceptive lawyer had almost hit the bull's eye. John Le Brun had been an unremarkable man until he won the election to become sheriff of Brunswick, Georgia. Although many people in Glynn County had heard that the Le Brun boy was brilliant, he had never had a chance to develop his potential. The War of Northern Oppression had come, and he had been wounded as a teenage soldier. His family had lost the money they had put aside to send him to William and Mary. He became a subsistence sea cotton farmer. Then he had been cheated out of the true value of his farm by a relative and left to find other work. By the simple act of talking with other men, he daily realized that he had far more common sense and native intellect than the vast majority of them. His dogged determination that justice be served, coupled with an unquenchable thirst to learn the business of criminal justice, gave him both the satisfaction of solving crime after crime and a commensurate degree of respect throughout his community. But only when the ultra-rich, exceedingly clever members of the elite Jekyl Island Club found themselves needing a murder solved did his gold-plated reputation expand beyond the Golden Isles. John had to admit that something inside him, beyond seeing that the law triumphed, compelled him to pit himself against amoral, immoral, and evil men and women who used their special talents for gain. He was the master chess player perpetually given the black pieces, needing to prove that he still possessed the stuff to best the worthiest of opponents.

"And ain't you sad about that skill?" John mocked his accuser.

"Without your insistence on bringing in the chief coroner, the fires and deaths would have been blamed on the *Neg Maron*," Carlisle complained.

"And you have no problem with gettin' innocent people hunted?" John countered.

"They would never have been found. I doubt if there's even a tribe of them near the Palmer plantation. My God, if you hadn't come to St. Lucia, Peter Palmer would never have left his home to meet you! It would all have been over in one night."

"Sorry," John called back. "They say 'timin' is everythin'.' The real cause of all this wasn't me; it was Penny Palmer's death."

"You're guessing about that, but it's a highly logical guess. I couldn't have made my play unless she were no longer living to inherit the plantation."

The two men exchanged their words in total darkness. John

strained his ears to estimate where Thiery stood, but the echoes off the many walls confounded him. "How did she die?"

Carlisle turned on his torch for the briefest instant, then allowed the passageway to lapse into darkness. "She was crushed by a fire truck answering an alarm. Don't you understand that I did this not out of selfishness but on behalf of all the downtrodden on St. Lucia?" As his mother had to Lordis, he detailed his plan to get more and more mulattoes and blacks greater stakes in the island, thus securing for them the right to vote. "Sugarcane is a dinosaur. Now that refrigeration has come to shipping, the banana will prove our salvation. My intent was to change Tristesse to a banana plantation."

Again, Carlisle risked turning on his flashlight, holding it out with his left hand at arm's length as he pointed his pistol where he supposed Le Brun hid. To his amazement, he found the detective standing directly in front of him at a distance of twenty feet. A millisecond after his light came on, John fired a shot at him. It passed through the armpit of his raincoat and caromed down the corridor, creating a multi-echoed din. Reflexively, Thiery fired back with two shots, aiming at darkness because his flashlight had fallen from his hand and shut off.

"Son of a bitch!" the lawyer shouted, dropping to his knees to grope for the flashlight, then retreating blindly to one edge of the corridor. "When you understood that it was me behind the plot, why didn't you stop? You know how unfair the social order is here. Bobby Johnson told me how fairly you treated a mulatto boy who had been accused of shooting a white man who coveted his girlfriend. He said you saved him from being hanged."

"That's right. But I also made sure he faced a trial. He served two years in prison. I already have one blind eye. You think I should have made my other one blind because I suspected you had a grand plan?"

"Our whites won't give up their stranglehold without

blood being shed," Carlisle declared. "Looking at the whole picture, four deaths would have been a small price for the cause of justice."

"Even though they were all innocent? Even a mulatto servant?"

Carlisle backed with stealth an extra twenty feet, angling to the opposite wall. "The Palmer clan was no more innocent than our mulattoes and blacks are guilty. They were casualties of war. Necessary sacrifice." As he spoke, he set his torch on the stone floor, flicked it on with his shoe, and sent a bullet into the room with the kegs marked "Gunpowder." The shot flew true, but no explosion occurred. A moment later, John darted halfway out from his hiding place and fired up the hallway.

"Dummy kegs. Just for show," John disclosed, after several moments of silence. "Good thing for you. I'd have been killed, but that many kegs would have cremated you and collapsed this part of the buildin'. You woulda been buried like a pharaoh in his tomb." His flashlight rolled into view, lighting the near third of the corridor.

Smiling broadly, Carlisle walked forward, straight down the middle of the access way. He picked up his flashlight and resumed his advance. "Revolvers have five or six chambers. You just fired your sixth shot. I'm sure you didn't bring extra cartridges with you." He raised his pistol and hugged the left wall, wanting to bring Le Brun into his sights from not less than a dozen feet. "I, on the other hand—"

John popped out from his concealment without his revolver. Instead, he held a two-shot derringer in his grasp. With no hesitation, he emptied both barrels into the lawyer.

Gasping both from his shock and from the impact of the two bullets, Thiery fell backward. His pistol slipped from his hand and spun away.

John raced to the fallen weapon, kicked it farther from Carlisle's outstretched fingers, and then picked it up. "I know. You reloaded." He bent for the lawyer's torchlight, straightened up, and shone it up and down his opponent's length. "For once, your linen suit, white shirt, and gray tie did not serve you. Almost too easy a target, even for a derringer."

"Am I dying?" Carlisle asked with a voice filled with pain.

"Can you move your legs?"

The lawyer succeeded.

"Then the bullet that passed through your elegant tie must have missed your spine. It surely hit your liver. The other one likely went through your intestines. You been what we call in my neck of the woods 'gut shot.'"

"Will I live?" Carlisle wondered aloud.

"Depends on several things. The damage I can't determine without undressin' you, figurin' how quick I get medical help here, and your will to live. That tie says you're fiercely brave. It also says you're willin' to shed blood for a cause. I suspect you didn't mean it to be your own." John put Carlisle's flashlight in his hand. "I'll hurry as quick as I can. You'll probably hang in the end, but you might could advance that cause of yours by usin' your skills in a courtroom."

# CHAPTER FIFTEEN

## July 9, 1910

"IT'S GENEROUS OF YOU to give up your Saturday evenin' to speak before the St. Lucia Island Club," John said to Richard Tubble. The pair had come down to Castries from Government House, where they had enjoyed an early dinner with their spouses. Lordis had stayed behind to fascinate an inner circle of government wives with tales of life in the New York City of 1910.

"Not at all," replied the lieutenant governor from the seat beside John. A government employee handled the horses. "Even though this will be a redundancy for many of those in attendance. They are, after all, also members of the Legislative Council."

John brushed self-consciously at the sleeve of his suit. "I don't believe they will have heard everythin' that will be said to them tonight."

"That's good."

John was certain it was not.

---

A GALA MOOD pervaded the first-story rooms of the clubhouse. It was packed to the far corners. Of the thirty-one surviving members, fully twenty-eight were in attendance. Folding chairs had been borrowed for the event. A raised platform had been constructed and a rostrum brought in. The evening meal was served buffet style so that members could elbow up to the tables and pick during what was expected to be a lengthy pair of lectures.

Richard Tubble began first, reporting with dignified gravity each event of the Palmer case in order, beginning with the death of Penelope Palmer Hollingsworth. The woman had indeed been crushed under the wheels of a Bath fire engine as its horses galloped to answer a call. The report via wireless radio of her death and its receipt by Sibyl Thiery had set the lethal wheels in motion. The reason for the Bath police delay in finding her had been because her husband did not run a tea shop, as Jacob Mansfield had incorrectly remembered. Rather, he owned and operated with his wife a bead shop. The shop provided beads, sequins, rhinestones, buckles, imitation pearls, fancy feathers, and the like for the decoration of dresses and hats. According to lawyer Lewis Norton, Penny's husband, Stuart Hollingsworth, was the prime candidate to claim the Tristesse plantation, although inquiries were being made in England to find blood relatives.

"It certainly would never have been that bastard Thiery," the owner of the Cul-de-Sac Sugar Refinery blurted out. "What dream world did he live in?"

Club President Raymond Scott called for silence and cautioned the group, many of whom were perceptibly drunk, to maintain an air of decorum.

Tubble continued, "You all undoubtedly have heard about the barefoot prints ruse. Molds one and three matched the right foot of Anton and two and four the right foot of Gilles Beaufort. Anton's match was found to have only a 10 percent chance of error. Owing to the unique deformity of Gilles's little toe, his mold was a 99 percent perfect match. That of Carlisle Thiery was judged to be about 75 percent sure."

Tubble explained how the unexpected presence of Peter Palmer at the club's greeting of John Le Brun and Paul Van Fleet had upset Thiery's plan, necessitating the theft of a straight-pointed shoemaking awl in order to frame Nigel Harvey. He then explained how Emeline Thiery had been tied to the theft of the awl. The official did not offer any of the backstory of Innocente Thiery, her relationship to the Palmers, or her effective exile to Castries. The information begged to be delivered, but the crowd of white men undoubtedly already had passed it among themselves.

All mentions of Carlisle and Emeline were in the past tense. Emeline had been shot in the heart and neck by Lordis and had died within seconds. Carlisle had managed to stay alive until the lieutenant governor's carriage arrived at the fort to transport him down to the city hospital, but he had died en route. The Le Bruns were pronounced innocent of their murders by reason of self-defense two days after their ordeals.

Apparently growing tired of hearing his own voice, Richard Tubble picked up speed in reading his typewritten speech. Hurriedly delivered facts indicated that he assumed all those gathered had heard about the involvement of the infamous Beaufort brothers, whom Carlisle had helped avoid long prison sentences over the theft of lumber and bricks. He slowed momentarily to inject the episode of the fer-de-lance attacks, tying them directly with the brothers and praising John for his adroit handling of the dangerous situation. The brothers, he assured the group, would soon enough face trials for the murders of the

Palmer quartet and of Abel Greenhut. Tubble tapped his pages against the rostrum.

"Justice has prevailed," he told the group.

A spontaneous cheer went up among the planters. From remarks passed near where John stood, the release of Nigel Harvey and George Turner from jail and their presence at the meeting seemed to be universally interpreted in the minds of those assembled that white men were good and unfairly demonized by people of color. Those who were of mixed race or black were the true demons.

"That damned lawyer pulled those logs out of the fire before," bellowed Nigel Harvey, "but this time they'll swing."

The group erupted into laughter.

John remained silent.

Encouraged to a postscript, Richard Tubble heaped praise upon both John and Lordis for their hiring of Abel Greenhut and for finding an answer to how such a cautious man as Carlisle Thiery would risk running barefoot through sugarcane field mud. Derisive laughter punctuated his last words.

"For an accurate account of how Mr. Le Brun and his wife dealt with the Thierys during the recent storm," Tubble concluded, "we must coerce the hero of the hour to speak." He stepped down from the raised platform, beaming at John and leading the applause.

John mounted the dais and slowly surveyed the gathering. It quickly fell into an expectant silence.

"We shot them in self-defense. End of story. I personally deplore the takin' of any person's life. Therefore, I'm unwillin' to share the details for the purpose of entertainment, as if it were the same as the trackin' of those two lions who killed all the railway workers in Kenya about ten years back." Heads nodded forcefully. He did not know whether they wagged in agreement with his code of ethics or in recognition of his African reference.

John looked down at the rostrum, staring at nothing as he gathered the thoughts that had been accumulating in his head for two weeks. Then he slowly scanned the group. "I will say this: if y'all think the deaths of Emeline and Carlisle Thiery have put an end to the issues that inspired them to act, you are gravely mistaken. Carlisle Thiery was a smart, worldly man, motivated by an egalitarian vision. While I will not say he did what he did for purely selfless purposes, he had a dream of improvin' the lives of people of color throughout your island. He knew the personal risk to his plan. Even if everyone in the Palmer clan was eliminated and the *Neg Maron* had been successfully blamed, he knew he could not lay claim on the plantation without—"

"No mixed breed will ever own a plantation," a voice declared from the middle of the listeners.

"—facin' a solid wall of opposition. As was so eloquently proven by the outbursts of two members just in the last ten minutes. If that attitude remains unchanged, it will someday spell an abrupt end to your way of life, gentlemen," John replied coolly. "Lawyer Thiery knew that the French part of your laws says exactly the opposite of those two bold pronouncements we just heard. In point of fact, a man of color who is fathered by the owner of a plantation can indeed claim it if no one else stands in the way. Y'all have just laws, but you're not willin' to accept them when it comes to black blood."

Two men stood in two different rows and worked their way toward the front door.

John did not pause. "Some of your forebears were guillotined in Soufrière durin' the French Revolution. A similar revolution is not impossible in your lifetimes. Isn't the history of the Caribbean the struggle of white men like yourselves workin' to become autonomous of your parent countries, even as the black have revolted again and again—the Haitian Revolution, Dominica, the Barbados Insurrection, the St. John Insurrection, the Jamaican Baptist War—for their freedom? You've lost thousands of workers due to noncompetitive wages, which is nothin' more than revolt with their feet. Those who can't leave will keep their numbers high with their children."

"You bet they will," Andrew Ashton declared. "They reproduce like feral dogs."

"They already outnumber y'all by more than twenty-five to one," John went on, unfazed.

Two more men rose and retreated, their faces clouded with anger. One was Nigel Harvey, who had only minutes before handed John fifty pounds for his work in solving the crimes. As he turned his back on Le Brun, he waved his hand in dismissing disgust.

"I am most sincere when I say I am not tryin' to offend anyone," John emphasized. "I have nothin' to gain from expressin' my observations; I am simply offerin' the perspective of an outsider. Your anxiety not to lose anythin' may cause you to lose everythin'. My family were farmers. We were surrounded by plantations. We and our neighbors suffered tremendous loss fightin' for the right of others to keep slaves . . . and losin' that right.

"If that won't convince you, look to Europe. Your paradise is not so isolated that you can be ignorant of the inroads the Communists are makin' in Germany, France, Hungary, the Netherlands, Italy, and Russia. Their ideas have crossed the Atlantic to the United States, so it's not impossible that they will take root on St. Lucia. People with nothin' have nothin' but their unbearable lives to lose in a revolt. Carlisle Thiery's attempt to grab part of the bounty failed. But, as the order of things in St. Lucia now stands, you risk experiencin' cruder, more widespread events. The riots two years ago in Castries and at the Cul-de-Sac Sugar Refinery could be an augur of things to come. Fear this more than you fear sharin' the governance of your island."

The unrest and murmuring had increased to the level that John had needed to raise his voice to be heard.

"Thank you, Mr. Le Brun," Raymond Scott said with tension in his throat, as he stepped up beside John and attempted to coax him from the rostrum. He smiled at the red-faced audience. "Progressive food for thought from the shores of the United States. Anyone desiring to debate our honored guest should take him aside and do so in a courteous manner. The rest of us will continue to eat, drink, be merry, and celebrate the triumph of justice."

# CHAPTER SIXTEEN

## July 10, 1910

THE LE BRUNS ARRIVED at the Castries dock twenty minutes ahead of the Van Fleets. Lordis and John had remained in the rented house on the Morne so that they had only chanced meeting them once during the week, on the Friday after the tropical storm. The Le Bruns had been sitting alone at an outdoor table of the Dolphin Café and had just ordered breakfast, making it impossible to avoid Paul and Minerva. The Van Fleets had received reports in bits and pieces of the Le Bruns' exploits on behalf of the Palmer family, and both were mightily impressed. Minerva, who had struggled for weeks not to look down her nose at Lordis too openly, was now acting like a private school freshman toward the Queen of the May. John and Lordis replied tersely to questions, but the bombardment continued unabated throughout the meal.

The third Sunday afternoon had at last arrived. The *Pindy*, several degrees handsomer with new coats of paint, was in the process of taking on her latest load of St. Lucian bananas. Two drivers the Le Bruns had never met picked up them and their belongings and were now supervising dock hands in the transfer of their luggage and bundled packages of gifts. The pair of drivers who delivered the Van Fleets also were unknown to John and Lordis, one a man so black that his skin seemed indigo when he turned momentarily to the full sun.

John advanced the film of his twelfth roll, focused the camera lens, and took two shots of the *Pindy*. One captured Captain Bobby Johnson on the bridge waving down at him, his smile typically wide. The last image John took was of Lordis and Minerva unaware of him, engaged in an animated discussion. From Lordis's bracelet dangled a new charm, a gracefully bent palm tree. He drew particular pleasure in the fact that his wife, game trouper that she was, had enjoyed the vacation immensely. The ironic element was that this happened not in spite of the murders and mayhem, the snakes, or the tropical storm but partially because of them. She who had defined her self worth in her twenties and thirties by serving three selfish men and in her forties by nurturing the children of another woman finally felt that she stood side by side with her celebrated and accomplished husband as a partner.

"You know, I was more than a trifle put out that no one invited me to last night's meeting of the St. Lucia Island Club," Paul confessed from behind John. "Once again, you were the center of attention. I assume you impressed everyone gathered."

"I would say that I made an impression," John returned.

"You must expand on the evening once we're out at sea," Paul said. He checked to see that Lordis and Minerva were engaged in their own conversation, then added, "Sixteen full days to get a true feel for this little island. Will you describe it as a paradise?"

"There is no paradise where there are humans. Eden proved that."

"Amen. Especially any place overrun with grindingly poor blacks. No matter how well-mannered they are, one can't help observing their pathetic villages and lifestyles. It's depressing."

"Is that what you'll tell your Manhattan Club and New York Yacht Club buddies?" John asked.

"Precisely. I mean, I have no doubt the amenities can be shipped in, all the necessities that a primitive paradise lacks. But a resort would need a high wall all around to shut out the truth. And how can one avoid seeing it when one visits the rum distilleries, the volcano, the beaches, the Pitons?"

John focused on the sweat running down the faces and chests of the black men hauling the North Americans' belongings up the gangplank. "Just so."

"What about you?"

"I'll tell the truth," John said.

"Exactly."

"Except not to Bobby Johnson." John watched Paul's eyebrows rise with surprise and curiosity. "No, he deserves a bit of punishment for his lack of candor in bringin' us here. Don't you think?"

A wicked smile appeared on the heavyset financier's face. "I do indeed. What do you suggest?"

"First, let's see if we can tromp the livin' daylights out of him at cribbage and chess. At the same time, Lordis and I plan to praise the island to the heavens in front of him. If he's bold enough to ask straight out, we'll say we intend to recommend it for the creation of one or more resorts. What about you?"

"Yes, he deserves that. I'll let Minerva in on our trick before we start up the gangplank." Van Fleet pivoted a slow full circle. "It truly is a wonderful island, though. Perhaps someday, when airplanes can fly this far from the States . . ."

"And when the island stops bein' a colony and the mulattoes and blacks have a greater share in its bounty and its runnin'."

Paul laughed heartily. "Don't hold your breath, John. That will be when pigs fly."

Le Brun thought back on his last visit to the Player's Club, where he had engaged in a debate over the solution to the mystery of the short story "The Lady or the Tiger?" He realized that, quite innocently, he and Lordis had stumbled upon an excellent proof of the argument John had presented. The white men were the kings of this land, and they behaved with a cavalier sense of entitlement and too little compassion toward the descendents of those slaves their forefathers had brought across the ocean against their wills in chains. Their mulatto progeny—results of white men's lust—had learned their superior attitudes and disdain from their fathers. Over the centuries, the resultant heartlessness had filtered down to the lowest levels so that the pure blacks looked down at the newly arrived natives of India. The Indians, learning in their land from the upper castes, likewise looked down on the indigent blacks with intolerance. The tiger was still behind the door. But if the one on trial were smart and educated, the other door could be chosen.

"I'm an optimist," John replied to Van Fleet. "In this age of marvels, I believe anythin' can happen."

# ACKNOWLEDGMENTS

I AM INDEBTED TO Dr. James Wiley, lifelong friend and authority on the history and geography of Central America and the Caribbean Islands, particularly concerning banana commerce. He suggested research books for *The St. Lucia Island Club* and later critiqued the novel. I was introduced to the island paradise while Jim was doing research, and my wife and I traveled there so that Jim and I could celebrate our identical sixtieth birthdays. Any inconsistencies of facts, both intended and innocent, are the fault of the author.

# ABOUT THE AUTHOR

BRENT MONAHAN was born in Fukuoka, Kyushu, Japan, in 1948 as a World War II occupation baby. He received his Bachelor of Arts degree from Rutgers University in music and his Doctor of Musical Arts degree from Indiana University, Bloomington. He has performed, stage directed, and taught music and writing professionally. He has authored fifteen published novels and a number of short stories. Two of his novels have been made into motion pictures. *The St. Lucia Island Club* is the fifth of the John Le Brun novels. The series started with *The Jekyl Island Club*, which was first published in hardback in 2000. Brent lives in Yardley, Pennsylvania, with his wife, Bonnie.